Notes for Return to the Hollow Earth

by

Rudy Rucker

1st Edition, Transreal Books, 2018.
Hardback Collectors Edition: ISBN 978-1-940948-33-1
Paperback: ISBN: 978-1-940948-37-9
Ebook: ISBN 978-1-940948-34-1

Cover design by Georgia Rucker.

Transreal Books, Los Gatos, California
www.transrealbooks.com

Contents

BASIC FACTS

Previous book was *Million Mile Road Trip*.
Return to the Hollow Earth was book #40 and novel #23.

Started the *Notes* on January 21, 2017.
Closed the *Notes* on August 16, 2018.
Notes word count 119,190 words.

Started *Return to the Hollow Earth* on April 27, 2017.
Finished the novel's final revision on August 15, 2018.
Return to the Hollow Earth word count 90,730 words.

For more info about my *Hollow Earth* books, and to view on online version of these *Notes* with clickable links, go to:

http://www.rudyrucker.com/thehollowearth

As you peruse this *Notes* volume you'll notice some dings and typos. Take these imperfections as evidence that you're reading an authentic writing journal, a working document that grew over time. And forgive me for not having the energy to polish my *Notes* any further!

ORGANIZATION

I started these notes while kicking around various ideas for a novel, and while writing some stories. Early in 2017 I decided to write a sequel, *Return to the Hollow Earth*. But then for a few months I got into collaborating with Paul di Fillipo on "The Lost City of Leng," a novella, a sequel to H .P. Lovecraft's novella, "At the Mountains of Madness." Our "Leng" tale mentions the Hollow Earth in passing. Co-writing it got some of the Lovecraft out of my system so I don't feel I have to put that stuff into *Return to the Hollow Earth*, to which project I then returned.

TITLE

FOR A HOLLOW EARTH SEQUEL

For shorthand, I can refer to a sequel to my *The Hollow Earth* as HE2, although I'm not quite sure of the actual title. The simplest would be *Return to the Hollow Earth*, but this to some extent suggests that a reader should read *The Hollow Earth* first (I'll refer to that one as HE1). And generally it's nicer if the books in a series seem to stand alone. But maybe that would be unreasonable.

I'm also tempted by the title, *Flying Saucers From The Hollow Earth*. I kind of like that one. Certainly it's a bit rich for some readers. But those squares aren't going to buy any of my books anyway. So why not let it all hang out.

Or maybe a title referring to the return of Eddie Poe to my cast! (An idea which didn't come to me until April, 2017.) Eddie is a box-office force, for sure. More so than the Hollow Earth. *Poe Redux* would be an easy title, slightly cryptic. And then I'd be saying that my book is "really" about Poe and about writers, as opposed to being "really" about the Hollow Earth and giant Lovecraftian sea cucumbers. I mean, which option will the average person (other than me) be more interested in reading about? Duh?

As of May 1, 2017, I started liking the idea of a really big twist—where Mason makes a 2nd trip into the Hollow Earth, but returns to our world in the year 2050 or even 2150 In this case it isn't totally a Poe book after all, so *Poe Redux* doesn't work. In this case, maybe *Return to the Hollow Earth* is still okay. I don't think I'd directly want to telegraph the hop to the future in the title, although maybe I'll find a way to allude to it.

FOR "MOUNTAINS OF MADNESS" SEQUEL

"Tekelili." "Beyond the Mountains of Madness." (Has been used.) "The Third Expedition." "The Cuke-Men and the Shoggoths." Decided on "In the Lost City of Leng."

WORD COUNTS

In September, 2017, My new Night Shade editor/publisher Cory Alyn sent me a list of the lengths of the ten manuscripts of mine that he plans to publish. And I added a couple more.

Titles in Order Of Publication	Word Count (K)
Spacetime Donuts	52
White Light	69
Sex Sphere	59
Secret of Life	60
The Hollow Earth	106
Saucer Wisdom	85
Mathematicians in Love	110
Jim and the Flims	91
Turing & Burroughs	85
Big Aha	103
Transreal Trilogy	214
Journals	417
Million Mile Road Trip	117
Return to the Hollow Earth	91

WRITING PROGRESS

November 3, 2017.

I'm about to finish Chapter 7, and I'm at 33K words and I'll hit 35k by the end of the chapter. So I'm averaging 5K words per chapter. If I do 20 chapters, I'll have 100K, which would be a reasonable match for the 106K of HE1. So I'm about a third done.

December 20, 2017.

Chapter 9 done. 46,300 words. A shade over 5K words per chapter. I might be half done by the end of January. I worry I'm running out of plot ideas. I'll just shoot for 19 chapters, and 95K words.

Jan 31, 2018.

57,800 words, and 11 chapters. I can get by with 7 more chaps, wrap it up at 18 chaps and ~95K words. I've more or less solved my plot problems, at least in broad outline, although there's still details to fill in. I feel like I might pick up speed, write two chaps per month, and get it done by June, 2018. Dreaming of rushing it into self-pub this summer.

Mar 13, 2018

73,600 words, and 13 and two-thirds chapters. If I can do 3 and a third more chapters I'll get 17 chapters and about 92 K words. That could be enough.

Mar 14, 2018

76,900 words, and 14 and a half chapters. I think 17 chaps is going to be enough, and then I'll have the Afterword as well. In fact the Afterword could just count as the final chapter, as I'm expecting to have some exposition in it.

April 5, 2018

83,800 words, and 15 and a third chapters. I'm now projecting 16 chapters and the afterword. I may only make it to 88K for this draft, although I often pick up a few extra K in the revision.

April 11, 2018.

It's almost done. 16 chapters at 88,350 words, with a short Editor's Note to come.

April 17, 2018.

And now it's really done, 16 chapters and the Editor's Note, at 90,800 words. Yeah, baby!

CHAPTERS DONE

#	Title	Pages	Done
1	Cape Horn	11	7/21/17
2	Shipwreck	7	8/31/17
3	Brumble	9	9/2/17
4	Roulette	12	9/11/17
5	Cytherea	12	10/14/17
6	Maelstrom	12	10/20/17
7	Ants	14	11/6/17
8	Tallulah	13	11/20/17
9	MirrorSeela	12	12/20/17
10	Fwopsy	14	1/24/18
11	Uxa	10	1/30/18
12	Twenty Eighteen	15	2/23/18
13	Impostor	12	3/9/18
14	Reunion	10	3/18/18
15	Rudy	10	4/2/18
16	Farewell	12	4/11/18

| --- | Editor's Note | 4 | 4/17/18 |

PACKAGING

If I were to publish HE1 and HE2 as a single volume, I could use the format I used for *Transreal Trilogy* which is 214K words in a 6" x 9" paperback with 640 pages. If HE1+2 is 200K it would run 598 pages in that same format. Might be fun to design a "sixty-nine" combo pack, with two front covers. In my Transreal Books editions, I sold *Transreal Trilogy* for $28 hb and $17 pb.

Using Kickstarter in 2014, I raised $7,300 for *Transreal Trilogy* from 170 backers. Independently of that, I sold 155 print copies (hb & pb), and 600 ebook copies. I'd do better than that with the brand new novel HE2 in the Hollow Earth package.

Not totally sure a single volume would be good. Maybe just for the hardback collector's edition, and the pb could be a matched pair of more manageable paperbacks. Or have the hardbacks be separate books as well. Costs a bit more for printing, but is slightly less work to design the editions of the hb match the pb. And there is maybe some collector cachet about a multivolume hb set. Can do an hb of the *Notes*, as well.

Looking forward, I totally don't see an HE3 in the cards. I'm too old for yet another solo land trek across this particular Antarctica. At least that's how I feel now, while the HE2 expedition is still underway.

NO OUTLINE

I never wrote a full outline for HE2 at all. I wrote a *sketch* outline of the ending when I was about to begin a version of Chapter 9 called "Seela and MirrorSeela." But it looks like I misplaced that one. And I wrote a few more outline sketches as I went along, and put them into my Writing Notes below. But usually I didn't stick to them very closely, at least not for long. Outlines are overrated.

TIMELINE

Check dates mentioned in HE1 manuscript on p. 108

11

In reality it was 1850 when Mason did that drawing I'd dated 1852, but I can change that.

Event	Date, Time	Mason / Eddie Ages
Poe Born	Jan 19, 1809	
Mason Born	Feb 2, 1821	0 / 12
Ina Durivage Born	Jan 19, 1832	0 / 12
HE1 Starts Mason Leaves Farm	April 30, 1836	15 / 27
MirrorMason Dies.	May 1, 1836	15 / 27
Sail for Antarctica.	June 1, 1836	15 / 27
Arrive in Antarctica.	Christmas, 1836	15 / 27
Fall through to Hollow Earth.	Dec 27, 1836	15 / 27
On the flower	Jan 1, 1837	16 / 28
Mason/Seela reach Core	May 1, 1837	16 / 28
Seela conceives Brumble	Sept 28, 1837	16 / 28
M, E & S thru Anomaly. Leave	Sept 29, 1837	16 / 28
Otha thru Anomaly. Leave	Oct 31, 1837	16 / 28
M, E & S thru Anomaly. Arrive. Earth. 12 yr gap.	Sept 29, 1849	16 / 28
MirrorPoe "kills " Poe	Oct 2, 1849	16 / 28
MirrorPoe Funeral (Age 40)	Oct 9, 1849	16 / 28
Mason starts writing HE1	Oct 10, 1849	16 / 28
Otha thru Anomaly. Arrive. Core. 12 yr gap	Oct 31, 1849	16 / 28
Mason sells rumby to Abrams	Feb 15, 1850	17 / 29
Poe show rumby to Machree	March 1, 1850	17 / 29
Mason finishes writing HE1	March 2, 1850	17 / 29
Mason entrusts HE1 to Coale.	March 3, 1850	17 / 29
Mason and Seela leave Balt	March 4, 1850	17 / 29
Machree buys rumby, reads HE1, robs Jilly	March 5, 1850	17 / 29
HE2 Starts Mason & Seela Ship NYC-SF	March 9, 1850	17 / 29
Purple Whale Sinks. Mason & Seela Board *Water Witch.*	May 13, 1850	17 / 29

Machree flies to SF.		
Arrive in California 4 pm. 99 days after depart.	June 11, 1850, 4pm	17 / 29
Seela's baby born, ~ 9 months after Sept 28.	June 12, 1850, dawn	17 / 29
Depart for North Hole	June 13, 1850, dawn	17 / 29
Arrive at Shrig Rookery	June 14, 1850, 6 pm	17 / 29
Fafnir attacks shrigs. M&S prepare to kill him.	June 15, 1850	17 / 29
Scare krakens. Ride shrig. Maelstrom closed.	June 16, 1850	17 / 29
Arrive at mirrorflower.	June 17, 1850	17 / 29
Leave mirrorflower	June 17, 1850	17 / 29
Arrive at Core	June 19, 1850	17 / 29
The full party enters the Anomaly	June 19, 1850	17/29
Eddie, Machree, Ina in SF (12 yr gap)	June 20, 1862	17-29
Eddie's 15 year Life on MirrorEarth.	1862-1877	*/29-44
Ina dies (33). Eddie goes in grave with her (44).	Jan 19,1877	*/29-44
Rudy starts writing *Return to the Hollow Earth.*	April 20, 2017	Call it 18
Mason, Seela, Brumble, Arf, Nyoo in Big Sur. (167 years + 9 months + 5 days gap,)	Sat March 24, 2018	Call it 18
Hitch to Santa Cruz	Sun, March 25, 2018	18
Get gigs at Good Times and Sparkle Wow	Mon March 26, 2018	18
Mason's article. Poe & Ina rise from grave. (141 years + 2 months + 1 week gap). Rudy joins them. Seela bails. Ride Lux to Sur for the Bloom.	Wed March 28, 2018	18
Return to Cruz. Mason Re-	Thu March 29,	18

claims Seela. Hatches Ned, Mason et al. leave for Pohnpei (Full Moon 3/31)	2018	

GEOGRAPHY

I don't use the word "Antarctica" as that word wasn't in use (at least on any map) until the 1890s. But people did speak of the antarctic region.

***

In the standard model, the Earth's oceanic crust is 5 miles thick, and the continental crust is 20 or 30 miles. These crusts float on the mantle, and reach a temperature of about 800 degrees at the upper edge of the mantle. The discontinuity there is called the Moho. The mantle runs about 3,000 miles down, and then for the last 1000 miles you're in the core, which is liquid on the outside and more solid on the inside.

They know all this stuff from seismic studies. I will have to assume that we have some ultradense rocks in the Hollow Earth which (a) get the Earth's mass up to what it should be, and (b) spoof the right kinds of seismic echoes, delays, and so on.

The Earth has a radius of approximately 4,000 miles. I might conveniently suppose that the crust of the Hollow Earth is 1,000 miles thick, and that from there it's 3,000 miles to the center. Or if that seems too thick, maybe just 500 miles thick and suppose the crust is really strong.

Since mass is a function of r^3, the ratio between a 4 thousand mile and 3 thousand mile radius Earth is 64 to 27. So the Earth with the inner part removed has a relative mass of 64-27, or 37. So to catch up on mass, the crust of the Hollow Earth should be 64/37 times as dense as expected, which is 1.7. Taking into account that the densest part of Earth is the core, which we're leavin out, we might suppose the shell material of the Hollow Earth is two times as dense as normal crust. If we want to slip to down to 500 miles thick, the inner part has a ratio 3.5 cubed which is 42, so then what's left is 22 in volume so it has to be 64/22 times as dense, which is triple, and that's okay too.

The temperature of the mantle where it reaches the crust,

mere twenty miles down, is about a thousand degrees Fahrenheit, and down where it meets the core, it's up to 7,000. Despite being so hot, the mantle is more or less solid, albeit plastic, due to the pressure.

If the Earth is in fact hollow, then the heating effect won't be so strong, and we might suppose that the temperature inside the shell doesn't go much above, say, 500 degrees. So, in an ocean situation, the five hundred or thousand-mile deep circulating water might not even be boiling.

So, look, I'll say the crust is 500 miles thick and three or even four times as dense near the center. And the temperature doesn't go over 2,000 degrees.

***

The North Hole maelstrom is 500 miles deep and, say, 200 miles wide at the top, and of a diameter of fifty miles near the center.

BOOK PROPOSAL

On Jan 4, 2018, I sent a draft of this book proposal to John Silbersack, with the first nine and a half chapters attached. John liked it, so I revised it a little (updating my notion of how the book ends) and sent it to Cory Ally at Night Shade on January 18, 2018, with the first ten chapters (the tenth being not quite done). The next day, January 19, 2019, Cory rejected it or, rather, suggested I resubmit it in about a year—after he's actually published some of the ten books of mine that he already bought.

***

Book Proposal
The Hollow Earth and **Return to the Hollow Earth**
Two Novels by Rudy Rucker. Agent John Silbersack.
January 18, 2018.

- [Reprint] *The Hollow Earth*. 1990, Hardback and paperback out of print, ebook in distribution. Revisions for a new edition in progress. 107,000 words.
- [New] *Return to the Hollow Earth*. In progress, completion planned by November 2018. 95,000 words.

I'm writing a sequel to my popular out-of-print novel *The Hollow Earth*. The sequel is called *Return to the Hollow Earth*. The two books could appear either as separate volumes, or as a single omnibus called *The Hollow Earth Narratives*. The books will be ready by November, 2018.

These two novels are mostly set in the late 1800s, and are written as narratives from the point of view of Mason Reynolds, a seventeen-year-old farm boy from Virginia. In my Afterword, I present these narratives as being authentic documents which I happened to recover—although most readers will understand that my claims are a playful hoax in the style of Nabokov, Borges, or Poe.

Summary of "The Hollow Earth"

Mason Reynolds meets up with Edgar Allan Poe, and they undertake a fantastic journey to the interior of our Hollow Earth, accompanied by Mason's one-time slave Otha, and by Mason's faithful dog Arf. They travel by ship to Antarctica, and then by balloon to the South Pole. They manage to break open the great plug of ice that covers the South Hole, and they fall through to the interior of the Hollow Earth.

One is very nearly weightless within the Hollow Earth. Although some part of the Earth's hollow crust, or Rind, is beneath your feet, the rest of the Rind arches high over your head, and the net gravitational force is nil. Our Hollow Earth is illuminated by branching beams of pink light that emanate from its central zone—like the streamers inside a 1980s plasma-sphere toy.

Mason wins the love of a Hollow Earth woman named Seela. She lives on the surface of a giant sunflower that's sprouted from the inner Rind. Eddie, Mason, Otha, Seela and Arf make their way to the core of the Hollow Earth. They find a zone of giant free-floating lakes, and a race of handsome and highly regarded people called the black gods, who are capable of riding the light streams with surfboards.

Enormous alien sea cucumbers called *woomo* float closer to the Hollow Earth's center—they are the source of the pink beams of light. The *woomo* light has the property of darkening people's skins, and before long, Mason, Eddie, and Seela are as dark as Otha and the black gods.

As it happens, there are two Earths, and the two are connected via a spacetime Anomaly at the Hollow Earth's center. This complicates the geography—but it opens up possibilities for the plot. Eddie, Mason, Seela, and Arf travel through the Anomaly and make their way to the other Earth's surface—which they call the MirrorEarth. The MirrorEarth is in fact the version of Earth that we readers live in. Mason's friend Eddie Poe encounters our Poe, whom he calls the MirrorPoe. MirrorPoe stabs Poe, who seems to die. And then MirrorPoe, as we know from our historical record, dies in the gutter.

Publication history for The Hollow Earth. Morrow & Co, hardback 1st edition, 1990. Avon Books, paperback 1st edition, 1992. Monkeybrain Books, paperback 2nd edition, 2008. Transreal Books ebook 2nd edition, 2012. Hardback and paperback now out of print, with ebook still in distribution. I am creating a revised 3rd edition of *The Hollow Earth* which will fit with *Return to the Hollow Earth.*

Summary of "Return to the Hollow Earth"

Mason and Seela are living in Baltimore in 1850. Seela is expecting a baby son. Although their skin is fading back to white, they're still being treated as black people. They set sail to California to start a new life amid the Gold rush. En route their ship founders off the Cape of Good Horn.

A giant flying nautilus arrives and saves them from drowning. This creature, called a *ballula*, hails form the Hollow Earth. It carries Mason, Seela, and Mason's dog Arf to a nearby opium clipper, where they find none other than Eddie Poe in a stateroom. He didn't die at the end of the first book after all; he was faking.

Eddie believes that the *woomo* within the Hollow Earth want him to return, and they've sent the *ballula* to help him. Eddie controls this very dangerous creature via a telepathy-granting *rumby*, a valuable gem from the Hollow Earth.

The group reaches San Francisco. Seela's baby Brumble is born. Eddie and Mason use their telepathic powers to win several thousand dollars in a gambling hall. Eddie uses the money to obtain supplies. And then the group sets off, riding among the tentacles of Eddie's enormous flying *ballula*.

As it happens, the North Pole has an open passage to the Hollow Earth—the great hole is a titanic maelstrom that runs through the Rind from the outer to the inner world. They ride the flying nautilus down through the maelstrom.

They land next to a thirty-mile-high jungle where some huge, flying creatures called *shrigs* are nesting. The shrigs have heads like pigs, and bodies like giant shrimp. Eddie proceeds directly to the core of the Hollow Earth aboard a shrig.

Mason and Seela make a detour to visit our MirrorEarth's copy of the great sunflower where Seela was born. Mason and Seela meet a MirrorSeela there. She doesn't like the life on her sunflower, so she accompanies Seela, Mason and Arf to the core. They ride to the core in a so-called fried egg, which looks something like an ancient flying saucer, although seemingly worse for wear.

It turns out that the rumby gems are in fact eggs of the *woomo* creatures who live at the core of the Hollow Earth. And it also develops out that the "fried egg" airship is in fact a living being, capable of reproducing itself.

Eddie and his merchant friend Machree venture into the Anomaly to gather a load of rumby gems, which they carry to the Earth's surface aboard the revivified fried egg craft. Due to the time warp in the Anomaly, they lose about ten years and get back to Earth in 1860.

As a result of a quarrel with the spiteful Machree, Mason and Seela get stuck inside the Anomaly at Earth's center for a period that, although it feels brief to them, uses up 168 years of Earth time. When they make their way out and ride the fried egg back to Earth's surface, the year is 2018.

Having noticed that I, Rudy Rucker, edited his first narrative, *The Hollow Earth*, Mason and Seela make their way to my house in Los Gatos with their dog Arf. My wife and I shelter them while Mason works on his *Return to the Hollow Earth*.

Meanwhile an antiquarian bookseller friend of mine unearths a manuscript that seems to have been penned for Mason's eyes—a manuscript by Edgar Allan Poe, dated 1860, well past the date when we believe Poe to have died. The manuscript explains that Eddie's load of rumby eggs hatched into a large number of *woomo*—who are hiding in a cave near Big Sur.

We learn, moreover, that the "fried egg" saucer planted a number of spores upon the walls of that same cave. For the past 168 years, the saucers have been slowly maturing on those stone walls like barnacles, or like shelf mushrooms. And the *woomo* have been maturing as well. And now they're ready to emigrate.

Mason, Seela, and Rudy come t understand that Mason's peregrinations have in large part been guided by the *woomo* to a racial climax: the *woomo* want our Earth to bloom like a dandelion that sends out a cloud of floating seeds. Each "seed" is to be a pair of *woomo* and a pair of humans inside a flying saucer. The *woomo* and the humans have been, although we never knew it, symbiotic all along. The entire history of our planet has been directed towards this cumulative blooming event which, will scatter our two races across our galaxy in search of new worlds.

Rudy Rucker (I) help Eddie and Seela liberate the saucers and *woomo* from of the cave. We overcome interference by some unexpected enemies. Working in secret, we enroll several hundred people willing to set out a cosmic quest

Mason writes about this in his *Return to the Hollow Earth*. But the final chapter is missing. And Rudy Rucker writes this chapter. One night, not so long ago, the saucers, the *woomo*, and the willing human passengers gathered on a cliff in Big Sur—and they took off, with two humans and a pair of *woomo* in each of the living fried egg saucers. Mason and Seela were the last to go. And they left their dog Arf in my safekeeping.

Possible closing words: "And if you don't believe this story, you can come see the dog!"

Praise for The Hollow Earth

Rucker never wants for new inventions…Irresistible. *Washington Post Book World.*
Jam-packed with Rucker's dada-gaga, aurora-borealism,

and gargantuan playfulness. Rucker is one of my all-time favorite writers. He warms the cockles of my heart and fires up the little gray cells.

Philip Jose Farmer.

Terrific...A thrilling-wonder sci-fi novel...Rucker's Poe is the most endearingly repulsive character I can recall having met in fiction.

Fantasy & Science Fiction.

Edgar Allan Poe would have loved this book — and so will you!

Robert Bloch, author of Psycho.

A craftily conceived adventure story, full of wonder, beauty and humor ...Goofily outlandish ...*The Hollow Earth* is a treat.

San Francisco Chronicle.

I never doubted that Mr. Rucker knew the way, and I never lost interest in the plucky young Mason and the redoubtable if reprehensible Eddie Poe, who encounters in real life every one of the nightmares he has so memorably set to paper.

The New York Times Book Review.

It's more fun than anything I've read in I don't know how long, and it's certainly the reigning king of the 'Hollow Earth' novels. Rucker has an enviable imagination, an astonishing ear for language, and a rare sense of proportion and humor. I wish books like this would come along more often.

James P. Blaylock, author of The Digging Leviathan.

Rudy has written the Great American Science Fiction Novel.

Marc Laidlaw.

TO DO

I list these in the reverse order that I fixed them (oldest ones appear last), and not in the order in which the fixes lie within the texts of HE2 and the revised 3rd edition of HE1.

- * Seela's disgust with shrigs in HE1.
- * Use "Tulku" title for Eddie at least once again in the final chapters.

- * How many woomo are there at the Gate? 60.
- * Double-check: In HE1, Mason should already notice that any "balance" between Earth and MirrorEarth is broken. And he needs to dial back any talk about balance in HE2.
- * Uniformize the HE2 sizes and colors of ants into HE1. (Only one mention in HE1).
- * Match the total count of Great Old Ones in HE1 and HE2. Call it fifty.
- * On the inside of the Rind, you would feel an outward pressure of maybe half a pound, due to centrifugal force from the Earth's rotation. Perhaps I should mention this in HE1 when I discuss that "gravitational ledge" zone where you're weightless. Mention briefly and in passing in HE1.
- * Check that I mentioned the freefall effect in a flying fried egg in HE1.
- * What about Eddie saying in SF that he lusts for Jewel. Neutralize that at the core, as by then he's with Ina.
- * HE1, Mason has a vision of a *woomo* at the moment when his time-line splits, that is, right after he kills the stableboy. Briefly hark back to this in HE2
- * Why didn't Eddie just get Mason and Seela to fly aboard Cytherea to the North Hole with him from the ship? Why did he let them go to San Francisco first? He wanted to get some equipment.
- * In HE1 I called the red-tooth dye "indelible." Take that back and say Seela's teeth have faded to white at the very end of HE1, so I don't have that to deal with in HE2.
- * Describe Mason drawing the "M.R. 1850" map the night before they leave SF. The woomo put some black, Asian, and Latino life essences into Eddie's sack as well. (And change the date from 1852 on the drawing.)
- * Mention early that a woomo can act as a womb.
- * Keep mentioning that rumbies are heavy.
- * Keep mentioning that rumbies have a vibe.
- * Mention early that a saucer needs a human presence for hyperjump. Woomo have partnered with humans forever.
- * Follow up on Mason's promise to program a Hollow

Earth game onto Rafaelo's Game Boy.
- * Put in numerous mentions that Arf doesn't like woomo.
- * Clarify that *veem* can mean either a half-*veem* or a full (double) *veem*.
- * Keep track of Eddie's box of rumbies on the trip from Evergreen cemetery to the meadow in Big Sur.
- * Duggie the male *veem* flies with his flat side up. On second thought, this is too confusing. Put it back, and allow the "lower" pilot to sit upside down, or turn the saucer so both pilots are sideways.
- * Dial down the explicit scene where Mason impregnates MirrorSeela.
- * The control panels in the veem have only one pilot's seat. The control is quite simple, It's a single joystick.
- * Eddie's "life essence" samples are in a third testicle.
- * Mention again near the end the bit about Machree being the stable boy.
- * In conversation with Mason, Rudy talks about how he realizes Mason's voice was in his head all along. And of course I'll mention this again in the Afterword.
- * Strongly prefigure Mason's decision to leave on the veem even if Seela won't come.
- * Nyoo stashed the rumbies in the Big Sur cave with Machree watching. Machree got half a dozen of them, but he kept going back to get more. Over the years, the ants moved into the cave. They wanted to be near the rumbies to eat woomo hatchlings, *or* to have a shot at the Bloom.
- * Hector's motorcycle has a sidecar with room for a kiddie seat and a passenger.
- * Ants eat woomo. It's hard for woomo to kill ants as they're shiny.
- * Set it up so Mason is writing HE2 in his head all along.
- * Search chest, make sure it's empty.
- * Make only six saucer babies.
- * Have Fwopsy and Duggie go into near-death stasis after they mate.
- * They gather only a hundred rumbies at the core.
- * Mason says he's not interested in Christianity. Jibe this with his church-going experience in HE1.

- * Eddie in HE1 is writing an epic poem called *Htrae* about their trip, but he's only writing it in his head.
- * When Mason glimpses the Duggie saucer inside the ice of the south hole—have the saucer be lifeless, as if in suspended animation.
- * Fwopsy mentions there's no mates around.
- * Mention in HE1 that Seela made some "money nets" and traded them for things in Baltimore.
- * Mason should immediately doubt his "cosmic balance" theory in HE2, as he remembers from HE1 that the worlds are not in balance anymore.
- * Uniformize, more or less, the speech style of the black gods. Make it a light-weight Ebonic. Mason says it's sort of in his head (given that they use tekelili telepathy). But Otha claims it's the "right" way to speak, and that the black gods came first. But give old Watcher a more formal mode of speech.
- * Although I like the "Oh, *woomo*, remember me," rap, it heavily clashes with my notion that each of the emigrant saucers must have two humans as well as two *woomo* inside. I could drop it entirely. Or go and say what people want to hear anyway: "But humans are too rich and subtle to be mere memory structures." And maybe they just "remember" things like krakens and fried eggs.
- * The fried egg is not a machine made of metal, it's a living organism. Hint only faintly at this in HE1, and have this effect grow in HE2, where the saucer is coming to life as it falls with Mason and the Seelas from the mirrorflower to the core. And then Nyoo and Skolder fully awaken it.
- * Have Eddie tell Ina who he really is on the ballula. She knows by the time they're at the core.
- * Uniformize and use "Central Anomaly" in HE1 and HE2, rather than just "Anomaly" in HE2, as I'd mistakenly been doing. Also make sure I use the alternate word "Gate" fairly often when the black gods are around.
- * Stress that the lock-step synch between Earth and MirrorEarth stopped when Mason and the stableboy shot at each other and the outcomes differed in the two

worlds.

- * Bring Otha back. What if he too came through the Anomaly, that would be cool. And forget about any Earth/MirrorEarth "balance" issue.
- * Eddie needs to describe his initial meeting with his helper *ballula*, Cytherea. I thought I wrote that, but I couldn't find it after all, so I put it in.
- * One of the baby krakens doesn't make it out through the closing maelstrom. Give the krakens a jittery solar-prominence-like edge. Like living flames, or like 3D Julia Sets.
- * HE1. Differentiate Jewel's more ordinary gems from her rumbies. Or, better, rumbies are the *only* gems she has.
- * Put more insects in the jungle. Have some really big ones.
- * HE1. Let's straighten out the shrigs' migration schedule and fit it with HE2. It'll be easier for plotting if groups of shrigs continuously migrate in and out, and there's no particular seasonality.
- * I should mention now and then that Mason's only 17, and that Eddie is 28.
- * Mention that Seela and Mason absorbed a lot of *woomo* light while the *woomo* were trying to roast the krakens at the North Hole—making them blacker than ever.
- * How many windows does the fried egg ship have? Windshield and two side portholes.
- * I think the word "Htrae" is confusing. Reduce usage in HE1 and HE2. Peg it as "Eddie's word." Fixed in HE2 and in HE1.
- * Clearly introduce Rind as being a formal, capitalized word.
- * HE1. Mention Yurgen and that he was the one blowing the reverberator.
- * Should mention Arf during the birth scenes, and let come down to the Eldorado with Eddie and Mason.
- *HE1. Mason mentions reading Euclid's *Elements*.
- * Weave in the fact that Machree is from Lynchburg, and have him hint at the fact that he encountered Mason in

the stable—we'll drop the bomb in one chap, then have a more discursive "reveal" scene before Machree enters the Anomaly with Eddie.

- * HE1. It might be tidy if they went into the Anomaly in September, 1837 and emerge in September, 1849 so the jump is precisely 12 years.
- * HE1. When they land in Antarctica, soon after "Jeremiah and Eddie were ashore now too," Eddie needs to say that he's coming on the balloon trip too.
- * For texture, make sure that Seela talks somewhat black. Or like a Pacific Islander, which is maybe a bit more Jamaican or Mexican in style.
- * HE1. Make the point that although shrigs mostly feed on garbage (like bottom-feeders), they *do* like to catch *ballula*s.
- * HE1. As they pass through the Anomaly at the center of the Hollow Earth, Mason has a vision that Seela is pregnant with a boy. Confirm with an aside near the end of HE1.

RECYCLED WORDS
BITS FROM HE1

I revised HE1 fairly extensively, mostly just doing grammar and logic clean-up, but also dialing down the exaggerated accents of the black characters, and generally trying to make the story more inclusive. Along the way I took the opportunity to make whatever tweaks I needed for a good fit with the action in HE2. And I made note of eyeball kicks and themes that I want to reuse.

To Do Items HE1

Page references are to the Monkeybrain Books 2006 paperback edition. I made notes on some action items.

- p.56. Reynolds mentions that the whale "Mocha Dick" may in fact be diving to the Hollow Earth when he disappears and then later reappears very far away.
- p 88. Arf puts feet up on railing and looks at Mason and

Eddie like a human.

- p 117. Mason notices that a rock from the walls within the tunnel is much heavier than a normal rock, heavier than gold. Perhaps the inner walls *are* gold? This would tie in with the Gold Rush. I think I required the walls to be extra dense so that the mass of the Hollow Earth would be close to the mass of our solid Earth.
- P. 117. Mason sees something like a giant manta ray.
- p. 123. Mason wants to eat something like a pig, but he never finds one. Maybe have pigs in HE2.
- p. 124. Why didn't Eddie write an expedition report when they returned? Why did he leave it to Mason? Why doesn't he write a report early in HE2? Might he try and plagiarize Mason's, somehow obtaining it from the bookseller Coale?
- P. 127. He hears big animals sloshing out of some of the floating ponds. Would be nice to see a couple of these guys.
- p. 132. Why did Quaihlaihle have such a strong reaction to Reynolds's redclaw pelt?
- pp. 124-135. Description of Seela. "Her eyes were hazel. Her nose was small and gently curved. Her upper lip was fuller than her lower lip; this upper lip was a smooth, kissable band, with only the smallest of indentations at its center. ...Her hair was yellow-blond. Her face was neat and fine, with a firm round jaw. Her eyes were greenish-brown, her teeth strong and white. Her limbs were pleasingly proportioned, and her body a wonderland of young womanly curves."
- p. 135. Mason says he didn't wear a full suit of clothes for six months (presumably his entire time in the Hollow Earth), but I think that was nine months, so I changed it.
- * Who was yelling through the reverberator on the big flower? A guy who was after Seela, perhaps? Might he play a role in HE2? [Yurgen]
- P. 142. Eddie is working on an epic poem about the trip.
- P 154. Add a diagram of the Flatland ER wormhole model.
- p. 166. "The North Hole was to be found in the midst of a

great blue sea. It was near midsummer in the north now,
so the hole was lit with bluish light—seemingly from the
open sky. The water around the hole glowed blue-green
with light as well. The North Hole was a vast maelstrom!
I strained my eyes, trying to make out if one really could
see clear through. Was that not a bit of the sun's disk that
I saw through the North Hole? With the hole wide open,
our trip would have been easier had we taken our balloon
north instead of south…were we willing to endure the
terror of floating down the wind-torn throat of such a vortex." I'll say there's a North Hole on MirrorEarth (our
world) as well, but then our boys will close it down when
they pass through it. Nice symmetry then, South Hole for
HE1, and North Hole for HE2.

- p. 167. I have the *woomo* tendrils going out through the
North Hole and now the South Hole in HE1. When they
rescue Mason from the shipwreck in HE2, the tendrils
wouldn't come from the South Hole, as our hole is
closed, so either they come through the sea, or possibly
arch down from the North Hole.
- The reason Eddie wanted them to go to MirrorEarth was
so he could see Virginia again (although by the time they
got there, Virginia was dead.)

Original Ending of HE1. March 2, 1850.

I'm checking what kinds of things I prefigured in HE1.
Note that, as necessary, I will in fact make some slight
changes to the old ending and to the two old afterwords. But
for reference I'll save the originals here. And, even though
I'm revising HE1 for a 3rd edition, I don't think I'll give it a
third afterword. I'll let any new afterword material go into
either the body or the Editor's Note of HE2.

Right now as I pen these words, it's the evening
of Saturday, March 2, 1850. All winter I've worked
on this narrative and waited tables at Ben's Good
Eats, making just enough money for our clothes and
our pleasures. Seela and I are almost white enough
to pass now, except for the fact that all the people
who know us are used to thinking of us as Negroes.

Seela's teeth are still red, but no matter. I've come to like them that way.

Tuesday morning we'll be shipping out for San Francisco on the *Purple Whale,* a clipper ship even faster than the *Ann McKim.* We have a cabin for two, and Arf will come with us. In the end we had to sell Seela's necklace jewel for the ticket money; the gem brought three hundred! We'll start a new life as white people out there; we'll be in San Francisco in time for our son to be born white and to have it easy. Maybe I'll find work at a newspaper out there.

Meanwhile, I'm going to turn this manuscript over to Mr. Coale at the bookstore. He says he'll try and get it published or, failing that, send it on to me in California when I have an address.

I'm excited about sailing around the Horn and being so close to the South Pole again. It's too bad this MirrorEarth doesn't have a hole down there, because if it did, I think I'd be tempted to go back inside, back to the wonderful Hollow Earth.

Original Ed Note to HE1, July 26, 1986.

Since I am guilty of the occasional science-fiction novel, I'd better make clear right away that *The Hollow Earth: The Narrative of Mason Algiers Reynolds of Virginia* is an authentic nineteenth-century manuscript and was *not* written by me. The original is available for inspection as catalog item *PS2964.S88S8 in the Edgar Allan Poe Collection of the University of Virginia in Charlottesville, Virginia. I first saw the manuscript there on March 7, 1985. It consists of 378 pages of parchment, handwritten in black ink. I have edited *The Hollow Earth* from a notarized Xerox copy of the manuscript.

I'm sure it would boost my desultory half career as an author to present *The Hollow Earth* as my own creation, but I'd be doing a big disservice to everyone. The simple fact is: Every word of *The Hollow Earth* is true, and we must all question our beliefs about the planet we live on.

***

What was the eventual fate of Mason Algiers Reynolds? The March 6, 1850, issue of *The Baltimore Sun* reports that the *Purple Whale* did indeed set out for San Francisco on March 5, but the June 10 edition of the same paper reveals that, tragically enough, the *Purple Whale* never made it around the Horn of South America and was presumed lost with all hands in a gale off Tierra del Fuego.

Grim news—but somehow I find it impossible to believe that Mason, Seela, and Arf could have died so simply. Surely, in the grand scheme of things. Mason's breaking of the great symmetry of the worlds must have had some higher goal. Even in a screaming gale and a shipwreck, would not Mason's uncanny luck and ingenuity have found some way to keep him, Seela, and Arf alive? Would not the Great Old Ones, who know all, have preserved them?

I am presently continuing my investigations and would greatly appreciate information about any post-1850 manuscripts that mention, or could possibly be attributed to Mason Algiers Reynolds of Hardware, Virginia, born February 2, 1821.

Original Editor's Note to HE1, 2nd Ed, Sept 26, 2006.

I'm grateful for this opportunity to bring *The Hollow Earth* back into print. In going over the text for the second edition, I was able to correct a number of misprints. And in order to make the text smoother to read, I've streamlined Mason's representations of dialect.

first edition of Mason Reynolds's account of his incredible journey. I had hoped the publication might bring in some leads regarding the reality of the Hollow Earth. But, until quite recently, only one really substantial bit of new information came my way, this being an original drawing that somehow ended up bound into a much-repaired copy of Augustus A. Gould, *Mollusca & Shells*, (Philadelphia : C. Sherman 1852). The volume is to be found in the Wilkes Exploring Expedition collection at the Bancroft Library of the University of California at Berkeley, filed as catalog item xfQ115.W6 v.12. I owe thanks to my eccentric and difficult friend Frank Shook for pointing this out to me.

The sepia ink on vellum drawing is initialed and hand-dated "M. R. 1852." Although I was unable to obtain permission to scan the fragile original, I've sketched a replica which is accurate in all essential respects.

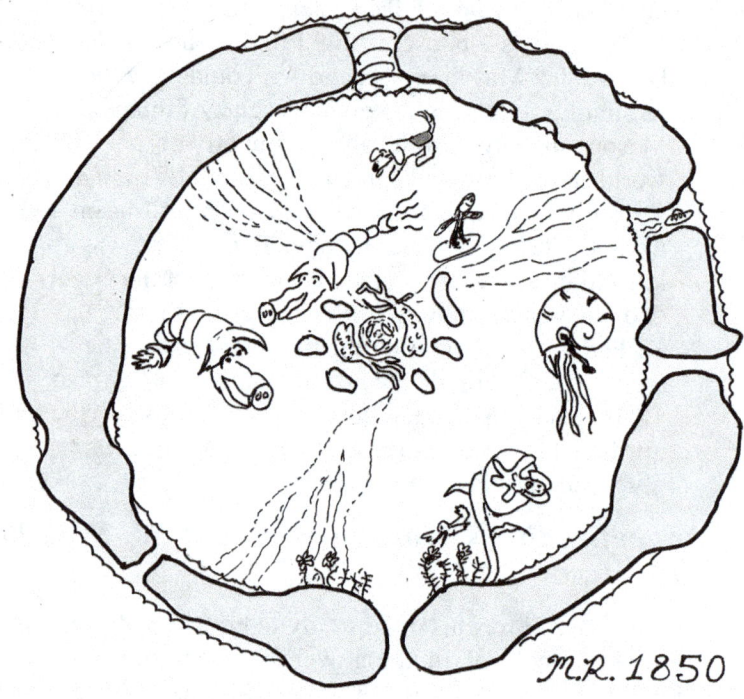

Figure 1: Mason Reynolds's Drawing of the Hollow Earth

A full twenty years have rolled past since I edited the In viewing the sketch, understand that it depicts a cross-section of Mason's Hollow Earth, sliced from pole to pole. The lumpy outer shapes represent the Earth's crust, partly overlaid with seas. Mason's Earth has Holes at both poles, and there are several additional holes passing through its seas.

The creatures within the Hollow Earth are not drawn to scale. *[Note that the image here was dated 1852 in the 2nd edition, but I changed the date to 1850 for the 3rd edition.]*

Running clockwise from the top, features to note are:

The maelstrom at the North Hole. Mason's dog Arf beneath it. A black god riding a lightstreamer. A gap where an ocean runs through Earth's crust, with a tiny "fried-egg ship" floating up through it—this corresponds to the hole near Chesapeake Bay. A *ballula* or giant shellsquid. A second ocean gap, in the vicinity of the Bermuda triangle. A flowerperson (Seela?) on a giant flower. A harpy bird above the inner jungle. The South Hole. A second lightstreamer. Another "blue hole" gap within the sea which is meant to lie, I believe, near Tonga and Fiji. A pair of *koladull* or shrigs. A third lightstreamer, which leads in towards the center where it meets the fan of a *woomo* or giant sea cucumber. The center also depicts six Umpteen Seas, another *woomo*, and the sphere of the Central Anomaly, with MirrorSeas visible within.

I am quite certain that this drawing could only have come from the hand of Mason Algiers Reynolds of Virginia. The reader will appreciate that I was immensely relieved to find the drawing, whose dating indicates that Mason survived the wreck of the *Purple Whale*.

Just this week, while editing this second edition, I've received some new and, I hope, reliable information concerning a manuscript describing Mason's later adventures. If my source is to be trusted, which is not at all certain, Mason or his son or possibly his granddaughter or some other relation—blast my informant's vagueness—did indeed make a return trip to the Hollow Earth.

For certain peculiar reasons not to be disclosed at this time, getting my hands on the second Reynolds manuscript may prove a labor of Hercules. But I have some small hopes of success. I set off soon for a trip to the Astrolabe Reef of

Fiji.

If all goes well, I will present new findings before another full twenty years have elapsed. And if I come up blank—
as is all too likely—no matter. The main thing today is that
The Hollow Earth will be out in a fine new edition. It's an
amazing adventure and, I may venture to say, a subterranean
classic of American literature.

—Rudy Rucker, September 26, 2006, Los Gatos,
California

Bladed Ropes from HE1

*I might use something like this to cut off the head of
Fafnir the kraken in HE2.*

At Eddie's direction, we gathered fifty of the
flowerpeople's sharpened shell knives and knotted
them into one of our precious silk ropes. The
flowerpeople were clever at weaving; in a short
time, the knives were arranged in a tight spiral along
the rope's axis, blades angling out. Eddie now revealed the elegance of his plan, and we cheered. ...

I fired a gunshot to frighten them, and then, while
our rapiers engaged theirs, Eddie, Seela, and I flew
inward past the blue flower and lighted on the vine
upon which the flower grew. No one bothered us.
We found the thinnest part of the flower's stem and
set to work pulling our bladed rope back and forth
like a team of loggers manning a double-handled
saw. The plant stuff was tough, but slowly we made
progress. Great quantities of sap oozed forth, lubri-
cating our cut. In the distance, the air battle raged on
with screams and savage yells. As the stem weak-
ened, the great blue flower gradually nodded away
from the ocean and toward the planet's attractive
center. We sawed like possessed souls. The flower
turned more and then, with a great, leisurely rending,
tore free. Slowly, slowly, it began drifting away
from the vine and inward towards the core!

Ending of "Saucer Wisdom."

*[For a time I was thinking of dragging Frank Shook into
HE2, although now I think I won't. But, yet, it could be that
Mason shows up and meets Rudy in 2018, in which case
something like this passage would be relevant.]*

"You know, Rudy, I'm really sick of you," said Frank,
suddenly flaring into extreme anger. "And now, thank God,
my part of our book is done and I'll never have to talk to you
again. I've been trying to get you to see how rich and wonderful a world we live in, to help you understand a little bit
of saucer wisdom, and it's like you're intent on just throwing
away everything I tell you."

"I'm sorry, Frank! I take it back! I do understand a little
bit. I just couldn't resist— "

"I am so fucking sick of people like you laughing at
me."

We didn't talk much more than that. We walked the rest
of the way to our camp, ate some noodles, crawled into our
tents, and went to sleep.

***

When I woke up in the morning, Frank Shook was gone.
No trace of him remained — and strangest of all, the tent of
his I'd been sleeping in was gone as well. I was lying there
on the bare ground of our campsite in my sleeping-bag, with
my glasses, clothes and water-bottle on the dirt at my side.
The money from my wallet, some three hundred dollars, was
gone. Oh well. The vision had been worth it.

***

I haven't heard any more from Frank Shook. I have no
idea where — or when — he is. Perhaps Finland? I have a
feeling he'll turn up again someday, so I'm saving his share
of the *Saucer Wisdom* money — minus three hundred dollars
— in a special account. My agent and I made several attempts to look up Peggy Sung, but we could only learn that
she'd moved from Benton to either Orange County or to
mainland China. And as for Frank's ex-wife Mary, the phone
number she gave me doesn't work anymore, I don't know
her last name, and nobody in San Lorenzo seems to have any
idea how to find her.

Maelstrom Scene from Hylozoic

The thin air thrilled steadily with a high-pitched vibration. *The ocean's surface was beginning to tilt, as if they were flying downhill.* This made the gray band along the horizon loom that much higher, *like a gigantic cataract rolling into the sea,* ranging to both sides as far as Chu could see.

Crosswise currents had begun ripping the sea to clotted foam. ...

And now, directly ahead of them, the ocean surface curved very sharply down, disappearing into darkness. With an effort Chu understood: *they were dots at the edge of a maelstrom that was hundreds of miles across.*

Duxy ...she opened wide her mouth and spit out her passengers...

With an abrupt lurch, Chu passed over the maelstrom's lip and *rushed headlong into the abyss.* He felt the sickening sweep of descent—but then the sense of falling ceased. Looking around, he saw that the rotational forces had taken over; he was circling around an immense funnel, unfathomable in depth, with glassy sides that spun with bewildering rapidity, bearing him along. It was a scene of terrible grandeur.

Round and round the six companions swept—not with any uniform movement—but in dizzying swings and jerks that sent them sometimes only a few hundred yards, sometimes several miles, and sometimes through a full circuit of the kingdom-sized whirl.

For the moment, they were too drained to think of fighting their way upward against the maelstrom's currents, or through the cyclone winds that filled its core. And so the six coasted on, roughly grouped.

Visible within the glowing walls were the innermost recesses of the subdimensional world, alive with forms that grew the more baroque the greater the depth beneath the Planck sea's proper surface.

The high, chiming sound within the immense spindle had taken on the quality of heraldic music. Chu formed a mental image of the whirlpool as the bell of an otherworldly trumpet whose mouthpiece lay in an infinitely distant land below. Gabriel's trump. And now, within his mind, the music segued into speech. The maelstrom's resident spirit was talking to him.

"I'm Beth Gimel..."

"We ain't done yet," said the pitchfork with a rough chortle. He executed a quick, vicious flip that catapulted Jayjay far out from *the maelstrom's glassy slope*. With snickersnack movements too quick to follow, he tossed Thuy and then Bosch in Jayjay's wake...

The *funnel of winds whirled* Bosch, Thuy, and Jayjay toward the central axis; ever tinier, they plummeted into the profundities below. *A momentary wobble in the wall* gave Chu a glimpse of the full length of the tube. The funnel's inconceivably *distant nether terminus* was marked by a blazing triangle of white light.

Curling his twin tines, Groovy clawed the air in exultation...Propelling himself counter to the whirlpool's currents, the pitchfork carved a steep gyre up the maelstrom's slope, shooting high into the air. At the last instant, he ...he became a lanky, green, three-eyed hillbilly.

So now it was just Chu and the maelstrom. He drifted for an indeterminate period of time, ever deeper, mesmerized by the chiming song that sometimes segued into the voice of the maelstrom's aktual. Beth.

As his *helical descent* continued, Chu's mind began feeling lighter than ever before, more agile. ...Chu ...was a loner. He was doomed.

But all the while, the whirlpool was changing. The sides of the vast funnel became less steep, the gyrations of the whirl less violent. The bottom of the gulf rose and, for a wonder, the maelstrom flattened out...A moment passed. A last fat bubble burbled from the depths, bearing within it—a glistening crow. He cawed, rose into the air, and circled Chu.

The Long Fall Passage from HE1

Here's a passage from HE1 about the inward fall from Rind to core, which seems to have lasted twenty or thirty hours. O January 4, 2018, I pasted into my HE2l doc and then revised it in there to recreate the effect in different words.

   ***

And what did we see? Though the air of the Hollow Earth is speckled with life, and cloudy in spots, we could discern a great deal. Behind us was the South Hole we'd come through, and the hole's surrounding jungle, and that great inner sea that stretched nearly a third of the way around the inner surface of the Rind. At the edges of the sea were two huge continents, and beyond these continents another ocean. All lines of sight that passed too close to the center of the Hollow Earth were warped, but it looked as if the over-all arrangement of land and water bore a rough and ready resemblance to the patterning of Earth's outer surface.

From our vantage point, we couldn't see directly through the South Hole. It occurred to me to try and see if there was a North Hole, but the confusion at the planet's center obstructed my view.

As we neared the twentieth hour of our fall, the appearance of the planet's center changed drastically. Though we were falling more slowly than before, the center seemed to grow faster than ever, swollen by some miragelike trick of space and light

The blue dots near the center could now be seen to be immense floating waterglobs, jiggling irregularly, about fifteen of them. Otha dubbed them the Umpteen Seas. The seas were arranged as if upon a sphere around the center, a zone in which gravitational equilibrium apparently obtained. The average Umpteen Sea held the volume of one of our Great Lakes or perhaps Lake Geneva.

The region beyond the Umpteen Seas remained visually indecipherable. It was brightly lit, with some stable dark objects and a curious lensing effect about the center, as if a spherical mirror were located there. This was the region whence the continual pink light-tendrils emanated. Something in the tight wrapping of the space near here made me think of a skittles spindle. Seen from the inner surface of the Rind, the view of the Hollow Earth was clear, yet here, near the Anomaly, things were as tight and warped as on the girth of a spinning spindle's stuttering tip. As we fell closer to the Umpteen Seas, the inner anomalous zone began looming so insanely large that most of the Hollow Earth's surface was eclipsed. Whichever way I looked, save directly outward, I saw nothing but the jiggling seas, the blotched inner region, and the rubbish around us.

Unused Summary of the Ending

This is from a draft Book Proposal which I then revised on January 18, 2016.

We have complications and rivalries involving Eddie, the other characters, the great *woomo* at the Earth's core, and some new creatures called krakens. The upshot is that Mason and Seela fall partway into the spacetime Anomaly at the Hollow Earth's core. They escape and, after various difficulties, they make their way back to the surface of our Earth.

But there's a twist. While Mason and Seela were within the Anomaly, two centuries flew by. When they return to San Francisco it's the year 2050.

Mason details the unfamiliar features of this future version of our Earth. Paramount among these is that, due to global warming, the Southern Hole beneath our Antarctica is now open, and the great maelstrom at the North pole is in full swing. There's a free flow of trade and tourism between Earth and the inner Hollow Earth.

And then Mason learns, and reveals, the true plans of the great *woomo* for our future, not to mention the schemes of the krakens—who hail from the Sun. And then Mason saves the day—we hope.

Although Mason finishes writing his second journal in 2050, he gets the *woomo* to pass the book back through time to me, Rudy Rucker, the purported editor of these two narratives in 2018. In the Editor's Note, I mock-earnestly discuss the significance of my new findings for the future of the human race.

Edited Central Anomaly Passage from HE1

Jan 22, 2018. I copied this passage out of my Ver 3 revision of HE1, and then edited it down so I can paste it into my HE2 manuscript as a starting point.

Eddie, Ina, Machree, Seela, Brumble, Arf and I were in the fried egg.

Rudy Rucker

I could glance back and see the Umpteen Seas spread out like a flock of blobby sheep. Due to the spacewarp in the Central Anomaly's spindle, the zone of the Seas looked flat, as did the innermost zone of the Gate itself. I could clearly distinguish scores or of the Great Old Ones upon the seeming plane, perhaps even a hundred of them. I also noticed some of the green airweed plants we'd harvested for our previous trip through the Rind's ocean—but we'd have no need for airweed this time, not with our fried egg Fwopsy in a fully restored state.

The *woomo* were pouring light energy onto Fwopsy, and she was basking in it, but greedy for more. We were drifting deeper into the Central anomaly. Above us, the Umpteen Seas were jouncing around like balls on a billiard table, merging and splitting at furious rate, like giant drops of rain in a storm.

"What's going on?" asked Ina uneasily.

"Time is molasses in here," Eddie told her. "The closer we get to the center, the slower our time goes. It's like being in dead, eh?"

And still Fwopsy dawdled. Beneath us was a *woomo* as big as sprawling town of San Francisco herself, and very nearly as hilly, what with the great warty mesa on her primeval integument. She was our friend Uxa from the last trip. She was channeling energy into Fwopsy.

"Hurry up," I urged Fwopsy. I didn't want my new home of California to be completely changed by the time I got back. The high-speed jiggling of the Umpteen Seas was hideous to behold.

"Time to close the door!" called Eddie.

"But first we ditch these troublemakers," said Machree. He shoved Seela, Brumble, and Arf out of the fried egg's door. We party and I were approximately in freefall, until we managed to find purchase upon one of Uxa's stubby protrusions.

Fwopsy the fried egg sped away under her own power. Out past her and the rushing Umpteen Seas, I could see the distant Rind of MirrorEarth, steadily turning, with the seasonal light pulsing on and off in the water-filled North Hole. Whole years were passing...dozens of them, and scores.

The mountainous bodies of the divine *woomo* were on every side of us, great warty barrel shapes bedizened with suckers, puckers, and subbranching fans. They lay in the plane between the two worlds, half here and half there, each of them slowly and steadily rolling over and over, like basking whales, and with their tendrils moving from one side to the other.

We passed through the Gate at the center of the Hollow Earth, and we were blinded by Light. Uxa was ripe with rumbies, the seeds for scores of more *woomo*, ready for the next iteration of the cosmic spawning that they called *woomo* blooming. And all the while the *woomo* ship that we called our Hollow Earth would be following its cause to its eventual destination, an inconceivably huge space spindle at our Milky Way island universe's core.

Once again I saw the secrets of the Great Old Ones.

Most planets are solid. Only a very few are hollow. It is only the hollow planets that have mirror counterparts. Each mirrored pair of hollow planets is umbilically connected, navel to navel, by a Gate at their shared cores. The mature *woomo* ride among the stars within linked pairs of hollow worlds like Earth and MirrorEarth.

Moreover, while on their great journey toward that inconceivably vast space spindle afar, the Great Old Ones would periodically cause their planetary craft to bloom, that is, they would send out seeds for fresh colonies of humans and *woomo*. And these seeds take the form of fried egg craft, each of them containing a man, a woman, and two *woomo*.

We'd rolled back to the MirrorEarth side now. Uxa said we'd lost more than a century. And here came the fried egg craft to pick us up again, Fwopsy. He motion was slowing as she approached. Uxa picked us up with one of her tendrils, and placed us on Fwopsy's rim. We crawled inside.

HISTORICAL INFO

Cape Horn in R. H. Dana's "Two Years Before the Mast"

Here are two excellent sets of Cape Horn passages from

Two Years Before the Mast by Richard Henry Dana. One is east to west in November, the second set is west to east in June. I have Mason on the *Purple Whale* going east to west in April (=October). So I'll make a judicious mix of the two sets.

Note that in the listing below, there are gaps between some of the quoted paragraphs.

PASSAGE FROM EAST TO WEST IN NOVEMBER (=MAY)

We found a large black cloud rolling on toward us from the southwest, and darkening the whole heavens. "Here comes Cape Horn!" said the chief mate; and we had hardly time to haul down and clew up before it was upon us. In a few minutes a heavier sea was raised than I had ever seen, and as it was directly ahead, the little brig, which was no better than a bathing-machine, plunged into it, and all the forward part of her was under water; the sea pouring in through the bow-ports and hawse-holes and over the knight-heads, threatening to wash everything overboard. In the lee scuppers it was up to a man's waist.

Throughout the night it stormed violently,— rain, hail, snow, and sleet beating upon the vessel,— the wind continuing ahead, and the sea running high. At daybreak (about three A.M.) the deck was covered with snow.

Towards morning the wind went down, and during the whole forenoon we lay tossing about in a dead calm, and in the midst of a thick fog. The calms here are unlike those in most parts of the world, for here there is generally so high a sea running, with periods of calm so short that it has no time to go down; and vessels, being under no command of sails or rudder, lie like logs upon the water.

A true specimen of Cape Horn was coming upon us. A great cloud of a dark slate-color was driving on us from the southwest. The hail and sleet were harder than I had yet felt them; seeming almost to pin us down to the rigging. We were longer taking in sail than ever before; for the sails were stiff and wet, the ropes and rigging covered with snow and sleet, and we ourselves cold and nearly blinded with the violence of the storm. By the time we had got down upon deck again, the little brig was plunging madly into a tremendous head sea, which at every drive rushed in through the bow-ports and over the bows, and buried all the forward part of the vessel.

For some time we could do nothing but hold on, and the vessel, diving into two huge seas, one after the other, plunged us twice into the water up to our chins. We hardly knew whether we were on or off; when, the boom lifting us up dripping from the water, we were raised high into the air and then plunged below again. John thought the boom would go every moment, and called out to the mate to keep the vessel off, and haul down the staysail;

For several days we continued driving on, under close-reefed sails, with a heavy sea, a strong gale, and frequent squalls of hail and snow. Our clothes were all wet through, and the only change was from wet to more wet.

Sea biscuit and cold salt beef, made a meal. Yet even this meal was attended with some uncertainty. We had to go ourselves to the galley and take our kid of beef and tin pots of tea,

We were now well to the westward of the Cape, and were changing our course to northward as much as we dared, since the strong southwest winds, which prevailed then, carried us in towards Patagonia. At two P.M. we saw a sail on our larboard beam, and at four we made it out to be a large ship, steering our course, under single-reefed topsails.

Albatrosses were our companions a great part of the time off the Cape. I had been interested in the bird from descriptions, and Coleridge's poem, and was not at all disappointed. We caught and ate one or two with baited hooks which we floated astern upon a shingle. Their long, flapping wings, long legs, and large, staring eyes, give them a very peculiar appearance. They look well on the wing; but one

41

of the finest sights that I have ever seen was an albatross asleep upon the water, during a calm off Cape
Horn, when a heavy sea was running. There being
no breeze, the surface of the water was unbroken,
but a long, heavy swell was rolling, and we saw the
fellow, all white, directly ahead of us, asleep upon
the waves, with his head under his wing; now rising
on the top of one of the big billows, and then falling
slowly until he was lost in the hollow between. He
was undisturbed for some time, until the noise of our
bows, gradually approaching, roused him, when, lifting his head, he stared upon us for a moment, and
then spread his wide wings and took his flight.

PASSAGE FROM WEST TO EAST IN JUNE (=DECEMBER)

A long, heavy, ugly sea, setting in from the
southward, told us what we were coming to. Still,
however, we had a fine, strong breeze, and kept on
our way under as much sail as our ship would bear.
Toward the middle of the week, the wind hauled to
the southward, which brought us upon a taut bow-
line, made the ship meet, nearly head-on, the heavy
swell which rolled from that quarter; and there was
something not at all encouraging in the manner in
which she met it.

Every now and then, when an unusually large sea
met her fairly upon the bows, she struck it with a
sound as dead and heavy as that with which a
sledge-hammer falls upon the pile, and took the
whole of it in upon the forecastle, and, rising, carried
it aft in the scuppers,

The waves were rolling high, as far as the eye
could reach, their tops white with foam, and the
body of them of a deep indigo blue, reflecting the
bright rays of the sun. Our ship rose slowly over a
few of the largest of them, until one immense fellow
came rolling on, threatening to cover her, and which
I was sailor enough to know, by the feeling of her'
under my feet, she would not rise over. I sprang upon the knight-heads, and, seizing hold of the fore-

stay, drew myself up upon it. My feet were just off
the stanchion when the bow struck fairly into the
middle of the sea, and it washed the ship fore and
aft, burying her in the water.

We were now nearly up to the latitude of Cape
Horn, and having over forty degrees of easting to
make, we squared away the yards before a strong
westerly gale, shook a reef out of the fore topsail,
and stood on our way, east-by-south, with the prospect of being up with the Cape in a week or ten
days.

And there lay, floating in the ocean, several miles
off, an immense, irregular mass, its top and points
covered with snow, and its centre of a deep indigo
color. This was an iceberg, and of the largest size, as
one of our men said who had been in the Northern
Ocean.

The sea in every direction was of a deep blue
color, the waves running high and fresh, and sparkling in the light, and in the midst lay this immense
mountain-island, its cavities and valleys thrown into
deep shade, and its points and pinnacles glittering in
the sun. All hands were soon on deck, looking at it,
and admiring in various ways its beauty and grandeur. But no description can give any idea of the
strangeness, splendor, and, really, the sublimity, of
the sight. Its great size,— for it must have been from
two to three miles in circumference, and several
hundred feet in height,— its slow motion, as its base
rose and sank in the water, and its high points nodded against the clouds; the dashing of the waves upon it, which, breaking high with foam, lined its base
with a white crust; and the thundering sound of the
cracking of the mass, and the breaking and tumbling
down of huge pieces; together with its nearness and
approach, which added a slight element of fear.

Cape Horn rig: thick boots, southwesters coming
down over our neck and ears, thick trousers and
jackets, and some with oil-cloth suits over all. Mit-
tens, too, we wore on deck,

43

Unsettling to sleep, lying, as I did, with my head
directly against the bows, which might be dashed in
by an island of ice, brought down by the very next
sea that struck her.

"Eldorado" Bayard Taylor, 1850

[A book of reportage from a trip to California, 149-1850.
I highlighted passages on my Kindle, and these appear here,
broken into paragraphs, one paragraph per passage.]

...the greater part of them mere canvas sheds,
open in front, and covered with all kinds of signs, in
all languages. Great quantities of goods were piled
up in the open air, for want of a place to store them.

The streets were full of people, hurrying to and
fro, and of as diverse and bizarre a character as the
houses: Yankees of every possible variety, native
Californians in serapes and sombreros, Chileans,
Sonorians, Kanakas from Hawaii, Chinese with long
tails, Malays armed with their everlasting creases,
and others in whose embrowned and bearded visages
it was impossible to recognize any especial national-
ity.

...the plaza, now dignified by the name of Portsmouth Square. the City Hotel, where we obtained a
room with two beds at $25 per week, meals being in
addition $20 per week. Adjoining it on the right was
a canvas-tent fifteen by twenty-five feet, called
"Eldorado," and occupied likewise by gamblers. A
friend of mine, who wished to find a place for a law-
office, was shown a cellar in the earth, about twelve
feet square and six deep, which he could have at
$250 a month. the town increased daily by from fif-
teen to thirty houses; its skirts were rapidly approaching the summits of the three hills on which it
is located...

The fresh milk, butter and excellent beef of the
country were...

...digging up the earth with knives and crum-
bling it in their hands. They were actual gold-
hunters, who obtained in this way about $5 a day.

After blowing the fine dirt carefully in their hands, a few specks of gold were left, which they placed in a piece of white paper. The presence of gold in the streets was probably occasioned by the leakings from the miners' bags and the sweepings of stores.

The little Post Office, half-way up the hill, was almost hidden from sight by the crowds that clustered around it. Mr. Moore, the new Postmaster, who was my fellow-traveler from New York, barred every door and window from the moment of his entrance, and with his sons and a few clerks, worked steadily for two days and two nights, till the distribution of twenty thousand letters was completed. Among the many persons I met, the day after...

...tolerable blankets could be had for $6 a pair; coarse flannel shirts, $3; Chilean spurs, with rowels two inches long, $5, and Mexican serapes, of coarse texture but gay color, $10.

...drinking, with a delight that almost made it a flavor on the palate, the soft, elastic, fragrant air...

At the United States and California restaurants, on the plaza, you may get an excellent beefsteak, scantily garnished with potatoes, and a cup of good coffee or chocolate, for $1. Fresh beef, bread, potatoes, and all provisions which will bear importation, are plenty; but milk, fruit and vegetables are classed as luxuries, and fresh butter is rarely heard of...we have choice of the United States, Tortoni's, the Alhambra, and many other equally classic resorts, but Delmonico's, like its distinguished original in New York, has the highest prices and the greatest variety of dishes.

...Montgomery street which fronts the Bay, are crowded with people, all in hurried motion. The eastern side of the plaza, in front of the Parker House and a canvas hell called the Eldorado, are the general rendezvous of business and amusement - combining change, park, club-room and promenade all in one. There, everybody not constantly employed in one spot, may be seen at some time of the day. The character of the groups scattered along the plaza is oftentimes very interesting. In one place are three or four speculators bargaining...

The appearance of San Francisco at night, from the water, is unlike anything I ever beheld. The houses are mostly of canvas, which is made transparent by the lamps within, and transforms them, in the darkness, to dwellings of solid...

There is no rest so sweet as that taken on the hard bosom of Mother Earth. I slept soundly in our spacious bed-chamber, undisturbed even by the continued barking whine of the coyotes. The cool, sparkling dawn called us up betimes, to rekindle the fire and resume cooking.

What with tents and houses of wood and canvas, in hot haste thrown up, the town seemed to have doubled in size. The dusty streets were thronged with people; goods, for lack of storage room, stood in large piles beside the doors; the sound of saw and hammer, and the rattling of laden carts, were incessant.

...the shrewd Celestials had already planted themselves there, and summoned men to meals by the sound of their barbaric gongs.

...but for the shadowy mountain-piles which lay along the horizon, seeming, through the haze, like the hills of another planet which had touched the skirts of the globe on its journey through space.

The beautiful crescent of the harbor, stretching from the Rincon to Fort Montgomery, a distance of more than a mile, was lined with boats, tents and warehouses, and near the latter point, several piers jutted into the water. Montgomery street, fronting the Bay, had undergone a marvellous change. All the open spaces were built up, the canvas houses replaced by ample three-story buildings, an Exchange with lofty sky-light fronted the water, and for the space of half a mile the throng of men of all classes, characters and nations, with carts and animals, equaled Wall street before three o'clock.

Portsmouth Square was filled with lumber and house frames, and nearly every street in the lower part of the city was blocked up with goods. The change which had been wrought in all parts of the town during the past six weeks seemed little short of magic

...there were hundreds of monte, roulette and faro tables, which were crowded nightly until a late hour, and where the most inveterate excesses of gaming might be witnessed.

...He was sitting alone on a stone beside the water, with his bare feet purple with cold, on the cold wet sand. He was wrapped from head to foot in a coarse blanket, which shook with the violence of his chill, as if his limbs were about to drop in pieces. He seemed unconscious of all that was passing; his long, matted hair hung over his wasted face; his eyes glared steadily forward, with an expression of suffering so utterly hopeless and wild, that I shuddered at seeing it. This was but one out of a number of cases, equally sad and distressing...

When I first landed in California, bewildered and amazed by what seemed an unnatural standard of prices, I formed the opinion that there would be before long a great crash in speculation. Things, it appeared then, had reached the crisis, and it was pronounced impossible that they could remain stationary. This might have been a very natural idea at the time, but the subsequent course of affairs proved it to be incorrect. Lands, rents, goods and subsistence continued steadily to advance in cost,

There was something exceedingly hearty, cordial and encouraging in the character of social intercourse. The ordinary forms of courtesy were flung aside with a bluntness of good-fellowship infinitely preferable, under the circumstances.

The most common excesses into which the Californians run, are drinking and gambling. I say drinking, rather than drunkenness, for I saw very little of the latter. The practice of drinking, nevertheless, was widely prevalent, and its effects rendered more destructive by the large amount of bad liquor which was sent into the country. Gambling, in spite of a universal public sentiment against it, grew and flourished; the disappointment and ruin of many emigrants were owing to its existence.

Note on Gold Rush Gambling by <u>*Gary Kamiya*</u>

The largest and most successful gambling resorts were found in the heart of the city, the old Mexican Plaza that had been renamed Portsmouth Square after the U.S. conquest. The entire eastern side of the square, most of the northern and part of the southern were taken up by gambling dens.

The first and most famous of these was the El Dorado, which opened in spring 1848 at Washington and Kearny. At first it was merely a 25-by-40-foot tent, but it was soon replaced by a structure made of rough wood boards for which the operators paid the astonishing rent of $40,000 a year.

The El Dorado's proprietor could afford it because he was raking in big bucks: The joint's daily turnover was said to often exceed $200,000. Other big gambling establishments on the square included the Bella Union, Dennison's Exchange, the Alhambra and the Parker House, where a group of sporting men led by the aptly named Jack Gamble paid even more than the El Dorado — $60,000 a year — to rent the second floor.

A typical "hell," as the gambling houses were called, was a large room with a row of pillars down the middle and a bar at one side, with the gaming tables on the main floor, surrounded by gilded furniture. The high-class houses always featured bands. Chandeliers hung from the ceilings, and the walls were covered with exotic hangings, large mirrors and pictures that one observer described as "French paintings of great merit, but of which female nudity alone forms the subject."

Women, painted or preferably real, were an enormous draw to lonely 49ers, many of whom had not seen the female form for months. One German visitor gushed about a special table in a hell where "a real living, pretty, modest-looking young girl, in a close-fitting black silk dress, her slender fingers adorned with rings," sold tea, coffee and sweets. The Alhambra featured a female violinist who was paid 2 ounces of gold dust to play for an hour a night.

Gambling was not confined to Portsmouth Square. Asbury wrote that "every saloon and hotel bar-room contained two or more tables of Faro, Monte or Chuck-a-Luck, while outside in the muddy streets roamed a horde of free lance Thimble Riggers and Three-Card Monte throwers." Some of those were children: One observer described one as "a precocious little blackguard of 14 or 15," who disdained to play for a bet of less than $100.

The gambling houses were nothing if not democratic. The authors of "Annals" wrote, "Judges and clergymen, physicians and advocates, merchants and clerks, contractors, shopkeepers, tradesmen, mechanics and laborers, miners and farmers, all adventurers in their kind — everyone elbowed his way to the gaming table, and unblushingly threw down his golden or silver stake."

According to the British artist J.D. Borthwick, the hells were frequented by "little urchins, or little scamps rather, 10 or 12 years of age, smoking cigars as big as themselves, with the air of men who were quite up to all the hooks and crooks of this wicked world (as indeed they were), and losing their hundred dollars at a pop with all the nonchalance of an old gambler."

Aurora from Bruce Sterling in "Storming the Cosmos"

(I think Bruce may have cribbed this from some polar expedition report. It's great stuff. I might use it in describing the climactic tunnel through space.)

There was an arc of rainbow light directly over-head, with crimson and yellow streamers shooting out from the zenith towards the horizons. Wide lu-minous bands, paralleling the arch, kept rising out of the horizon to roll across the heavens with swift steady majesty. The bands crashed into the arch like long breakers from a sea of light.

The great auroral rainbow, with all its wavering streamers, began to swing slowly upwards, and a se-cond, brighter arch formed below it. The new arch shot a long serried row of slender, colored lances towards the Tunguska valley. The lances stretched down, touched, and a lightning flash of vivid orange glared out, filling the whole world around me. I held my breath, waiting for the thunder, but the only sound was Nina's light snoring.

I watched for a while longer, until finally the great cosmic tide of light shivered into pieces.

UNUSED SCRAPS

On August 30, 2017, I took out some expository lumps I had.

Draft Outline

I wrote this draft outline in May, 2017, but I didn't stick to it at all.

1. Around the Horn.
2. California.
3. Eddie Poe.
4. The Burrower. Mason and Eddie go prospecting and they find a gnome-like creatures that can dig them all the way down to the Hollow Earth.
5. The Hollow Earth.
6. MirrorSeela.
7. Otha.
8. Into the Hole. Don't remember what the "hole" was, I guess I meant the ER Bridge in the Anomaly.
9. A Changed World. The Hollow Earth is changed over on the old Earth side, as the South Hole is open there (thanks

to Mason in HE1), and there's back-and-forth traffic.

10. The Future. They come back to the MirrorEarth side, and jump maybe two hundred years as they pass through the anomaly, and then they're in the future of we readers.

11. Problem.

12. Worse.

13. Resolution.

14. The End.

Describing Hollow Earth

Dropped this expository lump.

The thing is, you weigh almost nothing within the great airy space within the Hollow Earth's shell. You can don fins and kick yourself through the air, or navigate like a balloonist as do the giant nautiluses known as *koladull*, or jet about with giant flaming farts as do the shrimp-pig-hybrid *shrigs*, or ride the blasts of warm air surrounding the warm pink tendrils of the *woomo*s' light—as do the skysurfing black gods from the Umpteen Lakes at the Hollow Earth's core. So much to tell.

Backing up a bit, how so would a person be weightless within the Hollow Earth? Well, it so happens that the gravitational pull from the shell beneath your feet is at all times precisely counterbalanced by the pull from the shell doming above your head and to your sides. The great Isaac Newton proved this with his integral calculus as an exercise in 1670, never suspecting that the Hollow Earth is real. I'd mastered the details of Newton's calculation during my winter in Baltimore, and I enjoyed turning them over in my mind.

Counterfeiter

"I'm a counterfeiter as well," I blurted out, wanting to sound big. "Edgar Allan Poe and I, we printed a raft of bills. Down in Richmond. Cleared five thousand dollars."

"Poe again?" said Connor Machree. "You don't say."

This story of mine was new to Seela. "But why didn't you print us money in Baltimore?" she interjected.

"It's illegal," I said. "And it's not like we were prepared to skip town. Not like when I printed the money with Eddie in Richmond. We were out of there the next day."

"Illegal papers with pictures," said Seela, shaking her head. "Even sillier than gold." She had little patience with the fiddling fine points of Earth-surface finance. Back on the taut expanse of her native sunflower blossom, barter was the thing.

The Story of Poe and MirrorPoe

Dropped this expository lump.

There were in fact two Poes, living in parallel worlds—a linked pair of nearly identical Earths. One Poe was from my native world, which I call Earth, and one was from your world, dear reader, a world which I call MirrorEarth. Poe journeyed with me from the center of my Hollow Earth to the center of your Hollow MirrorEarth, traveling through an anomalous tunnel amid the *woomo* at the core.

An odd side-effect of my passage was that Poe and I slipped forward by twelve years. That is, when we emerged on the surface of your world's ocean near Baltimore, the Poe that we met there was twelve years older than the Poe I brought with me.

Roused to an insane passion, your degenerate older Poe murdered my poetic young Poe—killing my companion with a cowardly thrust of the sword. I sank my poor Poe's pathetic body into the Baltimore harbor. And meanwhile your Poe collapsed in the street, overcome by wine, remorse, and laudanum. *So happy*, were his last words to me, *so long ago*. I stole his clothes and left. He died a few days later, raving and calling my name.

All this and more was whirling in my head as Connor Machree studied me. I almost felt he could see into my mind. But he said nothing to suggest this.

Rescued by the Woomo

But, hark, here came a fringed streamer of light, and yes, at the core of the light was a frond, a branching feathery shape that was surely the feeler of a giant sea cucumber at the core of the Hollow Earth, the phosphorescent tendril of a *woomo*, the helping hand of a Great Old One. It was just as Seela and I had hoped. By now we were quite unable to move our limbs, but our two minds sang in harmony, joined by the rumby gem's mystic tekelili.

The sticky fan caught me, Seela, Arf and Crispus all in a bundle, and raised us high and higher above the storming waves. I drew in sobbing gasps of air. My circulation returned to the surface of my body, and I felt as if my skin were on fire. The pink light was all around. Seela coughed, and then managed a feeble whoop. We unlimbered our arms to the point where we could hug each other.

"It's an angel?" said Crispus, close at our sides. "Lifting us to heaven?" The storm clouds were still all around us.

"Better than an angel," I yelled across the roaring wind. "And we're not dead." In the distance another of the *woomo*'s tendrils seemed to writhe.

Through the stuttering lightning we rose, with the Great Old One's frond bearing us northwest and into the calm. The pink light around the tendril diminished to the point where we could see clearly though the night.

Machree Blackmails Eddie

"Those rumbies of yours that Connor Machree obtained, they led him to me in New York, in my persona of Goarland Peale. Machree dimly understood that I am a younger version of the MirrorPoe, that is, this world's superannuated Edgar Poe who was buried last November. Machree had some muddled notion that he might blackmail me. When in fact I am a nobody here, and my so-called secret identity is so fantastical that nobody would care. In exchange for his lumbering silence, Machree wanted the secret of how to reach the Hollow Earth." Eddie barked a short laugh. "As if it were a secret! Go through a hole at a pole! John Cleves Symmes and Jeremiah Reynolds expatiated on this topic at length while alive, little attention though they received."

Hollow Earth Giant Jellyfish

I think I'll bring these guys onstage during Mason and Seela's trip to her home flower aboard a zonne. Escaping them will be like when Captain Nemo electrifies his submarine, the *Nautilus*, to escape the clutches of a giant squid. I'm thinking of basing the creatures' species name on "Bruce Sterling."

"...the immense, ghostly jellyfish called *urbstegs*. A single *urbsteg* can seine a hundred cubic miles of air with its stinging tendrils, allowing nothing larger than a dung-beetle to escape."

Norwegian Kraken

Interesting bit that I dropped, but it's a case of "too much research" info if I include it. Found it on Google, natch. I did keep a variant of that Norwegian word for the name of the kraken in the maelstrom, I called her *Jumungo*, which is also a bit like the slang *humongous* or the variant *humungo*. But then I didn't like that and changed to Jormungo.

"*Jörmungandr*," said Seela. "She is the creature that spins the North Hole."
"But this is a word from Norse legend," exclaimed Eddie. "*Jörmungandr* is their version of the Ourobouros. The world snake who bites his tail. The unschooled might also call it a kraken."

Kraken Hive Mind

Initially I supposed that our tiny presences made little impression on Jormungo the kraken. I focused on the rumby at my wrist and felt for this kraken's vibrations. Her mind was ancient and vast, like an intricate maze, or like a city. No one voice from within her seemed to speak to me—perhaps I was beneath her notice. Or was it that she didn't have a narrowly focused mind at all? No one single soul, and in its place a—congregation of souls—whatever that might mean. Returning to my conception of her mind as a city, I seemed to see a vast round palace, filled with circular galleries and radial rooms, and within each room was a lambent yellow flame, and the flames held dark central spots that were like eyes. Jormungo was watching us after all.

Ants not Krakens

Around February 4, 2018, I first considered changing Jormungo into a giant ant. But I didn't like it. I kept the kra-

*ken. But then, on March 26, 2018, I decided it was too much
to have both krakens and giant ants, so I made the change.
Here are some of my now-unused scenes with the krakens.
I've now dropped some of these, and revised some of the
others to work with ants.*

And what of the kraken Jormungo? To my eye, she re-
sembled a centipede, that is, like one of those biting, fringe-
legged creepy-crawlies that Otha and I would sometimes
find scuttling about in the damp shade beneath the floor of
Pa's farm house in Hardware, Virginia. The kraken was,
however, three miles long. And she trailed, as Seela had said,
a limp pair of wings.

Jormungo's body was dark and glittering, no more than
two hundred feet wide, with exceedingly long and wiry legs,
and with, as I say, a folded pair of scalloped bat wings. She
lay sideways in the water around the maelstrom's hole, positioned like a bracelet, with her deep purple legs pointed inward. She was continually beating the glistening legs,
swimming in a circle, which is what kept the whirlpool spinning. I supposed she did this to irrigate the dozen large,
shiny, golden eggs along the midline of her pale belly.

The kraken's head was like a dark dragon's—burnt
black, with bulging eyes and with toothy crocodile jaws that
were firmly clamped onto her own tail. The tip of the tail
lolled to one side, waggling a pair of enormous, onyx sting-
ers.

Adding to the kraken's strangeness was that her body's
shape wasn't quite fixed. She seemed at all times to be in
flux. Her surfaces wobbled, her protrusions extended or
withdrew, and in silhouette she seemed to flicker or to flow.
This said, the kraken was more like a mountain than like a
cloud. And huge and long-lived.

***

The skinny centipede was, like his spouse, over three
miles long. His shape writhed against the sky like a narrow-
bodied silhouette, with his bat-wings and his hundreds of
devilishly lively legs in play, and every bend of his body
alive, his whole shape as vital as a flame. The jointed legs
were, many of them, over a hundred feet long, and Fafnir

was using them to skewer shrigs.

Once he'd impaled a shrig with a couple of legs, the victim would begin sagging and dwindling—Fafnir's legs served as hollow feeding-tubes and, vampire-like, he was draining the juices of his prey. Periodically he'd bend himself double and tear at the wizened, folded-up husks of those shrigs he'd impaled upon his writhing, fantastical limbs. He was dark as night and very shiny, with sheens of purple and green. The colors were continually shifting from his overall form's continuous play.

***

But a kraken's body is more like a fluid than like a stone, more like a vortex than like a wall. A kraken is, if you will, as solid as he wills himself to be. Encountering our poor stratagem of the thread, Fafnir let the strand pass through his flesh, healing himself in its wake, as if it were an oar in a river.

***

Our initial velocity was not so great as to prevent Seela and me from getting a good view of what the krakens were up to. The cloud of steam had drifted away from the sea. Below us, Fafnir and Jormungo were cavorting in the water— with a dozen newly hatched krakens at their side. The little ones had simpler shapes than their parents—they had curved bellies and round heads, perhaps a bit like rocking-horses, and they bore small metallic wings. The surfaces of their bodies had the same jittering quality as did the forms of their parents. No single feature of a kraken was ever quite still.

***

"Tell me more about the krakens," I said.

"They come and hatch their eggs every few hundred years," said Seela. "The *woomo* don't like them, but in the end they always want the krakens back. They like to have the krakens keeping North Hole maelstrom open." She leaned over and gave me a kiss. "You were right, wanting to save Fafnir."

"Why didn't you admit that before?" I asked.

"Well, I wanted to do *something* to jolt Jormungo," said Seela. "I wanted to see her hatch her eggs. And I wanted to see the maelstrom close." She smiled at me. "For reasons of my own."

I wasn't sure what she meant by the last remark. But notion of jolting Fafnir amused me. "In guess *almost* killing Fafnir was enough of a jolt."

"Exactly," said Seela. "Truth be told, I expected the thread wouldn't hurt him. I knew it would go through him. Krakens aren't made of normal stuff. I knew we'd rile him, and there'd be a ruckus and the maelstrom would close."

"You're a sly one," I said, getting the picture.

"I mean to keep you," said Seela. "You suit me well." She kissed me. I liked her with the dark skin.

"And what about the baby kraken who got away?" I said after a bit.

"He was meant to stay," said she. "They always leave one, to visit with the *woomo* at the core."

"The krakens and *woomo* are friends?"

"Kind of. The Earth's *woomo* and the Sun's krakens are on a big journey. In the end they want to go to different places. So they argue. But their paths don't separate until near the end."

"Tell me more," I urged.

"Nobody's ever told me the details. The journey is past the...stars? I never even knew what stars were until I came with you to Baltimore. Maybe we'll learn more about the journey later on."

***

It was that newly fledged kraken whom we'd seen hatched at the North Hole. The one who hadn't left through the maelstrom's hole. I recognized her psychic vibrations. She'd grown to some eight feet long, and she still had a round, curved belly and a round head. Her up-curved mouth was a melon-slice cut from her head, and she had saucer-shaped eyes. Her skin was more mauve than black, with a rippling iridescence. She didn't yet have those sharp centipede legs like her parents, although she had two rows of bumps where the legs would grow. She had bat wings, and a glowing pair of spines at her rear. The kraken hovered by our *veem*, peering in through our craft's door.

Seela had said the *woomo* and the krakens were partners, at least up to a point. But I also remembered how Fafnir and the *woomo* had been blasting intense rays at each other. So I was bracing myself for a fight. But our Nyoo seemed pleased to see the young kraken. The two of them had a rapid, wordless, tekelili conversation which, in its rough outlines, went as follows.

Kraken: I'm Skolder. You carry human partners?
Woomo: I'm Nyoo. I guide these humans to the Old Ones for the Bloom.
Kraken: It's past time for a *woomo* Bloom.
Woomo: The human named Eddie can awaken the *veem*.
Kraken: I will aid with my zap.
Woomo: May our races journey together in peace—until we part.
Kraken: Thou sayest it, Nyoo.

Nyoo bid us a temporary farewell, and flew out of our door. As if stimulated by the presence of the kraken, the *woomo* swelled a bit in size, growing into a warty sea cucumber some five feet long. The kraken narrowed her shape by pulling in her rounded belly, and by pressing her wings against himself. Nyoo widened one of her ends, and the kraken slipped into her like a spit through a chicken, like a sausage on a bun, like a dagger in a sheath.
***
Skolder the kraken slipped her rear end beneath the base of the *veem* and released a staggeringly powerful jolt. The fried egg grew livelier. And now a jagged gout of light zigzagged out from a *woomo* in the Central Anomaly. I recognized the *woomo* as Uxa. She was the one who'd helped me return to the Rind after my first trip to the core of the Hollow Earth. Uxa's energies haloed the fried egg in a radiance so great that the craft grew dark with light.
***
"I'll ride with you," said Nyoo, squeezing into the fried egg ship with us. "I'll help with the rumbies. Are you coming, Skolder?"

"I'm leaving," said Skolder after a moment's thought. "I want to be with my people inside the Sun. I won't forget you, Nyoo. And we'll help with your Bloom if we can." The small kraken, did a mid-air pirouette, then streaked off towards the North Hole, apparently intent on speeding through the water to the surface and then flying onward to the Sun.

Floating Protozoa

I liked this scene in a picaresque Land of Wonders sense, but giant protozoa don't connect to anything else in my HE2 plot, so I changed them into sunspots or urbsteg from the Hollow Sun, or possibly they're more like doorways to the Hollow Sun, that is, the mouths of hyperspace wormhole tunnels from HE to HS.

***

"Look," said Seela pointing ahead to a shoal of curious shapes—flexing blobs, darting blimps, whirling pods with whip-like tails, and long green loops like links of sausages. Somehow they weren't falling inward toward the core. The blobs had vacuoles of lighter-than-air gas to keep them adrift, the blimps had long rows of beating cilia, the pods propelled themselves with their flagellae, and the glinting green sausages had sparkling bubbles within the slime that filled their casings.

"Brobdignagian microorganisms!" I exclaimed, rummaging words from my store of learning. "Paramecia, amoebas, dinoflagellates, and algae."

"That's not how we say," replied Seela, with a laugh. "We just call them air eaters. Tallulah will gobble all she can. You and Arf and I can eat some too."

Our shrig was already feeding. Although the paramecia and amoebas were too large for her, she was harvesting bushels of the sausage-sized algal cells, scooping them up with her open mouth. Periodically she'd pause to masticate her catch, bursting the cells and releasing the verdant, effervescent slime within, and grunting with pleasure as she swallowed the slippery cud.

Seela leaned out from our perch on Tallulah's back to snag one of alga cells. It was over a foot long. Nimbly Seela sliced it across the middle, then handed me a half like a goblet. I lapped and sipped at the foamy cellular ichor, spilling out dancing droplets for Arf to snap from the air. The slime was grassy, but sweet, with a slight pungency. It slid readily

59

down my throat, slaking my thirst and restoring my energy. I snagged a second cell and then a third. A capital form of alimentation.

"Now for meat," said Seela, brandishing her blade. "A hunk of that sky-whipping guy's tail. A special treat."

Although none of the protozoa had eyes, they were aware of our bulky shrig's progress—I suppose they were alerted by our smells, our jostling, our sound vibrations, and perhaps our psychic emanations. The paramecia in particular were tracking us. They were glorious creatures, with rainbow highlights shimmering along their cilia, and colorful globules of food and fat and water within their gelatinous flesh. Each paramecium had what I thought of as a brain at its core—a mazy, intricately tangled mass of flickering tubes.

Meanwhile Seela was on the hunt. Her intended prey was a whip-tailed dinoflagellate, and she was steering our shrig its way. Sensing our approach, the creature beat its long flagellum against the air, spinning its body like a top, and caroming off whatever came in contact. Seela rose to her feet, checked her airfins, and handed Brumble over to me. Choosing her moment with care, she plunged into void amid the bustling protozoa, kicking her legs to speed her way. With no solid mater nearby, I feared Seela's sally might go badly awry, with her missing her mark, losing her fins, and endlessly tumbling inward toward the Hollow Earth's core.

But Seela had precisely timed her leap so that her body would interrupt the sweep of the dinoflagellate's tail. Seizing this thick, ropy strand in one hand, Seela slashed off a three-foot segment of the tip. And then she held the still-twitching bit of tail at such an angle that it propelled her back to our shrig. Cradling Brumble in one arm, I used my free hand to catch hold of Seela's leg.

She glued herself to our shrig again, and held up her prize, that is, a severed length of the protozoan's tail. After some diminishing shudders, the tail-tip fell still. Seela cut off a bit and began eating it, all the while grinning at me and exaggerating her chomps.

"Try it, Mason. We're masters of the Hollow Earth."

So I accepted a piece of her odd, fibrous catch. It was very chewy, like aged pemmican, with what I would call an off or a high taste, like spoiled meat, and the juices had the property of numbing my lips and tongue. I spit out what was in my mouth, and gave the rest of my portion to Arf. Of course the dog loved this offal, and he begged Seela for more.

Stunned by Seela's abrupt attack, the dinoflagellate was moving crookedly. Again I had a sense of contact with Tallulah's mind. Her energy was mounting like a wave. She sensed an opportunity. As Tallulah's mental activation peaked, she executed a great wallowing lunge, and seized the narrow end of the protozoan with her toothless but powerful jaws. The dinoflagellate failed to spin free. Tallulah burst a hole in its hide—and slurped down perhaps a hundred gallons of the, wounded creature's gelatinous body mass. And then our shrig bellowed in triumph. Swept into a close sympathy with my new friend, I raised my voice with hers, twisting my cries into squeals.

"What is *wrong* with you?" said Seela.

At this point three very large paramecia closed in on us, butting against Tallulah and dribbling corrosive fluid upon the hind part of her body. The shrig's roars turned to plaintive wheenks. More paramecia were approaching.

"Flame on!" Seela ordered the shrig, and we were off again, riding a burning plume of fart.

HE1: *Lightstreamers from* Warts

I used to have the lightstreamers coming from the warty bumps on the great woomo, but I found over time that I preferred viewing them as extensions of their tendrils—a better match, as the tendrils can then smoothly segue into the lightstreamers.

The rows of warts are used for sensing and for communication. The Great Old Ones' major sensory mode, other than tekelili union, is *electric*. Each of the tubes of light that flows out in any direction from the Central Anomaly emanates from one of the swaying mesas on their hides. When I watched attentively, I could see how the skeins of light darting through the inner sky were like giant ghostly versions of the tekelili beings' fans. Apparently, the dual, mirrored spinning of Earth and MirrorEarth makes the Central Anomaly an endless source of electric fluid, and the giant holothurians use their tube feet to manipulate the continual discharge. Before he changed his mind about the Great Old Ones, Eddie took this to mean that our planet is a giant body, with the trepangs comprising a galvanically active central brain benevolently working for the greater union of the whole.

MirrorStars in HE1

I'm thinking I might just want to double up the space by Earth and not do all of space. So I'm watering down this full Mirror rap in HE1:

Suppose that at the Hollow Earth's center there were a large shiny ball. Outside this mirrorball would be the Umpteen Seas, the Inner Sky, then the seas and forests upon the inner surface of the Rind, then the thick crust of the Rind, and then the outer surface of the Earth I came from, and its outer sky with Sun, Moon, and Stars. Suppose that all of this were imaged within the central mirrorball, so that staring into the mirror one could see Umpteen MirrorSeas, an Inner MirrorSky, a MirrorRind and, beyond the MirrorRind (were the MirrorRind transparent), a MirrorEarth beneath an outer MirrorSky with MirrorSun, MirrorMoon, and MirrorStars. Imagine all this and then imagine that the central ball is no mirror at all but simply a window between two worlds—an open airy window. This is what is true.

Unused Hollow Sun Ending.

I wrote this outline of an ending around December 27, 2017, and then decided not to use the Hollow Sun thing.
***

10. Drift

Seela is like, "Get it over with." Mason and MirrorSeela make love with Seela's approval. In the intensity of the *woomo* tekelili, it's like group sex. And they can sense that MirrorSeela is now pregnant. "And that's that," says Seela.

They see that stray young kraken, he's about twenty feet long, and he has it in for Hella, the baby *woomo*. Call him Skolber. He's needling her with his red rays. The *woomo* reacts, and there's a bit of a sky battle, and then, oh-oh, the kraken has called in a really big *urbsteg*, and they're falling towards it.

The *urbsteg's* interior looks like a big central tunnel. MirrorSeela agrees with Seela that it's a tunnel to the Hollow Sun. And Skolber the kraken gets hold of the *woomo* Hella and throws her into the *urbsteg*. And the *woomo* drags the fried egg with Mason, Seela, Otha and MirrorSeela after her.

***

11, 12, 13. To the Hollow Sun.

Go to the Hollow Sun and have adventures there, eventually managing to flee back through a Sun tunnel to the inside of the Hollow Earth near the Umpteen Seas.

***

14 & 15. At the Core

Eddie's still at the Umpteen Seas, he's having second thoughts about going back through the Anomaly. Machree is finding some rumbies with Jewel's help. Ina is in tight with Eddie, and she's doing something creative. MirrorSeela reveals that she's pregnant by Mason. She'll give birth to baby Bramble at the Umpteen Seas. She doesn't want to go back to her flower. She wants to stay in the Umpteen Seas with Otha.

***

16, 17. Crawl Through the Rind.

Eddie, Mason, Seela, Machree, and Ina want to return to the surface of MirrorEarth. They start out in the fried egg, thrown by Uxa, but this time the new kraken interferes and they continue flying toward the Rind and they crash into the ground rather than hitting the sea. That baby kraken and another kraken from the Hollow Sun are hassling them. Some Burrowers help them crawl into a tunnel through the Rind.

Crawl all the way through the rind and emerge in the Gold Country. And they meet up with that trans guy from the ship, what was his name? Crispa. Before they'd dropped him off in the Dakotas with some Indians, but we could have set him down by the American River near Placerville. Would be good to bring him back into the story.

***

18, 19. Back in SF.

Back in SF, Eddie can't publish under his own name, but

he sets Ina to reciting his stories and poems while saying she's channeling his spirit. His religion is doing well, thanks to Machree's sales of rumbies.

Mason writes HE2 while working for the newspaper in SF. He helps Machree import rumbies via the burrowers. Crispa can get in on this.

***

Editor's Note *to HE2*

Remark in the Editor's Note that someday the North Hole maelstrom will open up and the South Hole ice plug will melt.

Woomo "Remember" Other Beings

Kraken: I'll help you awaken your fried egg. I carry a zap.

Woomo: And in return—you wish me to remember you?

****

In return, the *woomo* provide the krakens with a kind of immortality, that is, they undertake to *remember* the krakens, just as they are.

This "remembering" is not to be taken in any vague or sentimental sense. If a *woomo* remembers a kraken, this means the *woomo* can at any future time bring this kraken fully back to life, unchanged, and with no sense of ever having left the scene at all. For a kraken to be remembered by a *woomo* is to come as close to immortality as these unexpectedly frail creatures may hope. But humans and the *woomo* have a higher type of immortality.

***

When our *woomo* Nyoo had wrapped herself around the kraken Skolder, I'd visualized her as memorizing every detail of Skolder's personality and form. And this had, I'd concluded, made her capable of regenerating a copy of Skolder at any future time. So, in a certain sense, Nyoo's store of Skolder-information was like an egg. And it didn't need to be soft and juicy.

Using his tekelili, Eddie Poe plucked my thought from my mind, made it his own, and presented it to the others.

"Consider the Gospel according to Luke," Eddie began. I found this opening incongruous, as Eddie was anything but a conventionally pious man. Preaching on, my friend intoned, "Saith the thief upon the cross: *Lord, remember me when you come into your kingdom.* Saith the Lord: *Today you will be with me in Paradise.*" Eddie paused and gazed at us, his eyes bright. "Remember me!" he exclaimed. "There's the axle of the wheel. Grant me a full memory of you, and re-building you is but a fiddling technicality—surely within the powers of a *woomo* or of a Son of God. We serve them in hopes of being remembered and reborn." Eddie's lips curved in a sly smile. He had an addendum. "In the much the same way," he added, "It is well to worship authors. They too have the power to remember their fellows, and to spawn simulacra of them anew."

"Eddie got part of that from me," I told the others. "I learned it from Nyoo, the newborn *woomo*."

Prefigure Seeing the Kraken and Nyoo

Over the weeks and months to come, I would reach a fuller understanding of what I'd learned, and of how my par-ty's tangled adventures fit into an upcoming *woomo* Bloom.

As I pen this, my second Hollow Earth narrative, I'm half a year older. I was seventeen when Nyoo enfolded Skolder, and the year was 1850. And now I'm eighteen, and the calendar year is—I hesitate to write the absurd number—the year is 2018. Yes, Seela, Arf, Brumble and I spent one hundred and sixty-seven years, eight months, and two weeks in the Central Anomaly—although for us, it was as an hour. In the words of the hymn: "A thousand ages in Thy sight / Are like an evening gone."

Read on, friends.

Kraken Explanation

I need to fit this in somewhere. It's too much if I bundle it with Mason's realization about the bloom that happens when Mason watches Nyoo and Skolder going at it.

- The krakens live in Earth's Sun and they tend it, like workers overseeing the firebox of a locomotive. The kra-kens make it less likely that our Sun might explode, which is all to the good. And the krakens use our Hollow

Earth as their mating and nesting ground, away from the turmoil within the Sun. The *woomo* don't like krakens, but they do appreciate having a maelstrom hole at the Hollow Earth's North Hole.

- The cause of the discord between *woomo* and krakens has to do with the ultimate destination of our conjoined Sun and Earth. Although both races agree on our general destination amid the stars, there is a final branching toward either a dark door a light door. The *woomo* want the dark door, and the krakens want the light.

Incest & Religion Rap

"How are one or two couples to engender a race?" said Ina. "Incest is a sin."

"Sin?" said I. "Have you and Eddie joined the ranks of washed-in-the-blood-of-the-lamb, purple-bottomed, button-holing, full-gospel, bible-thumpers?"

"What creative invective," said Ina, as if amused. "I rejoice in my personal resurrection, if you will. I've been buried for centuries, my high and mighty freethinker. Is a lack of faith required?"

Unused Setup for Mason Living at Rudy's House

On the theme of cutting and condensing, I must needs quicken my pace. I much still to tell, and I may be running out of time. As I write this, I'm at Professor Rudy Rucker's house in Los Perros, California, not far from Santa Cruz. It's June in twenty eighteen. My little family and I have been living with Rucker and his wife for four months. We took shelter with him after the disastrous publication of my *Good Times* article, "Lightsurfing the Hollow Earth." In return for Rucker taking us under his wing, I'll be letting him publish and take credit for this, my second narrative, *Return to the Hollow Earth*—just as he did with my first narrative, *The Hollow Earth*.

How my new narrative ends, I don't yet know. Uxa the *woomo* is pressing for the advent of the Bloom. The *veem* refuse to make a firm commitment to the Bloom plan. Seela categorically refuses to leave Earth in a flying saucer. The Hollow Earth ants have dragged all the rumbies into their burrow at the back of the Big Sur cave. And Professor Rucker is in the process of decrypting the documents entrusted to me by the undead corpse of Edgar Allan Poe. As I say, much to tell, and little time to tell it.

WRITING JOURNAL

January 21, 2017. Hollow Earth Sequel!?!

So, okay, I finished *Million Mile Road Trip* in August, 2016, and I (perhaps unwisely) sent it to my agent, and now the book's stalled in begging-editors hell. Jeremy Lassen at Night Shade says maybe he can make an offer in a week or two. Meanwhile I wrote some stories: "@lantis" with Marc Laidlaw, sold to *Asimov's*, plus "Emoticons" and "Fat Stream," a pair of short-shorts, also in "submission" hell for now. And I just started a story "Black Bucket" with Bruce Sterling. ["Emoticons" went to *Asimov's* as "Emojis." I eventually abandoned "Black Bucket." I couldn't sell "Fat Stream," but eventually I released it on the short-lived online Mondo2000 site.]

I miss having a novel to write on. Getting deep into it.

What to write? I often hark back to H. P. Lovecraft's *magnum opus*, "At the Mountains of Madness." I'd been thinking I might do a sequel to that story. But, really, my novel *The Hollow Earth* (or HE1) was already a kind of sequel both to Poe's *Narrative of Arthur Gordon Pym*, and a sequel to Lovecraft's tale (cf. the Great Old Ones at my Hollow Earth's core). And for that matter Lovecraft's tale is self-avowedly a sequel the Poe piece as well. So I might as well just do a sequel to Rucker's sequel to Poe. It's worth noting that the word "Tekeli-li" appears in all three.

I'll miss having Eddie Poe in the new novel. But perhaps Frank Shook can creep in. I noticed today that I mentioned him in my Editor's Note to the 2006 edition of *The Hollow Earth*. I don't think I could do H. P. Lovecraft as a character, I'm not obsessed enough with the man to twink him into reality as I did with my double Eddie Poe.

I've got "Mountains of Madness" and *The Hollow Earth* on my Kindle and I'm reading them. Not to sound too vain, but I'm a bit daunted by how classic and complete my HE1 is. I pray to the Muse I can come up with something worthy of that volume for the sequel. But there is, after all, also a tradition of sequels that completely fall flat. Not that I plan to go there.

A number of my concerns lie at the heart of *The Hollow Earth*.

- Living in Lynchburg, Virginia, near the home of my Rucker ancestors.
- Slavery and the ongoing tension between the black and white races.
- My father's alcoholism, and my own alcoholism and pot addiction. My similarity to Edgar Allan Poe, driven by an "imp of the perverse."
- My shame at not having a real job, and my pride at being a freelance writer.
- The architecture and physics of my design for a Hollow Earth.

What are some concerns that would come into play this time around? Why am I writing this book? What do I want from it?

- Being old, infirm, and ever-closer to death.
- UFOs and immortality.
- Longing for another great dive trip, akin to my Micronesia trip in 2005.

Speaking of longing for a dive trip, I'm also longing for another mental trip—most of my novels describe wonderful trips. Here's some of them.

- The subdimensions. (Spacetime Donuts)
- Transfinite mountains, the afterworld, and the white light. (White Light)
- Future worlds. (Saucer Wisdom)
- Bosch's world, subdimensions. (Hylozoic)
- The afterworld. (Jim and the Flims)

- Center of the galaxy. (Frek and the Elixir)
- 1950s beatniks. (Turing & Burroughs)
- Fairyland. (The Big Aha)
- The endless mappyworld. (Million Mile Road Trip).

January 23, 2017. Lovecraft, Title, Path, Worlds, Cast, Date.

LOVECRAFT

I am again reading Lovecraft's "At the Mountains of Madness." I love the part about finding the abandoned five-million-year-old city on an ultrahigh plateau in Antarctica, a locale which HPL suggests might be called the plateau of Leng. Possibly there's room for this city in my novel?. My character Frank Shook could have a connection to Lovecraftian elder beings and shoggoths.

But maybe I don't need shoggoths. I have enough crit-ters in the Hollow Earth as it is: giant *woomo* (or Great Old Ones), the shrigs (or *koladull*), and shell-squid (or *ballulas*). I also might mention immature *woomo* who are Lovecraftian ridged barrels called cuke-men. Lovecraft calls these the El-der Ones. In *Hollow Earth*, I suggested that the humans and the immature *woomo* cuke-men arrived in the ancient UFOs. Cuke-men could be, like an "instar" (earlier developmental stage) of the *woomo*.

PATH

Let's talk about how my characters will return to the in-terior of the Hollow Earth. I see several options.

* *Through a hole in the Antarctica.* Recall that HE1 starts in a parallel-universe version of Earth—which I'm calling UrEarth—and UrEarth has only a thin covering over its southern hole. Unfortunately, in HE1, I said our Earth lacks a South Hole. Possibly I could alter that. If so, then on our Earth the South Hole covering would be thicker, even though global warming is thinning it. Possibly I could have my characters punch through, as they did in HE1, but that would feel repetitive. But perhaps on the way back they might come up through the Southern Hole, at least part way. The long climb up would be fun, culminating in a futile

shrig-ramming or *ballula*-bonking of the ice lid, followed
by…see the next possibility

   * *Through a cave system.* Regular limestone caves bore
me. Dark and yarty. And of course Jules Verne's bogus, se-
cond-rate, middle-brow *Journey to the Center of the Earth*
uses a cave. But it would be okay to get into Lovecraft's
honeycombed maze of caves that lie beneath "Leng" in "At
the Mountains of Madness." It might be that my characters
in HE2 try to exit via the Southern Hole, find it too thickly
iced over, and make their way out through some of these
Lovecraft Leng caves. And maybe they encounter some of
the immature ridged-barrel Old Ones or the shoggoths.

   * *Through a hole in the floor of the ocean.* In HE1, they
came up through a Bermuda-Triangle type hole near Baltimore. They rode inside an ancient, abandoned UFO that had
belonged to the *woomo*, that is, the giant sea cucumbers
whom I call Great Old Ones. Suppose that in HE2, they use
this route to go down, using a modern hi-tech deep-dive
craft. The hole might be near Fiji. Quite reasonable.

   * *Via a maelstrom.* I adore giant maelstroms. (I have a
giant maelstrom in *Hylozoic* as well, although that's irrelevant.) Anyway, UrEarth has a stable giant maelstrom at the
North Hole. But our Earth lacks a North Hole maelstrom. I
commented on this difference on HE1 without trying to explain it. In fact I said our Earth lacks both a South Hole and a
North Hole. Possibly our Earth could now develop a North
Hole maelstrom, due to global warming. But I'd like for
HE2 to be consistent with the facts of our current world, so I
can't have a permanent North Hole maelstrom.

   * *Via a vortex thread.* I could have would be a thread-
like but fierce vortex thread that quickly comes and goes, or
maybe it's permanent, and it lashes about undersea. The
thread might be a tentacle from one of the Great Old One sea
cucumbers. It could explain the periodic disappearance of
giant supertankers at sea. In fact our boys could go down
under in such a supertanker, or as part of an investigation
into the loss of such tankers. The wild vortex threads pop up
on the surface all over the place, moving chaotically, like
one of those light-streamers inside the Hollow Earth. And it
could in fact appear near Fiji—aiding a trip downward in a

deep-diving vehicle.

TWO WORLDS

Recall that HE1 starts on an "Earth" (which I now call UrEarth) and ends on a "MirrorEarth," with the latter being in fact our own Earth…in which I, Rudy Rucker the editor, found Mason Algiers Reynolds's manuscript. It feels tedious to have the HE2 characters travel all the way back through to the old Ur Earth. Maybe my character almost goes through to UrEarth, but not quite. Sort of bounces off the Tekelili singularity-zone. Better: something comes through from UrEarth that my characters have has to deal with. Like for instance maybe those saucerian aliens are present in UrEarth and they're staging an invasion? No, Rudy, you just did alien invasions in *The Big Aha* and in *Million Mile Road Trip*. Think of something else. Maybe something good is coming through.

CAST

In my Editor's Note to HE1, I mention several people who might be in the cast. Me, Frank Shook, Mason, and Mason's child or grandchild. Supposedly there's another manuscript. Perhaps I find the manuscript and simply edit it. Or, in my search for the manuscript I encounter a path of my own to the Hollow Earth. And perhaps Frank Shook accompanies me.

If I bring in my character Frank Shook from *Saucer Wisdom*—which I do in fact long to do—then the HE2 novel becomes a dual sequel, that is, it follows up on both *Hollow Earth* and *Saucer Wisdom*. Kind of mind-expanding to imagine that. The new novel could be the third, and crowning, gem in trilogy of $_{hoaxes}$. The title could be—wait for it— *Flying Saucers From The Hollow Earth*. I'd thought I'd seen an ephemeral indie pamphlet-like print book of this title, but I don't see it on Google. I did find this link reprinting part of a *Hollow Earth* book by Raymond W. Bernard, with a reference to a (possibly imaginary) volume called: *From the Subterranean World to the Sky: Flying Saucers*. Maybe I've owned the Bernard book, the name sounds familiar. I ordered it from Abe Books in any case. And I'll root around in what remains of my Hollow Earth book collection from 1986.

Suppose the new novel is an adventure starring Frank Shook and me. We'd take the (stolen) dive vehicle to the Hollow Earth. Frank would do a deal with the UFOs. I'd escape by way of the long climb up through the iced-over Antarctic hole. Near the top I'd find some tunnel and make my way out through Lovecraft's Leng.

I didn't specify where Frank went after the end of *Saucer Wisdom*. He emptied the sleeping Rudy's wallet and left.

Maybe some larval young *woomo* are doing things on our surface, maybe they look like Lovecraft's cuke-men or Elder Ones.

DATE

I mentioned Frank Shook in the HE1 Editor's Note in 2006, when I was sixty. So my age in this new book would have to be between 60 and 70. Either the events happened quite recently, or about ten years ago—and I'm just now writing them up. Could be there's some significant new developments, e.g. Trump might be an alien sea cucumber— not that I'd seriously want to tie my book's timeline so closely to the ultimately evanescent phantasms of politics.

Note that when you pass through the ER-bridge between the two Hollow Earths, your time temporarily runs much slower than the outer world. When Mason went through the interface at the end of Chapter 13, he lost twelve years, that is, when he went in it was 1837, and when he came out it was 1849. And in 1852, he drew that map that's in my Editor's Note.

January 25, 2017. Bathyscaphes. James Cameron's Challenger.

Increase in disappearances of supertankers or (more interesting) tuna fishers in the South Pacific. (Cf. the start of "The Call of Cthulhu.") I could use the tuna ships I saw in Pohnpei. Frank Shook calls me. He's in Fiji or maybe Micronesia, and he's perhaps got a gig doing consulting on the causes of the ship sinkings. He's into sakau.

Note that in the Editor's Note to HE1, 2nd edition, I

mention talking to Frank Shook around 2006. I could beef that up a little and suggest that he's the person I'm about to go meet in Fiji. Or in Micronesia, which I know better, and which is close to the Mariana Trench. Or in Tahiti which is close to the tip of South America. [If necessary I could alter the mention of Fiji in the Editor's Note to HE1, edition 2.]

Maybe I get back in touch with Frank Shook via his ex-wife Mary?

Down in Micronesia, glowing vortex threads are dragging down the ships. Frank has made a deal with someone (TV show? Local government? Or his privately seen saucers?), a deal to find out about the glowing threads. He has access to a bathyscaphe. Or he knows how to steal one. I was initially thinking of a replica of the first manned bathyscaphe Trieste which, in 1960, set the world record by diving to the Challenger Deep, a 7-km-long slot canyon at the bottom of the Mariana Trench, 35,000 feet or 11,000 meters down, the deepest spot in the ocean, near Yap in Micronesia. Or, better, access to the renovated 2012, Deepsea Challenger, the second manned (solo) bathyscaphe to reach the bottom with none other than the director James Cameron aboard. I checked Wikipedia to find out what happened to Deepsea Challenger.

> Deepsea Challenger was donated to Woods Hole Oceanographic Institution for the studies of its technological solutions in order to incorporate some of those solutions into other vehicles to advance deep-sea research. On July 23, 2015, it was transported from Woods Hole Oceanographic Institution to Baltimore to be shipped to Australia for a temporary loan. While on a flatbed truck on Interstate 95 in Connecticut, the truck caught fire, resulting in damage to the submersible. The likely cause of the fire was from the truck's brake failure which ignited its rear tires. Connecticut fire officials speculated that it was a total loss to the Deepsea Challenger; however, the actual extent of the damage was not reported. The submersible was transported back to Woods Hole Oceanographic Institution after the fire.

Very suspicious, that fire, *hmm*? Was Frank Shook involved? Or, better, were certain Hollow Earth forces trying to prevent the re-use of the Deepsea Challenger? Cuke-men? Maybe the Australians wanted to use it to investigate the Micronesia ship disappearances, but some Hollow Earth agent tried to block them. A disguised conical Old One or shoggoth.

January 26, 2017. Crazy Triple-Decker Structure (Unused).

I'm starting to think of the "Return to the Hollow Earth" as including my first-person account of a trip with Frank Shook. Kind of in the style of *Saucer Wisdom*. That would be fun for me too, that style, although I'd also enjoy getting into the old-timey Mason Reynolds frame of mind. Maybe I'll do both.

I could structure the book as a triple-decker, with three layers.

(1) *Foreword*. I discuss meeting up with Frank Shook and going to the south seas to get hold of Mason's second journal.

(2) *Mason's Journal*. Describes the shipwreck, his time in San Francisco raising his son, his plan to return to the Hollow Earth, and possibly an account of a second trip inside—although I'd need to figure out how Mason's written account filtered out to us if he's still inside. Could be that Frank Shook and I get Mason's journal from a curious figure who later turns out to be a ridged-barrel Old One, or what I call a cuke-man.

(3) *Editor's Note*. My first person account of a trip to the Hollow Earth with Frank Shook, leading to a meeting with Mason, Seela, and Arf (or a descendent of Arf). This would be the longest part of the book.

So I'd have a modernistic and amusingly (to me) unbalanced structure for the novel, having the main action in the Foreword and Editor's Note. Like *Pale Fire* with the action in the footnotes, or like *Saucer Wisdom*, with the action in my account of my editing process rather than in the Frank Shook notes.

***

I have to figure out what happened to Mason. Unfortunately in my Editor's Note to HE1, 1st edition, I decided to sink his ship on the trip to San Francisco. So I might suppose that he, Seela, and Arf floated to shore on a beam of timber and walked or boated the rest of the way to California. We might suggest that a *woomo* tendril helped to rescue the three from the shipwreck of the Purple Whale—although it's not totally clear to Mason if this is what actually happened. (Or I could just change the Editor's Note.)

Mason and Seela live in San Francisco for a time with Arf, raising their son who's named, say, Silas. And then Mason and his family made his way to the South Pacific, to Fiji, Yap, Pohnpei or Palau. And then Mason and Seela make their way back inside the Hollow Earth, possibly bringing their son Silas along, or perhaps leaving him with an adoptive Melanesian mother.

Maybe Mason wrote up his journal before the trip and left that journal in Fiji and it passed down to Silas's grandson in Fiji. Or, maybe better, Mason's second journal describes his second trip to the Hollow Earth. And either he sent it back from there, or he brought it out himself, or he wrote it after his return.

I would still need to account for how Mason's 1852 drawing made its way into the rebound Berkeley copy of Augustus A. Gould, *Mollusca & Shells*, (Philadelphia : C. Sherman 1852). It would be enough, actually, if Mason left his drawing with a book collector in San Francisco.

In the second Journal, we learn that Mason lived near the Umpteen Seas. He and Seela dipped into the central anomaly at one point and lost about a hundred and fifty years, which is why he's still around. Me meeting Mason will be a surprise twist. And fun for me—to actually meet one of my characters from the past—in the *now*.

Maybe Mason's waiting for me in Fiji or Pohnpei. Expecting me. Told of my advent by some Hollow Earth agents. And we two have to do something together so as to, as per usual, save Earth. And that could be HE3—or it could be a long Editor's Note.

***

In HE1, I say that the *woomo* are aliens using our Hollow Earth as a kind of long-term generation space ship. They also take shorter journeys in UFOs and they lower cuke-man forms of *woomo* in fact arrived here with us in a UFO like pets, or like helpful bacteria. They're telepathic and they enjoy looking at our thoughts.

And the UFO they found in the Earth's core—who came in that? Humans and smaller versions of the Great Old Ones, these little ones like Lovecraftian Elder Ones, shaped like ridged barrels. The Lovecraftian ridged barrels are younger or larval versions of huge Great Old One sea cucumbers at the center. Perhaps we call them cuke-men. It seems that I might also come upon a village of the ridged barrels and, as I speculated before, there might be a now-abandoned settlement of them within our Earth's thousand-mile-thick surface, and this may serve as an exit route if it's not convenient to fly out through an ocean hole.

When Mason or I go inside, he and/or I should meet a village akin to Mason's flowerpeople, but different. A different tribe. Cuke-men and some humans who get along with them. (Note that cuke-men are androgynous.)

***

Rethinking this idea on May 1, 2017, I realize it would be a mistake to include Frank Shook. It's too much to expect that my readers have read not one but two of my background novels. And I should remove any mention of Frank from the Editor's Note of HE1, 2nd ed. I'm also doubting the wisdom of bringing in more of the cuke people aliens. I kind of got that out of my system for now by writing "In the Lost City of Leng" with Paul Di Filippo. The giant sea cucumber Great Old Ones are enough.

January 27-29, 2017. Mainly Mason.

I was rereading some of *The Hollow Earth* last night, and really enjoying it. It's written in the first person, always an easy style for me. Maybe I should just go ahead and make most of the book be a simple account from Mason's point of view. My triple-decker idea—it was just an avoidance technique. Avoiding, that is, the work of "becoming" Mason again, and the work of inventing a new plot.

Better to make the Mason journal be far and away the bulk of the book. Let the sequel be a sequel and don't get all weird and pomo and inside-out. Have HE2 simply flow from HE1 with new chapters. Mason's narrative tells about his second trip. I might have him end up by staying inside the Hollow Earth. How do I get his journal?

(a) Mason sent it out with a cuke-man as messenger. And I, Rudy the editor, got the journal from a shrouded figure wearing a muumuu and a burnoose with glinting eyes within. The figure has a piping Lovecraftian voice. And he's quickly revealed to be a cuke-man.

(b) Or Frank Shook and I steal the Deepsea Challenger and go inside the Hollow Earth and find Mason and he gives me his journal.

(c) Mason comes out and writes up his second journal and I find it with his descendants.

(d) I personally get it from Mason, who did a time jump via the Central Anomaly.

Okay, any of these could work. I'd like to have interesting travelling companions for Mason on his second trip. Perhaps he has Seela, and/or his son Silas, and definitely Arf, or Arf's son.

I had Otha and Eddie Poe as his companions in HE1, and that was great. But now Eddie's dead. Dig up some other famous companion…this would be about 1855. If I do Mark Twain or indeed, *any* writer, that's corny and obvious and a repeat of HE1 and, for that matter, Philip Jose Farmer's *Riverworld* series.

I Googled for San Francisco characters. Emperor Norton, famous nut—boring if he's really crazy, but maybe. Ah Toy, famous exotic Chinese prostitute and madam—nah. I don't know jack about Ambrose Bierce. Need some research. Read some history. "San Francisco at Statehood 1850).

Backing up—in terms of Mason's companions—for one thing I can make Seela a stronger character, she's a bit of a cipher in HE1, as I recall. His son can be a character with a bit of force. But, like I'm saying, I'd like someone with the force of Eddie Poe and/or Otha. I could make a character up. A Sta-Hi type prospector who Mason meets in SF, and the guy wants to go look for gold or, better, gems in the Hollow

Earth. There were some special gems that Mason and Seela got from the black gods, I vaguely recall.

I really need to knuckle buckle hunker down and read *The Hollow Earth.*

February 3, 2017. Rereading HE1.

This week I've been rereading the MonkeyBrain Books 2nd edition of HE1. I'm absorbing the story, and marking up the text a little for minor corrections for the 3rd edition. It's a strong book. Each chapter is about 10 or 12 thousand words long, and has the feel of a solid short story. Very nicely laid out, with a good strong climax in each chapter.

Makes me realize I'll need a strong series of incidents for HE2. I don't fully remember, but I think I more or less made up HE1 as I went along. Meanwhile going back and looping in the necessary foreshadowings and backlinks. The fact that HE1 came together so well wasn't due, in other words, to having a carefully thought out preliminary outline. As so often, I was winging it, counting on the Muse. But certainly I did have some high points in mind. My old "walk in the woods" model, like, "I'll head for that peak, and swing by such-and-such a lake, and walk through this particular canyon." But leave the details of the walk to the emergent terrain.

So my task in the coming weeks and months is to think of some high points I want to hit in HE2. Certainly there's the meta option of Rudy meeting Mason at the end, but before that I need a solid Hollow Earth adventure. And either it's Mason having the adventure or, as I've been suggesting, it's Rudy having the Hollow Earth adventure.

So many of the Mason adventures are particular to it being the *first* trip, a trip of exploration. I'm not sure I could make a second Mason trip as fresh. Maybe it *would* be better to have it be a Rudy trip. And I'd have a different slant on the things I'd see in there. Then I wouldn't have to skirt around the "as I said before" pitfalls of having Mason narrate the second trip.

February 12-14, 2017. Set Aside HE2?

Early in February, I put some effort into a failed version

of a story with Bruce Sterling, the working title was "Black Bucket." And we took a little train trip down to Santa Barbara and back for Sylvia's birthday. And I haven't felt like doing much on the "Return to the Hollow Earth" idea.

I've been on a mad Raymond Chandler kick lately. I read all seven of his novels and put together a lengthy blog post about them. His last two (out of seven) novels weren't all that good. Maybe I would do just as well not to keep trying to: "Do one more job, Louie, just one last job." Maybe 21 novels is enough.

     ***

As I've mentioned, I'm rereading HE1 2nd edition with an eye to republishing it as HE1 3rd edition. And that's worth doing. But I'm not seeing an HE2.

(1) Lack of character. I don't really think I could in fact regain that clear mind state of being Mason Reynolds again. That state came out of me living in Virginia, and of being a certain age. So maybe I could have a "Rudy Rucker" character (a la Saucer Wisdom). But that character, odd as this sounds, doesn't seem so accessible to me anymore.

(2) Lack of wonder. "Return to Ringworld" wasn't as interesting as 'Ringworld." Once you've written about a thrilling wonder like the Ringworld or the Hollow Earth, you don't have anything like so strong a card to play for a sequel volume.

(3) Lack of plot. I can't think of good reason for Mason to make a second trip into the Hollow Earth. Me fending off an alien invasion would be stale. Mason taking Seela back to her home flower seems boring

(4) Integrity. I feel HE1 is one of my great books. And I don't want to saddle it with a weak sequel. Running a "Rudy" character routine or dragging in Lovecraft's cuke-men would degrade HE1. The book went as far as it could, it's a perfect whole, leave it alone.

     ***

I think once again of Robert Silverberg's warning regarding a new novel at this stage of my career. "Make sure it's a good one, Rudy! Otherwise it casts a pall over your earlier ones." I think I dodged that bullet in *Million Mile Road Trip*, which came out quite well.

Annoyingly, *Million Mile Road Trip* remains in limbo. Jeremy Lassen still hasn't done anything about his grandiose suggestion that he might not only publish it, but also repub 9 novels from my Transreal Books backlist. Supposedly he was going to ask his boss a Night Shade for permission, but that still hasn't happened. I don't know why. He's scared to ask, or the boss has already said no, or he wants to just keep me on ice while he waits for his boss to "get on the Rucker train," as Jeremy kindly put it. I don't know. Thinking back to the time I sold him *Jim and the Flims*, I remember he kept me hanging for a few months, maybe four. I got the final word when I quite accidentally ran into the then-publisher of Night Shade at Richard Kadrey's birthday party.

I'm really itching to get *Million Mile Road Trip* out there. I wrote Jeremy an email suggesting that if he can't come up with something, I'll just do it via Kickstarter and Transreal Books again. So far, no answer. I'm getting closer and closer to taking the DIY route.

It's hard to get it up to start a novel when I still haven't published the last one. I wrote a few stories, but now my last two are in limbo, in the submission process. Three different people have asked me if I'd write an SF story relating to our current political situation in the US, what with the new idiot president. But somehow I don't feel like doing that. SF is my *escape* from the bringdown of politics.

I'm thinking I might just paint for awhile I sold eight of my paintings in the last couple of months!

Feb 15 - April 10, 2017. "Lost City of Leng" with Di Filippo.

[Later, on December 27, 2017, I put an edited and tightened-up version of this note into a blog post, promoting the appearance of the novella in the Jan/Feb issue of Asimov's SF.]

SEQUEL TO "AT THE MOUNTAINS OF MADNESS"

I want to write a 20 or 30 thousand word novella that's a sequel to Lovecraft's classic novella "At the Mountains of Madness," or ATMOM for short. Do quite seriously, a real push to make something great. Not a jape. But no need to be *too* serious about it, I suppose. Given that I'm more or less incapable of writing something that isn't, at some level, at least to me, funny.

The tale is related to the Starkweather-Moore expedition that Lovecraft's character William Dyer is inveighing against. I want to collaborate on it with Paul Di Filippo. Serious pastiche is one of Paul's fortes, and I enjoy it myself...I call it "twinking." Cf. my novel *The Hollow Earth*.

Maybe we'll call it "The Plateau of Leng" which was Lovecraft's indirectly intimated name for both the Elder One's city and for the landscape it was in.

Figure 2: Awesome Fake "Classics Illustrated" Comic Cover for ATMOM

By way of gearing up for this project, I'm working on a

Rudy Rucker

painting provisionally called, "At the Mountains of Madness." Based on the scene where Lovecraft's Dyer and Danforth are walking down along the friezes in the corridors in the millions-of-years-old lost Antarctic city of Leng.

As an aside, I found a nice online edition of "At the Mountains of Madness." The page includes reproduction of a truly bitchin' cover the Classics Illustrated edition of the book, shown a page or two down from here. It features a raging echinoderm Elder One or what I'll call a "cuke-man" waving a hapless dog and a man. Dig the frieze in the background, right? Love the guy cringing in his Antarctic furs. When I posted the image on Facebook, one of my more comics-savvy readers, Seth Kallen Deitch, informed me the cover is a fake. Wonder who the artist is. I just love those shades of green.

Looking up "At the Mountains of Madness" on Wikipedia, the closest thing to a sequel is Stross's "A Colder War" in *Toast* which I don't remember very well. Also this:

"Chaosium Games released a campaign book [that is, a connected series of battles, adventures, and scenarios] titled Beyond the Mountains of Madness for their *Call of Cthulhu* role-playing game in 1999. This book details the Starkweather-Moore expedition return to the ice to discover the truth about the Miskatonic Expedition. The book incorporates many of the aspects of the original Lovecraft story, including references to the Poe story novel The Narrative of Arthur Gordon Pym of Nantucket, [the artist] Nicholas Roerich, [and the characters] Danforth and Dyer."

The campaign book is on Abe Books for $120+ so fuck that, too expensive. Might be just as well not to read it anyway. Side thought: my characters can act as if they've read "The Narrative of Mason Algiers Reynolds" as well as "The Narrative of Arthur Gordon Pym."

Random idea: Have the characters be beatniks, a la "Yage Letters," searching for deeper kicks? Nah, that would be corny, also I just did beats it in *Turing & Burroughs.*

82

Would be more fun to do a full-on Cthulhu Mythos tale. Not that Ole Tentacle-Face actually needs to appear.

I just now wrote Paul to ask if he *will* collaborate on this, and he's like yeah, but not just now, he has commitments. I wrote back, "Went and read Kubla Khan just now. Possibly can work in some of my Hollow Earth stuff into our tale, seems logical that's where Coleridge's Alf and the river in ATMOM both ran. Stench of penguins at their indoor pen at the NYC central Park zoo. Riding down through the sunless sea on the backs of two penguins. The resounding *bonng* of freedom and air as our characters pop out into the Hollow Earth. And there in the far distance, at the Hollow Earth's Central Anomaly, there one can see *zonnng* the giant sea cucumbers, the true Great Old Ones.

Figure 3: Rudy and Paul at Lovecraft's Grave in Providence, 2003.

I pestered Paul some more. He said he was booked till

March 26, but he allowed as how he might have some "interstitial time." I was, like:

Aha. Secret interstitial high-quality Di Filippo time is on tap! I'm gonna frikkin' start the story this week. Time spent on the "wrong" project is always the sweetest.

First I'll make a few notes. I'm thinking the characters might be Starkweather and Moore, the guys who HPL's character says were about to make the second expedition. We can do it transreal style like I do with Bruce, I'll be one, you be the other. But we can write both characters, either one of us can write whatever. Say you're Moore. Moore is the narrator. He's from Providence. He's more of a practical guy. Starkweather is his somewhat flaky prof pal, and that's me. It'll be a team a little like Mason Reynolds with Edgar Allan Poe in the Hollow Earth novel.

Maybe we add in a woman as well. She starts out as Starkweather's wife, but she ends up with Moore. Starkweather dies or disappears near the end, he tumbles off toward the center of the hollow earth. He'll want to be with the giant sea-cukes at Earth's core. I'll get some notes together and write maybe 3 or 4 thousand words and send it to you in a week or two.

And Paul was like, "Go, man, go. Love it. It's been too long." So he's in. Great. Paul is great to work with.

***

I read Stross's "A Colder War" from *TOAST*, which is, as I mentioned a post ATMOM tale. As one would expect from Stross, it's very strong, and even a bit daunting. It's set in the Reagan years, and the existence of the "plateau of Leng" with the lost city of the Elder Ones (which might also be called Leng) is systematically covered up by the powerful nations—they signed a 1935 "Dresden Accord." Even Hitler signed.

In the end, to my relief, Stross's tale devolves into a WWIII disaster story, with Lovecraftian Old Ones appearing off-camera. On camera we have some star-gates to other worlds. Bleak worlds, not so interesting. And an emphasis on the *Evil* quality of the alien critters. He veers off into another area of the Cthulhu mythos, the Eater of Souls thing, and at the end we sense that the main character is *literally* in Hell.

I also read I. N. J. Culbard's graphic novel version of "At the Mountains of Madness." This one is nicely laid out, but somehow it's kind of weak. The buildings of Leng don't look alien at all...they look like Chicago. And the friezes get short shrift, and the cuke-men aren't so good, nor is the shoggoth, and the author writes the word "Tekeli-li" at least a hundred times in big red letters near the end of the book, which doesn't accomplish much. His big eyeless penguin is good.

One more source to check, suggested to me by Paul Di Filippo: Alan Moore and Kevin O'Neill, *Nemo: Heart of Ice.* I just bought it online. It came, I looked at it, a bunch of crap, unreadable. He, too, takes the sacred word *tekelili* in vain. The one good thing is a super-intense drawing of a shoggoth.

    ***

In any case, it looks like there's room for an immediate post-ATMOM tale involving the Starkweather-Moore expedition. To give it a bit of an outsider spin, it could be that our trio of characters (two guys and a girl) are *not* in the S-M expedition. They're freebooting drifters who go to Leng on their own, and have to outfox and/or save and/or be saved by the S-M crew. Or, no, better, let's say the S-M expedition has already been sent down and it was a fucking disaster with every single person killed and the support ships sucked down into giant maelstroms as well! Of course! Naturally this is covered up. And then our chracters skeeve down there while the world powers dither whether to send a yet-larger expedition including full military support.

Having just three or maybe four in the party would make the story's setup more lightweight. They'd need a special plane that can fly really far and high and carry a buttload of gas in expanded tanks, enough gas for the flight back, but that's doable with 30's tech, possibly modulo some slight rubber science tweaks. And they can *steal* the plane, so they don't really have to be that rich or well-equipped.

Figure 4: ATMOM in Astounding Stories, 1936

An issue I'm worrying about is how our guys will deal with the shoggoths. These seem to be group organisms like mold slime, giant slugs the size of a subway train with eyes and mouths spontaneously forming and dissolving all over their surface. Capable of moving as fast as, say, a running horse. How do you kill one of those with tweaked '30s tech? Projectiles seem fruitless. A flamethrower might work, but that's hella heavy to lug over the Mountains of Madness and down into the tunnels of "Leng." Need something trickier.

I'm thinking ultrasonics. Like a dog whistle. A shoggoth whistle. Breaks the thing up into amoebas. That "tekelili" chirp is how it holds itself together, an acoustic control system that marshals the protean cells of the undifferentiated tissues of the monster into form. You can carry the shoggoth whistle in your pocket! One of our guys, or the gal, invents it.

Juices starting to flow, Muse casting flirty glances my way, twitching her hem upwards.

CHARACTERS

How about the characters? For his character, Paul suggested Diego Patchen, a character name from his novella "A Year in the Linear City." Maybe we call him Doug Patchen so it's a different person.

Doug Patchen (27) is a young, eager reporter for the Boston Globe. He has some girlfriends, but nothing serious as yet. Doug has done stories on both of the other two male characters, which is how he knows them. He thinks the people in Arkham are full of shit and, as a reverse twist, this turns out to be, by and large, true. We're not going to see Cthulhu in this story.

Stan Gorski (45) used to fly a rescue plane for the Boston Coast Guard. He lost his pilot's license for drinking and for getting involved in liquor smuggling. (Prohibition ran from 1920-1933.). Works as a plane mechanic now. Has a wife and four kids. A tough guy, Chandleresque.

Dog. Gorski has a dog named Gurrr (?). Or maybe Hauhau, which is supposed to be the Polish imitation of barking. Or, no, give the dog to Doug Patchen, and use the name of Paul's former dog, Brownie, if that's okay with him.

Leon Bagger (37), a marine biologist. And Bagger's wife Ariel (32). Leon and Ariel are Australian. She's an artist, she does watercolors of sea creatures for monographs. Doug develops a huge crush on Ariel, who in turn flirts with him. Doug met these two while doing a Sunday supplement article on them.

I changed Ariel to Vivi, basing her on the sister of the Swedish adventuress and aviator, Ester Blenda Nordström.

Leon specializes in echinoderms (sea stars, sea urchins, sand dollars, and sea cucumbers, as well as the sea lilies). Especially sea cucumbers. Leon has been trapping sea cukes on the deep sea floor off Boston, in the Grand Banks. He had a problem in his research boat—it was sinking—and Stan Gorski rescued him. Leon and Ariel are visiting scholars at the Harvard Department of Invertebrate Zoology, part of the Museum of Comparative Zoology. The museum's echinoderm collection is one of the richest in the world. Founded 1860.

Figure 5: Ester Blenda Nordström, model for Vivi.

Leon gets in touch with Doug because he objects so strongly to the upcoming military attack on Leng. He found out via upper-echelon Harvard faculty club gossip. Leon feels the Elder Ones—whom he calls cuke-men or cuke-girls—are meant to be our friends. He wants Doug to help him organize a commando-like rogue expedition to Leng in the Mountains of Madness before the joint US-Australian military expedition goes there. Leon, who's quite a schemer, has gotten in touch with Stan as well. Stan is up for anything, with his background of bootlegger connections.

And—oh yeah, this'll kick it up a big notch—have a cuke-girl in the posse. She made her way to Boston (or at least to Melbourne) and connected with Leon Bagger to talk

Figure 6: Great drawing of a cuke-man. By Jason B. Thompson.

about the threat to her race. A little tricky for her to disguise herself as human. See the image below!

Name? Urxa for now. Or even Urxula, but that's maybe too much.

Great reveal when Doug meets the cuke-girl in Leon's

office.

PLANE

Figure 7: The Grumman Plane Stan Gorski Flew for Coast Guard Rescue, 1930.

I was briefly tempted by the <u>Dornier Do X</u> planes, also called a flying boat. In 1930 it was the heaviest plane in the world. It has six engines in a row atop the flat wing and six more in the back and is enormous inside, with fifty passengers and a crew of 19. But the Do X could only manage an altitude of about 1,500 feet. And they only built three of them. Too kludgy.

In ATMOM they have large Dornier seaplanes that land on deep snow, and I assume they are the *Wal* (Whale or Do J) planes. <u>Amundsen</u> used a Do J (range 500 mi, ceiling 12,000 feet). Ceiling matters as the highest peaks are 35,000 feet and the creepier mountains are 40,000 feet. But the pass to Leng is 24,000 feet. But Lovecraft just didn't worry about this. Or he was working from the fact that the plateau at the base of those mountains is at 12,000 feet. Range matters more, if we plan to fly direct to Leng from Australia.

For our novella, I like the <u>Dornier Do 24</u>, developed by Dornier for the Dutch Navy, mainly used by the Luftwaffe. All metal. Can carry bombs. Armed with Hispano-Suiza cannon and 2 machine guns. Crew of 6. Do 24 range is 1,600 miles, ceiling 26,000 feet. Had three Wright Cyclone radial engines mounted up on the overhead wing. You could fly it from, say, Sydney or Melbourne or, better, Ushuaia, capital of Tierra del Fuego, at the tip of South America, I'm saying you could fly from there to Leng if you managed to refill the gas tank on the way…you could manage that if you brought some barrels of fuel. Or, better yet, outfit the thing with double or triple size tanks of gas. The gas, by the way, was stored in "sponsons," which are stubby wing-like projections from the fuselage. Also gas in the tail, I suppose. If you double-size the tanks you can do 3,200 miles.

The Australian air force had a Do 24. Dornier is said (probably mistakenly) by one source to have developed the Do 24 in 1934, although another source says the first flights begun only in 1937. But I want a Do 24 planes at the end of 1933. We'll just fudge by saying they're using a prototype, specially commissioned, let's call it a Do 24x, with x for experimental, and with a nod to the giant Do X. But it's really a Do 24.

Figure 8: The Dornier DO 24.

To land a seaplane in deep snow is feasible, by the way although we might get Stan Gorski to add some ski-struts—or, simpler, assume the Exterminator mission guys have already done that, as well as enlarging the tanks.

Regarding range, again, I notice that, as of 2017, there are round trip day-flights over Antarctica from both Sydney and Melbourne, Australia. Round trip flight time is about 12 hours in a 747, and it's about a 6,000 mile round trip. If we don't tour around too much, that's not much more than 3 x 1600, that is, triple the normal range of a Do 26.

I'd been talking about going via Melbourne, but wait, looking at Google Earth, I see a shorter geodesic path that goes straight down along the west coast of South America. About 8,000 miles. The Do 24 range is, again, 1,600 miles, and if I've doubled or tripled the size of the fuel tank, I can do this in three or four hops.

If we fly straight down along South America, and it's about 10,000 miles. A Do 24 cruises at about 200 mph. So we're looking at a 50 hour flight, not too bad. Break it into five hops with the last stop before Antarctica in Ushuaia in Tierra Del Fuego. Except for the last hop, it's about ten hours each, not bad, do it in four or five days.

Boston - Kingston - Lima - Valparaiso - Ushuaia (in Tierra Del Fuego) - Leng

Maybe they push through and do the first two hops back to back to get away from any pursuit.

Boston - Lima - Valparaiso - Ushuaia - Leng

3,600 mi - 1,500 mi - 1,500 mi - 3,500 mi

18 hr - 7 hr - 7 hr - 17 hr

As I say, the distances aren't too bad, if we have a double size tank, although that last one is a brutal 3,500 miles in 17 hours, and you drain the tank. They won't have any gas to get back. Bagger and Gorski know this, but they don't tell Doug. They're counting on the cukes to carry them back. Urxula told them they would. They could fly 2,500 to get back to Tasmania. But that's hard too.

To keep things simple, let's say that we steal the Do 24x in Boston at the very end of December 1933, on New Year's Eve. Just checked and—how beautiful—there was a full moon that night. Perfect for a long flight.

To speed up the story, I'll double up the first flight, from Boston to Lima, make it an 19 hour death-run across 3,600 miles. Like they're scared of pursuit. And want to see if they can do a run like that.

To make things exciting, suppose that one of the other Do 24x planes sets out in pursuit a day later...but they lose him in Kingston. Anyway in the 1930s, they might not even be able to track where our guys are.

I was worried about having to hand-start the three engines of the Do 24x, but it seems like by 1930 some planes had <u>electric starters</u>. I'll just assume they have a set of those. And starting the plane in Antarctica won't be a problem as by then they'll be out of gas anyway…

DATE

ATMOM expedition starts from Boston on September 2, 1930, and when they get to Antarctica it's November 7, 1930. It's not quite clear when Lovecraft's story is written, perhaps in mid-1931, and the Starkweather-Moore expedition would be in the fall/winter of 1931. Maybe they're so bummed about Danforth's report in ATMOM that they postpone the Starkweather-Moore till, say, 1932? But, nah, I bet Moore and Starkweather just go for it in 1931.

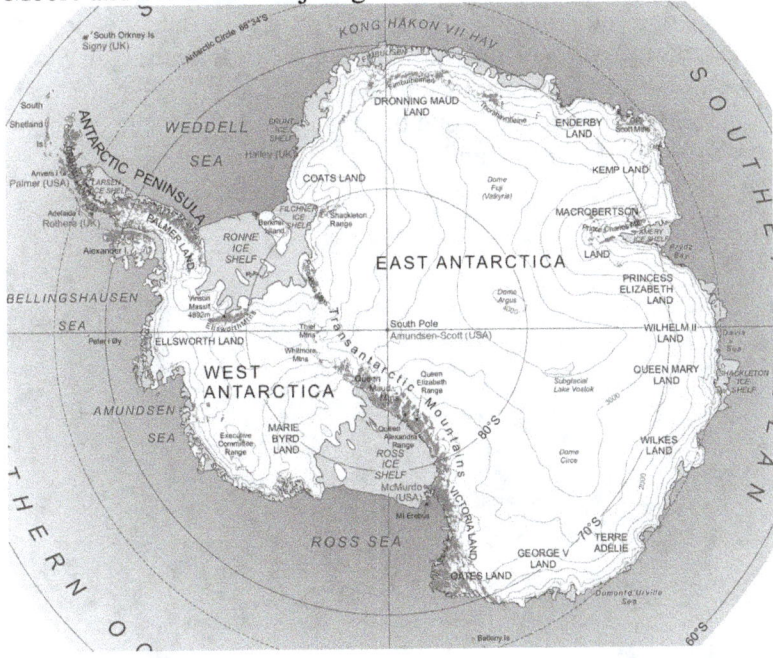

Figure 9: Map of Antarctica. Leng is by Lake Vostok.

And then I'm saying the S-M explorers were massacred by shoggoths—*despite the cuke-men's attempt to restrain the shoggoths*—and their ships disappeared into maelstroms. There may also have been some damage from mysteriously purposeful lightning bolt, as were observed by Dyer above the next peaks over (the true Mountains of Madness.) And it wasn't covered up, it was all on the radio.

After the utter disaster of Starkweather-Moore, nobody does a follow-up for a couple of years. Let's say this brings us to the end of 1933. And the US is planning a secret expedition, they're calling it the Extermination operation. And our guys steal the plane.

LOCATION:

Lovecraft's Leng is near Lat 76 15' S, Long 113 10' E. In East Antarctica, which is (I hadn't known this) the part of Antarctica that's in the Eastern hemisphere. It's close to being due south of New Zealand and Australia, and the closest airport might be Hobart in Tasmania, or Melbourne, or Sydney. It's on a plateau beyond the volcanic Mt. Erebus in McMurdo Sound. Beyond the Transantarctic Range. Inland from Queen Mary Land.

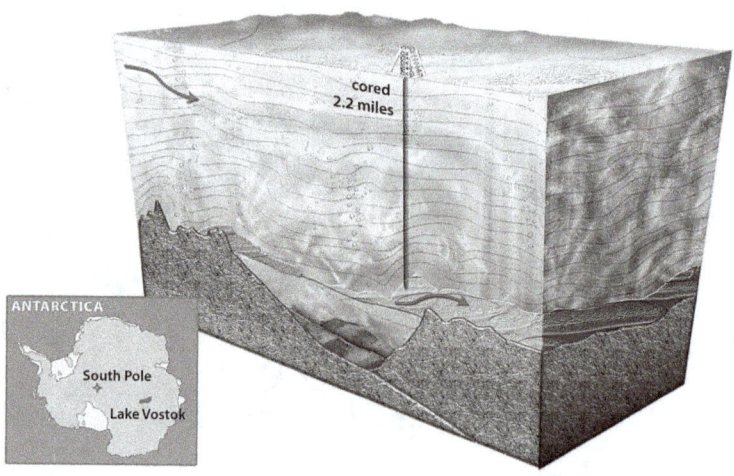

Figure 10: Lake Vostok

Turns out Leng is near the subglacial Lake Vostok , which Stross incorporates into his "A Colder War" of 2002. Lake Vostok's existence was suspected around 1960, and confirmed around 1990. By some uncanny vision or stroke of luck, Lovecraft writes about a warm subterranean lake beneath the Elder One's city of Leng. And William Dyer and the grad student Danforth or on their way there when the encounter the shoggoth.

Lake Vostok is at 77 S, 106 E, Also near the Southern "Pole of Cold," that is, the spot where the coldest temperatures occur, at 78 S 102 E. Record: -130 degrees Fahrenheit, in July, 1983. Temperatures rise only to -10 F in the summer season of December to February.

The surface of Lake Vostok is some 13,000 feet below the surface of the 12,000 foot thick ice, which puts the surface over 1,000 feet below sea level. This creepy lake is 150 miles by 30 miles, and is itself up to 2,500 feet deep. The Russians have drilled down to sample its water—one hopes without contaminating it.

Mason Reynolds, Leon Bagger, and I know, however, that a passage to the Hollow Earth lies beneath the lake.

THE THIRD THING

In AMOM, there's some third thing other than the cukes and the shoggoths. Danforth sees something in the sky as they were leaving, and Dyer tremulously writes about this. A list of things Danforth said. I edited out the boring ones.

> He has on rare occasions whispered disjointed
> and irresponsible things about "the carven rim",
> "the windowless solids with five dimensions", "the
> primal white jelly", "the color out of space", "the
> moon-ladder"; but when he is fully himself he repu-
> diates all this and attributes it to his curious and ma-
> cabre reading of earlier years.

And then I put these things into a vision that my Doug Patchen has.

You could also call the third thing the "Unknown Kadath." On the other hand, what if it's a *good* thing? Just for a twist.

OUTLINE, FEBRUARY 21, 2017

So if we want to write a novella, we need several blocks of story. Here's a first slash at it.

I To Leng! Tell back story and get our characters onto the plane to Leng.

II The Cukes. Leon enables them to find and to talk to a colony of cuke-men, who are agitated over the impending invasion. The cukes can hear radio waves, and generate them. They talk via the short-wave radio the crew brought along. The cuke-men are in some sense using Earth as a spaceship, riding it to wherever our solar system happens to be going.

III. The Battle with the Shoggoths. They use ultrasonics to wipe out the nest of Shoggoths beneath Leng. But not with full success. Maybe jealous Leon dynamites the entrance to the tunnel under Leng so that Doug and Vivi are trapped there—and then they have to exit via the Hollow Earth.

IV. The Lake. They flee go down into the deep subterranean lake, riding on the backs of cukes, who feed them air from their mouths.

V. The Hollow Earth. At the bottom of the lake is a hole leading into the Hollow Earth. Maybe it's just Doug and Vivi, or maybe Leon is with them after all, and he flips out and wants to fly all the way in to the center to be with the giant sea cucumbers there. Vivi becomes young Doug's lover. Stan Gorski gets drunk and fucks Urxula (maybe) or otherwise pisses off the locals and they have to leave in haste. Doug and Vivi get married.

VI. They make their way home and forestall further invasions of Leng.

NOTES, MARCH 20, 2017

We're going along well, nearly 14,000 words into the story now. I'm writing like a maniac—polishing, patching, and adding—fitting our word hoard into a seemly form. Putting a spandex Spanx body-shaper onto our textual shoggoth.

I think I'll drop any detailed Hollow Earth stuff, although perhaps the cukes can adumbrate it. Maybe their goal is to go down through Vostok lake into the Hollow Earth, and the shoggoths are hanging them up. We won't follow them through the lake and into the Hollow Earth—that would be "a bridge too far." We won't even explicitly say there's a star gate inside the Hollow Earth, although maybe there is one. Hollow planets are like stepping stones, or teleportation booths, you hop from one interior to the next.

At a lower level, I'm thinking that, during the battle with the shoggoths, Doug himself blows up the fuel dump, firing a Do 24 cannon blast into it because the boss shoggoth is right on top of the fuel dump at that moment. And Doug thinks he's screwed, but oh well, he saved the day for the cukes. And then the plane with frikkin' Teirney shows up, and those guys save him.

Not sure if Professor Leon is still alive in the end. Maybe yes, why not. The two guys were the dupes of Vivi and now she's gone and they're comrades in arms.

I'm assuming that Vivi is in fact a cuke, she's been one all along, and of course Urxula knew this, but Professor Leon didn't know, or maybe he does to some extent know. Vivi uses a "glamour," that is, hypnotic teep to make herself seem like a woman to them. She isn't actually speaking words out loud, only piping, and the teep makes it sound like words. Vivi enlisted Leon so she could get her ultrasound amplifier working, and so the cukes cold sing the shoggoth to bits. And it almost works, but there's a final white-slime shuggoth core that's immune to the music and it's rampaging up towards them, and that's the one that Doug blows up with the fuel dump—and maybe he's put the dynamite in there too.

I do still want a scene in those tunnels with the cuke hieroglyphs. Maybe Vivi and Leon and Baxter and Urxula go down there to lure the shoggoths out.

Two Issues

(1) Paul had the idea of them learning a shoggoth-language spell that would stop a shoggoth in its tracks. But why wouldn't the cukes know this chant, and be using it? Maybe it only works if it's declaimed in an ultrasonic treble which penetrates into the bodies of shoggoths.

(2a) A problem: If I have, like, a cubic mile of shoggoth, then blowing up the fuel dump isn't going to kill them. Unless—the shoggoths are flammable. And in the end, it's the flame thrower that turns the tide. Prefigure his by having the shoggoth in Ushuaia harbor catch fire, though that would be too obvious, have it smoldering, or have them see a plume of smoke behind them.

(2b) The fire is a little kludgy. How about this...I'd said that a lot of the Starkweather guys were killed by smart lightning bolts. Either I have to bring bolts back into our story, or I need to drop them. A nice option would be to have the lightning bolts recur in the grand finale of the battle against the shoggoths—we try and use the flame at first like Doug despairingly blows up the fuel dump under the shoggoth, shooting it with the cannon, and it looks like the slugs are terminally raging on fire, but then *whoops* the ultra shoggoth pinches out the flame and comes crawling forward—and that's when the storm kicks up and the lightning zaps the shuggoth mass into extinction. They could play across the mountains and kill of the castle-lurking shoggoths as well.

Oh, the kicker: Teirney is a shoggoth. Like a Trump appointee. The boys haven't in fact killed all the shoggoths. Just the wad of them that were blocking Vostok Lake (which needs a different name, make it Alph.)

End: The shoggoths are among us. (And somehow hint that Trump is one).

Or: If we want a clean happy ending, there can be one last lightning pop to kill Teirney.

Another problem: How do they refuel Tierney's plane?

Possible extra twist, the Mountains of Madness shrink down, and Leng totally disappears? But maybe that's too: "And then little Nemo fell out of bed and woke up." Why close down Leng for good.

I'm thinking the flying slugs are a distraction and maybe we should drop them.

Later. I put in pretty much all of these fixes and some new stuff, adding 4,000 words. And I attached the following outline to the manuscript I sent Paul.

OUTLINE FOR ENDING, MARCH 20, 2017

1. Vivi, Doug, and Baxter set out, armed only with .45 pistols and a Very flare. Also some good flashlights. We do a fast recap of ATMOM's trip down through the galleries, past the eyeless albino penguins, still further down and to the shore of a dark underground lake. [I'm nuts about those historical friezes, and later I'll elaborate on whatever you say about them. We can tweak them to impart some of the backstory.]

2. On the shore of Lake Alph, Vivi starts singing, Baxter is howling, they butcher a penguin and set off a Very flare. The lake billows and wallows, and here comes the biggest shuggoth ever. The whole enchilada. Like maybe the size of a battleship, or larger, like a cube that's 500 yards on each side. Like a big building.

3. They haul ass up to the surface, and when they come out of the tunnel, Vivi's screaming at Leon and Urxula to run the ultrasound speaker, but they're bumbling and fucking up. **Heroic Doug lures the megashoggoth to one side to save his girl.** Vivi makes it to the tent, she gets the machine working, she chirps out *"Hafh'drn 'ai nog fhtagn,"* all ultrasonic, and okay the shoggoth is frozen.

4. Leon noticed that the shoggoth in the harbor back in Ushuaia seemed like it caught fire, so he drags the flame thrower over to the megashoggoth and tries to light the big slug up. **A flying slug-man interferes.** A squadron of several hundred of them. Doug jumps into the plane and picks them off Space Invaders style. Meanwhile the flame thrower gets ruined. Oh shit.

5. Signs of the megashoggoth about to wake up. He happens to be stopped right on top of the fuel dump. Doug decides to sacrifice their future for the present. He gets the others to help him lug the crate of dynamite over to the megashoggoth and the fuel dump. They back off and get in the plane and **Doug fires the cannon.** Big explosion, all the dynamite and all the fuel.

6. The shoggoth is definitely damaged, good, but he's awake again, bad, but he's on fire, good, and the ultrasonic speaker isn't working anymore, bad, and now **the shoggoth bends himself in half, staunching out his flames,** double

bad. They run like crazy. They're screwed.

7. A bunch more of the cukes have come up from underground. Watching the spectacle. Waving their arms as if in prayer. A sudden storm kicks up from the Mountains of Madness. A fusillade of giant lightning bolts zaps the effing shoggoth into dust. Lightning even plays across the nearby mountains, eliminating any shoggoths or flying slugs that might be in those castles. Like a gum massager finding flecks of rotten food. It's all good. We've won.

8. Of course now they're stuck here with no fuel. But wait, here comes the second Do-24, with frikkin' Teirney inside. He's like a Trump appointee, a frog faced guy, a slimy Republican (though we don't flat out say this.) . He's mad that they killed the shoggoths. Vivi loses her temper and blows away Teirney and his plane with the cannon. His surviving crew have no loyalty to his cause. They beg our guys for help.

9. Fine, but still no gas. But, ta da, a stream of friendly cukes files by, like Hawaiian natives presenting leis, each of them expelling five or six gallons of primo aircraft fuel into the Do 24's tanks. They cukes can synthesize anything, you understand. Singing and dancing, the cukes disappear into the passages of Leng, bound for Lake Alph, the Hollow Earth, and mayhap the stars. Reveal (though the reader will have guessed by now): Vivi is a cuke. She's just been using what fantasists would call a "glamour" to make the boys think she was a girl. Telepathic hypnosis. Leon kind of knew all along.

10. So they load up their plane and fly back to Boston. The End.

FINISHING IT. APRIL 2-10, 2017.

Paul sent me version 6, pretty well wrapping it up at 17,800 words. He left out a couple of moves that I still might put in, and added some others, mostly better ones. In my previous ending outline of March 20 2017, shown above, I bold-faced a few twists I still want. I'll work some of those in, and then I'll go over the whole thing and try to get the tone right—I'd like it to be serious, although somewhat funny. And have consistent voices for the characters.

So okay, by April 6, I had the ending down, and I went through it to make the whole thing consistent. I also started reading another H. P. Lovecraft story, "The Whisperer in Darkness," which Paul had been talking about. He got his "planet Yuggoth" from there, also a guy Henry Akeley who had his brain packed in a can.

I sent Paul my version 7, he sent back a very slightly changed version 8, and then I dug in a worked for a week on the final version, number 9. As I wrote Paul about it:

"I went over the whole thing once, and went over the final part three or four times. Thickening and smoothing and logicizing. I made Leon a bit more of a bohemian. Added a couple of small eyeball kick scenes: a vision of Leng 100,000 years ago, and a view of Lake Alph, lit by Vivi's flare gun. The very last scene has the welcome feel of Jack and Neal on the road. And now it's 21K words and change. A novella, yes."

Paul sent it off to F&SF, and now we'll see. IMHO, a Hugo and a Nebula would be in order, but I've been wrong about such things before :)

It was really fun getting into this world, and now I miss it. Note that I added a Hollow Earth element to the story, which kind of nudges me to go back to HE2. I liked our character Doug Patchen for "In the Lost City of Leng." An unsure-of-himself young reporter in 1934. Could use a character like that for HE2.

April 20, 2017. So now, much to our fury and chagrin, Charles Findlay has rejected "Leng" for *F&SF* magazine. Too raw for his taste it seems, not po-faced enough. Numbnuts uptight entrenched mandarin that he is. So much for the visions of Nebulas dancing in my head. Like Eddie Poe's visions of treasure in his "Gold Bug" story. Well, *Weird Tales* rejected our man Lovecraft's "At the Mountains of Madness." And he pretty much gave up on writing fiction and died a few years later. Whoops! I sent "Leng" on to Sheila Williams at *Asimov's* and we hope for the best.

April 25, 2017. Yes! Sheila bought it. Such a relief. Now on to HE2!

April 13, 2017. Back to HE2.

So now with "In the Lost City of Leng" finished, and, as of today, "Black Bucket" decisively abandoned, I'm thinking again about *Return to the Hollow Earth*. HE2.

Doing the Lovecraft sequel as a standalone has slaked—or piqued?—my appetite for including the subterranean race of sea cucumber poeple. I do have a nice clear image of those "cuke" people now, and I might yet cast them in the coming epic.

But that other idea I had, of putting myself into the novel as a character, the idea of an ultra-transreal Saucer-Wisdom-style structure for HE2 seems silly and distracting. If I do HE2 about someone other than Mason (someone like me). I kind of need to recapitulate everything that Mason did in HE1—and that would be boring to write.

So the best option is just to have HE2 be written by Mason Algiers Reynolds, just like HE1 was. I can set this somewhat later in time, like have him be in his 30s or 40s. I could even have him be an old man, but who wants to read about an old man. Or if I do ever want to do that, save it for a putative HE3.

HE1 was purely picaresque. There was no specific goal, other than the lust for exploration. But, as the helpful Muse would have it, in the end a plot came together—hinging on the duality of the two worlds, and on Poe's theme of the double.

To draw him back into the journey in HE2, it seems like I do need a quest. A Monomyth-style tale, in other words. Suppose one of Seela's relatives comes up to get help. Some evil force is decimating the flowerpeople. Someone like Trump.

Drag in fresh aliens? Nah. We got enough aliens with the Great Old Ones. And the two Earths. And—I know I talked about this before, on Jan 26, 2017 but it's been three months—who rode those ancient flying saucers to Earth in the first place? I have to check what HE1 says. I think I said the ancient *woomo* came in the UFOs. Maybe they brought primeval humans along. And I'd been saying maybe they had some Lovecraft "cuke" men in it.

So, to start with, I'll get back to doing that reread & revise in HE1.

April 20, 2017. Hiking Zabriskie Point. Casting HE2.

Sylvia and I are on a road trip. We spent a night at Sorensen's Resort near Carson Pass. It was alternately raining and snowing.

I had a great Zen moment near the lodge, snowshoeing across a sodden meadow by a swollen, chaotic river, the snow dropping heavily, at a slight angle to the vertical, etching with white each damp dead grass blade and bosky spring twig. Me there on the bank, the rushing stream, my thoughts, the slightly off-kilter snow, the latent waiting growth all around, the insects under the tree bark, the protozoa in the moss in the stream, my breath, all of us together, no zap mind flash, just standing there, in the One, grateful.

Then we drove down the east side of the Sierras, and spent a night on Lone Pine, which was great. At the base of Mr. Whitney, With these awesomely knobby "Alabama Hills" below Then we drove to Death Valley to spend two nights in the deluxe Furnace Creek Inn.

Looking at Death Valley, I keep finding myself saying—"So *why* did we want to come here?" Today we got up before dawn and saw the sun rise at 6":15 am from Zabriskie point. It rose slowly for almost an hour, embossing more and more of the wrinkled rocks. I went off on a two hour "Badlands Loop" hike there, and by the end, I was completely lost, and having to scramble over these two hundred foot cones of dirt, getting a brief view of my goal, and then back into the maze, so very much like life itself.

Repeatedly of late, I'll have these flashes that the ambient chaotic natural processes around me are objective-correlatives for my psychic state, or for my right-that-moment interactions with Sylvia. This is in a good way. Like the world is thinking me, instead of me thinking the world.

On the badlands trek, I finally got some new ideas for how to set up the character roster for HE2.

How about this: Seela bore Mason a beloved son, and

Rudy Rucker

died young. Mason married a woman who is something of a callipygous Xantippe, I mean an attractive woman with a sharp tongue, and clever. Seela was maybe flat as a character, like an angel. Mason, now in his forties, makes a trip to the Hollow Earth with his son and his loudmouth new wife along.

Or it could be the same Seela wife with Mason after all. Seela could *grow into* the more acerbic and independent character I want. No need, really, to kill her off and replace her. Mason has an old wife, , such as mine. But maybe I don't want to write about own life, an old man with his old wife. On the one hand, the more transreal it is, the more good jokes I know, and the more emotion I can muster, on the other hand, writing about my wife (in a story that she will read) introduces constraints of taste and diplomacy, and could become overly mannered or stilted---due to my self-imposed restraint. Not quite sure how to go on this.

And do I in fact want Mason to have to bring a wife along on his second great adventure? In the transreal sense again, my novels are adventures for me, escapes, and do I want to have my wife with me? As it is, I do take my wife with me on my trips in reality. But maybe I want to do my imaginary trips on my own. Maybe that's more fun for the reader, too. I sometimes find novels about old marrieds doing things to be boring. Too domestic. As I say, the reader wants an adventure, too. Not just dinner with the cutely squabbling old neighbor couple.

Maybe Seela is dead, and Mason meets a new wife in the Hollow Earth, and she is in fact someone like Sylvia. Maybe Seela is dead on Earth but somehow is reborn inside the Hollow Earth. Come to think of it, I did kill off the wife for most of *Jim and the Flims*, and then brought her back at the end. Pretty much the same move. Jeez, I keep having the same ideas and thinking they're new. What's that word for that phenomenon? Cryptomnesia. Gotta watch that.

Or, um, what if Mason and Seela are both dead, and HE2 is the narrative of Mason's son who is traveling with his girlfriend. Or Mason's daughter, like a Thuy Nguyen character, traveling with a boy. Either way, now we're writing a novel like *Million Mile Road Trip*. And we need a third wheel, an

104

idiot—like the little brother in *MMRT*. Or we do the two-guys route, like in HE1. Mason's son and…"someone like Dennis." Like the two boys in *Mathematicians in Love.*

Groping, losing it. I'll have to rethink this anew.

***

Back to the Zabriskie point hike. At that time, or during the night after, I had a dream or a vision of a really huge McDonald's, like a golden Hindu temple, or a Vegas casino, wreathed in golden lights, with a facade as intricate as a neon cathedral. And when Sylvia and I left the Furnace Creek Inn to drive home, I was totally convinced that this McDonalds was an actual restaurant that we'd find down by the pawky bar and general store of the Furnace Creek Ranch oasis. And I was surprised the golden radiant neon McDonald's wasn't there, but then I thought it would be at Stovepipe Wells, and it wasn't there, and I thought it would be at Panamint Springs, and it wasn't, and then finally I admitted to myself and to Sylvia that I was suffering from a—hallucinatory delusion. Kind of scary. Like I'm losing my mind.

April 24, 2017. The Burrowers.

To get things rolling, a messenger from the Hollow Earth appears, a classic Monomyth opening. A " burrower."

Figure 11: Jeroon

I see up to three burrowers. My inspiration is some odd rocks I saw this week in the Alabama Hills near Lone Pine, California, below Mount Whitney. Three chthonic burrowers named Jeroon, Pahrump, and Bugg.

Figure 12: Pahrump

Jeroon is a variant of the mutant character from *Frek and the Elixir*, the man who's a head that runs around on two arms/legs. I liked his personality, and could use that again as well. He was called Jeroon, (My Bosch character in *Hylozoic* was Jeroen.)

Pahrump looks a little like Donald Trump, although I won't mention *that*. Possibly he looks like an enemy of Mason's in San Francisco. There could even be a direct connection between the apparently human enemy and this burrower.

Bugg might be like Franx from *White Light*. Note Seela poking him. He's Jeroon's friend.

Having three burrowers appear at once is of course too much. So Jeroon might be the main one, the messenger,

surprisingly well-spoken. And on the way down they encounter a hostile Pahrump. And then Jeroen's friend Bugg
saves their ass.

Figure 13: Bugg

April 25, 2017. Young Cast. Resurrect Eddie

Keep the casting simple. Mason and Seela, and perhaps
their son or daughter. I had been thinking of having Mason
be middle-aged, or even old (like me), but I think I'll have
Mason be 19. Start up three years after HE1. And Mason
and Seela have a child, maybe a little girl. The year on
MirrorEarth is 1863.

I guess they bring the three-year-old along, although
maybe that slow things down. Well, we might suppose that
Seela wants the child to see the homeland.

How about Arf? Mason and Seela brought him to California. He'll still be in good health, he might have been
three in HE1, and he'd be six now. So Arf comes too. And
how about Eddie Poe? I'll bring him back from the dead!

More on this point in a moment.

Mason, who, despite his young age, has been working as a printer and dabbling journalism. He's in trouble with a local San Francisco or gangster, and in some danger of losing his life. Mason exposed the man's grift. Taking a walk in the hills, Mason and Seela see a pink glow, it's a hair-fine tendril of a streamer from the Great Old Ones at the Hollow Earth's core. The streamer acts as a guideline for the burrower messenger Jeroon.

Some kind of war going on inside the Hollow Earth. We can suppose that, upon emerging within, they meet up with a tribe of humans different from the flowerpeople. They could be jungle people…call them junglers. They can be white like the flower people, or maybe a little darker, like Latinos, or maybe I'll have them be more like hillbillies. My glorious Kentucky heritage. Redneck hippies. Thuggish yet visionary. Like Roland Girling's friend Glenn in Lynchburg, VA. *Nostalgie de la boue.* I always like writing characters like that.

In the original Earth, Eddie and Mason disappeared in the Antarctic, and that was that. They jumped forward 13 years in time when they passed through the Anomaly on their way to MirrorEarth. In the MirrorEarth, they found that young MirrorMason had been killed by the stableboy. Our Poe is stabbed by the older MirrorPoe, and Mason sinks Poe's seemingly dead body in the harbor with a stone tied to his feet. Meanwhile the remorseful MirrorPoe dies of an overdose, in conformity with MirrorEarth's historical record. (Keep in mind that it's we readers ourselves who live in what Mason calls "MirrorEarth".)

And now in HE2, as adumbrated above, I'm going to say that our Poe *didn't actually die* in HE1. Poe's such a great character, I can't afford to lose him. One reason why he survived is that Arf, Seela, and Mason—although they don't realize it—are much hardier than normal, thanks to having basked in the light of Great Old Ones.

And the more relevant reason why Eddie survived is that his interment in the harbor was (using one of Poe's obsessions) a premature burial—orchestrated by Eddie himself!. A Poe-like proto-Houdini hoax. During MirrorPoe's attack,

Eddie was only stabbed once, or really just grazed, very lightly, and he only pretended to be stabbed many more times than that, slyly ducking the later thrusts of MirrorPoe's sword, like an actor taking a sword under his arm. Keep in mind that MirrorPoe was very drunk and opiated. When Eddie collapsed, he wasn't dead, he was only faking and lying doggo. And when Mason tied the stone to Eddie's feet, Poe made sure to flex his ankles apart so there would be wriggle room to extract his feet.

The 40-year-old MirrorPoe died shortly thereafter from drink and opium, but the 27-year-old Poe emerged from the harbor alive and well, like a risen Christ (as he is sure to say). He sneaks off to New York City, preying upon rich art-patron-type women as usual. He takes a false name—why not William Wilson, to amend the jape. To his chagrin, the disguised Poe is unable to sell anything he writes, as it all has already been written and published by the 13-years-older and now-dead MirrorPoe.

So Poe tracks Mason and Seela to San Francisco and demands to return to the Hollow Earth. He plans to retrace his steps back to his starting Earth, returning to his native locale, where he can still have his proper career. He doesn't initially grasp that, if we were to travel back through the Anomaly, he'd still be late, due to the loss of 13 years due to Anomalous time-speed-up. A forgotten man by now. And, probably there'd be an additional time jump from the second passage.

Poe has with him Griswold's two-volume collection of MirrorPoe's works—this way, thinks Poe, he won't even have to write all of his works himself. Turns out that Eddie himself wrote the famously scabrous obituary of himself under the penname "Ludwig," for the New-York Daily Tribune, October 9, 1849. And he helped Griswold trick Mrs. Clemm into letting him publish a collection of MirrorPoe's work. In these negotiations, Eddie presented himself as a cousin of MirrorPoe. He did have a cousin named William Poe, to whom he wrote a letter on Aug 20, 1835.

Eddie would do all this—why? Well, he *hates* MirrorPoe because (a) MirrorPoe tried to kill him, and (b) MirrorPoe has used up all of Eddie's career.

April 27, 2017. Started Writing HE2 At Last

Yesterday I was flopping around on the couch all day, and finally reached such a state of frustration and ennui that I wrote a few half-assed sentence for the start of HE2, although I wouldn't truly call that a start. Today is the start.

Around 11 am I drove down to Santa Cruz alone, had a late breakfast outdoors at Kelly's cafe, talked to my pal Vernon Head on the phone for a long time, then proceed to my favorite muse-contact / inspiration-spot on a cliff overlooking near the stone tower off Four Mile Beach north of Cruz. Sat there atop a cliff there watching the waves and seagulls and wind-rocked plants for an hour or two. Then scrambled down a gully to the sand, found a good long driftwood "stylus" (cf. the intended name *Stylus* for Eddie's lit mag), found a suitably damp patch of sand at the water's edge, and inscribed my by-now-traditional invocation of the muse, EADEM MUTATA RESURGO. "The same, yet changed, I arise again." Yeah! And now I'm at the Verve cafe on Pacific Ave in Santa Cruz. No rush to go home to Los Gatos, as Sylvia is going out early for a film-group dinner with friends in San Jose tonight.

On the cliff I was thinking about strange attractors, and about a short-short story I might write for *Nature* magazine called "Strange Attractor." The thing about a splash of foam off a rock—it's a pattern I recognize, a strange attractor, but there's no really simple geometric and accurate way to describe it. It just isn't a simple object. But it's a familiar spacetime pattern. A well-known strange attractor. Ditto for the body-forms and the motions of gulls in the wind. And the beating rhythms of the very stiff breeze on my face and on by windbreaker. And the flow of my thoughts—the various resentments, anxieties, and satisfactions. And sometimes, in some higher way, a pair of superficially unrelated strange attractors will seem to echo each other. So there might be a meta-attractor that has these low-level attractors as "leaves" or views. And, pushing it, there could be a single super-duper strange attractor which "is" reality, including my consciousness and all the physical world.

Whoah, a girl in high-hell boots, flowered skirt and

fuzzy red wool scarf turban walks past me across the cement floor of Verve Coffee, coming in through the April-breezy open door and the sun dappled sycamore shade. Clump clump. A straaaange attractor, baby. Can't see her now. Hidden in a geometrically inaccessibl2 nook of the curious 3D polyhedron of this room. Trace me no rays, bwah.

Vhere vas I? Ah, yes, the super attractor. Since "Strange Attractor" is to be an under-1000-word short-short, I can have the narrator and his doubting wife merge, melt, conflate into the epic Big Aha strange attractor like flies on flypaper or gnats in a Venus fly-trap, and there we bid the cast a fond adieu.

Anyway, after hanging on the beach, and after briefly but repeatedly hassling (via phone message) my UCSC freshman niece Tinsley Nugent to get together with me for a dose of uncle-type advice (she ducked out on the meet with this old man)—after these warm-up processes, I say, I came to Verve, cranked upon a nicotine patch and some Golden Oo-long tea, and transmuted the dross of yesterday's crude sketch of a start into a really quite wonderful 500-word opener for *Return to the Hollow Earth*,

I was reading Poe's essays and letters all day yesterday in this giant ebook compendium I scored online, and I got that voice back into my head, also (once again) my deep annoyance with the guy and his endless posing and bullshitting, so much like my own.

My latest flash on this front, which I know I already mentioned, is that the sly not-dead-after-all Eddie is the one who wrote the somewhat incendiary and scurrilous obit of MirrorPoe for the *Herald*, which appeared under the byline "Ludwig," and which later was attributed to Griswold. I got around to reading a printout of that obit lying on that cliff at Four Mile Beach today, laughing over it, and relishing the idea of Poe writing it himself. And slipping it to Griswold, and telling G that he was Poe's cousin, and that he'd help pave the way to make sure that G got the rights from Mrs. Clemm to publish a more or less complete edition of MirrorPoe's poems and tales. Poe deliberately writing the essay so it would *sound* as if Griswold wrote it. And G jumping on the chance for a taste of revenge and fame and money. I would *totally* do that if I was somehow around after I died, and if, like Poe, I had no surviving family to protect the rights for. "Great career move"—and I mean that seriously. Scandal sells.

I can have Mason see that obit—and Mason, too, will instantly realize or at least suspect that Poe is in fact alive and that he himself wrote it. This at the end of Chap One. And Chap Two goes on about their California life; it fast-forwards through a couple of years. And in Chap Three, Eddie appears.

So glad to have a novel to write again! Like, in the old days, scoring a full ounce of stony weed, with a sure connection for more. Twist Eddie up in his 'scripts and *smoke* him.

May 1, 2017. More Plot. Utopia/Dystopia. Mason to 2050!

And now I'm back to doubts about the HE2 project. The further into HE1 that I reread, the more I realize that, thus far, I don't have a plot for HE2 as strong as I had for HE1—in HE1, the grand discovery of the Hollow Earth was a big plot element, as was the MirrorEarth transition, the courting of Seela, Mason's relationship with Otha, and Poe's disastrous confrontation with his double, MirrorPoe.

I read that William Gibson has an alternate history + time travel book in the works, hinging on the Clinton-Trump election. The front page of the Sunday NY Times book section was given over to a near-future dystopian novel. Corey Doctorow just hit the stands with a near-future utopia. A market for near-future novels just now, and not especially humorous ones. Should I be writing one of those?

Another cause of doubt is my near-certainty that I won't be able to sell HE2 to anyone other than Night Shade who, by the way, still haven't finalized their contract offer for *Million Mile Road Trip* + my nine Transreal Books back-list novels.

Maybe my idea "Strange Attractor" could be the seed of a novel? It's not that big of an idea though. I have written a number of near-future novels—with not much public interest. I'm thinking of *Mathematicians in Love* or *Postsingular/Hylozoic* or *Big Aha*. The public just isn't go-

ing to break big for *any* of my novels at this point. I'm 71.
They never liked me that much anyway, not most of them.
Give it up, Ru. Vheenk, vheenk, vheenk.

***

But...remember that exhilaration I felt on Thursday,
April 27, 2017, when I walked on the cliffs in Cruz and decided to bring Eddie Poe back to life. The joy of *having a
book to work on.* I want that (conceptual) ounce of pot!

Well, let's give HE2 another shove. See if I can get the
thing rolling. Put my shoulder to the wheel. How can I add
more plot? For one thing, I can't just have everything be
happy and smooth—I have a tendency to want to do that, as I
love my characters—and I identify them with me, my
friends, and my family—and therefore I don't want to hurt
them. But a novel needs some harsh tokes.

Before delving into my newly budding ideas, I should
set some terminology. In HE1, Mason consistently refers to
the Earth that I (Rudy) live in as MirrorEarth. The book HE1
is published in MirrorEarth, and not in Mason's original
Earth. I'd like a clear word to use when I definitely want be
referring to Mason's place of birth. Well, let's call it
MasonEarth for today. I don't want to use something like
First Earth or Baseline Earth or Home Earth—as those
names seem to grant it an ontological precedence.
MasonEarth will be fine for the moment.

(1) Note that Mason's Seela comes from the inside of
MasonEarth. There undoubtedly is a MirrorSeela inside
MirrorEarth. Let's say that Seela loses her life in San Francisco. Murdered by Mason's enemies, who burn down the
shack that he lives in. So Mason has a motive for wanting to
go to the interior of MirrorEarth and seek out MirrorSeela.
We might as well assume that this quest will end in disaster.
MirrorSeela is married now, and her husband immediately
wants to kill Mason, who carelessly makes it clear that he's a
rival for Seela's hand.

(2) One question is whether anyone wants to go back
through the Anomaly to MasonEarth. *Eddie* might want to
do it so as to get his career back. In MasonEarth, Eddie

would be the only Eddie Poe, and he'd be free to publish his writing—without it already having been published by MirrorPoe. But there's not much reason for Mason to go back MasonEarth. But let's suppose that Mason gets stampeded into attempting the trip. Something is threatening him and baby Tuck, and simply to escape them, Mason and Tuck dive into the Anomaly on Eddie's heels.

(3) Mason and Tuck and Eddie start through the Anomaly and there's a screw-up, and Mason has to save Tuck, and even Eddie helps, and they're in there for quite a while, and Mason and Tuck and Eddie bounce out except it's about *two hundred years later*. *Yeah*, baby! Mason has jumped to, like, 2050 (although I won't precisely state the year). And now that Mason's in the future, we get to run some of that utopia/dystopia stuff I was wheenking for. That will be very cool. (By the way, I *could* have Mason hop to 2017 so that I, his editor Rudy Rucker, might personally encounter him, but nah, that would kill the action.)

Note by the way that they will be surprised to see more activity inside the Hollow Earth, and the South Hole and North Maelstrom will be open. At first they'll think they're in MasonEarth, but they're in MirrorEarth, which has changed in the intervening years, thanks in part to Mason's narrative, HE2 having appeared.

(4) Does Mason end up in *MasonEarth* 2050, or in *Earth* 2050? I'm leaning towards our MirrorEarth, as otherwise he's at a *double* remove, that is, in the future *and* on a different world. On the other hand, the future of Mason's original Earth might be more interesting than ours, as *they* have a South Hole and a North Hole. But, wait, I can assume that in MirrorEarth's future we've opened a path to the Hollow Earth as well.

And where does Eddie go? I *might* say Mason and Eddie split apart like two halves of an atom and Eddie flies off to Mason's Earth, where he wants to be, and he escapes the Anomaly fast enough to reach MasonEarth in 1870, so he can still have a reasonable career. But why put Eddie out to pasture like that? To be nice? Naw, I need to keep Eddie in the story. He gives it a nice jagged two-guys tone.

So, yeah, it's Mason, Tuck, and Eddie in the year 2050, on MirrorEarth, that is, in our own future.

(5) Now, what happens with Mason reading the HE1 and HE2 books? And, related question, how do I, Rudy, get my hands on these manuscripts which I'm editing and publishing?

HE1 isn't a big problem. Mason left the manuscript with bookstore-owner Coale in Baltimore, who never published it, but it ended up at the University of Virginia, where I found it, and published it around 1990. Mason reads it in 2050, and becomes interested in Rudy Rucker (dead by then of course) as his editor in the past.

Mason decides to write and to send HE2 to me to publish in the past. How will he send it? Metaphorically, he sends it to me via time-reversed email, à la Gibson's *The Peripheral*. But I don't want a lot of trans-time communication in my book. So I'll say that there's a special mechanism by which Mason transmits the book: it's handed to me by a Great Old One's pink tendril.

Possibly HE2 was not given to me at Mason's behest, it's just something that the *woomo* did.

So the HE2 memoir already exists in MirrorEarth of 2050 that Mason is in. It was (I hope) published in MirrorEarth around 2019. Mason learns of the second memoir's existence in 2050 before he starts work on writing HE2 himself. But he decides not to read HE2 before writing it himself. He goes on to write the whole of his HE2 without looking at my published version. Even though perhaps he sees the cover of a copy.

This way we water down the creatively vitiating effect of the *closed causal loop*. Due to cosmic synchronicity, Mason just so happens to write the same HE2 as the book that already exists because...everything fits. Blindly rewriting an extant book on instinct alone is an idea from a Jorge Luis Borges story, "Pierre Menard, Author of the Quixote." Even though HE2 is already in MirrorEarth's future with Rudy Rucker listed as editor, Mason and the Great Old Ones feel that Mason should send his HE2 back to me nonetheless, so as to validate what is a known part of MirrorEarth's history.

(6) What does Mason see in the future? Let's say that by then MirrorEarth has opened up the ice of its South Hole, and the maelstrom at the North Hole is once again open as well. This is basically due to global warming, or to the krakens I'll be mentioning later, although it may be that the publication of HE2, has helped bring this about. Our descendents will draw energy and trade from the Hollow Earth. There could be an issue with the Great Old Ones. In a fervent peroration, I urge the nations of the world to blast the South Pole with all existing stocks of H-bombs and A-bombs to get the ice plug open. I'm like: "Take Mason's advice from a happy future!"

I might perhaps write an eventual HE3 that's fully lodged in the "open poles" Hollow Earth, with our planet truly functioning as a star ship.

(7) Mason and Eddie get girlfriends in the future.

***

When Eddie shows up to meet Mason in California, 1853, he delivers a variant of some lines from an Easter-tide hymn called "The strife is o'er, the battle done!" I heard it in church yesterday. Tune from the 16th C. Words from the 17th C, with the original Latin title, *"Finita jam sun proelia."* Words translated into English in 1861, which is close enough to 1853 for my purposes. Eddie changes a few words.

The powers of Death have done their worst, /But *Poe* their legions hath dispersed; / Let shouts of holy joy outburst. / Hallelujah!

The three sad *years* are quickly sped; / He rises glorious from the dead; / All glory to our risen *Ed*! / Hallelujah!

I can totally see Eddie declaiming this.

May 2-3, 2017. Three Forms of Time Paradox

I see three main kinds of time paradox, with the second two being fairly similar.

- 1. Closed Causal Loop: A future event produces a past event that produces the future event, and so on. *The Free Novel*: My future self sends me a copy of a novel I plan to write. So I just publish the document as is. Nobody actually had to write it. It emerged.

- 2. Active Yes & No: I make a phone call to my past self, even though I have no memory of receiving such a call. Did I make the call? Yes and no. Examples: *Ineffectual Warning*. I have a bad accident, so the next year I'm motivated to phone my past self and tell him how to avoid the accident. If I don't have the accident, I don't make the call, so I have the accident, and I do make the call. *Grandfather Paradox*: I take out a hit on my grandfather. If he dies, I don't order the hit and he lives. If he lives, I order the hit and he dies.

- 3. Passive Yes & No: I get a phone call from my future self. But later, when it's time for me to make the call to the past, I don't do it. Did I get the call? Yes and no. *Selfish Gambler*. I got a tip on the Kentucky Derby from my future self, and I bet on it, and I won big, but then later I don't get around to passing that tip to my past self. *Welching Novelist*. The same as the *Free Novel* example, except this time, the future author doesn't bother to send back the novel to the earlier author. In particular, this is what we'd get if Mason *didn't* send HE2 back to me.

The Closed Causal Loop isn't a *vicious* paradox, and it generates no logical contradictions. The Yes & No paradoxes, however do seem to require some kind of resolution. Paradox #2 involves, if you will, a sin of *commission* on the part of the future agent, which #3 involves a sin of *omission* by the future agent. These paradoxes are sometimes referred to as Consistency Paradoxes.

The resolution most often used by SF authors is that of

branching time, as shown below. In the figure, the broad
paths are worldlines of possible universes. The worldlines
can branch. The dotted arrow-lines are paths of influence
from future to past.

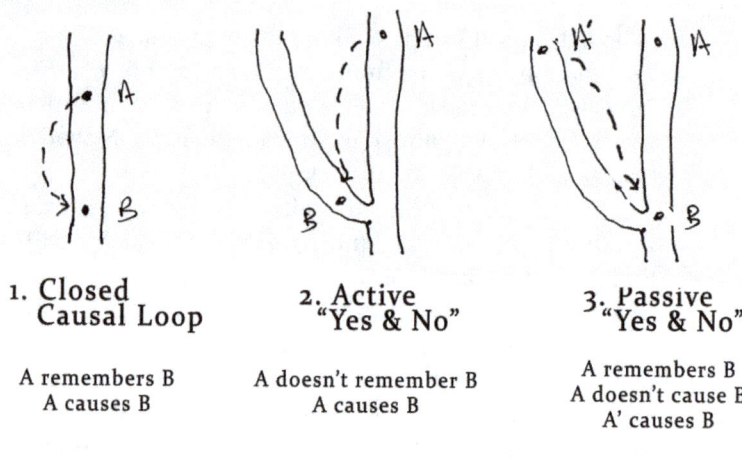

1. Closed   2. Active   3. Passive
   Causal Loop   "Yes & No"   "Yes & No"

A remembers B   A doesn't remember B   A remembers B
A causes B   A causes B   A doesn't cause B
                                             A' causes B

Figure 14: Three Types of Time Paradoxes

    The solution to paradox #2 is that A does something to
the past, but the action takes place on a branched-out stub of
A's timeline. The solution to paradox #3 is that the agent
who caused event B was in a different time branch, so it
wasn't necessary for A to do it.

    In the case of Mason not sending back the book, for in-
stance, we'd have to suppose that some good-hearted Mason
in a *different* timeline did send the manuscript into the past
of his timeline.

    In his recent time-travel novel *The Peripheral*, William
Gibson posits the emergence of a "stub" or fork or alternate
timeline for every time a future person "phones" the past. In
the image above, I visualize this by showing the stalk of our
worldline sending out a stub to meet the incoming signal
from the future.

    Gibson the allows the future person to continue phoning
back to the same stub over and over. It might be more logical to suppose that each successive phone call produces a
new sub-stub or sub-sub-stub—as shown on the right. But
this would be a conceptual hassle, obfuscating the action of

the novel. And, as long as you stuck to the path through the deeper and deeper stubs, the narrative would be the same.

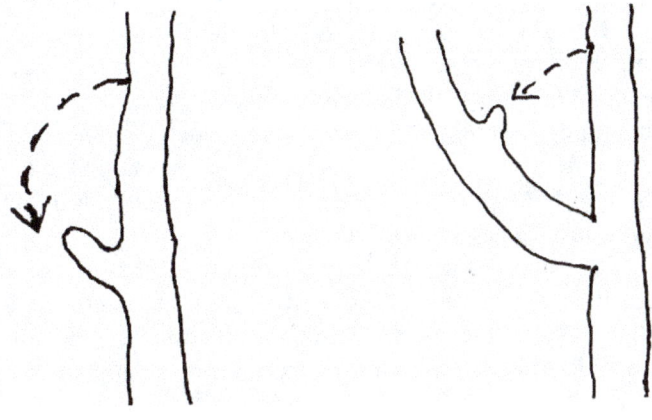

Figure 15: Gibson's Stubs

An issue that Gibson doesn't really get into is whether the world lines and stubs are actively growing while some cosmic meta-time elapses, or whether they might spring into existence fully formed, with the full future and past in place. If the latter, then you would kind of need to have a sub-stub model to make the thing make sense. So probably the former model works better for *The Peripheral*. And it helps that Bill specifies that the ongoing times of the stub and the main timeline are in synch.

***

I want to avoid having branching timelines in my novel *Return to the Hollow Earth*. Yes, I'm working with two Earths: MasonEarth and MirrorEarth. But I don't want the potential for *trillions* of them. Therefore I'll limit myself to the closed causal loop paradoxes, and not introduce and Yes & No paradoxes.

For someone sending messages or information to the past, it requires some care to avoid provoking Yes & No paradoxes that require a fork or a multiple timeline. But it's my feeling that if you tiptoe around gracefully enough, you *can* contact the past *without* forking time or provoking a stub. It's just a matter of being sure to do what already in fact happened. And a matter of being lucky enough that what you *want* to have happen *did* in fact already happen.

It could be—at least in my Hollow Earth cosmos—that you're literally *compelled* to do the necessary tiptoeing. *Particularly* if we always have to use a god-like giant-sea-cucumber Great Old One's tendril to touch the past. We can, I trust, depend on a hyperdimensional Great Old One to have enough finesse to avoid provoking forks—although they *will* allow closed causal loops.

Let me reiterate that there's nothing logically contradictory in a closed causal loop. If we think in terms of the universe a spacetime whole that arises all at once, then a closed causal loop is like a knot in the grain. A pleasing natural pattern.

A somewhat relevant remark that Kurt Gödel made to me in the 1970s: "Even if you know the future, this doesn't meant that you'll deliberately do the opposite of what you wanted to do." Here I'd need to recast this to "Even if you can change the past, this doesn't mean you'll deliberately change it to something different than what happened. Especially if you like what happened. And you may in fact take measures to *ensure* that the past happened as you currently believe it to have happened."

And be sure not to welsh on sending back something good you in fact got from the future way back when—lest you provoke a passive Yes & No.

I made most of this entry into a blog post on May 3, 2017.

May 4, 2017 Cape Horn.. Night Shade Joy. Muse Back.

I better have Mason's passage around Cape Horn as the first chapter. They're sailing in a clipper. Or at least I'll refer back to it. In the Editor's Notes I currently say that his ship *The Purple Whale* sank, but if I wanted to I could change that.

Here's a link to a Cape Horn section in Richard Henry Dana. *Two Years Before the Mast*. Surprising to read it…the passage took a week or two weeks. Seems like schooners didn't much use the Strait of Magellan, too narrow, I think. Horrible weather, rounding the Horn.

If a giant cuke saves Mason, Seela, and Arf with a ten-dril. Lifts them up from the sinking ship and places them on another ship or in a port. There weren't many ports down there in those days. Something like a port in the Falkland Islands, but that's the wrong way. If I go north to Valparaiso, that's a good port, which was widely used in the late 19th C. 1500 miles. The radius of the earth is 3,000 miles, so it's a real stretch for a *woomo* to reach that far. I guess it's reaching up through a sub-ocean hole near Antarctica. If I go to Easter Island, that's even further, 3000 miles, and there wasn't much action there at that time anyway. We could alternately have the *woomo* must set Mason's party won on another clipper ship nearby, or on a whaler although, by 1850 there weren't nearly so many whalers.

13,000 miles from NYC to SF around the Horn. Jeez. They typically sailed from New York, but I guess one might stop in Baltimore. Supposedly they could do the trip in 100 days, or even 89 days. The fast ones were called "extreme clippers." Or "sharp" ships, see page, Clipper Ships in San Francisco, this entry from 18511

"In the tremendous wind of yesterday, which made the whole bay white with foam, and caused sizeable brigs and schooners to pitch and roll, as they lay at anchor, like chips pawing over rapids, it was a study to mark the difference between the sharp clippers and the old fashioned, tub-prowed ships, as they lay at anchor, facing the tide and wind. One of the large, sharp ocean giants lay directly in the full range of the gale as it swept up from the Golden Gate, yet there was not a ripple at her bows."

And from 1852:

"It appears from records kept by the late harbor master, Captain King, that seventy-four vessels claiming and entitled to be called clipper ships, and averaging rather more than 1000 tons burden, had arrived in the port of San Francisco during the last three years. These records commence with the well known brig Col. Fremont, in May, 1849, and include the *Aramingo*, which arrived in May, 1852. The average pas-

sage was one hundred and twenty-five days. Some of the
fleet, however, made much more speedy voyages.
The *Flying Cloud*, which arrived in August, 1851, performed
the distance from New York in eighty-nine days. The *Sword
Fish*, also from New York, arrived in February, 1852, after a
passage of ninety days. The *Surprise*, arriving in March,
1851, the *Sea Witch*, in July, 1850, both from New York,
and the *Flying Fish*, in February, 1852, from Boston, respectively accomplished the voyage in ninety-six, ninety-seven,
and ninety-eight days."

That's 25 boats a year. March is a decent time to travel
as that's like September down at Cape Horn, and the weather
not too bad. I'm thinking you don't want to round the horn
in June-Sept up here, as that's Dec-Feb there. So probably 2
boats a month in the good months. So maybe there's another
boat nearby. Oh, there it is in the text: The Sea Witch in July
1850, from New York!

> "*Sea Witch* can be considered the first of the very
> sharp-ended full midsection clipper ships. She had
> little sheer, a straight keel with no drag, and marked-
> ly hollow bows. When loaded, the *Sea Witch* lay low
> on the water. *Sea Witch*, like other clippers, was
> built for speed. They could sprint at 20 knots and
> cruise at 16.
>
> At the time of her launching she was the most
> beautiful ship afloat: painted black with a bright
> stripe, her figurehead was an aggressive-looking,
> beautifully carved gilded Chinese dragon whose
> long coiling tail gave emphasis to her hollow bows.
> She was described as being rakish and heavily
> sparred, her mainmast being 83 2 long.
>
> *Sea Witch* was an opium clipper, which meant
> she was not only swift, but was also well-armed,
> mounting from 6 to 10 eighteen pounders. These
> armaments were necessary to see off the numerous
> Chinese pirates, who, in their fast *lorchas*, were at-
> tracted by the rich cargoes of silver and opium."

I'm learning that Mason and Seela actually need to embark from New York on their clipper. Not from Baltimore, which is just a Chesapeake Bay port. How would they get to NY from Baltimore? Did they have trains yet? Not really, at least not from Baltimore to NY. A ship *might* stop at Norfolk, but it wouldn't want to sail up the Chesapeake Bay to Baltimore. Mason and Seela could maybe leave a few days early to take a boat to Norfolk and then a boat to NYC. Packet steamers.

So happy today. As I emailed Marc Laidlaw at the end of the day:

> Ever since February, I've been working on a ten-book deal with Jeremy Lassen at Night Shade. Nine back-list Transreal Books editions, plus *Million Mile Road Trip*. Night Shade finally agreed yesterday to let me do a little Kickstarter on the side with an edition of 50 full color hardback "collector's edition" copies that I print up and offer as $150 prizes so I get some more money than their small advance.
>
> And now that's agreed, and they'll send the whole contract and Silbersack can look it over, but I think he's already negotiated most points. Now that it looks like I will get this deal, I realize I do want it. Did we ever decide on a title for the Zep and Del book of stories we wanted Night Shade to publish as well? Maybe just *Zep and Del*. The future is ours you see. Que sera, sera.
>
> I thought of another angle to really pick up the pace on *Return to the Hollow Earth*. I already blogged about it yesterday, so possibly you saw that already. In short, Mason and the not-dead-after-all Poe go back into the Hollow Earth. Poe wants to go back through the Anomaly to the original Earth he came from as he would have a shot at a literary career there. Mason goes along because right then something big is about to eat him. They get screwed up inside the Anomaly, stay too long, an end up being spit back out still on *our* side, that is…but now it's 2050 AD. Boffo!

It'll be a nice whipsaw to jump from 19th C steampunk to 21st C future utopia/dystopia/freakfest, all told in Mason's voice. The guy came before me, and he lives after me. So how do I get hold of this second narrative that Mason writes? He hands it to the febrile branch-wreathed-in-pink-light of one of those giant sea cukes, and the sucker hands it back through time to yours truly. Check and mate!\

So today I was happily reading up on clipper ships making it around Cape Horn. Mason's sinks, but the giant sea cukes pluck him up and drop him onto a nearby clipper. I found this actual ship *Sea Witch*. Arrived in SF right when Mason needs to. It was an *opium clipper*! Trading silver and opium back and forth, China-SF-NYC. Had cannons on it. The things people have done.

It took me three solid months of note-writing to get here. I thought I was done, out of the biz. I think my process won't work, and then, thank you muse, it does again. I start a DOC that's my writing notes for the book I want to write, and keep going back in there and wheenking, and trying ideas and discarding them, and pushing like it's a car mired in mud or deep snow, and finally I get so desperate and hopeless that I finally notice a tiny air hole or stock move where I might, if I just go and try it, might find some oxygen to breathe, even if it's dumb, and, gasping and sobbing, I claw my way onto a floating bit of flotsam and jetsam that I ride down into the roaring glorious maelstorm.

May 5, 2017. Stagecoach. Tweaks on HE1.

A little more info on opium clippers such as the Frolic. They ran a trade between opium from India to China, then bringing the profits back to, I guess, New England. As the opium trade went down and the gold rush picked up, some of the opium clippers switched to running Chinese goods to San Francisco…like silks, porcelain, jewelry and furniture. (Just as easy as running it around the Horn from the East Coast.) Another example. Water Witch had a triangle trade, taking opium from India to China, trading it for tea, and bringing the tea to London.

"The Furious Fifties" is the name of the area of Cape Horn, which is at a latitude of about 55 south.

***

So okay, Mason and Seela use a stagecoach to go from Baltimore to New York. Here's a coach description. I see in a photo that these coaches looked something like Wells Fargo logo coach. They traveled on gravel-fortified toll roads called turnpikes.

> The Concord Coach was built in six, nine, and twelve passenger sizes, though company records reveal that a few four passenger and sixteen passengers sizes were built between 1858 and 1864. Passengers were seated on two transverse, facing seats, in the usual coach fashion, and on one or two additional benches between the fixed seats. Suspended on the three-perch, thoroughbrace running gear, the body could accommodate a large amount of baggage, for there was a rack on top, another at the rear, and space in the front boot for that purpose. These Stagecoaches were painted in bright colors, and then highly decorated with painted scrollwork, oil paintings, ornate lettering, and gold leaf. The most common color was a red body on a pale yellow running gear, but varied combinations of green, red, orange, white, blue, yellow, olive, black maroon, etc., were also used.

> The coaches made about 6 miles per hour, and sixty miles in a long day. Distance from Baltimore to New York is about 200 miles via Philadelphia, so it would be about three and a half days in the coach. Call it four days, with Philly in the middle.

> Crude wagons began to carry passengers between Philadelphia and New York and in 1756. Travel time was reduced to two days in 1766 with an improved coach called the Flying Machine. The first

Concord stagecoach was built in 1827. Abbot Down-
ing Company employed leather strap braces under
their stagecoaches which gave a swinging motion instead of the jolting up and down of a spring suspension. The company manufactured over forty
different types of carriages and wagons at the wagon
factory in Concord, New Hampshire. Concord stagecoaches were built so solidly it became known they
didn't break down but just wore out.

Actually I might not even mention the stagecoach in
HE2. I kind of want to get the thing going and be on the
Purple Whale as soon as it opens.
***

I dug into my Ver 3. Revision of HE1 a little bit today. I
rewrote Eddie's death so it's possible that he wasn't killed—
before I had MirrorPoe stabbing him in his chest a dozen
times and blood gushing out— but now I have Eddie
wrapped in a cloak and he performs a loud and dramatic
"death scene" after the first touch of the sword. Not as dramatic as the original, but, hey, I gotta do what I gotta do.
[Unless I want to keep the more dramatic death and say that
the Great Old Ones sent out a pink tendril to fix dead Eddie,
but nah. The sly Houdini thing is better.]

Since it looks as if all the "round the Horn" clippers left
from New York or Boston, I set it up so Mason and Seela
will take a four-day stagecoach trip to New York to catch the
Purple Whale there.

And I mention that Seela's five months pregnant.

I'm saying that her pregnancy started on Sept 28, and
they arrived on MirrorEarth on Sept 29, but I'll double-check
this when I closely reread those sections.
***

I checked if here were any Blacks in California during
the Gold Rush.

In 1848 at the start of the gold rush there were
but a handful of African Americans in California.
Within two years there were over 1,000 and at the
end of four years there were more than 2.000. The

first black miners were sailors from Eastern whaling ships who jumped ship to go off and seek their fortune. This was a common problem for all ships who came to San Francisco. So many ships were abandoned they had to haul them out of the bay to make room for the incoming ships. These ships pulled onto land were used as housing, storage and jails.

So let's say Mason and Seela befriend a sailor named Crispus on the *Purple Whale* whom the *woomo* brings along with them for the hop to the *Sea Witch*, and Crispus goes gold hunting in the Mother Lode. I get the name from Crispus Attucks, an Indian/Black dockworker, who was the first person killed by the British in the American Revolution. Variant spelling is Crispa, I kind of like that better.

May 9, 2017. St. Elmo's Fire

From Wikipedia:

St. Elmo's fire is a bright blue or violet glow, appearing like fire in some circumstances, from tall, sharply pointed structures such as lightning rods, masts, spires and chimneys, and on aircraft wings or nose cones. St. Elmo's fire can also appear on leaves and grass, and even at the tips of cattle horns. Often accompanying the glow is a distinct hissing or buzzing sound.

I found some good stuff in Melville's *Moby Dick*, Chapter 119: "The Candles," which takes place after a typhoon near Japan. He refers to the coronas as "corposants." I edited it and morphed Melville's passage to get the following.

Each of the yard-arms was tipped with a pallid corona, a spike of St. Elmo's fire. The three tall masts bore white, tapering flames as well. Like supernatural candles before an altar. Except that these flames hissed; they sounded a sinister murmur that overlaid the purling of the waves.

The ensorcelled crew stood in a thick cluster on the forecastle, their faces gleaming in the pale phosphorescence, their assembled eyes like a far away constellation of stars.

Hubert cried out, " May God save us!"

At my side, Seela's red teeth gleamed a faint violet, as if they too were tipped by strange fire. Arf lay on his back, terrified. The tattoo on his belly glowed like a satanic rune.

May 10, 2017. The Shipwreck

So now it's time for the *Purple Whale* to sink. The *woomo* tendril will save Mason, Seela, and Arf. Do I save Hubert and/or Crispa as well? In any picaresque story, you have to dodge the risk of having character after character join on, like one of these children's books where each new character they encounter gets stuck to them, and by the last page you have this dog-pile parade of fifteen critters.

Saving Hubert here would be too much of a narrative load. This said, I do like Hubert as a character, and he'd be a good guy to have in San Francisco. Is there any possible way he could survive? Well, sure, he could float to the shore of Patagonia atop an empty barrel, and show up in SF a year later. On the other hand if I do that, it kind of deflates the drama of *Poe* also showing up, not dead after all. Just let Hubert go, I think.

Re. Crispa, I really would like to keep a black character, mirroring the presence of Otha in HE1. But how and why would he be saved by the *woomo* along with our main three? Certainly the *woomo* are partial to the "black gods" of the Hollow Earth. Or, simpler, Crispa happens to be standing with Seela, Mason, and Arf, and he just kind of gets lumped in. Maybe because he's holding Arf.

I see the ship sinking in a whirlpool, pulling them down, glowing pink light, a sticky branching tendril grabs them in a lump, like a net.

In the lead-up, I presently have two successive eerily calm scenes, the albatross and the St. Elmo's Fire. I should tie them together in some way, or merge them. Thing is, flat out copied the albatross and St. Elmo's fire scenes from *Two*

Years Before the Mast and *Moby Dick*, respectively, and they don't really have a fit with my story.

May 13, 2017. Gold Rush

I'm reading up on Gold Rush times. The anthology *Sketches of Early California* by Lewis and De Nevi has some nice contemporary accounts. A gold claim might be just 16 by 16 feet on a river bank. You wanted to dig down to the bedrock, and the gold was usually right by the rock. If the strata were edge on, there could be good pickings in the cracks between the sheets of slate. Coarse gold (chunks or even half-a-pea) is what they dreamed of, but mostly it was dust or flecks like cucumber seeds. Miners were pretty good about not stealing each other's stashes. To mark a claim you didn't do paperwork, you just started. You'd leave pick and shovel to mark your claim, although if you didn't come back soon enough, others would move your pick and shovel and "jump" the claim. When the roads were muddy it could take over a week to get to the gold country from Stockton or Sacramento. People would travel up the rivers to those towns. Three card monte was a popular gambling game. There weren't prostitutes up in the gold country, there weren't any women at all.

The first paper in San Francisco was the *California Star*, founded and run by E. C. (Edward Cleveland) Kemble, who bought out his Mormon boss. Kemble was 22 in 1850, and by then he'd merged with a paper from Monterey, taking business partners and the name Daily Alta California. Big fire in SF in 1851. In 1852 Kemble's partner Edward Gilbert was killed in a duel.

In later years Mark Twain wrote for this paper.

I found the whole *Daily Alta California* online! Insane amounts of historical data I can winnow through. Like a miner sluicing dirt through his "rocker." Looking for "color" (that is gold flecks like cucumber seeds) in the heavy sand that remains on the riffles of the rocker.

It's kind of cruder in SF at that time than is easy to imagine. They keep having huge fires and having to rebuild shoddy one-story buildings. Hundreds of abandoned ships accumulate in the harbor—their crews have run off to the gold country. Gold worth about $16 an ounce, but up in the gold country you'd spend that much getting two bottles of whiskey or a pair of boots. The population was only a couple of hundred in 1847, and ballooned up to two thousand (?) in 1850.

In a way, though, the research is just vamping, that is, my way of avoiding getting on with the tale.

May 18, 2017. Opium Clipper

I got two books by mail, *The India-China Opium Trade*, kind of academic and boring, and the exciting 1891 book by Lindsay Anderson, *A Cruise in an Opium Clipper*. Anderson is a bit of an Edwardian hack writer, using a lot of stock phrases, but the style is in any case so old-timey that it's a lot of fun. "Spanking along" meaning to be sailing fast. "Scud, scud, scud" to try and get away from a storm which is in fact a hurricane (typhoon), so they sail around in a four-mine circle all night long. "The ship was all a-taunto." Strange phrase which, however appears in other maritime books. In a big enough storm you might chop off your masts at the bases, lest you capsize.

The opium trade was originally a triangle, silver from England to India for opium, opium to Canton and Hong Kong for tea, tea to England for silver. The cutters had raked (back-slanted) masts for speed. Steamers began taking over from the clippers, and forward-raked bow sticking way out. Around 1850 the steamer boats had taken over most of the opium business, as they didn't sink so often. Some opium clippers turned to running household goods from China to San Francisco. They had V-shaped hulls (rather than U-shaped) for speed. Carried 7 or 9 cannons. The ship might be made of solid mahogany instead of oak.

Now, I wanted for an opium cutter to appear off South America en route to SF for Mason to land on. What reason would that ship have for being there? Well, opium's out of style. Need a new use for the cutter. Perhaps it's running household goods to SF to get gold, and then run the gold to China and get more goods, run them back to SF, get more gold there, then run the gold back to Boston. I was saying it was the Sea Witch (which belonged, I think, to a London company), but I could make up a different name for the ship and have more freedom.

The *Frolic* was wrecked near San Francisco off Mendocino, July 25, 1850. She <u>carried</u> a load of stuff from China.

> The treasure included ornately decorated camphor trunks, fine-colored silks, shiny lacquered ware, tables with inset marble tops, gold filigree jewelry, 21,000 porcelain bowls, candied fruits, silver tinderboxes, a prefabricated two-room house with oyster shell windows, toothbrushes, mother-of-pearl gaming pieces, ivory napkin rings, horn checkers, tortoise shell combs, silk fans, and scores of nested brass weights used by San Francisco merchants to measure their goods.

No lives were lost in the crash. Insurance paid the owners off. Was it a deliberate scuttle?

Back to the question of the opium cutter being off South America. It's 6,000 miles from Hong Kong to San Francisco. It's 13,000 miles from New York to San Francisco around the Horn. Much more efficient to get stuff from China. Well, let's say this boat is just changing over. And it reported back to its home port in Boston.

As I said before, I ought to stop researching and get down to writing the novel again. In any case, I would like to finish the *Sea Witch* scene before shifting gears to revising *Million Mile Road Trip* which, really, I need to get down to pretty soon if it's going to be done by August 1. Will take about a month to revise. I'm going to be on a trip from May 24 to May 31, and probably won't do much writing in there. But if I start on *MMRT* on June 1, that's probably soon enough.

May 24, 2017. Eddie's on the Sea Witch!

As I write this note, Sylvia and I are flying east to Swarthmore for my class of '67's 50th reunion. The flight isn't bad. We paid extra for "comfort" seats. Changing in Minneapolis, landing in Philadelphia, spending 2 nights there, then hit Swarthmore early on Friday. I kind of wish we were already going to S'more on Thursday night, but last time (40th?) we went for three nights, and it seemed like too much.

I noticed a new senility thing lately. Well, twice it's happened. I dream something, and then when I'm awake at some later point I think it's something that *really* happened. First was the giant temple-of-light McDonald's I dreamed I'd seen in Death Valley, and then in the car I was looking for it. Second was this week, I dreamed I saw the name Ytrombo, and I said it was an odd name, and Sylvia said, "That's one of Penny's relatives," so a day or two later, I ask Penny, "Do you really have a relative with the last name Ytrombo." And she's like, um, no. Disturbing. What if this happens more and more as I segue into the twilight. As death nears, the border between life and dream fades. I remember the last time I visited my grandmother in Hanover she was a little like that, glancing under the table we sat at and saying the footstool had been flying around under there, and then stopping herself as she (I think) realized she'd mixed a dream into reality.

Well, maybe I can use the name Ytrombo in HE2. A gift from my befuddlement.

Listening to earphones off my iPhone. Dylan "Stuck inside of Mobile with the Memphis blues again." Best song ever. A whole novel.

Back to HE2. I need an episode on the *Sea Witch*. Captain Ytrombo. Default is a silky villain, very traditional style, snobby, foppish, pointed mustachio, Like Captain Hook, basically. Or a bewildered bureaucrat. Or Mason's father Pa, that would be a kick, but it would be too big. Somewhat dashing and reckless. Missing the opium trade. Maybe he's a smoker.

I'd like it if Captain Ytrombo and the *Sea Witch* have something to do with the rest of the novel. I do worry I'm already I'm slipping into picaresque on this one, which is not a style I always find engaging to read. *Million Mile Road Trip* was already quite picaresque.

As it happens, picaresque is, I think, a typical late style for an aging author who's losing his marbles, It takes focus and energy to visioneer the hidden machineries of a vasty plot. But I'd to do that here, so therefore I need a plot-element event aboard the *Sea Witch.*

Maybe later the *Sea Witch* will take Mason, Seela, Arf, and Poe to a drop-off point for traveling back into the Hollow Earth? Well, nah, I don't want to have to go to sea again, too much of a repeat. I'd rather they go down there with those burrowers I talked about already. You know: gold rush, mining, holes in the ground, natural cavern, tunnel.

What if the *Sea Witch*'s crew deserts the ship in SF, and Captain Ytrombo or one of his men or his wife joins Mason? No, that gets into this metastasis thing, where in every chapter somebody new joins the cast, like in one of those kids' books where on each page a new animal gets stuck onto the parade. Already we've got Crispa, and Poe is on deck.

What if Captain Ytrombo is from the future? Well, hmm, the central anomaly can quicktime you to the future, fine, but I don't see an obvious way it could take you to the past. Unless we did a Gibsonian retrograde-time-link running a peripheral. Naw.

Oh, wait! It's Captain Ytrombo who brings Eddie to San Francisco. In fact Eddie is *already* on the *Sea Witch.* Yeah. Now we've got a ping. Now there's something happening. Now the scene has a point. And the captain has never heard of Poe, particularly, and Poe is already using a pseudonym, like perhaps the anagram Goarland Peale (see more on his pseudonyms below).

To make this work, we need to assume the *Sea Witch* left New York a full week *after* the *Purple Whale.* Giving Eddie time to get up there. So I need to weave in a bit about the *Sea Witch* speeding past the *Purple Whale* as they start on their wallowing struggle westward below Cape Horn. And that way, later, the *Sea Witch* isn't so unexpected an apparition and, mainly, it makes sense to have Poe on there.

I'd originally planned to save Eddie's appearance for later. But—I've learned this a zillion times—it's a fool's strategy to hoard up your exciting reveals. Spend freely the coin of the muse, and more shall be granted.

I do still want to have a long chapter or even two with Mason and Seela in SF, but I can do this with Eddie for a time in the background out west, and then he screws up and comes to Mason demanding that they head back into the Hollow Earth pronto. To start with, Eddie goes up to the gold country to write about it, but then he gets his ass in a sling.

In the gold country, Eddie is writing featurettes for the *Daily Alta California* where Mason works, he's using a pen name. Bashford Clokk. Burberry Crouton Excelsior. Or, better, one of those anagrams he used for signing the Bank O' Kentucky bills in HE1. The ones I had were: Peale O. Garland; A. Prodegal Lane; Learn A. Godleap; E. Apalled Groan; Loan A. A. Pledger; Gaol Pan Dealer. I'll tweak the first of those to be Eddie's name on the ship, and for his pen name, I'll think of a new anagram—like Ragland Ealope or *Grandee Polala*. That last one is good. Grandee Polala. The inflated title and the mockingly silly surname are the kind of thing Eddie might like, see, e.g., his characters "Tarr and Fether." Grandee Polala. There was a woman writer who sent dispatches from the gold country under a fanciful pen name. Naturally Eddie will get into a feud with her.

May 28, 2017. Swarthmore 50th Reunion Wrap-up.

On the plane to Louisville now. Reunion's over. Very touching, I just about started crying after the reunion colloquium in the amphitheater in the woods, where they also held our graduation, back in 1967, the start of the Summer of Love, and a month before Sylvia and I got married. The accumulation of time—like a steady fall of snow that's slumped into a huge drift, higher than my head, nearly covering my house. The familiar or semi-familiar faces of my classmates—many of whom I in fact hardly spoke to in college, but they're comfortable background figures. Everyone was being kind, and I found myself being quite empathetic, certainly more so than I used to be, a humble man worn smooth by the slow polishing of time, the endless jouncing against others, wearing down the corners and the crests.

Sylvia and I found "our" tree, a big old beech near Crum Creek, where I carved our initials in perhaps 1965. It's SB + RR, with the SB on top, ladies first. The letters now stretched wide, smoothed out, and lifted a foot or two higher above the ground than they were 52 years ago, when freshly incised.

Roger Shatzkin and Don Marritz are, as I always say, comfortable as old shoes, creased and worn to a warm shine. Kenny Turan looking, at least to my eye, Hollywood, with a well-trimmed shock of white hair and, *mirabile dictu*, a pale summer-weight suit jacket.

I gave away five or six of my books, various titles. I'd laid them out as a display on the "Show & Tell" table at dinner, which everyone pretty much completely ignored. And after dinner, rather than schlep the books home (and I do have a lot of spare copies kicking around), I gave them away. My set-at-Swarthmore SF novel *The Secret of Life* went to Kim Tingley, a tall Virginian, always a bit intimidating, we tended to insult each other all the time in the old days, a way of relating…I remember once telling him, "Mockery is the tribute mediocrity pays to greatness," and he in fact liked this *bon mot* so much that he memorized it back then. This was also a guy who might, returning from the shower jump naked onto a chair and holler, "Blow me!" at the other boys. This weekend he said how impressed he was that Sylvia and I had stuck together for so long, saying this sincerely. So I cut him some slack and gave him what was in context, the best book to get.

I gave copies of my art book *Better Worlds* to Elizabeth Daniels and to Don Marritz. Elizabeth was a class above us and she married Tom Large from our class. I had a crush on her Freshman year, and even now enjoy listening to her talk. She's very contrary. My physics-major friend Arne Yanoff got *Saucer Wisdom*, I think he'll get a kick out of it. Like me, he feels that what we see and know of the world around is the thinnest of veneers upon the Great Unknown Reality beneath. Arne helped me understand the confusing "chain rule" of calculus in the fall of Freshman year, 1963. He taught me to think in terms of infinitesimals and to view the rule as $dz / dx = dz / dy * dy / dx$. I gave my respectable historical novel on Bruegel, *As Above, So Below*, to class secretary Muffin Reid, a sweet and fun-loving nice woman.

And I gave *The Fourth Dimension* to my older friend Ted Nelson the 79-year-old computer/web/hyperlink guru, who is himself a Swarthmore grad, class of 1959 I think he said. At the end of our class dinner I was stiff, and I was dancing next to the table where Sylvia and our friends sat, getting into the 60's play-list that Roger Shatzkin had crafted, feeling good in my dancing, and Sylvia pointed behind me, and there was Ted, of all people, conjured up from Silicon Valley mist.

July 20, 2017. Drop HE2 for a Novel of the Future?

I spent a month and a half closing my ten book deal with Night Shade Books, I have more details about the whole thing in my separate *Million Mile Road Trip Notes* document. My main work was doing a final revision of *Million Mile Road Trip.* (Final for now, anyway, although the effin' pub date is 2019, so probably I'll do another polish in a year or two.)

And now I'm looking at the 3,800 word stub I have written on HE2. And I'm going *hmm*. It's rough, and it needs more conversations. Seela, Mason, and Crispa need to expand as characters. Seela in particular is kind of vapid, like a dream princess, and Crispa is but a pale shadow of Otha.

But more than that, I'm not entirely sure this book is a good idea at all. At least not right now.

It'll be hard to sell—I mean, a sequel to an out of print historical SF novel? Maybe Night Shade would buy it, but it's not clear if I'd want to be selling books to Night Shade right now, as they have a ten-book backlog of me as of last month. And, seriously, there's no way I could sell HE2 to Tor. I could of course self-pub it with a Kickstarter. But somehow the appeal of that channel is wearing thin.

Another problem is that I don't really have—unless I'm forgetting something—a plot for HE2. Mason and Seela would return to the Hollow Earth, have some kind of hassle in there, bounce off the *woomo* again, and end up in 2050, and then do something else, but who knows what.
***

One element I felt excited about in HE2 was that future-hop move, I came up with it on May 1, 2017. My idea was to have the latter part of HE2 be set in 2050—and do a little fancy footwork to send Mason's future journal back to our era. The 2050 scenario seems fresh—as opposed to reprising

the trip to the center of the Hollow Earth, which is wonderful, but it's been done by me already. And I can't face writing up the goldrush San Francisco days stuff. I don't want to
do historical research. I want to make shit up.

So today I'm thinking I should just do the future part and
drop the HE thing? Do a completely different novel?

***

If I bail for a novel of the future, could I find a way to
repurpose the 3,800 words I already wrote for HE2? Not
sure. Wouldn't hurt to polish them a bit in any case, just this
week, to have something to do. There's a longshot chance I
could shift it to he future, and use it as an opener for my future novel.

Like, the rounding the Horn thing could be about some
contemporary or future people, like hippies maybe, dropout
types, re-enacting the old ways, it's a fluke, them taking that
boat, a recreation of an old boat, doing it for kicks, and the
pink tendrils of the *woomo* are an unknown deus-ex-machina
force majeure.

***

Maybe I just abandon HE2, and just let my current
Chapter One (and maybe a Chapter Two and even a Three)
of HE2 be an Appendix to HE1. Write enough to round them
off. I'd hate to waste my Chapter One now, as it's pretty
good.

Well, we'll see.

July 21-22, 2017. Maybe I Can Do HE2 After All.

So I've marked up my printout of my stub on HE2, and
I'm editing it, and adding conversations, and thickening it up
as I type in the changes. Rucking it up. And now I'm thinking maybe I could get it going.

HE2 still is an obstinately non-commercial route to
take…a sequel to a historical novel about the Hollow Earth.
But if I'm having fun writing it, what the hey. I'm thinking
of a two-in-one edition.

So here I am revising, and having fun doing it. 1,500
new words in a day. I'm getting some conversation going
between Mason and Seela. They were kind of goodie-goodie
in HE1. Paralyzed by high emotion. Like the bride and

groom on a wedding-cake. But in HE2 they're starting to be like a married couple, with more give and take. Seela's a bit quarrelsome.

July 23-25, 2017. HE2 Plot.

Okay, I fixed HE2 Chapter One, and now it's time to see if I can think of a plot. Or if I can even write a Chapter Two. Huge uncertainty regarding the plot, and the viability of HE2 as a project. And the uncertainty is a drag, as what I really want is to be dreaming and writing. Well, let's see what I can think of.

***

Mason and Seela get to SF, they have the baby. Eddie is hectoring Mason and Seela to get them back to the original Earth via the Anomaly at the center of the Hollow Earth. That's why he followed them to California. He can't get any traction as an author, given that MirrorPoe already published pretty much everything that he might think of writing.

Mason doesn't want to go back to the Hollow Earth just yet, although Seela herself would like to see her family. She says they should summon a *woomo*, but Mason doesn't want to do that, and then they actually try it, but it doesn't work, as they can't get together the level of fear or tekelili intensity to make it happen.

Eddie is offstage for a bit, he goes up into gold country, and writes dispatches as Grandee Polala. Mason gets a job at the *Daily Alta California*, Mason is publishing Eddie's dispatches, and that goes well enough at first.

[The Daily Alta *was run by Robert Semple, who had the only steam press in the west, started in 1849. I think Edward Kemble was the editor at first. Remember that I have some more refs in my* Gold Rush entry *above. A quarter of San Francisco went up in a fire in May, 1851, and the* Alta California *was burned out then. I think Mason and Seela will leave right around then. In 1850 there were about 2,000 people in town. Many abandoned ships. One, the* Niantic, *a whaling vessel, had been dragged ashore to serve as a store.]*

The newspaper job is a repeat of HE1. And so is the bit about Eddie as a struggling writer. Cryptomnesia alert! So I have to fast-forward through that stuff very quickly in HE2, almost in passing. Eddie writes something that gets someone mad at him—maybe a purportedly fictional tall tale involving Jeroon the Burrower — but it's really true, some Burrowers are coming up from the Hollow MirrorEarth for gold, and the Mormons are working with them.

Ed comes back to SF. And then, thanks to Eddie, Mason is suddenly facing a duel. And then it's May, 1851, when they have the big fire, with a sheet of flame covering half the city. They're being driven along by the fire, and being shot at by Eddie's enemies, and they're about to die.

They make their way down to the harbor to escape the fires and the gunmen. They take shelter in a beached ship that's a store. The *Niantic*. The killers throw a flaming torch onto the ship. A *woomo* tendril drags the ship into the water, and overturns it so they're in a bubble of air in the hull. And then they sink all the way down to the Hollow Earth.

That's a decent Chapter Two.

***

And then—what happens inside the Hollow MirrorEarth? Maybe some enemy humans are in the Hollow Earth as well, brought by the burrowers. I can imagine a Burrowers Team vs. Sea Cucumbers Team.

A bit of fighting. Seela doesn't make it to the Hollow MirrorEarth flower as she'd be extra there, an uncanny duplicate. Instead they get into a different landscape, maybe a place where the burrowers hang out, it looks like the Alabama Hills above Lone Pine, CA.

So now Eddie and Seela want to go through the Anomaly at the core to get back to the proper Hollow Earth, and from there Eddie intends to go back to his proper Earth, in which, at this point, he's simply viewed as lost at sea, without all that much written yet, so he could have a fine career, assuming he's not in trouble for that counterfeiting jape.

But it's too boring if they actually get all the way back to our original Earth.

***

So I was thinking I could have the passage through the anomaly get screwed up, and they lose two hundred years and end up in 2051, and are still on the MirrorEarth side, that is, our side.

But then…I don't know. More and more, the time-jump feels like a desperate and awkward move. Although if it was a Jules Verne / Captain Nemo steampunkish future, it could fit. Or have a big UFO thing in 2050. Like the Great Old Ones are piloting our world to its goal. But I don't feel especially interested in that scenario.

***

We could suppose that the Great Old Ones simply won't allow a second passage through the Anomaly. I could make up some bogus reason why not. You can't pass through the anomaly more than once, and that's that. But maybe later they do let Poe through so he can go home.

***

So let's see if I can make a novel-length HE2, *without* the jump to 2050, and without going back to Earth. How?. Start writing Chapter Two, and then Three, and see what happens. Tend the garden and see what grows. Maybe there's enough juice in the wonder of the HE. I could have fun coming up with some new animals and plants and topography—and have the older ones do new things. The shrigs and the *ballula*.

Bascially, it's like I'm Niven writing *Ringworld 2*. I always had that same longing to write a *Frek 2*. To further explore the wonder of that world I made.

One hassle about the HE series is that I have the two worlds, Earth and MirrorEarth, and that's confusing, and a pain in the ass. Like it's so complicated if Seela and Eddie want to go all the way home.

MirrorEarth --> Hollow MirrorEarth --> Anomaly --> Hollow Earth --> Earth.

***

By the way, I can't remember what were my characters' ostensible motives for going through the Anomaly in HE1. I mean really I was doing it so their lives could jibe with our known past, and so I could have the double Poe encounter, but were the characters thinking something? I'll have to look it up.

July 20-23, 2017. *"Juicy Ghosts"*

CORY DOCTOROW'S *WALKAWAY*

July 20, 2017.

I just read Cory Doctorow's new *Walkaway*, and it's so modern and relevant. I posted a big review of it on my blog. He does a lot of stuff with converting people into "sims" that live in the cloud as ghosts that are embodied on Earth via sensors and such effectors as drones. It's the move I introduced in *Software*, some forty years ago, and now it's back, much stronger than before. Why shouldn't I pick up that tune once more? Call it, like, *Juicy Ghosts*.

I'm thinking that's the, like, popular topic now. So I wouldn't be oversaturating the market. And I'm the old grandee, the master of the trope. And maybe even work in some of the Gibson-style time travel moves that I was discussing on May 2, 2017. And for sure work in some politics. I'd like to step forward to help raise the nation's consciousness lest Trump be reelected in 2020. It's my civic duty, you could say.

"Juicy Ghosts" could just be a story or novella instead of a novel. Like I can do the move of people becoming like ghosts, in the cloud, gloating over Earth, running in quantum computational strata, and then they notice there are "real" ghosts there already. Twas ever thus!? Maybe the "real" ghosts have an issue we have to solve.

Theoretically, I could segue into the "Juicy Ghosts" story in the proposed 2050 section of HE2, but that's too much of a shift, I think. And a waste of the "Juicy Ghosts" idea.

CHRIS BROWN & POLITICAL SF

July 23, 2017.

Sylvia and I went up to Borderlands Books in SF and saw Chris Brown talking about his novel *Tropic of Kansas*. I've been reading it on my Kindle, it's very political, along the lines of *1984*. Chris is a charming guy from Austin, TX, maybe 50 years old, a lawyer, author of numerous fantasy stories, and this is his first novel.

We had dinner with Chris, and Michael Blumlein, and Joseph & Rina of Tachyon Books, and, out of the blue, my

Night Shade editor Jeremy Lassen, who was working (!) at Borderlands, something he does a couple of days a month, partly to keep his hand in, and partly for the money, as he's not all that well paid nowadays, as an employee of the NY-based Skyhorse who are the owners of the Night Shade imprint.

I told Chris my notion of having someone move their mind/soul into the cloud, and I remarked that chip-based computers wouldn't actually be powerful enough to do the necessary personality-maintaining crunch, and I explained that we'd be using matter-computers, that is, quantum computational chunks of (somehow) tamed matter. And I said that when my character transfers to that platform, he or she senses that something else is in there, and it's a "real" ghost. Turns out all along people's ghosts have been migrating up into the hylozoic and panpsychic matrix of rich matter.

As Corey has it in *Walkaway*, the cloud sims have a weak form of Earthly embodiment in that they can use very rich sensors in our world—eyes, ears, tastes, smells, and even haptic touch probes. I see these things as little bundles, sensos they're called. Or gnoses. "The gnose peered at him, sniffing the currents of air, cocking its ear to one side, and running its phinger along his forearm." Or knose?

And I was saying I'd layer on some political element as well. Chris loved this, he said only I could do it. This morning, reading the daily report on what our current President has recently tweeted, I feel so amped up for protest. Bursting. I think would feel good to write a hard-core rabble-rousing political novel. This seems to be a good time for that, historically speaking.

On the one hand, current-events novels don't age well. On the other hand, look at *1984* and *Clockwork Orange* and *Man in the High Castle* and *The Trial*. To universalize it, things have to be not too close to our world, I think. *Mathematicians in Love* had a political flavor, as did the *Postsingular* diptych. Nobody noticed.

This said, I don't like being sour and bitter. I like sunny and sense-of-wonder. I've always wanted to see politics wither away, rather than becoming even more central. So maybe I invoke some ghosts that simply executes every single Republican oppressor. Of course the French-revolution-type "off with their heads" strategy never ends well. It runs wild, turns against the splinter groups within the revolutionary party, and provokes Draconian retaliation from the enemies.

Could my juicy ghosts do something other than killing the pigs? Dial up their empathy? Allay their fears? Give them prophetic dreams? Group hugs instead of the guillotine.

***

You know, if I wanted to just get it over with, I could write "Juicy Ghosts" as a thousand-word story for *Nature*. I bet they'd buy it. But I think they only pay $100. Make it a bit longer and try it on *Light Speed* or *Terraform*.

***

If I do hop to the future in the second half of HE2, I should make sure that it's the 22nd century, not the 21st. This suggested by a remark by William Gibson in an interview today. He's, like, "In the old days everyone was dreaming about the 21st C. And now we're there, so why aren't people dreaming about the 22nd C?" Well, maybe we just haven't gotten around to it yet. But it's a good idea. They jump to 2150. Three hundred years.

And I could of course have a dystopia there. But maybe something funner. I don't really need to write a political dystopia novel. I mean, I did that plenty of times, e.g. in my very first novel, *Spacetime Donuts*.

August 2, 2017. Going to the Daily Alta Office.

I know this is a thematic repeat of Mason going to look for Poe at the *Southern Literary Messenger* offices in HE1. But, hey, writing is what our boys to. The *Daily Alta* office was somewhere on lower Market or Montgomery street I think. It was lost in the fire of 1851. But now we're on Monday, July 8, 1850, the birthday of Brumble Reynolds. Eddie drags Eddie off to the Alta office. The editors were, according to my microfilm of the paper, E. C. Kemble and J. E. Durivage. Don't know, as yet, what those two birds are like. Maybe a Mutt / Jeff or Hard cop / Soft cop thing. The paper at this time had ads on the front page and then a little bit of news on the second page, and the rest was mostly legal announcements or ads.

Again repeating HE1, we may well suppose that Poe will want to get drunk after the interview at the paper. Or that the interview may adjourn to a saloon. Or he goes on a gambling spree.

Creepy thing: the guy who was on the *Purple Whale* with Mason is at the bar in the saloon. And yet Mason thought he saw the whole ship sink, and immediately there-after he caught the very fast cutter Sea Witch direct to SF. So how could he get there? Did a *woomo* help him? Or a bur-rower?

***

More info on Edward C. Kemble (1828-1886) who was on the masthead as the editor of the Daily Alta, along with J. E. Durivage. Note that he was only 22 in 1850. Closer to Mason than to Eddie Poe i age.

> Born Nov. 11, 1828, in Troy, N.Y., Kemble was known as the "boy editor," as he became interested in journalism early in his life.
>
> At 16, he worked as a printer on a weekly Mor-mon publication. *The Prophet*. His employer, Sam Brannan, envisioned an empire in California where his sect could worship without persecution. His plans included starting a newspaper. When Bran-nan's group sailed west to San Francisco, the non-Mormon, adventurous Kemble was with them.
>
> Kemble went to work immediately in San Fran-cisco, typesetting for an advance extra of Brannan's paper, The California Star. In April 1847, Kemble and another young printer, John Eager, were placed in charge of the newspaper by Brannan, who left for Salt Lake City to meet a westward migration of Mormons.
>
> Following Brannan's return in September, 1847, Kemble was made editor officially. He was then just barely 19 years old. Kemble readily became in-volved with local politics, and in April 1848 he was elected clerk of the town council.

When gold was rumored to have been found on
Captain John Sutter's land near Sacramento, Kemble
went to investigate, but he found no gold.

When he returned, Kemble called the supposed
discovery "All Sham" in bold-face type. "A superb
take-in as ever was got up to guzzle the gullible."
His scoffing was to cause him embarrassment for
years to come.

In any case, a month later every man in San
Francisco was digging for gold at Sutter's mill.
Kemble had done his best to put down the rising tide
of "gold fever," as he called it, but eventually the
rumor became obvious fact, and even Kemble himself left to try his luck at the mines.

In late September he returned to San Francisco
and bought The Star from Brannan for $800. The
paper later joined with California's first newspaper,
The Californian, which was suffering great losses
because of ownership changes. It became the Alta
California, the only paper in the territory at the time.

The Alta entered into the work of forming a pro-
visional government and reforming municipal matters in San Francisco; it became "the people's
organ." After the paper was on its feet, Kemble traveled to Sacramento to establish a sorely needed
newspaper there.

Despite many problems, Kemble on April 28,
1849, published the first issue of The Placer Times.
He returned to San Francisco in June, 1849. The Alta became one of the most profitable newspapers in
America, but in 1851 and 1852, tragedy and setbacks
struck the paper.

On June 22, 1851 the sixth great San Francisco
fire burned out The Alta. Despite large financial
losses, it continued publication, but over a year later
a greater blow to Kemble and The Alta struck. Kemble's partner and close friend, Edward Gilbert, was
killed in a duel. To Kemble the loss was like that of
a brother. The Alta continued to prosper, but Kemble's heart was no longer with the paper.

You have to dig to find stuff on Durivage. He came from New Orleans to San Francisco via Chihuahua in 1948. He worked on the Picayune newspaper in New Orleans, and they serialized an account of his overland trip. There is an eight page article called "Durivage of the Picayune." Published in 1995 in San Diego by the Westerners Corral. He traveled through Tucun in Sonora in 1849. I found some of his *Picayune* dispatches excerpted in "Salt Dreams; Land and Water in Low-Down California" by William deBuys and Joan Myers. Durivage had a tough trek through the desert getting from Mexico to California. He's a breezy, fairly amusing writer, Durivage—he's not unlike Poe in his elbow-in-the-ribs humorous journalistic style.

August 17, 2017. Back From Wyoming.

Sylvia and I were on a road trip for two weeks, drove 2,400 miles to Wyoming and back, out through Rt. 50 in Nevada, back through Rt. 20 in Idaho and Oregon. The whole nuclear family of 13 met at Isabel's for a week: the two of us, the three kids, their three spouses, and the five grandkids. Fabulous. So touching. Now some more or less random thoughts on things to do with *Return to the Hollow Earth*.

***

I thought about the novel off and on during the trip, and even did a few touch-ups to the novel. I made Connor Machree into an ongoing character—my assumption at present is that a *ballula* or shell-squid or giant balloonist nautilus is the creature who rescued him from the sinking *Purple Whale*. Machree will be working with a faction inimical to the "good" Hollow Earth people.

***

Looking ahead, I might bring Otha back as a character inside the Hollow Earth—and I'm talking about, the younger Otha from Mason's Earth who stayed with the black gods near the Anomaly, and not about the older Otha whom they encountered in Baltimore.

Recently there's been a lot of controversy in the news about tearing down old statues of Confederate generals and politicians. It makes me slightly uneasy about mentioning slavery in *Return to the Hollow Earth* as well as in *The Hollow Earth*. I hardly know what I'm talking about, re. slavery, and I'll need to do my best not to be offensive. So maybe I shouldn't be too eager to bring Otha back onstage.

***

Speaking of time and age, however, it now occurs to me that if they go back through the anomaly to the original Hollow Earth, it'll be a dozen years later, due to the time the lost on the first passage through the anomaly, and possibly many more years later in the event that they spend overly much time on the passage through the anomaly.

It might be good to steer clear of more trips through the central Anomaly. It's just too confusing for the readers if I keep going back and forth between the original Earth and the "MirrorEarth" where we now are. They don't want to know about there being two Earths. It's enough to just have the one Hollow Earth where this novel is set. The fact the Earth is hollow is more than enough.

If I still want to do that big hop forward to, like, 2150, then I could still use the Anomaly for that, or the Great Old Ones, but they don't actually go through the Anomaly. They, like, bounce off it. Eddie Poe gets them to do it, as he's so eager to go back to his roots.

***

Years ago I wrote a scene in the jungle of the *Hollow Earth* that I didn't use. I wonder if I can find that bit. In any case, I do like the idea of blundering around inside that perhaps miles thick tangled jungle again.

***

As always, it would be nice to have a bit of an outline of the chapters ahead. The proverbial story arc.

August 18-28, 2017. Making Corrections on HE1, Edition 3.

Aug 18, 3017. Before going further, I want to finish marking up and typing in the changes to put into Version 3. I'm in a bit of a fucked-up situation as I now have two (differently) marked-up "master" copies of the Monkeybrain Books edition of Version 2. I'd worked on the initial "Master #1" master a little since 2006, and then more intensely during 2016-2017, and then I couldn't find it so I started putting corrections into a "Master #2" master at some point in 2017. And it looks like some sections were corrected in both the masters copies, and some in one, and some in the other, and I'm not even sure which changes I've typed in.

So what I have to do now is work through all of both the masters in their current state and enter all the changes. It's doable. And while I'm at it, I'll mark up the rest of the book and type all that in, so I'm totally *au courant* on what's in it. And when I finish HE2, I can do one more pass on HE1 to enforce consistency.

***

Aug 19, 3017. Okay, I typed in all the changes from Master #1 and from Master #2, and I'm now in the process of marking up the remaining chaps 9 through 15 and typing in these changes. It takes nearly a day to do a chapter, so I'll be at this for nearly a week.

As I go along, I'm cleaning up Otha's dialog somewhat. Making it less like Jim in *Huckleberry Finn*—which book is kind of apt analog of *The Hollow Earth*. The industrial-strength full-minstrel accent is fun, for the writer, but for today's readers I think it comes across as racist. Like I changed all the uses of "fo" to "for," and "goin" to "gonna." This said, I am still giving Otha's dialog a bit of a colloquial quality, although I can still rethink that later on.

I also was more forthright about Pa raping Turl, and I'm trying to make Otha's resentments a bit sharper. Here again I worry I'm overcorrecting.

***

Aug 21, 2017. Finished correcting Chapter 11 today. Four more chaps to go. I'm kind of staggered by how much action, incident, and eyeball kicks I put into HE1. It's comforting to remember, however, that I made it up as I went along. I'm hoping the muse will be with me on the journey into HE2. But clearly the watchword will be *don't let up.* Pedal to the metal all the way through, ringing ever more changes.

***

Aug 22, 2017. I revised "Chap 12: Tekelili" today. Lots

of stuff about the Central Anomaly, the two Earths, and the *woomo*. I was at the beach in Cruz with Sylvia, went swimming, peaceful there, a Tuesday.

I love Mason's epitaph, the way it doesn't quite make sense, or is ambiguous, "What Laughing Heart Has Died In Vain" Could mean (1) *What* a laughing heart he had, poor kid, and he died for nothing, and it sucks. Or could mean (2) No laughing heart has ever died in *vain*, there was a higher purpose to his life. Or it means a third thing I can't quite express. The epitaph is like an ambiguous figure.

***

August 24, 2017. I stopped referring to the Great Old Ones as Tekelili. *Woomo* and *tekelili beings* are enough aliases to have around. Better to save "tekelili" for what I elsewhere call "teep."

I was going to say (in passing) the MirrorEarth is not a mirror image of Earth, but a copy, But then, upon rethinking it in terms of what I know about passing through an ER bridge, I realized that the MirrorEarth *is* an mirror image, *but* when you pass through the Gate, you too are turned into your mirror image because then you're "lying on the different side" of space. So when you go through the Gate into the MirrorWorld, everything looks normal. You match. And if someone comes through the Gate to visit you, he or she looks normal as well. They flip to match you.

I've decided to have a North Hole in MirrorEarth as well as in Earth, and (as discussed in the next note) that way our boys can balloon down through MirrorEarth's North Hole but (for consistency with what is now know of our MirrorEarth), they'll clumsily ruin the vortex and close it up, possibly causing the earthquake of 1851 in San Francisco.

Finished "Chap 13: Through the Spindle." Should it be "Through the Gate"?

***

August 28, 2017. I finished the revisions today.

August 23, 2017. How To Get Back Inside? Thrashing.

GETTING BACK INSIDE

As I go over HE1 for the version 3 revisions, I keep fretting over how Mason and Eddie and Seela get back inside the Hollow Earth in HE2.

(a) Caves are boring and dirty.

(b) The South Hole on Mirror Earth is sealed over, and we wouldn't want to do a repeat of breaking the ice open.

(c) Going through the ocean via a submerged hole in the crust is a trick I used in getting from MirrorHtrae to MirrorEarth at the end of HE1. Also, though I don't explicitly mention it, the *ballula* at the start of HE1 must have come up through a hole in the sea floor. And we know that whales go through. So diving down into the sea is an obvious method. But you'd be sinking down, like a thousand miles, which is physiologically dicey—although I pretty much glossed over this in HE1, and could do that again. Maybe they'd have some special gas. But face it, another dive is dull. If I do go with the dive, I could have them ride down in a refurbished UFO. But maybe I don't want the UFOs to take over. It's kind of enough to have the Hollow Earth, isn't it?

(d) I could have them sail or balloon down through a maelstrom at the North Hole.

I mention in passing that Earth has a maelstrom North Hole in HE1, but I'm not using it at all. I also say that MirrorEarth doesn't have a North Hole. In order to have a North Hole in Mirror Earth, either

(d1) I revise HE1, so we see a North Hole (and revise the Editor's Note to wonder why we don't see it now). And then the boys the North Hole on MirrorEarth, but they somehow ruin it and close it up, Ruin the vortex or something. So that after HE2, the "MirrorEarth" we live on looks the way it's supposed to.

(d2) I leave HE1 the same, but I have the boys temporarily *create* a North Hole. This would require a really big paddle, being spun by a *woomo* tendril perhaps. Make the paddle out of ice by using explosives to separate off an ice sheet? Well, ice is awfully brittle. Ultra ice? An adamantine mineral discovered in the gold mines? This is too much trouble.

If I take either of these routes, how do they travel through the raving windy vast ultratornado of the North

Hole? I already have a big sailing sequence rounding the Horn in HE2, so I don't want to sail down into the North Hole. I did have a balloon thing in HE1, but I could use a balloon again, that would be fun. Or I could ride a refurbished *woomo* flying saucer through the hole. I guess Crispa can be flying it. Or maybe Crispa and Otha. But, again, I'd kind of like to lay off on the UFOs. I mean, fuck the UFOs. Hollow Earth ought to be enough. The UFOs are just a little backstory decoration.

***

Another idea I had on the beach: what if I went ahead and traveled to the Hollow Sun! That would be something fresh. When *Hollow Earth* came out in 1990, there was an article about my novel in the paper in San Jose, and a young but weathered homeless guy came by my office to tell me this news, I'll quote from my autobio *Nested Scrolls*:

> The guy says, "The sun is cold and hollow. That light you see overhead is just the interaction of some special rays from the sun with our upper atmosphere. I used to be a very famous surfer, you know. Look."
>
> He pulled out a page torn from an encyclopedia with a grainy picture of someone on a wave. "That's me. Inside the Hollow Sun."

Well…maybe that guy was the muse, helping me in advance. Like seedy Mercury, messenger of the gods. So, do I work in a Hollow Sun? Kind of tempting. but…it's a lot of trouble to get from Earth up to the Sun. Of course there could be a shortcut trapdoor at the center of the Hollow Earth. We'll see.

***

What about that sinister unexplained guy Connor Machree, he could somehow be involved in the Hollow Sun. I was thinking that when the *Purple Whale* sank, he must have ridden a *ballula* that came up through the ocean near Antarctica and carried him to San Francisco. Do I want to stay with that? And about the feelers of the *woomo* that save Mason…do I still want those to come up through the ocean? Might as well, if a *ballula*'s coming up that way too. *Or*, I could have the *woomo* tendrils snaking all the way out the North Hole and down. And if I do that, maybe the *ballula* should come through the North Hole? On the other hand the original *ballula* in HE1 came through an ocean-floor hole near Antarctica, which is kind of convenient. I think I now added an aside in HE1 where I explicitly refer back to this. (I'm not totally sure which changes I end up actually doing, as I cycle among HE2, HE1, and these *Notes*.)

THEN WHAT?

Revising HE1, I'm struck by how clean and linear and straight-through the plot is. They go into the Hollow Earth, go to the center, through the Gate, up to the MirrorEarth surface, Eddie gets killed by his double, and they're done.

In HE2, I seem to be groping for some kind of intrigue between two factions. A *yawn* war. Can't I find a straight-through story? The obvious thing would be a re-wind, so they end up back on the first Earth. And then perhaps, in various ways, back-to-square-one sucks. And then to save the situation, they plan for a third journey to fix things for good. Forget it. Don't write a sequel that puts me in hock for a Vol 3!

Of course in HE1, all these effects were new, with big sense of wonder. So on the rewind to make it fresh, I'd have to be doing things a bit differently. Like riding a *ballula* through the North Hole, that's good. And then they get hung up with a totally different MirrorHtrae tribe, not like the flowerpeople. More like crocodile people in the jungle.

And going to the center has to be different. Riding a shrig. Maybe they bomb right through the Gate just to get that part over with. But they lose 300 years and it's 2150. And Otha is dead or something. The flowerpeople are screwed up. And back on the original Earth, Eddie wants to have a career now, but oh-oh nobody digs his style as it's decades (or centuries?) later. So then there's no happy or even interesting ending. I don't think I can make the *deep* future jump work at all. Better drop that.

I'm seeing the *Ringworld II* problem bigtime. No more sense of wonder. So then? I could just double down on the wonder of the known scene. And throw in the Hollow Sun glimpse as a lagniappe.

THRASHING...

Fretted over the story all night long in my dreams, half-awake. Worked on revising "Chapter 13: the Spindle" today. Lots of nitty-gritty details about the Gate in there, and about MirrorEarth vis-a-vis Earth.

I decided definitely to say that MirrorEarth has a North Hole. And then in HE2, my boys will balloon through it—either on a hot air balloon or on a *ballula*—but as they reach the inner Rind, they'll have some kind of fuck-up that closes the maelstrom. The waters of the vortex starts, like, widdly oscillating. An instability. Maybe there's some *really* big monster in that ocean. A kraken.

Re. Mason moving to the future, I could dial that back and have him just hop up to 2018 and I meet him in Fiji. The *Saucer Wisdom*-style Rudy-meets-his-character routine I was thinking of a few months ago. Only I don't literally bring in Frank Shook. Mason Reynolds is the Frank Shook.

As for the Hollow Sun? Well, if I balloon through the North Hole, encounter a Kraken, and have Mason jump forward in time, I'm not sure I need the Hollow Sun.

I still don't know how to handle. Connor Machree. Maybe he isn't human. So he just, like, swam to SF from the shipwreck. Maybe he didn't have a *ballula* save him. Or maybe he's a *ballula* in disguise. On maybe he's a sinister guy who has, like, a *pet* or *partner* or *boss ballula* who ends up hanging around 1850 San Francisco, then the boys could steal it, or convert it to their side, which would be totally cool.

Maybe Machree's angle is to get some of that really heavy ore from inside the crust.

August 24, 2017. Dodecagems, or Rumbies

I want to have very dense matter in the Hollow Earth's crust. The best way to do this is to have stable transuranium elements. Gold and Lead have atomic number about 80. There is a short-lived element 120. But I want something much higher. Like 300 or maybe even 600. Re. 600, there is a four-dimensional regular polytope with 600 vertices, called the 120-cell, it's sort of a 4d dodecahedron, John Conway calls it the dodecaplex, we could also call it a hyperdodecahedron. It's made of 120 dodecahedra and has, as I mentioned, 600 points. And somehow the energy fields of a nucleus can settle onto this 4D configuration. Suppose we call the element dodecaplexium. It's about 7 times as dense as lead. Awesome.

Turns out Poul Anderson wrote a story, "Lodestar," and a novel *Mirkheim*, about a heavily cooked planet or star remnant made of "ultrametal" with, I think, an atomic weight around 300. And the stuff is, it turns out, essential for some galactic spacecraft drives. On August 15, 2017, I ordered Poul's books and will read them.

Metal, per se, isn't as interesting as gems, so let's suppose that my character Jewel's gems are made of a dodecaplexium compound and they're called, say, rumbies. With shifting pentagonal faces. Quivering.

It seems we could also have curiously-shaped *beads* of dodecaplexium, possibly on Seela's necklace. But it's cleaner to just have the one kind of dodecaplexium decoration, the dodecagems, that is, rumbies, and never mind the beads.

I don't really like that name "dodecagem," it's too mathematical. Pompous. Not romantic. Let's try for something else. Turn on stream of glossolalia! Maybe something more like fire drop or god tear or holy eye. No, these are all too corny and obvious, like cheesy SF in a 25-cent paperback from Woolworth's in 1959. Hypergem. I don't think they used the prefix "hyper-" all that much in 1850? William Rowan Hamilton wrote about quaternions in 1843. Quaternogem is pompous. Gustav Fechner wrote "Space has Four Dimensions" in 1846 as Dr. Mises. Tessaract comes from 1888. But these gems aren't actually meant to be particuarly 4D, it's just got that atomic number 600 from the 4D dodecaplex polytope. Quintaplex, like a dorm room. Rhyolite. *Woomo* egg. *Woomo* dingleberry. Jingleberry. Dazzler. Space hole. Eye tunnel. Vortex. Whirlie. Mirrormaze. Snub cube. Fivevif. Twelvlewt. Wheet. Fleenk. Gahoink. Rubby, you can't stop touching it. Also it's close to ruby. And it's a cozy word. I like it. [In Saskatchewan, a rubby is an alcoholic bum who lives in garbage or rubbish, but never mind that, nor will I worry about the other Urban Dictionary meanings.] I stayed with rubby for a week, and then I changed it to rumby.

August 25, 2017. Aha! But Still Thrashing.

Today I went for a walk, wading in the headwaters of Los Gatos Creek above Lexington Reservoir, gravel bed, clear stream, not really enough time, but I got in forty minutes, and my new round of ideas for the HE2 story started coming clear.

Connor Machree has a pet / tame / ally *ballula* that he's hiding in the SF Bay. Mason, Eddie, Seela, the baby, and Arf will steal it, enslave it, and use it to fly down through the North Hole.

At the bottom of the great maelstrom, an immense kraken will lurch out from the thousand-mile-deep ocean. Eddie or Mason or Seela will do a maneuver which throws the vortex into such a wobble that it closes over.

Connor Machree is after them because he has seen and obtained one of Seela's dodecagems (or rumbies) that she got from Jewel. These gems are seven times as dense as normal matter, as they are largely made of Element 600, which has a geometry based on the 4D polytope called the dodecaplex or the 120-cell. We can suppose that, being cooked up within the bodies of the Great Old Ones, the rumbies are imbued with a tekelili-potentiating quality. So if you have one, you can read minds.

I was saying Connor Machree is a bartender, but that's maybe dull. Better if he's a jeweler who found out about the rumbies from the guy in Baltimore who saw Jilly's and Seela's rumbies. Maybe as soon as Mason and Seela left Baltimore the jeweler broke into Jilly Tackler's and stole her rumby at gunpoint, and rushed it to New York, and Connor Machree looked it over, both Jilly's and Seela's rumbies, and somehow they're powerful enough that Machree gets in touch with a *ballula*, and he jumps onto the Purple Whale with Mason and Seela, tracking them, and then deliberately sabotaging the ship, but why do that?

Somehow Connor has enlisted a *ballula* to work with

155

him. *Or vice-versa.* The *ballula* might be Connor Machree's slave-master! Yes. Is Connor surprised when the *ballula* sinks the *Purple Whale*?

And *why* does the *ballula* sink the *Purple Whale*? Perhaps the *ballula* figures this will bring the *woomo* to show their tendrils as they rescue Mason. And the *ballula* knows he can save Connor and would, if necessary, perhaps have saved Mason and Seela as well.

When the *ballula* causes the wreck of the *Purple Whale*, Mason sort of sees it in action, but he doesn't realize what he's seeing. It's the *ballula* that twists the ship at just the special "wrong" angle so the wave splits it in two. And, again, glimpsed but not mentally parsed, Mason sees hints of the *ballula* tentacles in the water, and unknowingly sees it making off with Connor Machree—then carrying him safely to San Francisco.

***

What is the *ballulas*' status vis-a-vis the black gods, the flower people, and the Great Old Ones? Are *ballula*s at all intelligent?

Given that a *ballula* has a "facial squid-bunch of tentacles," it would be natural to see them as Cthulhu-like baddies. But that's too obvious a move. Better to do a reverse and have them fact be a force for order? (Like the way the critters in *Spaceland* who looked like devils were the good guys.) Maybe the *ballula*s are trying to block the destabilizing asymmetries of having Mason and Eddie move world-to-world, and the potentially world-wrecking effect of having rumbies in the hands of surface-dwelling humans. They could play a role like the "time cops" in time travel novels.

Vision of a *ballula* wearing a Sherlock Holmes tweed deer-stalker hat and puffing on a Meerschaum pipe. Except Sherlock's face is a facial squid bunch of tentacles. Vision of an incredibly fine *ballula* tentacle, it stretches out the window, and down along the street, and into Mason and Seela's room and it takes a tentative nip of their new baby's heel, sampling the tissue, and the lad bawls and the tentacle scoots away.

August 26-28, 2017. Machree, Ballula, & Rumbies.

Thrashing.

As I said, Machree could be a tekelili-controlled slave of the *ballula*. Or, again, it could be the other way around. Or they could be allies, which would be a more stable situation.

Maybe the two rumbies are like a pair of psychic walkie talkies.

Does Jilly Tackler still have her rumby, or has she been robbed? Maybe by a *ballula* hovering over Baltimore, with its tendril slowly creeping in through Jilly's open window.

Back up. What would the *ballula* want from Earth's surface? Basically they just like to eat people, so far as I know.

And are the *ballula*s in any way enemies (or agents) of the giant *woomo*? As I said before, I'd like steer clear of having an interspecies war—to me, exploration is more interesting. But if there were to be a war, what would the two or three species be arguing about? Where our Hollow Earth should eventually end up? Whether to go public and move freely between the inside and the outside? Whether to allow free passage to our unknown brethren from within the Hollow Sun?

If the *ballula* care about rumbies, they would like to be making forays to the zone of the *woomo*, down in the central core, but the shrigs or *koladull* are often feeding there, and they attack *ballula*s on sight, so the *ballula*s can't go there.

Might I assume that Machree has one of the rumbies with him. Would be a nice scene to have Machree *show* Mason the gem shortly before the ship goes down. And maybe their shipboard sailor friend Crispa has the other gem?

Getting into a *Lord of the Rings* thing there, which isn't necessarily a bad idea. Maybe there aren't many rumbies at all.

The *ballula*s crave rumbies because they don't have tekelili, and the gem will give them that. As I said before, maybe Machree has acquired the rumby that Mason and Seela sold to the jeweler—this would have happened during the few days it took Mason and Seela to travel from Baltimore to New York.

***

August 28, 2017.

I finished revising HE1 for Ver 3 today, so now I really have to figure out what's happening in HE2 so I can start writing on it again.

* I have a clear image for a scene them riding the *ballula* down through the North Hole maelstrom. I can see them sitting on the inner edge of the nautilus cell, legs dangling, with the great buoyant shell behind and above them, and a tangle of tentacles all around them, and the big shiny eyes, and the beak not very far away. They have to be on very good terms with the *ballula*. And then, just when things start to go sour, here comes the Manhattan-sized kraken! That's good for a chapter.

* And I have an image for a scene of the *ballula* floating in the SF Bay and the boys befriending it there. Maybe they feed some San Jose cows to it. Sunset. Herding the cows into the shallows. The twisting tentacles, the unhappy, surprised *moos*.

But how does the *ballula* show up in our world. Well, let's suppose it followed our boys through the ocean, a bit at a distance, and they didn't see it at night. Then maybe it gets Jilly Tackler's rumby with a sly tendril. And it wants the other rumby, but that one is in the pocket of Connor Machree. So it follows the ship down around the Horn.

* Machree has a rumby, and he wants more. The jeweler in Baltimore resold the gem to Machree, and he's on the trail of Mason and Seela. Machree and the jeweler don't get it about the Hollow Earth. He thinks Seela is from some exotic South Sea island, and he wants to track her there.

Why doesn't the *ballula* just *eat* whoever has the rumby—in particular Machree—and get the prize that way? We know from the scene on the antarctic beach that the *ballula*s are completely ruthless. But in the scene at the Horn, the *ballula* decides to make Machree into an ally because—why? The *ballula* knows that rumbies come from the Hollow Earth's, Central core, so Machree is of no help on that front. Well, maybe having Jilly's rumby has transformed the *ballula* into a kinder being.

***

Let's suppose that Eddie "borrowed" Mason's manuscript from Mr. Coale. In order to do this, he returned to Baltimore right after Eddie and Seela left for New York. Then Eddie might bag the manuscript, and possibly get on the *Water Witch*, perhaps leaving a day or two after Mason, with some kind of plan about finishing and publishing the book together. But he doesn't like the way that Mason writes about him.

Maybe the boys team up with Machree. They don't really care if Machree gets more rumbies, that's his business. And if they ride the *ballula* together, that's great.

They have to leave in a hurry, as Eddie has provoked someone in San Francisco so much that they want to kill him.

***

Found a good picture today in the Wikipedia entry on SF History: Gold Rush. I keep having to grasp that SF went from population 1,000 to 25,000 in a single year.

Figure 16: San Francisco Harbor at Yerba Buena Cove in 1850

With Yerba Buena Island and the misty Berkeley hills in the background. This spot is somewhere around today's Ferry Building or today's base of the Bay Bridge. Treasure Island isn't there yet, as it was created from dredging. The buildings are a little more solid than I'd realized; I'd gotten the impression that at this point a lot of the buildings were still cabin-tents.

Back to my worries about rumby, Machree, and the *ballula*, I think the thing to do next is to print out what I have on HE2, and mark it up, pushing in some of the stuff that I want to see, and worrying about the whys and wherefores later.

Now I'm marking up and revising the start of HE2—at this point I have 9,500 words, twenty-three of my typed pages, which is about one and a half chapters.

August 30-31, 2017. Revise Chap 1 of HE2. No Thrashing.

In the mark-up, I see some heavy expository lumps that have to go. Road boulders that the reader will stumble over. The story must seamlessly draw in the reader in, even if they haven't even read HE1. But—the controlling author asks—how will they know what's going on Well, they won't, so accept that, but if new shit is happening they won't care that much, and *eventually* things will be clear.
***

I wonder if I could have *Eddie* write some of the chapters? That might be fun, and it would be a way of getting in some exposition of the back story. Eddie's narrative could start during the trip through the ocean up to Baltimore—he noticed that a ballula was following them. Or he can just tell all this in an extended discourse, like a story within a story, I could even indent it.
***

Thinking back on my revisions for HE1 Ver 3, I worry that I ruined it. But mostly I was just clarifying actions, and toning down the black accents, and I think all that's for the good.

The questionable changes I made were:

(1) Saying so much about the rumbies (formerly just called jewels, and then dodecagems, and then rubbies).

(2) The watering down of Eddie's murder—removing

the dramatically fierce repeated stabbing of the sword through and through his breast. The subtextual sexuality of the thrusting is pungent and, come to think of it, I lifted the phrasing from Poe's "William Wilson" tale of a double. Wouldn't be wise to so lightly discard that peak. Also I had them sink him with his clothes on so that they don't see that he's not all that wounded.

But, look, I want Eddie to be able to say he was *faking* his death. That's a good move. All I have to do is have MirrorPoe stabbing Eddie's "cloak" instead of his "breast." If do "breast," the dude is frikkin *dead* after *that* shit.

I briefly entertained the thought of having Eddie die but be *resurrected*. How? Resurrected by a rumby gem he's wearing. Or by the touch of a sly *ballula* tendril, come in search of the divine rumby that Eddie has somewhere about his person. But Eddie is nude? Well, perhaps there were three gems, and Seela let Eddie wear one in a necklace of his own, so then we have Eddie with two necklaces, one with the rumby, and the other with the teeth, and the teeth one is gone, but he was buried in the water with that amulet necklace with the rumby, and maybe he wasn't nude anyway. Balls in the air.

It *would* be useful for the plot if Poe has one of the gems, and if he at least he knows about the jeweler Machree who's after the rumby gems.

Suppose the *ballula* followed their UFO up from the Hollow Earth, and it doesn't resurrect Eddie but it's in awe of his rumby. A ballula won't just *take* the rumby and eat the rumby's erstwhile owner. It wants to, like, *serve* the wearer of the rumby. So Eddie was faking, but he does have his rumby, and when he comes up to shore the ballula shows up, underwater, and shyly touches Eddie's rumby, and the ballula becomes Eddie's pet or mascot.

I wonder if Eddie should tell this info in conversation or should I have him write it out, and he hands it to Mason to read and that's a chapter in HE2. Easier to just have him say it. If I do a chunk, it only slows things down, and I want that fast careening downhill speed like in HE1.

Note that Eddie *does* have the manuscript for HE1 with him. He bagged it from Mr. Coale. He wants to work a book deal with Mason. He wants to go back to the Hollow Earth and write a sequel to Mason's narrative.

A problem with the ballula meeting Eddie in the harbor is that the ballulas are quite large, and this one might not fit under the ocean's surface if the water's only 30 feet deep, and people would see it. So okay, like I said, it hides underwater when Eddie walks to a deeper spot or something.

And then we're set for Eddie to be pals with, or master of, the *ballula*, which is great, much better than that prick *Machree* being pals with the *ballula*. Eddie sent the *ballula* to save Mason and Seela, but mainly it was looking for the rumbies that Machree had, heh.

Machree doesn't get saved. Fuck him. I hate him anyway. And it's the *ballula* who saves Mason and Seela, I don't use the *woomo* frond like I said before. It's overkill to have both a *ballula* and the *woomo* saving people from the foundering *Purple Whale*. But I will keep the pink light from the *woomo* as, first of all, it's a beacon for the ballula and, as a practical matter it makes Eddie and Seela turn black again, and it's nice to know the *woomo* are watching.

And what about Crispa? Well, why not let the *ballula* save him too. Slightly reluctant to save him because I don't want that Bremen Town Musicians kind of thing with an agglutinating cast of characters. If I've got Seela, Mason, and Eddie, do I really need a fourth character right off the bat? And have it be such an obvious reprise of the Otha character? What plot function would Crispa play? Well if I do keep Crispa, I'll have him be a woman disguised as a man, so we get an *aha* out of that, so it's worth while. I was calling him Crispus, but I like Crispa better. More unisex.

***

August 31, 2017

So okay, like I mentioned above, Poe is faking and not dead. I gave him an extra necklace with a rumby, and they sank him into the harbor with it. They didn't have the heart to strip the amulet gem from the sad corpse. And they left most of his clothes on so they don't notice that he was hardly stabbed at all.

And like I say, I won't have Eddie write a chapter for HE2 about the ballula meeting him. He can just talk a lot about it. Don't drag it out and make a big thing of it. Tell people what's happening and move forward.

And the ballula worships anyone who wears a rumby.

Eddie's ballula went on a mission to fetch Machree and his rumbies, and it ended up saving Seela and Mason kind of by accident, because Seela grabbed the rumbies from Machree at just the right moment in time. It's a kind of unvoiced joke that Eddie wouldn't actually worry about saving Mason and Seela, that's how Eddie is. And like I said, I'll kill Machree in the sinking of the *Purple Whale*, and I won't have him pop up in the casino in the San Francisco chapter like I was going to. Let him go. Or? And we can have more jewelers show up hunting for rumbies later on if we want to.

Anyway, for now, I'm inclined to stop outlining and be done with thrashing, and to start interactively massaging the sacred lines of the revealed HE2 text and fixing things as I go. At some point it's easier to discover the changes as you type them, rather than precisely planning them in advance. If I do it interactively I don't have to fuckin *think*. The text dances with me.

And today I pushed for eight hours and I got Chapter 1 "Around the Horn" fully revised. And now I can go on to Chapter 2 "San Francisco." I'm done thrashing. Kind of. For now.

September 2, 2017.

I finished revising what I had written on Chapter Two as well. For now I still have Connor Machree reappearing. He's black like Mason and Seela. Apparently the *woomo* light carried him all the way to SF. He's in a bar, Mason just sees him in passing. Not quite sure if I want to keep him around. He could start trying to get back the two rumbies that Seela took off him. This could lead to some hostile action, prompting an earlier-than-expected departure. Eddie clarifies that he now has Mason's HE1 manuscript, not that it matters, as it's just going to kick around unpublished until editor Rudy finds it around 1986, some 116 years later.

September 4-11, 2017. Finish Chapter at Eldorado.

September 4, 2017.

I'd planned to do a scene in the newspaper office, and a

scene of Eddie getting drunk and losing some money gambling, and Eddie sparking a duel that Mason will have to fight in. I might skip the scene at the newspaper office, as I don't feel excited about it, it's too much a replay of HE1. What about having Eddie go straight in the Eldorado in the morning on their way, supposedly, to the *Daily Alta*, and Eddie loses his money and get drunk before noon.

Really I'm eager to get our party on the way to the North Hole. I don't want to have to do endless historical research on SF and the Gold Country in 1850—I mean I've done some research already, but it's a black hole if you get into that. I'd like my boys to skip town within a week, riding on Cytherea the ballula.

By the way, I was going to call the ballula Cynthia, but Cytherea sounds more like a Poe name for a maiden. Cytherea is in fact an alternate name for the goddess Aphrodite—supposedly Aphrodite was born near the Greek island of Cytherea, which is also spelled Kythira. (And also, I notice on Google, Cytherea is the name of a porn star, "known for ability to ejaculate while having sex acts" (i.e. she pees in the air), but, *yucch*, never mind that!)

September 5, 2017.

I could speed up the departure by having Connor Machree go after Seela and the boys—he's trying to get back the two rumbies that Seela took off him when he was on the point of drowning in the wreck of the *Purple Whale*. And he might get violent about it. And the tendril of the ballula could play a role.

Who's in the travel party? Well, Eddie and Mason of course. And Seela, but it doesn't seem like it would be realistic to bring Seela and the newborn Brumble onto the ballula before at least a week has elapsed. Seela's tough, sure, but we gotta give her a week of down time. So I'll have to vamp for a week. And what about Crispa? Do I have to bring him, I mean her, along to the Hollow Earth? What plot function would Crispa serve?

What if Eddie fell in love with Crispa, that would be something. Note that I was also considering linking Eddie with Jewel. But, really, I tend not to see Ed as having girlfriends. Although with Jewel he could get into his literary gigolo thing. Trying to get more rumbies out of her. So, okay, no romance between Eddie and Crispa.

I guess I could leave Brumble with Crispa in SF, and have her be, like, a nanny, but that's kind of dull, and I don't think Seela would go for it. Or I could kill off Crispa in San Francisco, as part of the ongoing skirmish with Machree. Always good to have a death to amp up the plot. But is it racist and cisist to kill off my black trans character? Like how it always happens in action movies—the black and/or trans one is the first to die. Like how I killed off Dirk Peters in HE1. Maybe Crispa kills Machree? And then she has to flee? Or she gets something going in SF for when they return? But probably it'll be years later when they return. Well, sigh, if Crispa comes to the Hollow Earth, then, as I said, I have to find something for her to do. She can be Seela's pal.

September 7, 2017.

I went back and altered HE1, Ver 3, so that Jewel is Eddie Poe's type, thin and strange, rather that robust and womanly. A haunted maiden, not a rich widow. And I set up a little affinity between them so that now in HE2, Eddie can actually say Jewel is one of the reasons he wants to go back into the Hollow Earth. And Eddie knew about Connor Machree before setting off after Mason and Seela.

September 9, 2017.

Now I've added this occult society, the Order of the Golden Frond, and they pray to the *woomo*, although they don't realize what the Great Old Ones are. Connor Machree and Annabel Whistler are in the society. (The society is inspired by the Order of the Golden Dawn, which was formed around 1880, as an offshoot of the Masons which, unlike the Masons, welcomed women as members. The "Frond" is a subtextual reference to *woomo* arms.) As Annabel's boyfriend, Poe turned them on to the tekelili power of his rumby. Machree wants to get more of them, and Eddie has told him of the Hollow Earth, but Machree keeps thinking it's an island. Eddie makes a deal to show Machree how to get there from California, and gets money from him. Tells Machree how to get the other two rumbies, and how to follow Mason and Seela. Says they'll meet in SF, and hopes

Machree won't show up.

Does Eddie in fact instruct his ballula to sink the *Purple Whale* and to save Mason and Seela? If I do this, then Eddie is a mass murderer (of the crew and passengers of the *Whale*), and then he becomes unusable as main character who you want to root for. Suppose Eddie tells the ballula just to fetch Mason and Seela, and it's the ballula's *own* idea to sink the ship. Eddie is supposing that they'll get to SF in advance of Machree, and they'll leave town before he gets there.

September 11, 2017.

So I worked out most of the back and forth with Machree. Did several revisions. I wrote a closing scene where Eddie and Mason go into the Eldorado and use their rumby tekelili to win $3,000. Pip the porter is, they don't quite realize yet, a spy for Machree, and he's going to bring in Machree, and they're going to leave town in a hurry.

September 14-15, 2017. Machree Read Mason's HE1.t

Sept 14, 2017.

In my HE2 draft thus far, I've been saying that Eddie has possession of Mason's HE1 manuscript, I had some idea that Eddie wanted to get in on publishing it. I don't think I'd said exactly how Eddie got the manuscript from Coale.

But it would be more interesting if Machree has read Mason's HE1 manuscript, and he's using the info as a guide to the return trip to the HE that Eddie and Seela both will want to do. In this case, the actual manuscript for HE1 plays an active role in HE2—and that would be a fun "meta" move, a way of doubling down on my hoaxing claim that HE1 is a physical manuscript that I found in the U. Va. Library. Internal consistency! You can see that Mason's manuscript is real, since it's documented in HE2! And it'll be simpler if we leave it with Coale in Baltimore.

I like this new idea a lot.

So now I need to work out a precise timeline for putting into play the contents of the Mason Reynolds HE1 manuscript that Coale has. While I'm at it, I'd also should get a timeline of what Eddie was up to during the nearly nine months apart from Mason. I want, in particular, a timeline for Eddie's involvement with the Annabel Whistler, the Order of the Golden Dawn, Connor Machree and the rumbies.

Sept 15, 2017.

As the timeline now stands, Mason finishes the manuscript on March 2, 1850, and he leaves Baltimore on March 4, presumably entrusting the manuscript to Coale on March 3, the last day before he and Seela leave. As I researched before, they took a four-day stagecoach ride from Baltimore to Manhattan with a stop in Philadelphia, arriving in Manhattan on March 8. And they ship from Manhattan the *Purple Whale* on March 9, the next day.

Machree has a constrained window during which to: (a) Read the HE1 manuscript, (b) get the two rumbies, and (c) get aboard the *Purple Whale*. To make things dramatic, suppose that Machree reads HE1 in Baltimore on March 5. He makes an immediate snap decision to get both rumbies, and then to get in touch with Mason directly. But Mason is gone! So he engages a private carriage for an express trip to Manhattan. He would have preferred to forestall Mason from getting aboard the *Purple Whale* at all, but by the time he's in Manhattan, Mason and Seela are aboard the *Purple Whale.* Machree is brought aboard the *Purple Whale* at the last minute by the boat that fetches the pilot as they leave the harbor.

And what about Eddie? Before leaving on the *Purple Whale*, Machree tells his Order of the Golden Dawn contacts that that he's following Seela and Mason. And the Order passes the word to Eddie.

At this point Eddie doesn't know that Machree has read the HE1 manuscript, and he hasn't read it himself. But he decides to get the jump on Machree anyway.

Mason mentions the manuscript to Eddie on the *Water Witch*, and Eddie makes remarks about possible publication, and about Mason's possible insults and *lèse majesté*. And maybe later, Machree gives Eddie a verbal précis of the HE1 manuscript while the whole party is aboard Eddie's ballula, and this way we can have more discussion of the book.

But wait, did I say, *whole party"* Well, yeah, clearly the next right thing is for Machree to muscle his way onto the

Return to the Hollow Earth expedition. Perhaps by kidnap-
ping Brumble!

That's a lot of revising and weaving-in to do! Which
makes me glad. Means I've had another visit from the Muse.
As confirmation of this, I just now was struck by a need to
excrete—and, with one flex, I effortlessly laid a smooth 16-
inch turd in the bowl. "Auspicious," as the *I Ching* would
say.

Rather than listing the requisite changes here, I'll just go
into the novel manuscript and search for all mentions of
"Machree" or "manuscript" and make the needed changes as
I find the spots. Focus on the "territory" (the novel document) and not the "map" (this notes document). I'll also
comb through Poe's narrative dialog aboard the *Water
Witch*, and in Portsmouth Square. And the reveal of
Machree's knowledge is in the scene where Machree catches
up with Mason and Eddie in the street.

September 16-18, 2017. What Happens in the North Hole?

Sept 16, 2017.
So it looks like before departing for the North Hole,
we'll be loading up Cytherea the ballula with Mason, Seela,
Brumble, Eddie, Crispa, Machree, and Arf. That feels like
too many. Like I said before, why do I have to have Crispa at
all?

In the balloon across Antarctica in HE1, I had Mason,
Otha, Eddie, Peters, Reynolds, and Arf. The same count,
and somewhat analogous roles, with Seela ~ Otha, Crispa ~
Peters, and Machree ~ Jeremiah Reynolds. As I mentioned
before, I killed off Peters fast. And then killed Reynolds.

If we *can* ditch Crispa and Machree, we've then got our
crew down to a workable core: Mason, Seela, Eddie,
Brumble, and Arf. I like to imagine that the passage to an
underworld strips characters away.

I have to keep remembering to mention Arf, sigh. That
always happens when I give my hero a dog. Like Gyro
Gearloose's ever-reacting Li'l Bulb. Did Arf do anything
much on the trip in HE1? I'll have to search and see. But I
guess I'm stuck with him. Maybe this time I can think of

something important he can do.
***

I was talking to my mathematician friend Nathaniel Hellerstein on the phone, and he thought that my North Hole is likely to be at least, say, a hundred miles across, given that it's 500 or a thousand miles long. And it takes something pretty drastic to create a big enough wobble to close a hole that size. The humans aren't likely to be able to close it with a simple bump or blunder. And that's where the kraken might come in. The kraken might be, like, the gatekeeper of the North Hole. He can close or open the neck of the maelstrom.

Or I can ignore Hellerstein's possibly mistaken caveat and claim that maelstrom necks down to a really small size in the middle. Think of how big, broad eddies in a stream tighten down to tight vortex threads that snake down to the bed of the creek. Think of a tight tornado. Twisting like mad in the thin part. Suppose the South Hole maelstrom does neck down to fifty yards across in the middle. Or ten yards. Or five yards. And it's buffeting the ballula shell. Insane spray and whirling. Big scene.

And the beady-eyed kraken appears there at the tight neck. Rapping or scraping on the shell like whatever it was in Dylan Thomas's poem, "Altarwise by Owl-Light,"

> Old cock from nowheres and the heaven's egg
> With bones unbuttoned to the half-way winds,
> Hatched from the windy salvage on one leg,
> Scraped at my cradle in a walking word.

By default, I see the kraken looking like a crawfish. Feelers, eyestalks, thin claws. But maybe I can come up with something gnarlier. My guys *imagine* that the kraken wants to eat some or all of them. They think it's a Scylla and Charybdis situation, with the kraken as Scylla, and the vortex as Charybdis.
***

Crispa by some heroic act rides or joins with the kraken just as the kraken closes up the maelstrom—*gloop*! The rebound of the surface-tension-membrane on the underside the

Arctic sea is like a trampoline—*spang*—it flings our crew, still ensconced in their ballula, out into the inner sky of the Hollow Earth. [Or, as mentioned in the Sept 21, 2007 entry, maybe, save the pinch-off till the return trip through the North Hole at the end of HE2.]

Crispa isn't fact dead, and she can reappear a little later on. And it can turn out that the initially off-putting kraken is good. Okay, but then I can't say that he wants a human sacrifice at the tightest point of the North Hole vortex thread. I'd have to reframe that. Suppose the kraken didn't really want to *eat* anyone, he just wanted to enlist a rider, or a speaker, or an interpreter—who turns out to be Crispa. And, like I say, if Crispa links up with the kraken, they can return to do a big save near the end of the book.

***

Sept 18, 2017.

So how do I ditch Machree? Maybe when they're in that whirling panic, and the kraken appears, Machree is trying to throw baby Brumble to the kraken, imagining the kraken is seeking a human sacrifice, although the kraken is in fact it's seeking a symbiotic human partner, and not a meal.

Crispa nobly offers herself in Brumble's stead, leaping at the kraken, who does not in fact eat Crispa, but instead— gnarly, dude!—incorporates Crispa into the kraken's body. Like those fish where the female captures a tiny male and makes him into a vestigial sperm-dribbling organ situated near her cloaca.

Mason is so infuriated at Machree that, via the power of the rumby, and over Eddie's protests, he tells the ballula to eat Machree. And this is about to happen. But then—once again, a tendril of *woomo* light saves Machree, bearing him off towards the center of the Hollow Earth. "Borne as if on angels' wings," says Eddie. "The High Adept of the Order of the Golden Frond of which I shall be the Prophet."

Okay, great, love it, but yet again I ask, why actually *do* the *woomo* help Machree? *Cui bono*? To what end?

Let's review. The *woomo* got lightly in touch with Machree via the Order of the Golden Frond, and more deeply via Eddie's *woomo*, and via the two rumbies while Machree briefly owned them.

Suppose the *woomo* wanted Machree to join in the return to the Hollow Earth because they want to use him for a purpose. Remember Axis Sally and Lord Haw-Haw, who broadcast on the radio in support of the Axis in WWII? The *woomo* want Machree to be their voice for broadcasts or visions for citizens on the outer surfaces of the MirrorEarth and the Earth.

They've made some tentative contacts via the Order of the Golden Frond which—news flash—Eddie Poe himself founded during his nine months on MirrorEarth. He started it with Annabel Whistler as a money-raising scam. But it got away from him.

And now the *woomo* want a broader presence. But why? Well, maybe they just want to use the human race as, like, a sense organ. A kind of retina. Us watching the skies. Preparing for—I won't say yet. But maybe it's an invasion from the Hollow Moon and/or from the Hollow Sun. And the krakens are the allies of the *woomo*. All the creatures inside the Hollow Earth are, approximately, allies, like the entities within a living cell. Although, yes, shrigs eat ballula when they can, and ballula eat humans, but that's how it is in a chaotic living biome like a cell or like a Hollow Earth.

Sept 21, 2017. When to Slam the Maelstrom?

I'd considered slamming the maelstrom on the way in, but maybe I want to save the maelstrom-closing for the end, when they're on the way out, and the *boing* can launch them up into the air above MirrorEarth's North Pole. Doing the pinch on the way in might be too many events at once, slamming it right after saving the baby, threatening Machree, Machree being saved by a *woomo* tendril, and Crispa jumping out to merge with the kraken.

And if they don't boing on the way in, they could settle down somewhere on the inner surface of MirrorHtrae and some little adventure. Like there's a fire. Or they visit the mirror version of Seela's flower.

Could work better to do the slam at the end of HE2, and Crispa shows up with the kraken to close the maelstrom because something's chasing Mason, possibly the *woomo* tendrils, goaded by Machree. By now the *woomo* will be incorporating Connor Machree's mind, see, and maybe Machree doesn't want our gang to make it out—I'm thinking by then the "gang" might be down to just Mason and Arf.

And it would be interesting if, at the end of HE2, we've (seemingly, although if there's an HE3, one never knows) banned the *woomo* from access to the surface of our Earth. More in line with our experiential reality. I mean, until now I'd figured the tendrils could go through the ocean wherever there happens to be a "blue hole," like by Antarctica, or by the Chesapeake Bay, or (maybe) Fiji. But I could ban that, and require there to be a hole. Constraints are good for a story, as they provoke solutions. If this is where I'm going, then the *woomo* tendrils that reached the *Purple Whale* at Cape Horn in HE2 didn't come up through the sea, they came through the North Hole and bent down. And I'd have to review HE1 and my existing start for HE2, and make sure I don't have any *woomo* tendrils coming through the ocean, but just through the North Hole. (Done.)

If the MirrorEarth North Hole gets closed off during Mason's return at the end of HE2, that has to happen before the Amundsen-Ellsworth 1926 Transpolar Flight over the North Pole, riding in a dirigible called the Norge. (By the way, the Peary (1909) and Byrd (1926) attempts are by now discredited.)

So if Mason comes back and slams the North Hole shut so the ice can freeze over the pole, this ought to happen before 1910 or so…or before 1900 to be safe. So he could only have an up to a fifty-years-into-the future jump this time. I'd been toying with the idea of him jumping clean up to 2018 and meeting me in person. But If I want to keep that, then I'll have to close the North Hole maelstrom earlier—like during their descent—and then have Mason coming back via some other channel such as, once again, a bathyscaphe ride up through a blue hole, which isn't as exciting…although if he rode a ballula to Fiji that would be a little different than riding an ancient alien UFO to Chesapeake bay like in HE1.

Re. Mason's time jumps, if he goes back to the original Hollow Earth, and then back to Mirror Hollow Earth, he'll be doing two jumps. The first could be, say, 12 years like in HE1, and, if I wanted, the second jump could be anything up to 38 years, to bring him back at 1900 at the latest. Not that there's any special reason to make it 1900 instead of just another 12-year jump, with the round trip bringing him back at 1874. Would be kind of relaxing if the time slip was always the same.

Yet again, I might not send Mason through the center at all. Maybe it's just Eddie and Seela who go through. That could be a big farewell scene. Seela would go back to her flower, and Eddie could count on his pet ballula to carry him up through the South Hole and to Baltimore, it would be, say, 1862, and he could kick his writing career into gear. He might well have brought two volume of collected Poe writings along to make things easier. Note that two volumes of the four-volume Griswold edition came out in time: *Tales* in December, 1849, and Poems and *Miscellanies* in January, 1850. And he's run some scam about where he'd been for so long—if he happened to have a copy of Mason's HE1, he might even publish it himself. Or better he'd just write one. Or by the time he got back, people would have noticed the now-open South Hole. Fodder for a possible HE3...

And note that if Mason came straight back through the North Hole, he'd get back to San Francisco in 1851 or 1852 (depending on how long he stayed in the Hollow Earth this second time), and that drawing I "found" in Berkeley could well be dated 1852, and his second narrative could well have recently turned up in San Francisco as well.

***

Re. Eddie and Seela going on through the Anomaly without Mason—what if *Eddie* has in fact won Seela's love. Awesome plot twist! And we're set up for that—Seela doesn't like Eddie, and he's not all that interested in her, so if they then fall in love...classic. What if Mason keeps the baby? That would be cute. Would Seela give him up? Maybe, or maybe Mason would kidnap him. Maybe Seela wouldn't care that much? Certainly Eddie wouldn't particularly want a baby.

But I'd rather keep Eddie, although I could live with losing Seela.

September 28 - Oct 3, 2017. Louisville. Mammoth

Cave.

Sept 28, 2017.

Sylvia and I came to Louisville for me to give a talk at the "Idea Festival" yesterday. My title was "Welcome to Your Cyberpunk Future." I was tense about it, but I worked up a good draft for it, and it went really well. One of my best talks ever. I killed, as the stand-up comedians say. A great review in the local online paper today, and the Idea Festival paid me $5,000.

I have hopes of visiting Mammoth Cave while we're here—like for Hollow Earth research—in fact I perhaps unwisely planned for the trip to last six nights so we'd have tome for the cave, but now I'm not sure I can make it happen, as it's a two hour drive either way, and Sylvia and Georgia don't want to do it. Maybe I could just go with Embry?

I have jet-lagged insomnia again tonight, our third night. Lying awake, fretting over a minor pre-bedtime quarrel with Sylvia. I was thinking I might now get off the gerbil-wheel by writing something about the Poe / Hollow Earth book, but that's not happening. It's about 3 am. Fuck it. Maybe I'll have another try at going to sleep.

Oct 2, 2917

On the plane home now. Bored on my ass. I was trying to read Darryl Gregory's *Spoonbenders*, but it's like it's written for schoolchildren, it's so dull and corner and obvious and—spare me—the first scene is about a boy jacking off while peeking at his female cousin through a hole in the wall. So banal.

Then I tried to read Jeff VanderMeer's *Annihilation*, which is more literary in it's aspirations, but in a hackneyed way. Purple patches of prose, and the plot seems to be some kind of winking-and-shrugging *X Files* deal. "Stranger than we can imagine!" But what happened? "I can't say, I can't put it into words, I can't tell you yet!" In other words the author doesn't know, and can't be bothered to figure it out, and he plans to vamp and mystify for the full length of three short-weight volumes. "Fine writing and big ideas." Feh!

And yet these books are best-sellers, within the SF field,

and my sacred texts are spurned. *Wheenk*! And I was sucker
enough to waste about $15 on each of them. I might still try
Spoonbenders again, but nix on VanderMeer. I might add
that he's refused to include me in any of the anthologies he's
edited. Oh, well, really he's a fantasy writer, and he can't
help it if he can't plot a novel.

They guy next to me on the plane is watching the new
Bay Watch. How is it that, to my eye at least, the characters
on that show look so deeply unintelligent? How can I judge
that at a glance? The blankness of their foreheads. Like, no
lines of worry, no glow from the mystic Third Eye. The
simplicity of their facial microexpressions. Frozen counte-
nances, earnest in concentration, trying to remember their
lines. Maybe they'd enjoy *Spoonbenders* or *Annihilation* if,
that is, those entertainments were TV shows or movies instead of books. And, god help me, today Marc Laidlaw,
chuckling over my comments on VanderMeer, tells me that
Annihilation is in actual fact slated to become a movie.
Good fit, of course, as SF movies tend not to have coherent
plots either. But fine writing and big ideas, yes!

Oct 3, 2017.

I'm home now, and I want to write up some remarks on
Mammoth Cave. As I mentioned on Sept 28, a few paragraphs back, I was eager to go there—a famous tourist spot
near Louisville that I'd only visited once, at a young age, and
hardly remembered. I was thinking it might be of some research value towards HE2.

Brother Embry drove the two of us down there in his
Porsche, past Elizabethtown, near Glasgow, an hour and a
half on the freeway—when I was a kid it took more like
three hours. Later we drove back partly on a two-lane back
road, balm to my soul, those rolling green Kentucky fields,
little ponds, beautiful horses in the fields, little white-painted
clapboard houses and churches, creaky old wooden tobacco
barns for drying the harvest, some of it visible right now,
five-foot-long sheaves hanging upside down. Tobacco is
slipping in value as a crop—I look forward to seeing Kentucky get into growing pot.

I had only the faintest of memories of Mammoth Cave,
of the entrance, it's a portal in the side of a gully, twenty or

thirty feet high, and inside the ceiling arches higher, up to fifty or even a hundred feet at times, with gray rocks and cave dirt all around, the path with railings, the path itself hardpacked dirt or stone, and, surprisingly, no dripstone or stalactites in view. Turns out the cave is the path of a former underground river, the Green River, which by now is running along a fresh tunnel that lies several strata lower—it keeps burrowing deeper, with the slightly acidic water eating through the limestone.

The channel we walked in was like a big subway tunnel, with electric lights illuminating the yellow/orange bands of stone. Kind of boring, actually. We were in a crowd of about 120 people, walking very fast, Embry and I trying to stay near the head of the pack to be near Ranger Ashley, a talkative young lady. At one point, beside a large rectangular formation called the Giant's Coffin, she turned out the electric lights, and then she extinguished the candle of her single lantern, and it was amazingly dark. Not one photon coming in, and deeply silent. Like being totally blind. You'd have a really hard time trying to walk out of there alone— particularly in the old days when the cave didn't have paths and railings

Ranger Ashley told us a great story about a guy in the old days who was lost, and he blew out his candle, expecting to see the light of some other candle not too far away—but it was all black and, oh-oh, he didn't have a match to light his candle and he was alone in the dark for 39 hours. He thought he heard footsteps—which was in fact the sound of his hammering pulse in his inner ear. To drown out the sound he began banging two rocks together, and he was still banging them when they found him.

We wriggled through a narrow spot called "Fat Man's Misery," and that was kind of fun, although I worried about my weak left leg giving way, and me falling down and popping out my hip or being unable to get up. I brought along a hiking stick of Embry's and was glad for it. The hike was really quite taxing, and eventually were 300 feet below the surface, so low that we were in a zone that fills with water when the yet-further-underground river when it's running high in the spring. Then we had to climb a seven-story-high staircase, like the "fire stairs" in the corner of an office building, exhausting, I was drenched in sweat.

What a joy, then, to enter the "twilight zone" where we could see faint light from the land of the living, and even greater joy, to see the green leaves of the trees, and the faint blue Kentucky sky, the breezy, living free world up there. Like how it feels whenever I get out of the hospital, like after my spleen fifty-five years ago, and after my stroke more recently.

October 3, 2017. Leaving for the North Hole.

So, okay, back to making plans for HE2. I only wrote a couple of hundred words in Louisville, but it looks like Eddie will be taking along Mason, Seela & Brumble, and Arf (I still keep forgetting to write him in)—taking them aboard the ballula shell to ride through the North Hole. On the first day in San Francisco (and the night thereafter) the baby was born. On the second day (and the night thereafter), Eddie and Mason won money at roulette and Eddie loaded the ballula with supplies. On the dawn of the third day they leave.

I'm tempted by the thought that they might duck out of letting Connor Machree come aboard the ballula. And I'm not so sure if Crispa is coming either. As I've said before, I'd basically like to ditch those two. Although, come to think of it, in my earlier entry of Sept 16-18, 2017, I already sketched a scenario for getting rid of those two supernumeraries during the passage through the North Hole—that is, there's a crisis, Mason threatens Machree, a *woomo* tendril saves Machree, and Crispa dives into the maelstrom to join forces with the kraken.

Backing up a bit, why would Eddie even *consider* letting Machree come along on the expedition? It can't be that Machree pushes his way aboard the departing ballula by means of say, threats with a gun or unmanly threats against the baby. For at any moment, Eddie could tell the ballula to kill Machree and thus be done with him. There has to be something that Eddie still wants from Machree. The answer to this depends on the nature of Eddie's ultimate plan. Does he want to be a plagiarist, or a prophet?

- *Plagiarist.* I had been thinking that Eddie's plan is to push all the way back to his initial Earth and to have a writing career there, a life of plagiarizing himself from his collected works in the form of the Griswold edition he gets on MirrorEarth. In that case he has nothing to gain from Machree. But perhaps he *doesn't* want to go back to the original Earth, perhaps he views it as in some sense a grim tomb, and the thought of self-plagiarism bores him. Even if this is not Eddie's plan, I'll leave open, for now, the possibility that he might go back to the original Earth with Seela after all. Re. the possible return, I can complicate it by having the *woomo*, be reluctant or, alternately, eager to facilitate such a trip.
- *Prophet.* Suppose that Eddie plans to win the hand of the black goddess Jewel in the Hollow Earth, and to return to MirrorEarth with a supply of rumbies, with Jewel as his wife, then to enlarge the Order of the Golden Frond and be a socially prominent prophet, and to write a madder-than-*Eureka* theory of the universe, and to write greater fictions than ever, and to write the *Return to the Hollow Earth* with Mason, and to open a permanent trade and cultural link to the Hollow Earth—well, then perhaps Eddie would see some use for Machree as his assistant.

I like the prophet scenario better. It's more grandiose. It's just like an author to dream of having wild success in fields he is in fact totally unsuited for. Explorer! Prophet! Socialite! Metaphysician! To get the ball rolling on the book again, I might go in and do some light touches to weave in Eddie's prophet plan. And then write the leaving-in-the-ballula scene. I kind of imagine someone on the ground shooting a rifle at them as they leave. Some enemy that Eddie has made while assembling the equipage.

***

By the way, I don't know if I mentioned that, late in September, 2017, I split each of the two original chapters in two. So now I have four chapters done, and I'm working on the fifth. I split the old first chapter at the shipwreck off the Horn, and I split the old second chapter after the birth of Brumble.

The current four chaps have lengths of, respectively, 11, 6, 9, and 11 pages—as measured in my current typescript format.

In wanting to go for longer chapters, I'd been thinking in terms of emulating the structure of the impeccable and unsurpassable HE1. But then I decided shorter chapters for HE2 would make the book easier for me to write. And shortish not-necessarily-uniform-length chapters might conceivably make the book more approachable for the reader.

By the way, re. structure, at some point I should decide *when* Mason is writing up the HE2 manuscript. He might even be writing it up as the events are going along. In time this will be revealed to me. Reminds me of an insight I had years ago when I was starting to write *Twinks* in Lynchburg, Va. Which I now duly tweeted:

"Early stages of writing a novel. Like I grubbed a crystal out of the dirt, and am rubbing a facet to see the tiny moving patterns within."

And Isabel responded, "Finding a worthy crystal is a stellar start."

October 5-6, 2017. New Keyboard?

Oct 5, 2017. My beloved old Microsoft Natural Elite keyboard's numeral **1** key wasn't always working, so I bought a new wireless Microsoft Sculpt online, and I hate it. It's has the number pad on a separate piece, which is weird, and the keys don't click or travel as much, and it's not at a nice angle. Maybe I can fix the old one, like take it apart and air blow it for scraps of food. There's six little screws. Or maybe I can get one online. It's vintage, so I can get one in the box for about $150 or a used one for about $70. Devotees claim it's the best keyboard ever.

Oct 6, 2017. Well, I took apart the old keyboard, and it was really weird inside, like a jellyfish, with rubbery egg-carton stuff under the keys, and the circuit for "noticing" the key strokes was "trace sheets" of clear plastic with printed-on frosty circuit lines. Very *Wetware*. And I cleaned it...blew out ten years worth of sandwich crumbs...but I felt confused putting it back together and I did it wrong somehow, maybe something with the trace sheets, and now it

Rudy Rucker

doesn't work at all, dead as a doornail, so for now I'm using the Sculpt and, ya know, maybe it's not so bad. The biggest part of my problem with it is that the key layout is a bit different, so I can't use muscle memory to find the End, Delete, Arrow, and so on.

On the other hand, the fact that the letter part of board (without the number pad) is smaller than the Natural Elite is, maybe, a good thing…as this way it's not such a reach to go over to the mice I keep on either sie of the board. And the fact that the keys have less "travel" up-and-down is, I don't know, maybe it's okay. Takes less time per key, although you get a bit more of a "slam" against your fingertip each time as you bottom-out quicker. I guess I could type more gently, like I do on the laptop. Tickle the ebonies. So maybe I'll stay with it.

In any case, today I'll try reassembling the old keyboard a different way. On my work bench in the basement, yes, geekin' out!

And, well, I did reassemble it, and it still doesn't work, so screw it, put it in the basement, and go ahead and love the new one.

***

More fetishistic tech purchases—I ordered a Google Pixel 2 phone for $750 yesterday. Supposedly it has the best camera of any smart phone, and that's including the iPhone 8 Plus and even (I think) the iPhone X in the competition. As well as hardware, Google focuses on AI and, I love this, the sensor has "split pixels" (that is, two one-micron-separated sensors per pixel) instead of multiple lenses like Apple does. The deal is to capture a bunch of images for each shot, and AI them together to kill motion blur and, if you want, to put in bokeh, and to make up for low light.

On the photo front, I got a great shot of a chair on our deck in the light of the full moon last night, on my Fujifilm T100X. I had the ISO up to 12800, which is insane, and f / 2.0 at 1/3 second exposure.

Excited about the impending port from iPhone to Pixel, I looked up how to move the Contacts info via the iCloud, and how to put my songs onto the Android, and how to leave Apple Music for Google Play, which sounds good. Like I'm

180

emigrating from one tech kingdom to another.

October 7-8, 2017. All Aboard!

Oct 7, 2017.

So I got Cytherea the giant ballula up in the air now with Mason, Seela, Brumble, Eddie, Arf, Crispa, Machree, and now Ina aboard. Six adults, god help me, and taken together they must weight a thousand pounds.

Ina turned up at the last minute, unseen in the fog on the street outside Mrs. Mackie's hotel, and the ballula snatched her up with one of his tentacles. The fog a subliminally supplied objective-correlative for my uncertainties about the passenger list, and Ina pushing her way in, as she's growing into an increasingly interesting character.

If Cytherea is lugging a thousand-pound load, how's she going to lift herself? Say she needs to lift twice as much, that's a thousand kilograms. She lifts by being full of hydrogen, which weighs next to nothing, so her the lifting force is roughly the same as the weight of the displaced air, and air weighs 1.3 kg per cubic meter, so to lift, say a thousand kilograms of ballula + load, we need to displace about 800 cubic meters of air, which could be approximately a prism of 5 x 160, and 160 is about 3 x 50 or pi x 7-squared, so we'd need a shell that's five meters across and with a radius of seven meters. An opening that's fifteen feet across, and a diameter of 40 feet for the big shell. Make that a bit larger. The opening is twenty feet across and the diameter of the big shell is sixty feet.

Okay and how about propulsion? How does a ballula move through space? Did I get into that in HE1? All I can think of is some type of blatting with a cephalopod-type siphon. Oh, right, "I screamed and pointed as the monstrous shell rose into the air, righted itself, and began—with thunderous spewings of gas and liquid—to speed toward us." A type of jet propulsion, not wholly unlike the shrigs' use of flaming farts. I'm not confident that you could get up much speed that way. We'll have to suppose that a *ballula* (or at least Cytherea) is clever at finding and riding jet streams and winds. For already, Cytherea has flown around the Horn from New York to San Francisco in the wake of the *Water*

Witch. Not to mention making that extra detour back to the Horn to rescue Mason, Seela, Crispa, and Arf from the wreck of the *Purple Whale.* I'll weave back a mention of that.

. Cytherea's going to need a lot of energy for this long haul to the North Pole. I should let her dip down and devour a cow or a moose now and then—we'll have a scene on that.

Maybe during one of these stops Crispa jumps ship, as it were. Perhaps to join an Indian tribe. As I've mentioned, I really have no handle on Crispa as a character. Just eager and ingenuous, which is dull. Crispa needs a twist, I need some character trait to weave in, some obsession, some hobby, anything at all really. I mean, sure, she's trans, but so far that's just an opportunistic add-on, If I want to keep that, I need to build it up. I'm uneasy about seeming sexist or, heteronormative, or overly cis in writing about Crispa being trans. But maybe I could get some juice out of it. Need backstory.

Oct 8, 2017. I had a good day yesterday, and I fixed the Crispa thing. Gave her a backstory—she'd always wanted to be out in the wilds, and now she left the ballula to join an Indian tribe while the ballula makes a pit stop to eat a whole bison and part of another one.

I'm thinking that, with a meal like that, the ballula ought to double her volume and thereby her lifting power—so I'm upping her dimensions by a factor of cube-root-of-two, which is about 1.25 (figured that out in my head in the movie theater last night while waiting for *Blade Runner 2049* to start, noting that 5 cubed is about the double of 4 cubed). So now Cytherea can lift two thousand kilograms. So it's fine if she eats a literal ton of bison.

October 12-14, 2017. Balancing MirrorWorld vs. World

(In the title of this entry, I use "World" to stand for "Earth & Hollow Earth" and "MirrorWorld" for "MirrorEarth & MirrorHollowEarth").

I wrote some backstory for Ina into the novel, very dramatic—so much so that it may later turn out that she was exaggerating or even lying. In any case, I've finished a

Cytherea chapter with them travelling across Canada and the *ballula* eating a buffalo on the way. Crispa left them to join a tribe of the Indians in Canada. Ina is a strong character, maybe she's Eddie's girlfriend-to-be.

And now I have a new chapter coming up, "North Hole." They're right at the edge of the maelstrom now. I'll take another look at some plans I made for the trip through the maelstrom back in Sept 16, 2017—although by now I think some of my ideas have changed. Also I'll copy some quotes from Eddie Poe's story, "Descent into the Maelström" here.

Okay, I reread that earlier stuff, and now I'm not sure I even want to see the kraken on the way in. Or let's say we barely glimpse him, but don't get involved. And the kraken can still close the whirlpool on the back. Or maybe the kraken nearly kills Machree and once again the *woomo* save Machree.

***

I still need to do something with Machree. He's such an uninteresting character at this point. We don't hate him enough to kill him, and I can't see the *woomo* really wanting him for anything. But they *did* spirit him from the shipwreck to SF, and I don't want to drop that. I need more backstory for Machree. There has to be some reason why the *woomo* are moving him around. So, okay, what is it?

Eureka, I have solved it! (As summarized in the drawing above.) Let me explain.

It turns out *woomo* need Machree to balance out the two worlds. If you move someone permanently from one world to the other, then you have to move someone else the other way. But we'll say that if you only stay temporarily in the other world and then go home, It's okay.

Suppose that, as I'm now thinking, Eddie and Seela go back. And suppose Mason stays on the MirrorEarth. Then Mason is the only person that's out of balance. And I can fix this if I Machree emigrates to the original Earth.

MirrorMason died young on MirrorEarth, shot by the MirrorStableboy, but his place was taken here by the Mason of Earth who moved here. Now—here's my big kicker—suppose that *Machree* on MirrorEarth is in fact the grown-up MirrorStableboy. So in symmetry with the Mason thread, we can have the Machree thread where his Earth version (the stableboy) died young on our Earth, but that stableboy's place will be taken by the MirrorStableboy (that is, by Machree) who moves permanently back to our Earth.

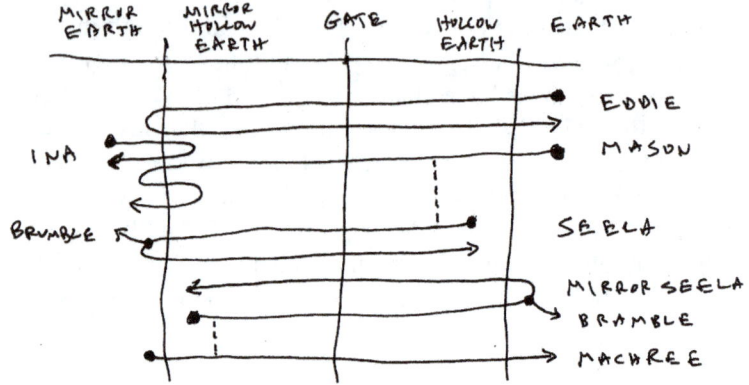

Figure 17: Rococo Worldlines for the Twin Worlds. (First Draft. Final Draft in Fig 19.)

In other worlds, Machree goes through the Anomaly over to old Earth with Eddie and Seela. And then Mason can be allowed to stay on MirrorEarth without destroying the cosmic balance.

And it fits that Machree in our world, which, again, Mason calls the Mirrorworld—it fits that Machree (the grown up stableboy) is, say, 12 years older than Mason, because Mason had that forward time jump when he went through the anomaly. So Mason is 17, and Machree is 29. Perfect.

I'll work in some preliminary hints of the backstory where here on MirrorEarth, Machree grew up in Lynchburg, worked as a stableboy, shot MirrorMason, made his way to NYC and became an assayer and a jeweler.

Having read Mason's HE1, Machree fully understands that he's the stableboy whom Mason shot on Earth, and MirrorMason was the country boy whom the stableboy (Machree) shot on MirrorEarth. But for the moment he's not telling Mason about this. He *has* mentioned that he's from

Lynchburg, and that he knows Mason is from there, and that he and Mason have some shared history—but for now Mason isn't getting the picture. The age difference is distracting him. Machree will do a reveal a little later on—whenever the story needs a goose.

***

Another *big* point to think about: Brumble. Brumble is an asymmetry in the population count. He's only present in one of the two worlds, and there's no duplicate version of him. There *are* other asymmetries that I'm not worrying about—most of these all stem from the fact that in one world Mason died and in the other world the stableboy died. Also there's asymmetries relating to Poe and Seela and Machree as well. But none of these is a *population count* asymmetry. But, as it now stands, Brumble is only born in the one world, with no balancing-out baby born in the other. What to do?

Rococo option: On the fence. I suppose I could maroon poor Brumble inside the central neck of the anomalous Einstein-Rosen bridge between World and MirrorWorld, and thus have him not affecting either world's population count. And there he might take on a divine quality, overviewing millennia. Seems a little harsh on the little baby, though.

Simpler option: Two Brumbles. Here's a much better solution. I'll say MirrorSeela has a baby too. Call him Bramble. Mason and the gang connect with MirrorSeela when they stop in and visit the Mirror-Hollow-Earth's flowerpeople on their flower. The father of MirrorSeela's child must be, in symmetry, someone from MirrorEarth.

Okay, so who is the father of MirrorSeela's Brumble?

Rococo Option: Machree father. if I want to overcomplicate things—the father could be Machree, who maybe takes a liking to MirrorSeela. And then in full symmetry, MirrorSeela could give birth to Machree's baby on the old Earth, and MirrorSeela might then eventually return to her native flower on MirrorHollowEarth. This is the option shown in the Rococo Wordlines figure I drew. I didn't think of the rococo Two Brumbles version until I drew this figure, and was looking for ways to make it as symmetric as possible. This is an example of the value of my logical-mathematical approach in writing Notes for a Novel. The logic suggests plot threads. On the other hand, sometimes the threads are a bit too gnarly—as mathematics often is. So this is also an example of the weakness of the logico-mathematical approach. We elaborate complexities for their own sake.

Simple Option: Flowerperson father. The father could just be a MirrorEarth flowerperson. And Bramble could just be born on the MirrorFlowerpeople flower. This is the option show in the figure below. If all we're doing is counting heads, then it doesn't really matter if Brumble and Bramble are both born on the MirrorEarth side, as long as one of them ends up back on the Earth side.

Balanced Option: Mason gets MirrorSeela pregnant. Somehow she hasn't had a baby yet, even though she's twelve years older than Seela. And this way there's a more precise balance between Bramble and Brumble. They have the same father and, genetically, they have the same mother. They could even be identical. That would be kind of interesting, the "same" baby, yet not the same. And Mason fucking MirrorSeela could precipitate (or be caused by) a breakup between Mason and Seela.

The balanced scenario is shown in figure below. I've revised this picture a lot of times, with the latest version from October 20, 2017. The dotted lines indicate approximately when Mason impregnates Seela and MirrorSeela, and eventually Ina.

Summing up, Eddie doubles back so that's balanced, ditto for Ina. Seela/Brumble balance with MirrorSeela/Bramble. Mason balances with Machree. Those two are the only ones who emigrate for good.

One more thought. The whole reason for the imbalance came from the Schrödinger-type split when Mason and the stableboy shot at each other. You might say that incident split the universe in two and caused the Earth/MirrorEarth duality. Getting cosmic, I could even say that the split propagated *backwards* as well as forwards in time. There have always been the two worlds *because* of that fork moment when Mason and the stableboy shot at each other. What made it happen? Perhaps the *woomo* did it. Maybe I should weave back a sly sea cumber lolling in the hay-manger in that barn—kind of kidding about that, but maybe Mason could have a glimpse of a *woomo*, although not knowing what it is.

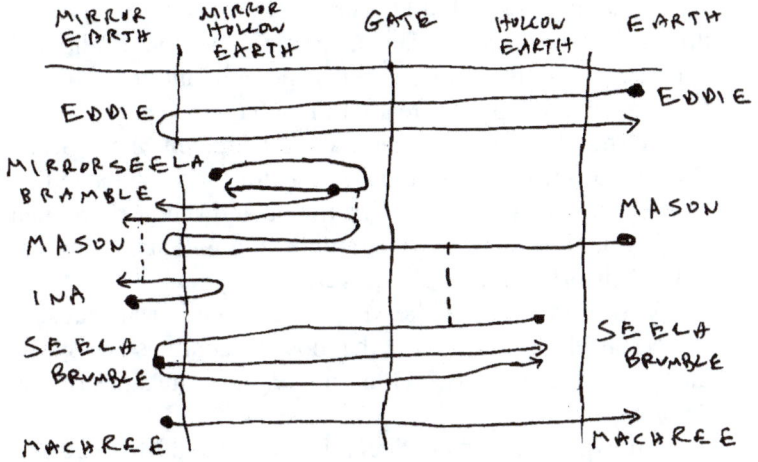

Figure 18: Balanced Population Worldlines for the Twin Worlds.

Yet another thought. For purposes of balance, I think we might require that Mason and Machree don't have any more children. Mason had the two Seela/MirrorSeela babies, and one lives on each side, that's nice and balanced. He shouldn't then have a singleton baby with Ina on MirrorEarth. And Machree shouldn't have a singleton baby over in the Hollow Earth or on Earth.

Maybe poor Mason should at least get to keep the baby Bramble.

***

Summarizing the upcoming events I'll be writing about: they go into the Mirror Hollow Earth for awhile, and they visit the MirrorFlowerpeople, and MirrorSeela is settled in with MirrorYurgen. MirrorYurgen and MirrorSeela are twelve years older than Seela, which feels weird. They don't have a child.

187

Seela's old boyfriend Yurgen was is just a sidelight in HE1, he only gets a few paragraphs (that I still need to write into HE1 Version 3). He was the guy playing that giant horn.

Seela kind of wants to hook up with MirrorYurgen, just for a quickie at least, but he's creeped out by her, and he thinks the whole party—Seela, Brumble, Mason, Eddie, Ina, and Arf—he thinks they're freaks and evil, and the MirrorFlowerpeople are ready to lynch them.

So they flee to the center and the Umpteen MirrorSeas. But MirrorSeela comes along with them for the ride, and ends up that Mason fucks MirrorSeela and she gets pregnant, and in due time she'll have Bramble, and will stay with him in the MirrorFlowerpeople flower.

MirrorOtha isn't in the Mirror Umpteen Seas because he stayed on MirrorEarth—but that doesn't count as an asymmetry, as at least the two Othas are on opposite sides of the Anomaly.

Anyway, then Eddie, Seela, Brumble, and Machree all go through the Anomaly together. Mason wanted to keep Brumble, and Seela said it was okay, but the *woomo* snatch Brumble and put him with Seela for the sake of symmetry, and then they're all gone, and it's just Mason and Ina. They fuck like crazy with the black gods for awhile, and they get some more rumbies from MirrorJewel, and then they go back up to MirrorEarth. And at some point maybe Mason figures out that a lot of what's happened has been "about" preserving the symmetry.

***

Later, after Mason and Ida and Brumble get back to SF, Mason dutifully feels like he has to kill Cruickshank on Ina's behalf, but at that point Ina tells Mason that her big story about Cruickshank murdering her father was a lie, and that in fact Ina's father is still working at the *Alta* newspaper. Maybe Ina wasn't even a prostitute and Cruickshank wasn't a pimp. And Pip isn't even her brother. But by now Mason loves Ina anyway. He writes HE2 and gets a job at the paper.

***

An issue to consider: when Seela goes back to regular Hollow Earth, Yurgen will be twenty-four years older than her.

Simple Option: Seela is quite casual about who she
sleeps with, as the flowerpeople are the opposite of Puritans.
So she does not in fact feel compelled to hook up with her
old boyfriend Yurgen when she eventually gets home to her
native flower. She'll probably pick a younger guy.

Rejected Rococo Option; In order to keep Seela from being too young for the aged Yurgen, what if I say that when
you go through the Anomaly in the reverse direction, it
jumps you back in time instead of forward, but I don't think
I want to do that.

In any case, I *might* say that they are careful to go
through the Anomaly really, really fast this time, and they
only lose, say, a year or two, and then Seela's only a 13 or
14 years younger than Yurgen which might be workable.
And it would be handy for Eddie to only have been gone 13
or 14 years, I mean in terms of resuming his literary career,
and assuming he ever gets back to the surface, which of
course we will assume.

What about a mate for Machree? There's no absolute
need to send him back to the original Earth. Eddie doesn't
care about bringing him along. And it's enough for the
woomo, in terms of balancing out Mason, if Machree is in
the original Hollow Earth and not on the Mirror side.

I could suppose that Machree hooks up with Jewel, as
it's rumbies he cares about. And instead of getting into importing rumbies up to the surface, maybe Machree just gets
into trading them within the Hollow Earth. Or I could say
that Machree's homosexual. And then, as a bonus, he would
not in fact have "violated" Ina while sharing her room.

So does Eddie bring a woman back to Earth? Well...no.
But that's to be expected, isn't it. He'll find one back home
anyway. He never lacks for admirers and patrons.

I don't want to explicitly "queer" Eddie and pair him up
with Machree. But they could perhaps hang out together in a
kind of nerdy way like the narrator and the detective Auguste
Dupin in "The Mystery of Marie Roget." Like Watson and
Holmes.

***

By the way, as Mason is narrating, we don't necessarily

189

find out what happens when Seela goes back to her original flower. Or what happens to Eddie. Or to Machree. So all that stuff I was just saying is off camera.

But it would be nice for the reader to know it, so let's suppose that the *woomo* will let Eddie and Mason have a psychic visionary staring-into-the-sky "Face Time" conversation at the very end of the book so as to wrap up the "what ever happened to" questions.

And I'm *not* going to save the "what happened to" stuff for a possible HE3. I'm not going to lie that long. I'm going wrap up HE2 tight and final. A diptych, like *Postsingular/Hylozoic.*

***

I was telling Sylvia about balancing the people out, between World and MirrorWorld, and that it was the *woomo* enforcing this, and she asks, "Why? Why do they care?"

And the reason I came up with is this. If the World and MirrorWorld get out of balance with each other then the tunnel connecting them will snap, and the *woomo* won't like that, as they live on the hypersurface of the tunnel, and they draw energy from the counter-rotation of the two Worlds relative to each other. Possibly they could survive as two separate colonies, in two unlinked Worlds, but maybe they wouldn't like that.

Or, who knows, maybe they would. Maybe they'd be grateful to Mason for bringing down the house of cards. Like you're balancing a plate atop a long stick balanced on your back-tilted forehead, and someone knocks down the stick and the plate and you're, like, "*Whew*, now I can stop doing that."

Anyway, if I wanted a cataclysmic ending the tunnel could snap. But, again, that's kind of rococo.

***

Basically what I'm doing in this long Notes entry is vamping. Like I'm scared to try and write the North Hole passage chapter. But now I should just go and do it, and make the most of whatever pops up.

October 15, 2017. Sick. Books Per Year.

I've had a chest cough ever since Louisville, two weeks

now. I usually get this about once a winter, I cough and spit for up to four or even six weeks in a row. I seem to have weak lungs. The annual plague came early this year, I picked it up on the trip. I get depressed when I'm sick this long. Postviral depression is the technical term, it's a real thing.

In church today it occurred to me to pray for health—petitioning the white light and the kind, bearded, hippy face of Jesus. I thought of all my maladies—my leg continually and perhaps forevermore sore from the bungled hip operations two years ago. The growing pain in my right shoulder. My inability to sleep deeply through the night. My unreliable and stented heart. My hemorrhagic-stroke-damaged and now seizure-prone brain. The ache in my chest from the weeks of deep coughing. My increasing absent-mindedness—like, the other day I went for a hike on the cliffs by the sea, and when I was there I realized I'd left my sandwich and my bottle of water on the shelf next to the front door, and I felt so old and so sorry for myself that I almost started crying.

The writing, it's almost like physical therapy. Embroidery. Crossword puzzles. Having a bit of fun moving words around.

Just now I updated out my old Books Per Year Excel chart to convince myself I'm still in the game.

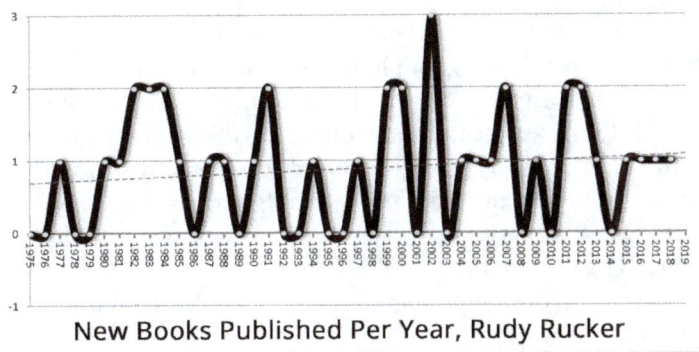

New Books Published Per Year, Rudy Rucker

Figure 19: Book Rate from 1975 - 2019.

Let me explain the last five data points on the right. I finished and self-pubbed *The Big Aha* in 2013. No fully new book appeared in 2014, although that year I published a revised second edition of *All the Visions*. I finished and self-pubbed my *Journals* in 2015, and I'll count it. Self-pubbed the *Transreal Cyberpunk* antho with Bruce in 2016—as far as I recall, it's fair to count new anthologies as books in this chart. I'm going to count *Million Mile Road Trip* for the year 2019, even though I finished it in summer, 2019, but it won't be out from Night Shade till 2019. And to fill out the chart, I'll count *Return to the Hollow Earth* as being published in 2018, as I may well be self-pubbing it as soon as it's done.

So actually I'm hitting a book a year, which isn't so bad after all. And the trend line looks good—I'd say the average rate has picked up since I retired from teaching in 2004. I was putting so much time into CS in the mid-nineties that the book rate was low, although I did have that anno mirabilis three-book year 2002, when my Bruegel book *As Above So Below*, *Spaceland*, and even my Software Engineering text came out at about the same time.

October 16, 2017. The Maelström

Poe wrote his "A Descent into the Maelström" in 1841, and the HE1 Eddie left Earth on 1839, so this tale would not be in our Eddie's memory—although by the time I'm writing about, he would have read MirroPoe's version in the Griswold collection.

I've been thinking about what drives the maelstrom and where the water goes, and how much air goes in. This isn't like a drain, after all. As the level within the maelstrom descends to the surface of the Hollow Earth's sea, the gravitational pull goes to zero. Probably the pulled-down water drifts up around the sides of the maelstrom, and possibly big bubbles of the pulled-down air are coming up around the North Hole's mouth as well.

Here's a drawing, with a *woomo* light-tendril going through the North Hole.

But what's driving the maelstrom's swirl? I'm thinking of a six-hundred-mile long millipede who's biting her tail, like the world snake Ourobouros, but this is an icky centipede kind of thing, lying on her side kicking her little swimmeret type legs, I'll call her a kraken. She's doing this because she's a filter feeder and likes the flow, she has ba-leen-like gill rakers between each set of legs. Six hundred miles is excessive. I'll pinch the hole down to one mile across, and have the kraken be five miles long.

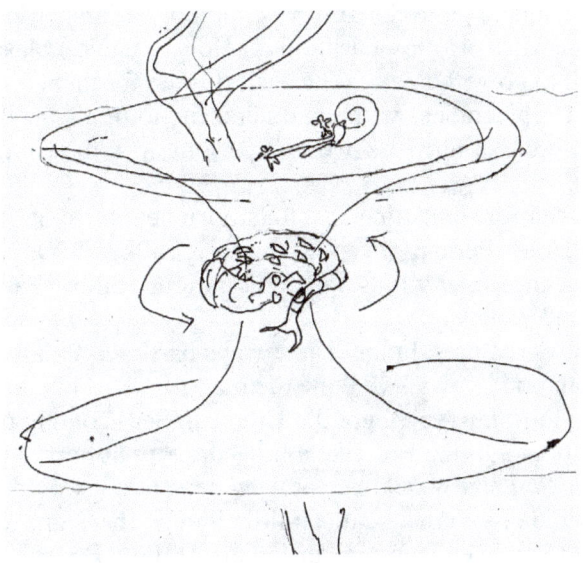

Figure 20: The Kraken in the Waters Around the Double-Funnel North Hole

Historical note: A tail-biting creature like Ouroboros is depicted in the "Enigmatic Book of the Netherworld" in King Tut's tomb which, however, was only unearthed after Eddie's time. But the Ouroboros symbol was common in medieval times, especially in alchemical documents. Another classic mythological world-snake is the Norwegian Jörmungandr or Jormungand, also known as the Midgard Serpent. Eddie might have known some of this.

I can imagine some leakage back and forth between Norse lore and the knowledge of the Hollow Earth flowerpeople. Surely at least one Viking ship came through the North Hole.

October 18, 2017. Baby Hollow Suns. "Zonne."

Okay, I've gotten through the North Hole maelstrom. Eddie wants to go through the Anomaly to the original Earth. Ina says she'll go with him. Machree might go with him. Seela wants to go to the mirror version of her home flower near the MirrorHollowEarth South Hole's jungle. Mason's willing to go with Seela. The easiest route for them is to fall to the Umpteen Seas with the others, and to light-surf down from there. Possibly the two groups split up at the Umpteen Seas.

I need for something else to happen near the exit of the North Hole. Perhaps a visit to the shrig rookery? Or perhaps an encounter with some other curious Hollow Earth creature? A new one.

New creatures, hmm. I'm always partial to flying jellyfish, but god knows I've done them a lot. I also like living water globs, but we've got the Umpteen Seas coming up. How about a living fire, like a little star, but hollow, a baby *Hollow Sun*, that would be cool and new, and it would set up a possible link to the "real" Hollow Sun. Perhaps our real Hollow Sun even lays eggs inside our Hollow Earth.

I've been wanting to mention a Hollow Sun, but I'd been holding back—silenced by that Puritanical inner voice that says, "Too crazy, too wild." To hell with that voice.

So, yeah, some baby Hollow Suns. Not all that big. A couple of hundred yards across at most. How do you get inside one of these suckers without it burning the shit out of you? Well, it could open up a vortex in its surface and you *whoosh* inside. Where do you sit? The Hollow Sun has a magnetic field that holds an iron-ore-containing stone platform in its center. Or maybe it's a big rumby stone, yeah.

How do you see out? Psychic emanations of the little Hollow Sun that are amplified by your rumby stone platform.

Colloquial word for one of these guys? Sizzler. Sol. Solly. Zun. I found a page listing "sun" in a bunch of different languages. Naturally Hungarian is different from all the romance languages: "nap." Czech is good: "slunce." Others: xemx, hnub, zon. I think I'll go with *slunce*. Or maybe not—two hours later I couldn't remember that word "slunce." Kind of has bad vibes. Slum, dunce, silence. Maybe keep is simple and use *zonn* or, maybe *zonne* is better.

The resting-place at the center of a *zonne* might even be one of those antique "fried eggs" or flying saucers like they found in HE1—but maybe I don't want to reactivate that thread just now. If anything, I could say the *zonne* is a type of interstellar vehicle itself, and set things up for some rivalry between the ancient saucerians and the ancient *zonne*-riders. For now I'll go with a kind of bench or sofa made of a single rumby stone.

Weave back a glimpse or twos of the *zonnes* near the North Holes in HE1, one or two sentences is enough.

What is the actual name of the *zonne* who saves them? I kind of want to say BeeBee. That was a girl's name in Louisville. Was there a BeeBee Blakely? I met a CeeCee in Louisville when I went there to give the talk. DeeDee, GeeGee, JayJay, MiMi, RuRu, VaVa, YuYu, ZiZi. I guess BeeBee is best.

What is she like? Female. Speaks only in teep, I suppose.

And let's suppose that the ballula's attack on the Moby-Dick-type whale is radically unsuccessful. The ballula is crushed, and my guys barely escape into the maelstrom's waters, buoyed on the flotsam and jetsam of whatever "equipage" Eddie had brought along.

This would be a golden opportunity to kill off Machree, by the way. And then the difficult-to-write character Ina could be the one who goes over to old Earth to balance Mason.

October 20-21, 2017. Itinerary Sketch.

I did the whale scene, and I decided not to kill Machree, I'll have the *woomo* snatch him up to the Umpteen seas with one of their tendrils—which is totally annoying for the others, especially for Ina, who has it in for Machree. I think I'll stick with sending Machree through the Anomaly with Eddie, and hanging onto Ina for Mason.

Not sure now about the zonnes. I'm guessing they live in the caves where the shrigs are? That time Otha got swallowed by a shrig, the shrig didn't eat him on purpose, he was wrapped in garbage. They're not man-eaters. So our gang goes over to the shrig cliff kind of hoping to ride one.

Figure 21: My Artist Friend Bef's Sketchbook Drawing of a Whale.

Eddie, Ina, and Machree manage to get aboard a shrig—it's migration season, they're going back into the center to feed. Seela doesn't want to ride one. She thinks the shrigs are too disgusting, also she doesn't want to bother with a big detour, and thirdly, she knows a secret way that she doesn't want to tell the others, whom she doesn't much like.

So Seela shows Mason the zonnes in the caves. And they ride a zonne. This is better than having Seela and Mason up to the Umpteen Seas and then go out to the MirrorFlower, and then (later) come back to the Umpteen Seas to send Seela off with Eddie. Better to have them go straight to the flower, riding in a zonne. And good to have a reason for the zonnes.

I redrew my map of the characters' lifelines to match.
And now I'll sketch a sequence for upcoming events.

- *Woomo* lift Machree to Umpteen Seas.
- Eddie, Arf and Ina ride a shrig to Umpteen Seas. It's migration time.
- Seela, Brumble, and Mason ride a zonne to Mirrorflower.
- MirrorSeela and MirrorYurgen are married, but have no children. They have group sex with Mason and Seela. Seela doesn't like it that much, she thinks Yurgen is too old, and he's slobbering on her. But Yurgen is hot for Seela. And Mason, surprisingly, has quite a thing for MirrorSeela. Something about her—maybe he likes older women, not having had a mother. He wants to live with both Seelas. MirrorSeela thinks that might be fun, but Seela's not particularly into it. Yurgen wants to kill Mason—*he* wants both the Seelas too. So Mason and the Seelas head up for the Umpteen Seas in their zonne.
- MirrorSeela reveals that she's pregnant by Mason now. She'll give birth to baby Bramble at the Umpteen Seas. She kind of wants to go back to her flower, but she's worried about Yurgen being mad about the baby. Seela says she's taking Brumble to the old flower, and she won't have any entanglement there, and she'll find a young guy.
- Eddie, Machree and Seela go through the Anomaly. Ina stays, she wants to go back to San Francisco. MirrorSeela goes back to MirrorYurgen on her Mirrorflower. She tells Mason he can keep Bramble, as MirorrYurgen would be too jealous.
- Mason, Ina, and Bramble go back to Earth. Ina and Mason fall in love. And Ina gets pregnant.
-

Eventually I can make a nice thing about the Mason/Machree duality. This fits with the fact that I don't plan to write an HE3. Duality = Two volumes! (Beware the synthesis...)

October 26-30, 2017. Jungle, Shrigs, & Krakens

Oct 26, 2017

So now we've landed in the jungle by the sea: Seela, Mason, Brumble, and Arf plus Eddie and Ina. Isabel sent me a photo of a moa and an elephant bird today. Maybe I'll work them in. I don't see trying to cook and eat one. Riding some of them away from the kraken attack would be good. But, wait, we're in zero-gee, so you wouldn't ride these guys like horses. They're legs would be more flexible, I think, grabbier, and much shorter, so they're more like penguins. Might as well have little wings.

Oct 27, 2017

I got a thousand words done today. I'm calling this new chapter "Shrigs" for now, and the next one might be called "Zonne." At the start of the current chapter they screw around in the jungle and we have some descriptions of shrigs. I already did those things in HE1, but, you know, the weightless Hollow Earth jungle is really cool, and it's fun to be there, so why not write about it again. Like, it's not like James Bond only goes into a posh casino *once*, and not like there's only one barroom gunfight in the works of Louis Lamoure. It's okay to do something again, if you make it a little different.

Rereading the HE1 jungle scene, I realize it has more eyeball kicks than I have in my HE2 draft for this scene as yet. I need to layer in some more stuff. Slime molds. A different way of making a fire…some trick they used with the black gods. Eddie needs to have a tinder box. Eat a moa egg? Or have a really impressive ant colony in a hollow log.

Somewhere I have a jungle-scene for HE1 that for some reason I deleted…I wonder if I could find it again. The setup was that they fell asleep with a fire burning, and a log caught on fire, and this big beetle they called a "fire bug" showed up and squirted liquid on the fire.

I'll need some kind of tension in the shrigs scene. The deal is that Eddie and Ina want to hitch a ride on a shrig. And it's not totally dangerous because shrigs don't deliberately eat people. They eat garbage and dead stuff, although they *do* make an exception for *ballulas*. In HE1, I did a scene where the "black god" Shrighunter (and then his pupil Otha) wrapped themselves in garbage so a shrig would gulp them down and then they could ride in the shrig's gut and, at some point, hack their way out. But perhaps Eddie and Ina balk at so noisome a stratagem.

The largest moa *Dinornis maximus* (1) and the largest Elephant bird *Aepyornis maximus* (2). Both birds lived until relatively recent times and may well have been seen by primitive man; their colours are hypothetical.

Figure 22: Moa and Elephant Bird

Oct 28, 2017

But looking at the jungle is just "vamping," that is, killing time. There has to be some action in this chapter. Somehow everyone almost gets killed. A kraken attack would be good. Like what if there's a second kraken, the "husband" of the kraken who circles the maelstrom's throat. And the *woomo* get involved in a battle among our crew, the shrigs, and the krakens—maybe our guys kill the husband kraken,

and the wife kraken comes down from the inside the maelstrom, and the uneasy *woomo* zap her to death, and meanwhile the maelstrom has slammed shut, what with no kraken
swirling the water at the throat.

And thus we permanently close the North Hole of
MirrorEarth (which is our actual world). I'd been meaning to
do this *eventually* but, as I always tell myself, it's best not to
hoard for later the "big scenes" I've thought up. Stop vamping and *do* the next big scene, and trust in the muse to tell me
more big scenes for later, when "later" actually rolls around.

The kraken-shrig-*woomo* fight is a real "double-page
spread," as Bruce Sterling condescendingly refers to florid
high-adventure SF scenes. But I love this kind of scene. I
might even start a big painting of it this week.

So yeah, there's two krakens, the one who's whipping up
the central maelstrom---the female. And we've got the husband Kraken who eats lots of shrigs. He brings food to the
maelstrom whipper wife. There's tens of thousands of shrigs
for him to eat in this locale, they're numerous as the sky-
darkening passenger pigeons of yore. The cliffs they live in
are the sides of a dead or quiescent volcano. And a tube of
the volcano goes down into the Rind and emerges in a subterranean cliff in the hole where the Arctic Ocean runs down
to MirrorHtrae.

And, as I've already described, that female kraken is
swirling the maelstrom into existence. Her partner brings
food to her to keep the swirl going. What's up with that?
Well, she's nesting, duh. She has big red eggs fastened to her
underside, in fact I'll write in a bit about Mason noticing
those when he was riding down through the maelstrom's
hole. The mother kraken plans to hatch a bunch of baby krakens into the maelstrom and they're supposed to zoom up
and vector through Earth's atmosphere and into interplane-
tary space. Krakens are, in other words, outer space beings.

What's the relation between the krakens and the *woomo*?
Symbiotes. The *woomo* like to have a kraken making a maelstrom—it gives the *woomo* an easy path to push their tendrils
outside, particularly if the south hole happens to be iced
over, as is the case on MirrorEarth. Our Earth/MirrorEarth-
combine more or less belongs to the *woomo*, it's their inter-

stellar spaceship. The *woomo* are incredibly powerful with their light streams, and they can fairly easily kill the krakens, so they're doing the krakens a favor by allowing them settle in here and make their maelstrom nest at the North Pole.

Even though the *woomo* have greater power, there's some tension and paranoia in their feelings about the krakens, as on some worlds where the *woomo* were too lax, the krakens have, gone rogue and flown into the center and managed to kill and eat the *woomo*. But, again, the *woomo* can potentially kill a threatening or out-of-control kraken with a focused light-stream.

In general, to be on the safe side, if the resident krakens don't in fact keep the maelstrom open, and if they show signs of going rogue inside a Hollow Earth, the *woomo* will indeed do their best to kill the krakens for self-protection. This said, it's not a total slam-dunk for the *woomo* to kill a kraken, as the krakens are fast. I kind of see the angry Mom kraken as flying a very rapid upward zigzag path, and the light-zap only gets her after several unsuccessful attempts.

My initial thought is that it's Eddie who starts all this up. He's making friends with the shrigs, and decides he should kill the husband kraken, by way of doing the shrigs a favor. It doesn't occur to him that the end result of this will be the closing of their exit route, that is, the closing of the maelstrom at the North Hole.

So how does little Eddie kill a four-mile-long kraken? "Give me a lever, and whereon to stand, and I shall move a mountain," pronounces Eddie, purporting to quote Archimedes. A thousand farting shrigs maneuver a mountainous asteroid-like boulder into a certain position, as Eddie requests.

And then Eddie pulls against an adamantine lever send this giant boulder towards the stone lip of the kraken's burrow, doing this just as the kraken is starting to crawl out to eat two hundred shrigs. The asteroid-like rock cuts off the kraken's head. *Goosh*! A Niagara of sick smeel!

The husband kraken dies with frantic tattoos of his legs upon the Rind's stone. The anxious wife kraken creeps down to see what happened to her partner. Meanwhile the maelstrom closes. The mother kraken is infuriated, she chases our guys around, and kills a lot more shrigs. The *woomo* zap her with a warning ray, meaning to herd her back through the tunnel where she can get back to work on the maelstrom.

Mad with grief, the mother kraken buzzes up into the sky, meaning to attack the *woomo*. They redouble their rays and crisp her into bacon.

Eddie and Ina leave, borne upon a palanquin by a joyous swarm of shrigs. At Seela's insistence, Mason and Seela remain hiding in a cave.

October 31-November 1, 2017. Killing Kraken.

I wrote another thousand words on Oct 30, 2017,, setting up the ideas that the kraken at the core is gravid with eggs, and that she has a husband. I wrote a scene of our crew going up into an overlook in the canopy of trees and seeing the husband kraken emerge and eat about a hundred shrigs and impale another hundred on his sharp legs to take back to his wife like franks on toothpicks, like cocktail snacks.

Call the male kraken Fafnir (after Wagner), and call the female kraken Jormungo, after the Norse myth.

I wonder if a hundred shrigs is enough of a meal for a three-or-four-mile-long kraken. Need to balance that against how many shrigs are here at the rookery, and how often the krakens eat. Let's do the math. (I revised this a few times.)

- I want to say that, to feed himself and his wife, Fafnir kills 20 shrigs a day, 10 for him and 10 for his wife. That's 600 a month, and about 6,000 in a year. If the shrig population is 80,000, they lose about 10% of their population a year, and that's sustainable if they breed at a faster rate. They take turns coming to the rookery for three months at a time, so there's a typical rookery flock of 20,000. So now we work backwards from that, adjusting the relative sizes of the krakens and shrigs.
- Krakens are ribbon-like parallelepipeds 5,000 meters long, 20 meters across, and 10 meters thick. Volume is 1,000,000 cu. m. A tidy million cubic meters.
- I'll say krakens eat 1% of their body mass a day, which is like me eating two pounds of food a day, which is reasonable. 1% of a million is ten thousand.

- Large shrigs are, say, sideways cones 50 m long and 10 m in diameter. Twice as long as whales. A cone's volume is one-third of a cylinder's, so that's about 1,250 cu. m, Call it a thousand cubic meters, as some shrigs are smaller. So ten of these guys is ten thousand, which is that one percent of a million cubic meters.
- I'll go over the HE2 draft and HE1, to make the sizes of the shrigs and krakens consistent throughout. Shrig is 150 feet long and 30 feet wide, about twice the size of a whale. A kraken is three miles long, sixty feet across and thirty feet thick. Quite skinny.

I want our party to kill the kraken Fafnir. How and why?

Unworkable Plan. Eddie will get a hundred or a thousand shrigs to be hovering over Fafnir's hole, and they'll build up momentum to bring down the rock so its inertia cuts the kraken in half or smashes his head. Problems: The kraken might dodge, as the approach is ponderous. Hard to time the approach. And how does Eddie convince all those shrigs to work together? I don't think I can make this work. It'll trash the reader's willing suspension of disbelief.

Better Plan. Seela finds some monomolecular-filament-type strand that can cut off the kraken's head with almost no effort. The strand is from, let's say, a certain kind of vine, the thread vine. And the ends naturally adhere to chunks of the stalk, so they can use those for handles. In HE1, by the way, they used a bladed rope with shell knives braided into it. Used it to cut the stalk of the blue flower where their enemies lived. But it might be too much trouble to make a bladed rope that's long enough to cut across the kraken's neck.

And now a question of motive. Why would they want to kill Fafnir to aid the shrigs? Seela doesn't like the shrigs. Mason doesn't much care about them, although he thinks they're funny. Eddie is mainly interested in helping himself. And in any case, they would not be killing the kraken as part of any quid-pro-quo deal with the shrigs—as the shrigs are so stupid you can't possibly negotiate with them. So it has to be Ina. A whim of hers. She thinks the shrigs are cute and pathetic. And she prevails upon Eddie and Mason with her outré charm, and then Seela grudgingly helps them get the filament, even though she has a feeling it's a very bad idea.

Back to the thread vine. Seela has heard of them, and Eddie takes great interest. They break off a stub, using fire, as it's uncuttable, then whittle through to expose the inner thread, which has a shimmer as if electricity along it, then pull that sideways and it cuts its way free of the vine, and then they burn the other end to make a handle. Pulling it through the jungle it clears out a swath of vegetation.

Back to the kraken's meals. I think he'd better come every day, instead of once a month, so our guys don't have to wait so long for the next raid. Say Fafnir and Jormungo each eat 10 shrigs a day. Hard to chew up such big things. He sucks out their juice with his legs which are in fact hollow tubes. Like a vampire, in a way. And then he chews up the wrinkled rinds of the formerly bulbous shrigs.

November 3, 2017. Don't Kill the Kraken

Woke up this morning and decided I shouldn't kill the krakens. It would make Mason and his friends too unlikeable. Too much like my brother Embry flying to Africa and, in his first week there, killing a world-record crocodile while this harmless (?) old creature slept peacefully on the banks of the Nile, where he spent every day. Embry shot it with a telephoto-sight sniper rifle, from a mile across the river. This always outraged me, although at some level I share Embry's pride in his feat, and in fact I think I own a belt from this poor croc's hide, or maybe I gave it to Rudy Jr. or somebody else as it made me feel bad. I'll have to check. In any case, I don't want Mason to be like a trophy hunter. Don't want him to murder the wondrous kraken Fafnir the moment he first sees him.

So...now what I do instead? Well, I've been setting up this killing for over a week and don't want to waste all that planning and writing. So the thing to do is to have them *start* to kill the kraken, but then kraken goes free. And the escape should be pegged as an act of good will on Mason's part. He gets into some rumby teep with the unexpectedly intelligent and empathetic kraken, and then he throws down his end of the monomolecular-filament-type hundred-meter garrote that he and Seela are holding.

And then I might break, and start the next chapter, which would be, unless I change the numbering, Chapter 8.

***

So in the next chapter, the freed kraken immediately goes into a shocking and unprecedented orgy of shrig-killing, skewering two hundred shrig corpses on his long sharp legs, and then, heavily laden with his catch, he worms back through his hole. And then he collects his wife Jormungo, and they *leave*.

Mason follows their progress via teep (I'll need to use this odd p.o.v. as there's no practical way he can visually watch the scene with his naked eyes). The cold of outer space cracks Jormungo's eggs open, and two dozen small krakens appear. They and the parents ride off into outer space, riding solar energy lines, and heading maybe for the planet Jupiter. Or maybe—aha!—towards the sun, as the krakens are in fact native to the Hollow Sun.

The dim-bulb shrig realize that, for them at least, the departure of the krakens is a good thing, so they'll be happy, and ready to give rides to our heroes. Who tells the shrigs the krakens are gone? Well, maybe as Fafnir enters the tunnel for the last time, he squawk-shriek-roars, "Farewell, flying pigs!"

At this point it would be overkill to introduce the "hollow mini-sun" zonne beings I'd been planing to use as an alternate means of transport. So we'll say Eddie and Ina catch a ride on one shrig, and Mason and Seela catch a ride on another shrig—despite Seela's distaste for these creatures.

Mason and Seela use their rumby power to control their shrig so he *isn't* going to fly to the center as he would normally to. Instead he flies towards Seela's mirrorflower near the South Hole. As they start out, riding on the shrig's fat back, Mason and Seela they see the maelstrom sloshing closed, how awesome, Seela is, like, "Now you have to stay in here with me, Mason."

I could save the *urbstegs* jellyfish things for later, but, oh hell, why not do it now—never vamp and postpone big scenes. So Mason and Seela's shrig will indeed power though the filigreed tentacle net of an *urbsteg*, flaming a path with shrig-farts, and in fact Mason and Seela will have to take shelter within the shrig's disgusting stomach contents.

And then the shrig poots Mason and Seela them out onto the mirrorflower, and it's a new chap. We'll get Mason and Seela into a Jane-Austen-like social interactions and shifting love-triangles thing. Some readers will want a break from of all these heavy FX scenes I've been doing.

"Hi, Yurgen! Let's fuck!"

"Wow! You look like a younger version of my wife Seela. *Sure* I want to fuck. We'll get my wife in on the action too. And your boyfriend. But, um, can you two take a bath?"

November 4, 2017. What's the Third Act?

This morning I stepped back a bit and took a long view of my progress. Finally got a Chapter Outline started. The fact that this took me till now is an indicator of how totally no-outline and without-a-net this HE2 project is.

Number crunching reveals this: When I finish the scene of going off to kill the kraken and then letting him go, I'll have about 35K words, and seven chapters, and I'll be a third done. So this finished chunk of the book, the first seven chapters, it's my Act I: getting my characters back into the Hollow Earth and slamming the maelstrom.

With two acts to go, I need twice as many events as I've already described. I worry about this, as I already have had so much stuff happening. I don't as yet see all that much ahead. But, remember Rudy, it's always like that. The muse feeds me one scene at a time.

I do have a rough idea of the second act. It's all that back-and-forth of the balanced worldlines diagram a few weeks ago. I figure the second act runs from the trip to Seela's mirrorflower all the way to the start of the trip back to the surface of MirrorEarth.

And the third act is whatever Mason does back on Earth. He's with Ina. She's kind of flaky and he doesn't initially like her that much, but they fall in love. What else happens? Well, in HE1, I had the Poe/MirrorPoe conflict to stoke the third act. But right now, as I keep saying, I'm basically blank on Act III.

Well, what if I go back to my idea of having the third act be in the year 2050, like I was saying on May 1, 2017. I'd abandoned that idea as being too baroque, but maybe it's not so dumb after all. It would be a big effort to dream up the Earth of 2050, but it be a big wow of a payoff. And then I'd for sure have something to write about in Act III.

By the way, the time-jump might happen because some-one like Eddie drags Mason into the Anomaly against his will, and he fights his way back out, like running in quick-sand, and those two hundred years fly by.

If I do the time-jump, there's all that niggling bullshit about HE2 being published in 2018 even though Mason Reynolds actually wrote (correct tense?) it in 2050. Looking back to that May 1, 2017, entry on this topic in these writing notes, I see some preliminary bullshit about how to finesse that, not that I'd at all want that particular sideshow to be-come a big thing. Famous last words.

I could cut myself some slack and have the time-jump and just jump to, say, 1990, an interesting time. Or to 1918, which would be cool. Mason would come to my house and we'd work on his book together. And, as I mentioned be-fore, somewhere in these notes, I could add an earnest pero-ration, warning that climate change would surely open up the South Hole once more, and perhaps even invite a return of the maelstrom-spinning krakens to the North Hole.

Yet again, if I don't want to face the time-jump, I could have something about the Hollow Sun in Act III. I'm men-tioning right now that the krakens come from the Hollow Sun, doing this as a quick aside, but if needs be I could delve into that later on. But I have a feeling it would be overkill. Just keep the Hollow Sun as a background thing, not quite serious.

November 7, 2017. "Goalie's Anxiety at Penalty Kick."

I've brought Mason and Seela to the edge of the tunnel where the kraken Fafnir is going to stick out his head. And now I'm anxious about the scene I have planned. (That cap-tion above is the title of a 1977 Wim Wenders film that I haven't yet seen.)

Originally the kraken was fairly soft, like a centipede, and he was going to die. Then I decided, reverse, to have Mason balk at the killing. And, double reverse, I'll have Seela yank the string despite Mason's hesitations, and this way the killing *would* happen, if it were possible. But, triple reverse, they can't in fact cut the kraken's neck, as the kraken is made of some very strong material, as he's from the Hollow Sun.

And then I planned to have the kraken kill a lot of shrigs and fly off to the Sun with his wife. I already have a scene of kraken killing shrigs, so this seems like a repeat, but I'll do it anyway, rapidly. And then, the main thing is that the kraken and his wife leave Earth.

Why exactly *would* the kraken and his wife leave after the assassination attempt? Can I find a better reason than "it is written"? The kraken can use the thread to cut loose Jormungo's eggs? Or they were waiting till "the time was ripe". Or something in Mason's thoughts urges him on? But Mason doesn't particularly know anything important. Or maybe the *woomo* get involved?

Yeah, Fafnir is going so apeshit that the *woomo* start zapping him, and Jormungo comes in to back him up, and it's like a freaky shootout in a crack house where a big deal's gone wrong—cops, agents, dealers, junkies, double agents, all blazing away with shotguns and pistols—and the krakens are, like, "Fuck this shit, we're outta here."

I need to write some of this today. I'll just write the scene more or less the way I was going to do, and work in that last type of explanation.

Two hours later: Boom! I wrote eight hundred words, and it's coming together well. It's gonna happen.

November 9-10, 2017. Enormous Protozoa?

So I got on a real roll over the last three days and finished off the kraken scenes. I wrote, like 1,500 words a day three days in a row, totally nailed it, with more and more inspirations arriving along the way, ensuing in quick forays back through the text to prefigure and to keep things consistent.

And now Mason and Seela are riding a shrig across the empty space of the Hollow Earth, heading for Seela's mirrorflower, but I need for something to happen during this journey. Earlier I'd had a notion of a narrow escape from some giant jellyfish called *urbstegs*, but now I want something different. Seela and Mason and their shrig Tallulah are hungry and thirsty. Flying about 6,000 miles is a lot to ask.

I want a floating island. A floating tangle of plants doesn't exactly work in the middle of the Hollow Earth, as the weak gravity would pull it down into the center. I do have a "gravitational shelf" near the center, that the Umpteen Seas sit on, but I don't want to use that trick twice. The floating islands have, lets say, *cilia* that they beat to stay in place. The idea of cilia suggests that they're giant *protozoa*. I've always liked the idea of giant protozoa in our atmosphere—I read about those in a UFO nut book once, and I think I referred to them in my story, "Guadalupe and Hieronymous Bosch," or at least when I was *planning* the story I was thinking about alien UFOS that are in fact giant protozoa.

Suddenly I really want to call them "The Isles of Langerhans." Just to be silly. Like the Firesign Theater. I "know" that The Isles of Langerhans are, um, something anatomical, let's see...Google that...The much more commonly used phrases are the Islets of Langerhans or Islands of Langerhans. Little patches of tissue in your pancreas which produce insulin and its opposing hormone glucagon, also a third thing. My mother had diabetes, and when she had too much insulin and had a scary violent insulin reaction in the night, we'd in fact give her a shot of glucagon, sometimes I'd be the one to give her the shot. I never knew that's what glucagon was, I'd kind of thought it was like glucose sugar. Langerhans noticed his islets in 1869.

So if I use that name I don't relate it to the "real" Langerhans. (Unless I want to claim he visited the Hollow Earth before his discovery.) I just use it for an in-joke, a semi-private goof. Or maybe use a word that's just similar to Langerhans. Or different. I've got it: The Greeks had the Fortunate Isles. From this Wikipedia reference, I draw three quotes::

"Plutarch, who refers to the Fortunate Isles several times in his writings, locates them firmly in the Atlantic"

"The islands are said to be two in number separated by a very narrow strait..."

"For fantasy author J.R.R. Tolkien, the Fortunate Isles and other mythical islands such as Avalon, Atlantis, etc. used to exist as a separate continent in the West...but drifted out into space as the Earth became spherical (from flat), in order to prevent mortals from reaching it."

The last quote is good, as, in a sense, the Hollow Earth *is* Atlantis, so if the Fortunate Isles are associated with both, so much the better. Maybe the Fortunate Isles used to be near Norway and got sucked down through the maelstrom into the Hollow Earth.

The Fortunate Isles are in fact a pair of paramecia, steadily beating their cilia so as not to be drawn into the center. They have chlorophyll, and they live on light, like algae.

   ***

Now *why* do I want to do the Fortunate Isles scene? Why not just go to the mirrorflower and get on with the romance stuff. I guess I'm worried the romance stuff will blow past really fast and then I'll have too much space still to fill in the novel. So I was thinking I could just throw in a random picaresque grotesque-travelogue scene.

On the other hand, I just did a travelogue scene with the krakens, and I feel like I ought to have it be more like linear plot for a little while, instead of just unrelated pearls on a string. And I guess I don't feel all that much like inventing the race of people who live on the hovering paramecia, partly because I'm concerned these people will in some way "steal the thunder" of the flowerpeople. If I don't work at it, the Fortunate Isles are practically the same as the mirrorflower. I'd have to come up with something to make the Isled different.

If we do encounter the paramecia people, I think it should be quite brief. And look out, or one of them will sponge on and join Mason and Seela on the shrig. What if they found Crispa there? That would be kind of nice...I feel a little bad about having dismissed Crispa from the cast, as I liked her. But getting Crispa down there...how would I do that? I guess she would have come via a downward passage through Indian caves. But for god's sake, I've been wanting to get it down to just Mason and Seela, so stay with that for a few scenes more. I can bring back Crispa quite a bit later, when they're making their way back out to the surface, somehow she'll help them.

What would be fun to write about the paramecia people? I'm thinking of these Herodotus type characters, vaguely remembered…men with one big foot at the bottom, people with giraffe necks, Bosch-character people in other words, people with leopard spots, silky wings, a head that is a single large eye, a man with his mouth in the middle of his belly. Poeple with no heads and their faces on their chests. People with horses hooves. With giant dangling ears. Six arms. Dog heads. Tails like mice. Not all that interesting, they're just chimeras.

Might the paramecia people be exiles from the Hollow Sun? I once heard in some cartoon that the people on the sun are thin and naked and they're always running.

Or, simpler, the paramecia people could be Norsemen or Vikings. Like I was saying before, maybe the paramecia islands drifted down through the maelstrom from the sea off Norway.

A few days later (after Windycon)

I don't feel like making a big thing of the Fortunate Isles. Just a colony of giant algae and paramecia with some dwarves living on them. They eat some spores off the algae and move on. But maybe I need to make a big thing, because I need scenes to fill the book. Maybe I'm just facing a (temporary, one hopes) failure of the imagination, and can't think of good stuff for the islands.

Fuck thinking. I'm too fried to think. I'll just start writing the next scene and see what happens.

Nov 11, 2017. At Windycon

Maybe the flowerpeople should be in some way like the people at this SF con I'm currently attending as GoH (fanspeak for Guest of Honor), it's Windycon in Lombard, Illinois, an hour's drive out of Chicago, at a Westin hotel isolat-

211

ed in an enormous mall parking lot across from a JCPenney store. A small con, about a thousand attendees, I'm very much at loose ends here, and wondering why I came.

If I could turn this experience into a scene it could make it more fun. I wrote a couple of sort of funny emails about to the con people to Marc Laidlaw, very catty, although, as the con ground on, I eventually gave up and opened my heart to mine hosts. But here, just for kicks, are some extracts of the emails.

I've only met two people who've read some of my books, a long time ago, can't quite remember them, "I really need to go back and read some of your new stuff." Another guy had a free preprint of *Postsingular* that he got from a reviewer for 25 cents. He brought it for me to sign, but hasn't read it.

Nobody talks about lit, about SF. Why am I here, I've spent my whole life avoiding these kinds of scenes, and here I am again.

In my head, at the pre-con staff dinner tonight, I had this Martin Amis or Kingsley Amis voice going, as in, respectively THE INFORMATION or LUCKY JIM. The man across from me had a thin waist-length bearded pigtail. *of course he did.* A guy had a fancy cane with a crystal ball head set into a pronged clamp and the ball kept falling out and rolling across the floor. *of course it did.* A massive woman leaving the buffet line, having spent seven minutes in it, carries a plate piled so high it looks like a bundle of kindling wood. *of course it does.* For my room-treat the con organizers gave me hand sanitizer and herbal tea and a generic packet of cheese crackers, *of course they did.*

And *of course* I feel guilty and ungrateful for looking down my nose at these dear and all-too-human souls. This is their little festival, their source of joy, their gay holiday of fun and magic, and they look forward to it, and work on it, and plan for it, and make all the pieces come together, and I the aloof interloper—I sulk and sneer. So I'm a horrible person. What a payoff. I'm bored and unappreciated, and now on top of that I'm guilty about being unhappy.

"Why can't you just relax, Rudy?" says Sylvia's voice in my head. "Be happy for them that they're having fun. They're touching. Love them." Well, maybe Sylvia wouldn't go that far. Maybe that's Jesus's voice.

One pleasant person I met so far, non-zombie, was a woman named Barb who sells T-shirts her husband designs. Great image of Cthulhu modeled on the Sheppard Fairey poster of Obama. "Cthulhu for REAL Change." Talking with Barb was my most enjoyable half hour today—encoutering a fellow human being amid the zombies in this limbo.

I'm looking forward to my panels and my big talk! Previsualization: My handlers lead the circus animal from his cage in the shadows behind the tent. He blinks at the bright light, slightly confused. The attempts a growl, someone throws a soda can at him, he snarls. Kafka territory.

[Three days later.] I'm unbelievably tired. I did about four panels in the last two days, a reading today, and a big keynote-type speech last night although only about 40 people came to see it. But I did good.

Anyway, I got through it, and there were a few good moments amid the weariness and ennui. I kept being polite to people, even delivering a saintly homily at the opening ceremony about how it warmed my heart to see their joy at their little communal festival.

Nice to everyone except for a woman next to me on a "What are your fave books? Panel. It was all the GoHs on the panel, like GoHs for science, art, videogames, writing (me), and *signing* in the sense of translating talks into sign language in real time. The woman next to me was in fact the signing GoH, not handicapped herself, she just happened to know ASL, she was some kind of English teacher.

She wouldn't shut up about these dipshit fantasy
books she loves, lavishing cliché praise upon them,
going back and forth with the moronic videogame
GoH who did his best to dominate the rap after pro-
nouncing himself (for no reason) the "moderator."
And this woman next to me is like: "*The Princess
Bride* is SO much better than *Catcher in the Rye*,"
and I'm like, "Well, they're different." And she's like
"No, *Catcher in the Rye* is whiny garbage," and,
without looking at her, I deliver what is, for me the
mild-mannered prof, a withering put-down. "And
you're an...English teacher? *Hm*." And then I go on
talking about some other book.

I'd like to say I won't ever go to a con again, but
World Con is in San Jose this summer, so probably
I'll stop in there, and they will actually have some
fellow writers there for me to wheenk with. But, no,
I don't think I'll ever fall for being GoH at a small
regional con again. They gave me airfare, three
nights in the hotel, and $150.

And now, to sleep, perchance to dream...of three
mile krakens from the Hollow Sun.

I left the con for three hours to go see the *Thor:
Ragnarok* movie on an Imax screen in a 19-screen AMC theater across the parking-lot, between the hotel and the
JCPenney store. What an overdone heap of bombast and
glitz, that Thor flick. Fun at times, though. Jeff Goldblum
was great, teasing Thor and saying "the ass place or ass
land" instead of Asgard. So Beavis and Butthead. And you
could order food from your seat in the theater, I got an open
flat bread with a Philly cheesesteak on it, so delicious in the
dark, gobbling it like a wild animal (released from my cage
in the shadows behind the tent).

I hung around at the book stand of Greg Ketter of
Dreamhaven Books of Minneapolis in the dealer's room of
the con. He was the one guy who had some of my books for
sale, and I know him from way, way back. Nice to be with
him, and there were even a couple of true Rucker fans who
turned up at his stand and bought some books, a nice woman

named Valerie had a bunch of them. Finally I felt like I was a Guest of Honor. And then I made a short speech at the Opening Ceremony, and then I did my "Welcome to Your Cyberpunk Future" talk with a lot of Q & A afterwards. They tried to tape it for me, not sure yet if it worked.

On the last night, I had dinner with Ketter and Valerie and Ketter's wife and Valerie's grown daughter at a Mid-western chainlike eatery, the peaceful browsing herds of the prairie around us. I'm been eating such unhealthy food.

November 19-27, 2017. Mirrorflower. Plot.

Back in Los Gatos. After I did the GoH gig at the Windycon SF con in Lombard on my own, Sylvia and I had a good visit with Georgia & Co., then spent three days in a hotel Chicago, which was great. Highlights: the big shiny bean sculpture, the blues club Kingston Mines, the restaurant The Dearborn (2ce), the Chicago Art Institute (2ce), and the now-defunct Chess Records studios where Willie Dixon, Muddy Waters, Little Walter, Bo Diddley, and the Rolling Stones all recorded. Willie Dixon's family owns the place now, and one of Willie's descendants gave Sylvia, me, and an English guy a very long tour—he talked a lot. By no means an over-visited spot!

I did a little writing on the road. I extended the travel chapter with a fairly brief stop among a colony of large pro-tozoa, without having any native humans living there—I'll save the primitive humans for the mirrorflower.

***

This morning when I woke up in Los Gatos, Sylvia showed me a very funny video of an extremely lively young Kirgiz woman doing a cover video of the Bee Gees "Stayin' Alive," using a beef bone for the microphone, a handmade straw broom for the guitar, and ending up by going back into her yurt carrying a teapot and a basket of dried dung-patties (for heat, I guess)—casting a come-hither look. It was like getting an email message from the Muse (mediated by the Facebook home page of something called Trash Kultura) "Here, Rudy, have your flowerpeople be as jolly as this."

I also spent an hour looking at images of a painting we saw in the Chicago Art Institute, shown below. And here again, I thought this might help with the flowerpeople. I'd like to write a scene like what we see here. Hell, I'd like to be *in* this scene.

Figure 23: Arnold Böcklin, "In Der See," 1883.

I didn't really do much with the flowerpeople as characters in HE1, and this time I can fill them out a bit more. They'll be crazy about Arf, like before. I can have the now-older Yurgen blowing on the reverberator. I'll revise the HE1 chapter a little bit first, I think, setting up some prefigurings, and then I'd like to do a mirrorflower chapter where they settle in for some days, and we have some of the rhythms of daily life.

    ***

I need to get straight what happens on the mirrorflower. I had an Itinerary Sketch before, I'll copy it to an Outline section up in the first part of this *Notes for HE2* document, and then I can keep editing it. I need an outline more when I'm in the second half of a novel than when I'm in the first half. In the second half you have to fill things out, and pull the plot together. In the first half, you can just write whatever comes to mind.

The outline I have at this point is too thin, and it won't get me all the way though twenty chapters. It needs more wows. I have a few farfetched ideas, although at this point they feel random and unmotivated. I'd like to get something like the organic unity that HE1 had. But here's a short list what I've got, and I might add to it later.

- Bring on the Hollow Sun creatures. We already have the krakens. Maybe there's some of those round zonne guys I talked about before.
- Have Mason jump to 2018 and meet me, doing a Frank Shook in *Saucer Wisdom* routine.
- Jump him to 2050 and do a *Futurama* number. If he comes back in 2050, he could open up trade between our Earth and the inner Earth.
- More about the *woomo* and the humans arriving came in those ancient UFOs?
- Maybe the shrigs are in fact smart?

Outlining can be a way to avoid actually writing. Or, more accurately, to work your way up to writing. Typically, I outline for awhile, and then I give up on the outline and just get back into dreaming up scenes one at a time, and writing them, which is, after all, the point of the exercise. And once I start writing, the plot logic fills in secondary ideas for things to do.

I'm always telling myself: Don't worry about the parts that are way far ahead. Just keep doing the next part and, muse willing, it'll all come together.

***

So, okay, what's on deck for the mirrorflower chapter?

Mason and Seela park Tallulah the shrig in the jungle near the mirrorflower. MirrorSeela and MirrorYurgen are married, but they have no children. Mason and Seela meet them right away, it's kismet, like the way they met MirrorPoe right away when the boat picked them up in HE1. Like a magnetic attraction.

Mason and Seela settle in with Yurgen and MirrorSeela, sharing a petal pod for a week or two. Seela still doesn't want to have intercourse, as she so recently gave birth, but maybe she brings off MirrorYurgen once or twice for old time's sake, but she's not into it, as she thinks Yurgen is too old. He's of course slobbering on her, excited by her youth, her fecundity, her milk.

For his part, Mason loves making love to MirrorSeela. Something about her—maybe he likes older women, not having had a mother. Or, put more simply, he's glad to get laid at all, as it's been at least a month and maybe more. And MirrorSeela does look exactly like Seela, just twelve years older, and a little more comfy and worn.

Let's say Quaihlaihle the queen is dead here, too. Symmetry. Come to think of it, she's been dead for twelve years. (Or maybe not? But she was a dull character.) The new queen Fleeka might pose a problem of some kind. Maybe she's loaded on *juube* all the time. Perhaps the tribe kind of wants Seela to be the new queen, as she's so unusual. They're impressed with Arf, and Mason gets a younger kid named Nurr to be Arf's groom. Things are going pretty well, but then Mason finds out that MirrorYurgen is planning to kill him. He wants both Seelas for himself, and he wants to have Brumble for his son. Fleeka the bad queen wants to kill Seela as well, which complicates things.

Not quite sure if this is he right strategy for getting them off the mirrorflower and onward.

Perhaps a fight with the blueflowers is in the offing, but I won't again use Poe's trick of sawing through the stem of the enemies' flower. Actually in HE1 they exterminated one colony of blueflowers, but presumably there are more blossoms of the two colors. The yellowflowers vs. the blueflowers.
***

Now it's a few days later, it's November 27, 2017. Reprising what I already wrote in this note: my idea is to re-read the flowerpeople sections of HE1, and make notes (or at least mental observations) of things to include in the upcoming HE2 flowerpeople chapter. Although I keep not doing this....

Conversely I'll tweak in a few changes to the HE1 scenes so there's good continuity—in particular I'm putting

Seela's beau Yurgen into HE1. He plays what I'm now calling the *reverberator tube*, and he's a bit of a coward. I managed to start work on the edits to HE1 while Sylvia and I
were up in San Francisco visiting Rudy Jr. and his family for
Thanksgiving.

REMEMBER

The sound of the reverberator tube in HE1: "A roaring,
almost human sound, oddly warped and amplified. Droning
blabber."

* I used the word flowerpeople in HE1, so it's fine here.

Insects in the jungle, glittering beetles flying on the
flower. Huge ocean next to the jungle with the flower, it
curves up into the sky. Like a wave.

* The village center is a hexagon near one edge of the
flower, a hundred yards wide with doors on the cells around
it.

* Huge blob of water at the center of the blossom, with
small blobs on some of the cells. A hole in the center of each
cell with stubby petals around it.

Necklaces of crystals, shells, and carved bits of wood.
Most of them are bare-chested, with a loin cloth. They lick
each others' faces in greeting.

Three juube beans per cell, the size of watermelons. The
liquid is albuminous, slick. juice was something like sweet-
ened eggwhite, with a bitter aftertaste. It was invigorating,
and a bit dizzying.

Quaihlaihle was albino.

HOLLOW EARTH LANGUAGE

Pulpul for airfin.

Ahnaa bogbog du smeeepy flan? Mii'iim doc janjee Girl
taking Mason captive

Ah'mbaa na toloo klick gorwaay Girls laughing when
Mason asks to be set free.

Lamalama tekelili? Quaihliahle greeting Otha.

Bogbog doc janjee! Ombondoohoo! Quaihlaihle telling
them to free the captives.

Emthonjeni womculo. Thul'ulale. Seela calming down.

Sini lindile. Nansi Seela. Seela introduces herself.

Ma'aassong. How Seela she says "Mason"

Nicabange orlooah Are you going to take off these pants?

Gooba'am Is that cool?

Nicabange smeeepy doolango Seela catches hold Mason lest he fall into sky.

Quaihlaihle shange yejazi, I never liked Quaihlaihl

Dmbagolo laaa nuinullee orbaahm. Welcome to the Umpteen Seas.

TO DO HE1

* Seela should mention that she thinks Yurgen is stupid.

* Yurgen ducked the battle with the blueflowers, as he's a coward.

TO DO HE2

* Make sure Mason and Seela are quite black when they get to the mirrorflower. I think it's kind of funny to keep turning them black over and over again—it kind of makes a point about how it actually *is* for black people. Wake up every day and—black again!

* HE1. Yurgen sabotages Mason during a battle by weakening his airfin beforehand.

* I'd thought Yurgen would be a strong jock, but as I write, he's coming out as a thin musician. I started to make him a total juube addict, but maybe that's too pat.

* Mention Seela's kind-of father Ogger. MirrorOgger.

Remember that Eddie was writing an epic poem called "Htrae" about the Hollow Earth.

Decide what to do about the *Htrae* word. Should I use it? Seems needlessly confusing, actually.

November 28-December 1, 2017. Puttering.

I'm moving slowly on the flowerpeople chapter. I don't know why I can't get around to rereading the old flowerpeople chapters from HE1. Today I worked all morning on a blog post, and Sunday I spent the whole day editing my recent photos.

***

Different topic: I'm reading Christopher White, *Other*

Worlds, Harvard U. Press, pub date March, 2018. I love the book, and I'm working on a blurb for it. Here it is:

Ver 1. Nov 28, 2017

"*Other Worlds* is a magisterial and deeply satisfying work on the history of a peculiarly modern idea: the fourth dimension. This esoteric concept points beyond the quotidian world, and Christopher White's volume shows how readily the notion of hyperspace blends with human spiritual aspirations. The fun is that White makes his history into a juicy narrative, rife with geniuses, scientists, charlatans, impresarios, and artists of every stripe. The depth of research and wealth of information is stunning. One almost feels the author has surveyed our times with an all-seeing, higher-dimensional eye. A book to treasure, a feast."

Ver 2. Nov 29, 2017 (Mailed this off).

"*Other Worlds* is a magisterial and deeply satisfying history of a peculiarly modern idea: the fourth dimension. The author focuses on the entanglement between human spiritual aspirations and the notion of hyperspace. The fun is that he makes his history into a juicy narrative, replete with geniuses, scientists, charlatans, impresarios, and artists of every stripe. So incisive is Christopher White's research that one suspects he has access to an all-seeing, higher-dimensional eye. A book to treasure, a feast."
***

On November 29, I finally printed out my HE1 flowerpeople chapters in their current state and am reading over them, noting things to adhere to, and making a few more fixes.

Read and fixed all day November 30, too, putting the changes into HE1, Ver3. I added this thing were Eddie is working on an epic poem about the trip and he calls it Htrae, and I'm going to reduce the use of that word by anyone but Eddie as, I think, it confuses the readers. Eddie might even say, in HE2, that the word Htrae is "his" and Mason shouldn't use it in writing HE2. I think maybe I got it from Nathaniel Hellerstein in the first place. I'm thinking Eddie's

first line for his epic, and I remember the jingling, enjamb-
ment rhythm e of Shakespeare's "full fathom five thy father
lies…"

*Full fathoms they fell / To the land of Htrae / Within
mother Earth's warm rind.*

The fathom thing doesn't make much sense here. And I
ought to have all iambs.

*I fell through ice to Htrae— / A world within the hollow
rind / That humans deem firm Earth.*

I'm wondering why MirrorSeela stays with
MirrorYurgen if he's a coward and a stoner. There has to be
something attractive about him, I guess it's his music. It's,
like, hypnotic. And maybe he can sing really sweetly. But
why hasn't MirrorSeela gotten pregnant by another man?

Oh, and I gave a name to the "old man" whom Seela
rooms with in HE1, the guy who may or may not be her father, kind of a *juube* stoner. In naming him, I went with my
private joke tradition of Tuckerizing my old pal, roommate,
drinking buddy, and fellow writer Gregory "Gregor" Arthur
Gibson. I scrambled Gregor, dropped one of the R's and
came up with Ogger. Great name. In *Spaceland* there's an
Uncle Arthur who falls down dead at a family dinner, I
think. And a gargoyle-type monster called Gargor in *Frek
and the Elixir*. My hero's roommate Ace Weston in *Secret of
Life*, of course. I know there's some others, but can't think of
them just now. Leave it to the grad students…

December 1, 2017.

It's interesting to be thickening up the flowerpeople
scenes in HE1, and now, I hope, I can go back into the
flowerpeople scenes in HE2 and have them be rich as well,
but different. A good MirrorYurgen reverberator concert
would be a nice idea, I can work on the hypnotic quality of
the music and it's power over MirrorSeela. The sound is, I
figure, like a big didgeridoo. I remember when Sylvia and I
stayed in a hotel in Sydney, Australia, near the Circular
Quay—there were a bunch of buskers playing those things,
the sound thrumming in the air all day long.

Okay, finally finished marking up HE1 Chapters 10 &
11 and putting all the changes into HE1, Ver 3. As adumbrated, along the way, I came up with a number of fixes run-

ning through both HE1 and HE2, which is why it took so long.

And now I can reread the HE2 flowerpeople section, just a few pages as yet, and start getting the rest of that chapter moving. It really helps that I developed Yurgen as a character in the new Version 3 of HE1.

Looking ahead to eventual publication, I'm doing so many changes to HE1, that I think it might be best to publish the two volumes as one, that is, the revised HE1 Ver3 with HE2. I'm nearly ready to ask my agent John Silbersack to approach Cory Allyn at Night Shade about it. They have an option, so we need to try them first, and maybe they're the best place for me, as I do like the covers they're making for my 10-book run with them. Although if there's not strong interest, we could try someplace else, I suppose…if there is anyplace "else" that would in fact consider publishing a new novel by the septuagenarian RR.

December 1, 2017. Letter About "Being High"

Synchronistically enough, just after I put "Ogger" into my manuscript yesterday, Greg Gibson happened to write me today, and he mentioned drinking, and I wrote back something about my thoughts on the topic these days. And then I revised this passage on Dec 4. 2017, with an eye to perhaps sharing it with others.

> I was at my AA meeting yesterday, and I was thinking about how I sometimes miss the buzz, the cheer, the immediacy of the fix, the yellow quality the light takes on, the relaxation in my muscles, the sense of peace—we call this "euphoric recall".
>
> But then I remind myself that all those nice effects of pot and alcohol are things my brain knows how to do. They're neurological processes Smoking and drinking used to nudge my brain into being high. But, as I say, during my time being sober, I've noticed that my brain can in fact generate an inner buzz.
>
> That is, I can feel high and relaxed---just out of the blue. The junkie author William Burroughs used

to refer to this effect as "the inner Man," using "the Man" in the sense of "my dealer." I like to talk about "the Muse," and I think of her as a woman.

The catch is that the Muse doesn't get me high at the snap of a finger. I'm never quite sure when she'll show up—it's not like me slamming a bourbon or lighting a jay—but the Muse *does* keep coming by.

The thing about waiting to be high—there's a surf analogy I like to use. You're out there on your board waiting for the waves. In the sea. Or I compare it to the weather—if you don't like the weather right now, I just have to wait a few hours, or wait a day, and have the patience to wait without having to take something while I'm waiting.

The good feelings come more often when I'm doing things like being loving and empathetic, or walking or biking outside, or writing or painting, or listening to music, or even just staring off into space with my mind blank and with perhaps a slight (traditional) trickle of drool.

And generally I'm not hooking into good vibes when watching TV news or stewing over my ever self-renewing grudges/fears/remorse! Re. the second problem, I have to tell myself, over and over and over and over: Let all that go, be mindless, be high, be in the now, open your heart to love, bask in the White Light which is everywhere.

I've always loved the White Light. We're stained glass windows, and the White Light is shining through us, and that's why we're alive. The Light, as I say, is everywhere, all the time. Reminding me to unwrap the barbed wire from around my heart.

December 8, 2017. Balance and the Two Eddies

I'm having second thoughts about eliminating Eddie Poe by sending him back through the Anomaly. He adds a lot. Even having him missing from the last chapter or two I've felt the lack. Maybe he won't go through the Anomaly after all. Maybe he changes his mind about that. And Ina hooks up with Eddie for good.

Perhaps he'll plan to come back to our Earth and start a career as a writer. He thinks of claiming his death was a hoax, but Poe didn't do that in our world, so we can't do that, or maybe he tries it, but nobody believes him. So he tries using a new name and—funny/sad kicker—he has very little literary success, illustrating how capricious such success is. That's harsh on Eddie. There is, I feel, a schlock element in some of his work, but the finest stuff really is genius. Suppose he is still undeniably great, but his style is out of fashion already, or that our Poe is viewed as an imitator.

And then Eddie turns to a different career. There was that thing about the poet Rimbaud abandoning writing at 21, roaming the world, and settling down as a coffee merchant in Harare, Ethiopia till he died at 34 of cancer. Could Eddie possibly do a move like that? That could be interesting. I can see the travel, can't quite see Eddie as a merchant. Running a gold mine? Kind of humdrum, that, but maybe he'd have a rumby-type angle.

***

But wait, what about the balance issue? Ridiculous solution for Eddie: send Tallulah the shrig through the anomaly to in some sense emulate him for balance. Nah.

Let's just say Mason was completely mistaken in his analysis of the balance between worlds. It's funny for Mason to be wrong. And then I'm free to think about the emotional weight of the plot turns.

So with my self-created straitjacket of balance discarded, I'm thinking it would be nice to have Mason keep Seela and Brumble and, hell, why not keep MirrorSeela and Bramble as well. That's so much more satisfying.

One problem here. I came up with the "balance" thing as an explanation for why the *woomo* gave Machree special treatment. So now I need to find a new explanation.

It might still have to do with balance, but applying only to the case of Machree and Mason. They're a singular connection because of that chiasmus thing of Mason killing Machree on Earth and Machree killing Mason on MirrorEarth—back at that Lynchburg stable. So the *woomo*

225

just wanted specifically to toss Machree through the Anomaly. And maybe then Eddie talks the *woomo* out of applying the balance rule to him, if they were even going to do that. In any case, although initially he wants to go back to Earth, maybe he changes his mind.

Suppose that I state the reason for tossing Machree as "entanglement" rather than "balance." Not quite the same thing could happen with Poe, as he's only one person. But even so, the actions of Poe have altered the histories of the two worlds anyway.

And returning Poe or Machree to one world or the other doesn't really undo the fact that the Earth and MirrorEarth are no longer copies of each other. Especially given that they closed the North Hole maelstrom just now in HE2. And that they opened the South Hole ice plug on Earth in HE1, leaving the MirrorEarth ice plug in place.

***

Remark added on December 15, 2017.

Moving onward, I'm realizing how liberating it is to release myself from the "mandatory balance" shackles. I can have MirrorSeela and Seela both go up to San Francisco with Mason. I can have good old Otha pop up in the Mirror Umpteen Seas, having come through the Anomaly out of curiosity. I can keep Machree around and have him try to get into rumby imports. I don't need to send Eddie off through the Anomaly and back to the original Earth. In other words, I get to keep my full cast of characters. Yes, I did want to get Eddie, Machree, and Ina offstage for awhile, but I don't want to lose them for good. They're fun to have around. And bringing back Otha—wonderful!

I do like the bits where Mason makes his deductions about the consequences of the Cosmic Balance Principle. But now, all along, I'm deflating his claims by means of asides to the effect that later he'd find out that he was wrong.

December 9-13, 2017. Fried Egg & Woomo.

I'm not writing much this week, as the Christmas tide is rolling in. Daughter Isabel is in town, and she was staying at our house. We went to the beach at Santa Cruz one day, and San Francisco the next day. Visited my *A Skugger's Point of*

View painting on display at the Luggage Store Gallery at 6th & Market. Hit a Southern Black Art show and a Mexican pyramid show at the DeYoung. And I started a big new painting of a shrig, which eventually became *Shrig and Krakens.*

I got a few pages done of the mirrorflower chapter, but now I'm stalled. I got maybe too much into the slobbering about sex with MirrorSeela. And I had plans for a new queen of the mirrorflower, but queens are boring, even if they're albino black gods. And I was seeing MirrorYurgen as being a physical threat to Mason, but now I'm seeing him as kind of feeble and spaced out.

At this point I don't have enough scenes for the mirrorflower, and I don't know why/when Mason and Seela will want to leave. But I *do* have two scenes. (1) MirrorYurgen really plays well, and everyone is tripping out. (2) Mason gets to fuck MirrorSeela, although ostensibly this is going to be just the once, as she's loyal to her "sister" Seela, and she only wants to use Mason to get pregnant. But maybe Seela isn't even jealous and later it develops into a lasting threesome, which will be okay in San Francisco. (Resume slobber mode!)

But I still need a wow on the mirrorflower, a treat, a surprise, some reason to want to write the chapter. So let me return to my oft intoned dictum:

Squander Your Wows. *Don't hoard your wows—use them as fast as you can. The Muse will provide more.*

I had in mind some eventual HE2 wow involving the saucers, and I was going to use that when Mason was back in the Umpteen Seas. But right now I'm "dying," in a stand-up comic's sense of the word. That is, I'm in danger of boring the audience. So…"Voila!" [*Brisk double hand clap. Assistants wheel an ancient metal flying saucer onto the stage. Pink light glows from within the saucer.*]

- The "fried egg" (flying saucer) that Mason rode out to the Chesapeake Bay in HE1 is on the mirrorflower. It sank down to the bottom of the sea, through the Rind, drifted out into the sky of MirrorHtrae , and was tugged toward the South Hole by a curious shrig, and was salvaged by

227

the mirrorflowerpeople as a trophy.

- It would be amusing to have a tiny newborn *woomo* sitting in the fried egg. Not a queen, but a tribal totem.

I love the idea of that saucer sitting in the mirrorflower's hexagonal village square. And love the baby *woomo*. Mason gets to hold it. It rides along in the flying saucer. Talk about *larvae*! (My nickname for the grandchildren.)

Not quite sure what precipitates the trip to the core. As I said, I don't see MirrorYurgen as threatening Mason's life. I like the idea of them falling upward inside the fried egg.

In any case, the departure should, naturally, be turbulent. Some of the mirrorflowerpeople are trying to kill Mason, Seela, Arf, and/or MirroSeela. Why? Let's say that the seemingly listless (but secretly spiteful and jealous) MirrorYurgen has uses the enchantment of his music to whip up the tribe against our crew.

***

Okay, I was busy with the family, a wonderful reunion. And then I was doing an update of my online *Complete Stories*. But on Tuesday, Dec 12, 2017, I went to the library and sat alone, with no wireless, and got some writing done, about a thousand words. Pent-up scenes pouring out. It always feels so good and relaxing when I can sink into my work. My happy place.

I've got Mason, the two Seelas, Arf, and Brumble in the mirrorflowerpeople's village, with Seela and Mason about to take a nap. When they wake up, MirrorYurgen will be doing a show on the reverberator tube, and the tribe will be carrying around, as in a procession, the little *woomo* who has hatched inside the fried egg, displaying the *woomo* around like the Sri Lankans displaying the Tooth of the Buddha upon an the back of an elephant in a religious parade. Or, maybe she's just glowing with pink light inside the fried egg, that's simpler.

Tallulah, as it turns out, is a regular at the jungle beside the mirrorflower. And she's the one who hauled the fried egg to the mirrorflower. She's one of those synchronicities I'm weaving in. I'm not even sure I'll ever explain them. I just like the aura of "mysto steam" they add. And when I'm almost done with the novel and I see what I actually have, and what I actually need, then I can make up some rubber-science-bogosity-generator-type reason having something to do with the two Earths being linked. Like when Philip Marlowe paces back and forth and gives a rapid-fire explanation of the logic of a Raymond Chandler novel on the second to last page of the book.

Rudy Rucker, *Return to the Hollow Earth*, December 12, 2017

Figure 24: Climax on the Mirrorflower

Tallulah was going to carry our crew to the core, but it'll be more lively (and heart-breaking) if some of the mirrorflowerpeople warriors to kill Tallulah when she comes over to pick up Mason and the two Seelas. The killers are the same two guards who met Mason and the Seelas as they came in, Kurt and Kong, and then they'll be the ones threatening Mason as well. They kill Tallulah both to stymie Mason, and because: *"Thar's a heap o' good eatin' inside, my friend!"* I was sentimentally reluctant to kill Tallulah, but I gotta go for that huge, tragic *wheenk*. Poor old Tallulah, I love her so.

And, as I was saying above, it'll be the effect of MirrorYurgen's music on Kurt and Kong that precipitates the departure. K & K will be hanging over MirrorYurgen like the drunk guy staring at the bagpiper in Bruegel's *Peasant Dance*.

And then K & K start after Mason, and he gets the gang into the fried egg, and Seela has cut the tethers on the fried egg, but it's stuck there on the flower, and MirrorSeela tries to push it off the flower's edge, but it won't move so she hides inside the fried egg again, but then the mini *woomo* Hella kicks into gear, pushing with a beam of pink light,. Or Tallulah shoves the fried egg loose as a final favor during her dying flutter. And then they're airborne, and falling towards the core.

By the way, what's it like inside the fried egg? Quote from HE1. I'll reuse this with edits.

The inside of the ship was fully gutted. There were three shattered stands that must have held seats; also, there was an alcove that could have housed bunk beds like those on the *Wasp*. Behind the alcove was a bulkhead sealing off a third of the craft's hemispherical bulge—I imagined that within the sealed compartment there might be a stove to produce hot air. The craft had a porthole on either side and a long, thick-glassed view port right in front of where the seats had been. Beneath the view port was a slanting panel with the broken-off stubs of what must once have been controls. Watcher said that the black gods' ancestors had broken off all the pieces they could use for ornaments. Numerous hieroglyphs adorned the cabin: a circular frieze of them wound around the walls, and hieroglyphs in oval cartouches were engraved near each of the vandalized controls. Some of the hieroglyphs seemed to show the fan-capped barrels of the Great Old Ones; others looked like that poor forked radish, Man. Had Man and the Great Old Ones used the fried eggs together in ancient times?

December 14-15, 2017. Rumbies are Woomo Eggs.

I still need to figure out how that *woomo* started growing inside the fried egg? I was thinking of some kind of aether ray transmission, but then it occurred to me: why not have the rumby stones in fact be *woomo* eggs! This is a great idea, it's a sword that cuts three Gordian knots.

- Given that the black gods find the rumbies in the core, excreted by the *woomo*, it's quite reasonable that rumbies are *woomo* seeds.
- If the rumbies are *woomo* seeds, this explains why the rumbies have teep power. It's tekelili!
- If the rumbies are *woomo* seeds, this explains why the *woomo* care about the rumbies, which in turn explains why they take a special interest in Machree.

Expanding on the third point: the *woomo* care about Machree because he wants to import rumbies to the surface of MirrorEarth, and this would increase the odds of rumbies escaping into interstellar space and landing on another hollow planet. We're talking *very* long-range planning here.

So rumbies are *woomo* seeds. Perfect. I had this idea the other day, Dec 12, walking down the stairs on my way out of the library after a big writing session. A bolt from the Muse. I ended up spending several hours on December 13 and 15, going through HE1 and HE2, incorporating, and subtly paving the way for, this new rumby=*woomo*-egg wow. I made sure to keep mentioning "tekelili" in connection with the rumbies, and stressing that they seem alive.

I still need to explain how a rumby got into the fried egg and hatched before Mason and Seela even show up. Keep in mind that it's hard to move things from the core out to the Rind, as the gravity runs the other way. Shrigs and ballulas carry some things, and *woomo* rays can push things, and black gods can surf the light rays all the way out.

I could have MirrorJewel happen to ride a light ray out
and trade a rumby to MirrorSeela for some juube beans. Before the fried egg even got there. Or, no, to keep it simpler,
I'll just say that the *woomo* send down a ray and gave
MirrorSeela a rumby. The *woomo*, being masters of space
and time, always know what's gonna come down. And then
the *woomo* get Tallulah to drag the fried egg to the
mirrorflower, and MirrorSeela's rumby uses its tekelili to tell
her to put the rumby into the fried egg.

But then what provoked this particular rumby seed to
hatch? It couldn't just be the vibrational energy of the fried
egg, as we've already had rumbies inside the fried egg before, like when Mason, Seela, and Eddie rode the fried egg
up through the sea to MirrorChesapeakeBay—and those
rumbies didn't hatch at that time.

So let's say that in order to hatch the rumby in the
flowerpeople's fried egg, the *woomo* hit it with a special
zap. Once again, the *woomo* know all. So they'd know to do
this. So that's cool.

But, um, one more question: What was the *motive* of the
woomo of the core for getting that baby *woomo* to hatch inside the fried egg? I'll say they wanted the newborn *woomo*
to shepherd the fried egg back to the core.

Why the *woomo* even *want* that fried egg back in the
core? Let's say they like having a fried egg around—for
Frisbee-tossing possible future guests out through an ocean
on the Rind.

And why do they need a *woomo* pilot for the fried egg's
trip from Rind to core? Couldn't the *woomo* at core just use
remote tekelili to force Tallulah to release the fried egg into
the air so it falls to the core on its own? Or have told Tallulah just carry the fried egg all the way to the core. *But maybe
the fried egg would then have been grabbed by some as yet
unknown enemy on the way in.* So the fried egg, in other
words, needs a sly *woomo* pilot to run the gauntlet to the
core.

The as yet unknown fried-egg-kidnapping enemy can't
just be a ballula or a shrig, as the *woomo* seem able to control those guys. The only obstacles so far who stands up to

the *woomo* are (a) a stray kraken or two and (b) vagrant tunnels to the Hollow Sun.

So okay, the enemy is a rogue kraken. Let's say it's one of those newborn krakens from the North Hole. I'll alter that scene so that one of them didn't make it out through the closing maelstrom. I like using a kraken instead of yet another kind of critter. "Don't put in too many critters, Ru," as Sylvia sometimes admonishes me. As if.

But, wait, I will have another kind of critter. For I need to have nature of the kraken's attack to be more dramatic than just biting. The kraken tries to push or drag them into a wormhole that goes to the interior of the Hollow Sun! *Now* we're getting somewhere. A wow for the next chapter. I don't want my characters to actually *go* to the Hollow Sun…that's overkill. But to peep in through the Gates of Hell, as it were, that would be good. The krakens and the *woomo* are in some sense competitors.

—*Answers prepared by Professor Rudolf v. B. Rucker, Ph.D. (Piled High and Deep).*

Extra Credit Problems:

Q. I need to rule out the option of the *woomo* dragging in the fried egg by using a light ray as a "tractor beam," such as it used to deliver a rumby to MirrorSeela, and which it used to carry Machree to safety when the *Purple Whale* sank.

A. The cunning of the enemies is so great that the fried egg needs an onboard pilot for rapid response. I should mention this in passing.

Q. Why was the fried egg in HE1 able to easily cross the sky between the core and the MirrorRind without incident?

A. The wise *woomo* Uxa put sufficient spin on the fried egg so that it avoided any dangerous shoals. And it helped that the fried egg was moving really fast. Maybe on the way out this time, they won't be so lucky.

December 17-18, 2017. Denizens of the Hollow Sun?

I'm thinking more about the nature of the obstacle that my crew encounters while riding the *woomo*-piloted fried egg from the mirorflower to the Umpteen Seas. And in the previous entry I suggested it might be a rogue kraken, but I need more.

Another angle might be something involving those (seeming) giant protozoa I had in the previous chapter. I'm not happy with those guys, as they aren't a good fit for the other creatures, as HE2 isn't all that much about gigantism. Admittedly, there *are* some oversized trees, scorpions, flying pigs, nautiluses, flowers and so on. So I *could* come up with a rubber-science explanation for the giant paramecia.

But it would be useful if can find a way to link the "giant protozoa" to creatures from the Hollow Sun. First of all, they're jellyfish instead of protozoa. If you're looking at a blimp-sized blob, calling it a flying jellyfish makes more sense than saying it's a unicellular protozoan. And then I want to add the twist of them being in some sense from the Hollow Sun or, better, *tunnels* to the Hollow Sun. When Tallulah ate most of what seemed to be a dinoflagellate, per-haps she was in fact eating thermonuclear aether from a dis-embodied solar prominence.

We've seen them in a fairly benign form already. But now when they reappear they get more menacing. Maybe they unleash those big nets I'd talked about at one time, when I was calling them, I think, *urbsteg*. And the *flying saucer*, oops!, *frying egg*, oops!, *fried egg* barely evades them on the way in towards the core. The *urbsteg* are kind of like protozoa and kind of like jellyfish but they're from the Hollow Sun, I tell you!

***

So I went back and changed the giant protozoa to *urbstegs* in my HE2 manuscript. They have as-yet-unexplained glowing stomachs at their core. I'll have my crew meet a big *urbsteg* while drifting to the core inside the fried egg with the *woomo*, and, as I'll say, I'll make clear that those glowing cores are wormhole tunnels that run to the Hollow Sun. And like I said, to make it better, a rogue kra-ken will be trying to nudge them into the urbsteg, and then perhaps the kraken falls in itself, and it'll be one of those newborn baby krakens that didn't make it out through the maelstrom.

And I'm eventually going to say that the *urbstegs* are living sunspots—I've always loved the notion that sunspots are alive, I wrote about that in *Frek and the Elixir*.

December 22-27, 2017. Hollow Sun. Lizzie Doten. GANs.

I was off for Christmas up at Rudy Jr's with family from Dec 24-26, a great time. I started this note on Dec 22, and then came back and finished it on Dec 27.

So at this point, they're in the fried egg—Mason, Seela, MirrorSeela, Brumble, and Arf. Falling inward. Seela says "Get it over with," and Mason fucks MirrorSeela. It's kind of cheerful. Thanks to the *woomo*, they have so much tekelili that it feels like a three-way and they can even tell that MirrorSeela got pregnant. "So that's that," says Seela.

They open the door and enjoy the breeze. But now they see the stray kraken, he's about twenty feet long, and he has it in for the baby *woomo*. He's needling her with his red rays. The *woomo* reacts, and there's a bit of a sky battle, and then, oh-oh, they're falling towards an *urbsteg* with a big central tunnel.

And MirrorSeela tells them it's a tunnel to the Hollow Sun. There's been a lot of that action during the twelve years that Seela skipped over. The kraken gets hold of the baby *woomo* and carries it into the hole, like time our Arf picked up the neighbor's miniature dachshund puppy in his jaws. Nice glimpse of the inside of the Hollow Sun, Mason like dangling in there on a woven rope of some kind, and the two Seelas pull him out.

The fried eggs keeps falling toward the core, and nothing is bothering them, and then a sky surfer shows up and maybe it's Otha, if I want to bring him back. And that could be a chapter's worth.

***

And at that point I'll be about halfway done, depending whether I want twenty or just nineteen chapters.

But—as I keep saying—I don't have enough plot for the second half. I mean, they're all together in the core, and have some affairs and quarrels,, and then what? Not enough paint to cover those other two big blank walls of the room I'm in.

Rudy Rucker

Let's revise and reformulate the options I mentioned <u>last month</u>.

- Have Mason jump to 2018 and meet me. Or ump him to 2050 and do a *Futurama* number. If he comes back in 2050, he could open up trade between our Earth and the inner Earth.
- Trans-Rind prospecting activities back on the surface of the Earth. Lots of rumbies. Eddie's cult takes off.
- An intrigue or political struggle between the *woomo* and the krakens at the core, which culminates with a visit to the Hollow sun.

(1) I don't see much plot juice in me meeting Mason. I mean fine, but so what, and we've been there with Frank Shook in *Saucer Wisdom*. My initial idea of jumping to 2050 is better. First thought, best thought. And in 2050, Mason gets the holes open, and starts cranking up inside/outside trade and tourism. Could have a climate-change angle, in that the warming North Pole would get the maelstrom going again in 2050.

Thing is, that's a whole other book. Climate change in 2050. It breaks the whole cozy Victorian-era set of HE1 and the first half of HE2. Can't I find a way to work the story without time jump?

(2) The second option goes back to an idea I had while visiting Lone Pine, CA, that is, some intense ultra-deep mining project, in search of rumbies, and the tunnels are produced by those critters I called, um, <u>burrowers</u>. I could introduce the burrowers as follows. A *woomo* like Uxa flings the fried egg towards the underside of the Pacific ocean. But an *urbsteg* or a kraken screws up their flight and they crash land on the underside of the Gold Country And something's chasing them, and some burrowers show them a tunnel to the surface. Not that I like tunnels very much, but we could compress the process and perhaps add some vault-temples. And then maybe they're importing rumbies big time and maybe Eddie's cult takes off. What was it? The Order of the Golden Frond. How do we fit this into our Earth's known history? Could Eddie become a different writer, perhaps an

236

unsuccessful one? I could research contemporary Poe imitators. Martin Gardner used to talk about James Branch Cabell. Huysmans didn't write in English. Eddie himself wrote a very long and ranting essay about Longfellow plagiarizing Poe's poetry. I found an interesting angle in the Wikipedia entry on Poe.

> One trend among imitators of Poe has been claims by clairvoyants or psychics to be "channeling" poems from Poe's spirit. One of the most notable of these was Lizzie Doten, who published *Poems from the Inner Life* in 1863, in which she claimed to have "received" new compositions by Poe's spirit. The compositions were re-workings of famous Poe poems such as "The Bells", but which reflected a new, positive outlook.

Lizzie Doten (1829-1913) was known as a spiritualist trance-speaker, who gave performances of her work in, for instance Boston, and attributed many of her poems to Poe, even saying that he spoke through her as she recited them. Eddie could *totally* be in with her. In 1850, she'd be 21. One of her performances, in Baltimore, 1863, was "The Streets of Baltimore," about Eddie's death in 1849. It's great stuff, very much like what Ed would write. And it's a fairly close copy of "The Raven."

> Nay, with deep, delirious pleasure,
> I had drained my life's full measure,
> Till that fatal, fiery serpent,
> Fed upon my being's core!
> Then with force and fire volcanic,
> Summoning a strength Titanic,
> Did I burst the bonds that bound me —
> Battered down my being's door;
> Fled, and left my shattered dwelling
> To the dust of Baltimore!

I'd maybe want the Eddie imitator to start up earlier than 1860, but if I did use Lizzie Doten, I could just mention the performances in the Editor's Note.

(3) The third option I mention above is to have some kind of power struggle at the core. I'm seeing the Hollow Sun krakens and *urbsteg* as the rivals of the *woomo*. The payoff is an excursion to the Hollow Sun. I've been telling myself I'd leave the Hollow Sun for a possible HE3. But once again, I'll invoke my principle:

Squander Your Wows. *Don't hoard your wows—use them as fast as you can. The Muse will provide more.*

So go ahead and do a Hollow Sun chapter or two here and now in HE2. And then I can still use the option (2) after the I do the (3). If I do Hollow Sun in HE2, then I don't even need to write HE3, so much the better. And then my HE2 is stuffed with action.

Figure 25; "It's starting to look at lot like Gansmas."

What's been holding me back re. the Hollow Sun is "the shooter's anxiety before the penalty kick," or the fear of the blank canvas, or a self-induced failure of the imagination. It's not that I *can't* think up a landscape for the Hollow Sun. It's that I haven't been able to bring myself to *try*. So now I'll start dreaming on it. Go.

    ***

My starting point is a Disney TV cartoon from about 1955, about possible extraterrestrials, and about the dullard ancients imagining the denizens of the Sun as being naked and continually running. Naked because it's hot there, running because the "ground" burns their feet, I suppose. But now they'll be running around on the inside. But wait, no gravity in there to glue you to a surface to run on.

Unlike the Hollow Earth, I don't need to have pink streamers for light from the center. The underside of the Sun's surface glows.

Maybe there is a ball inside the Hollow Sun. Like Earth, only it's in a very large spherical greenhouse with a very bright sky. Forecast: sunny. A world like the old SF image of planet Venus. Cloudy and it's always raining. Brontosauruses bellow. Or even have the inner planet be hollow, à la John Cleves Symmes, who had hollow worlds within hollow worlds. A hollow planet with an Anomaly inside. Overkill, no, don't do it. I'd rather not have a planet in there at all. Stick to a big open space with weird shit flying around.

Probably, for the sake of symmetry I'd have an anomaly at the core of the Hollow Sun. So there can be a MirrorSun for MirrorEarth as well as a Sun for Earth. And shit is riding in the Sun's Anomaly zone. Krakens. Rather than seas of water, they have seas of…plasma?

The critters in the Hollow Sun—they need to be different. I can't just use dinosaurs or jellyfish or telepathic fungi (well, *maybe* telepathic fungi, as in Lovecraft's "Fungi from Yoggoth.") Whenever I decide on the look of the Hollo Sun denizens, I can go back and tweak the krakens to match. At present the krakens are just big flying lizards. I'm thinking something more Julia-set-like around the edges.

Figure 26: Uncanny Valley in Celebrity Face Space.

Maybe those GANs videos I've been looking at this week could help. Generative Adversarial Networks, it's a new thing in deep-learning neural-net AI. I found out about them by way of Bill Gosper, who turned me onto a kid named Neal Bickford who mentioned them on his blog. I got an image-processing app called Prisma that was trained with GANs methods to, for instance, make a photo look like graphic-novel comic art, and I took a photo of our Xmas tree and posted it.

Marc Laidlaw commented, "It's starting to look at lot like whatever Gansmas looks like." And that just slayed me.

Cousin Barbara had a very apt one-word comment: "Nostalgia." Brimming so high.

GANs generators can also produce animal-like figures based on points in a high-dimensional "latent space" of parameter vectors that are (via unknowably complex neural networks) converted into critters. As the controlling parameter vector wanders in latent space, the visible critter is continually changing. The Hollow Sun critters are protean.

So, yeah, I want the critters who live in the Hollow Sun to be GANs-like. In German, *gans* can mean "goose" or (as *ganz*) "the whole." What do I call one of these critters. A sun goose? Or use Sheckley's great word *ganzer* from *Mind Swap*, I don't think I ever used that word of his before.

Joking previz of a scene:

> "I ate the whole Gansmas ganzer," said Eddie
> Poe. His jaw lengthened and his head was that of a
> crocodile, but then, with a fillip, the head became
> that of a simpering maid. And it wasn't Eddie Poe at
> all. "Kiss me?"said the morphodite Eddie-thing.
> "See the mistletoad?"

Could go bananas/apeshit and write the Hollow Sun chapter in spaced-out Joycean pun-riddled quack-quack paralanguage. Would be fun for me. Perhaps less so for the reader. But I want to go there. The book is, after all, for me.

Here's a <u>video</u> of a guy explaining GANs. And a video <u>demo</u> of a full *hour* of continually morphing GANs-algorithm-generated "celebrity faces" with many, many uncanny valleys between the grinning peaks. This is the effect I want to use for the critters who live inside the Hollow Sun. It'll have to be handled properly, or it's tedious. Surrealism overdose. Like describing a dream. Maybe if it's better if they're static in the uncanny valley, rather than morphing all the time. Or maybe they only morph once in a while. Like a square dance where suddenly everyone jumps up and mills around, and then they split up into pairs of partners again.

"Howdy podner." My interlocutor had the head of a horse, but with the sly smile of a pirate. One of his eye sockets was empty.

And the krakens could have a bit of that look, they could

241

be constantly changing their precise appearance. Protean, like I said. Like solar prominences or, as I mentioned, like attractors in the variations on the Mandelbrot set

Figure 27: "Rudy's Horse" in the Rudy Set.

I do hope it could work to have the language go really kerflooey in the chapter. Like I did visually in the Million Mile Road trip chapter where they whip past dozens of planets, but be doing that with words. A tour de force. And if it bores you , dear reader, then please just frikkin' skim it. And it should still sound a bit like Mason's voice. Steampunk surrealist writing that isn't mannered or corny. Interesting challenge.

***

I kept thinking about having the krakens be writhing ganzers—though really I think I'll still call them krakens anyway, as it's a easier word. I mean "ganzer" in the sense of something calculated by a GANs algorithm or, in a richer zone of the CG vein, having them look like details of the Rudy set.

Figure 28: Shrig and Three Krakens

And then on the afternoon of December 27, 2017, I went and put three of these guys into my painting of the shrig.

I went back and revised the krakens by the maelstrom to have more a fractal look. And I made the *urbsteg* be a little more like Julia sets or sunspots than they currently are. And then I'll do the upcoming kraken, *woomo*, and urbsteg ambush scene in the new chapter,

I'd like to get on with it and write something new and not keep revising. Or, more likely, dither a bit longer, jumping back and forth in the existing text to fix it so I can make all the elements work, turning my attention to whichever end of the workbench appeals at any given moment. Mitering, dovetailing, blending. It's such a lot of work to be writing a novel. And I get tired of it. But then I take a few days off and I'm ready to go again.

January 3, 2018. How Long to Fall to the Core?

I need to straighten out how long it takes to fall to the Earth's core. I looked up "terminal velocity" on Wikipedia, and they pointed out that in freefall, your speed increases until the gravitational attractive force is balanced by the force of your drag against the air. Now the attractive force towards the center of the Hollow Earth is rather low.

Frankly I don't quite recall why there's a central attractive force at all—I just kind of put it into HE1 so it wouldn't get stagnant in there. I suppose it's caused by the presence of the central anomaly. Anyway, it's not a really strong force like you'd feel from Earth on the outside. Note however, that if you fall long enough in a vacuum, even a slight attractive force can jack your velocity up to an exceedingly high value. But, again, the central gravitational force is rather low inside the Hollow Earth, so a relatively modest drag force can stymie the pull, and limit you to a rather low terminal velocity.

A desideratum here is that I don't want these falls to take an extremely long time, as this stalls the action. I can live with 50 hours (roughly two days), but no more than that.

In HE1, they fell most of the way inside a flower blossom which was quite massive—contributing to a higher terminal velocity. But, on the other hand the blossom was, rather shaggy, what with the petals, so the drag was fairly high. In HE1, without thinking about it too much, I suggested that the fall would take about 30 hours, which indicates a terminal velocity of a 100 mph, which seems excessive—but, again that blossom was really, really heavy.

In HE2, I have Mason remark that the terminal velocity for a falling person might only be 30 mph, leading to a fall of a 100 hours, which is a physically reasonable, although it makes for an awkwardly long trip. Note here, that a person is fairly dense, and in Earth's atmosphere a falling person's terminal velocity is on the order of 120 mph—but, once again, he central pull inside the Hollow Earth is low, so the acceleration could plateau at some modest level in the face even a low amount of drag.

When they actually *do* fall to the center in HE2, they're riding inside the saucer-like "fried egg." Suppose this craft can (thanks, perhaps, to some steering-rays from the *woomo* on board) be coaxed into falling sideways—rather than wildly tumbling or, worse, skimming back and forth like a falling feather. In this case its drag might be quite low, and it could reach, let us say, a speed of 60 mph. And in this case we'd have a fall time of 50 hours.

So let's stick with the fall time of 30 hours in HE1, but mention the fact that the blossom is heavy.

And in HE2, we'll go with a fall time of 50 hours, and mention that the fried egg is light, but that it's drag is low because it's falling edge-on.

Okay, fine. I went and worked all of these corrections into HE1 and HE2.

January 1-5, 2018. Groping for More Plot.

Still waiting for the Muse to drop off the script for the chapter about the fall from the Rind to the core…and the chapters after that.

By way of inveigling Her, I'm working on an outline, off and on. I'm numbering my upcoming "Fall to the Core" chapter as #10, and I've set a total of nineteen chaps for my goal.

Another thing on the burner has been to send a proposal for HE2 and the reissue of HE1 to Cory Allyn at Night Shade. If he turns me down, maybe I try Liz Gorinsky at Tor…I've always had a feeling she might buy one of my books, although I could be completely wrong. She's sort of semi-friendly when I see her. I think she's shy. I'm so deaf I can never really hear her voice. Possibly she thinks I'm a horrible old sexist pig. We'll see…

Anyway, with Dave Hartwell dead, I'd like my agent to try *someone* besides Night Shade so I have a backup. Or of course there's still the Kickstarter/CreateSpace route. But in any case I'll send it to John Silbersack first.
***

I had an idea for a Hollow Sun Ending, but I woke up on Jan 1, and I'm like, "Happy new year!" and I'm happy, and then I think about that ending, and I'm all, "What a mess." So I'm reworking the ending.

We don't need to go to the Hollow Sun at all. Forget that. It would be a desperado move. And I can drop my passing fancy of having sun-tunnel wormholes inside those *urbsteg* giant paramecia. We've already got the Anomaly as a type of wormhole, and it would clutter the conceptual apparatus to have another kind of wormhole. But for spice, I *will* still say the krakens come from the "Sun." But I won't use the phrase, "Hollow Sun," that is, I won't use it unless I need something extra at the book's end.

***

For the action at the core, I'll have a some of them flying straight back to the Rind, some of them falling into the Anomaly and passing through, and some falling in the Anomaly, staying too long, can coming back on the same side, and it's the year 2050.

As I've mentioned, as a sidelight I might as well work that routine about climate change opening our North and South poles to the Hollow Earth. It's high concept—a weighty plot idea that fits into one sentence. And a fun twist on climate change SF—which is usually kind of dystopian, minatory, and banal.

I forget, how was I going to get Mason's 2050 HE2 manuscript to editor Rudy Rucker in 2017? Oh, right, a pink *woomo* ray magically delivered the manuscript to me. Or maybe it was that extra kraken delivered it. How could I have forgotten that?

Quoth Dr. Rucker: "And what a great day it was when my completed manuscript arrived without me having to write a word of it!" Never forget that Ph.D. means "Piled High and Deep."

And see my May 1, 2017 entry for my first inspirations about the 2050 option.

Anyway, the rest of this entry will hold some ideas about the rest of the book. I can't see all the way to the end of the book—in fact I'm still a few chapters short— but I can see a few chapters in.

***

10. Fall to the Core

Mason has hopes of making love to MirrorSeela, but in the intensity of the *woomo* tekelili, it becomes clear this is never going to happen. But they have so much tekelili that their affectionate mutual vibe is a little like sex anyway. And, even better, MirrorSeela milks some sperm out of Mason, with his help, that is, she starts a handjob that he finishes, and MirrorSeela captures a gobbet from the air and presses it deep into her furrow. Hot!

I love this scene, and I even think it's kinkily funny, but I'm also worried that I might seem like a slobbering horn-dog old lech for writing it. And possibly this impression is enhanced by my multiple mentions of Seela nursing Brumble.

"But younger guys like Cory Doctorow are putting more and more sex scenes into books like *Walkaway*," I protest. And then a voice says, "Sorry, Rudy, you're old, and the rules are different for you, and anyway, Anyway, Corey wrote about tender twens having het and gay sex (although with one wise older woman mixed in). And he didn't mention conception and nursing mothers."

I'll leave my scene in for now, and see if it still works on the next full re-read. Meanwhile I *will* continue trying to hold myself back.

***

On the way to the core, they encounter the stray young kraken whom Fafnir left behind. He's about twenty feet long, and he does something with Hella, the baby *woomo*. Call him Skolber. He's needling her with his red rays. The *woomo* reacts, but then it seems like the *woomo* and kraken are friends. They fly off together.

Mason and the Seelas make it to the Umpteen seas and are together with everyone.

***

11. Repairs

Eddie's still at the Umpteen Seas, he's having second thoughts about going back through the Anomaly. Turns out the black gods can go back and forth through the Anomaly with no time lag. So Jewel and even Otha might be there. MirrorSeela reveals that she's pregnant by Mason. She'll give birth to baby Bramble at the Umpteen Seas. She doesn't want to go back to her flower. She wants to stay in the Umpteen Seas with Otha. And Machree is finding some rumbies with Jewel's help.

Meanwhile Ina is in tight with Eddie, and she has a knack for turning his stories into mental movies. She's also good with her hands. Eddie, Ina, Mason, and Seela get into repairing the fried egg. The baby *woomo* and the kraken are gilding them.

***

12. Two Centuries

Once the fried egg is working, Eddie, Ina, and Machree fly back to "our" MirrorEarth's surface—they fly to the North Hole and make their way up through the column of water, with an eye to flying to San Francisco. They carry a buttload of rumbies with them. Eddie and Ina plan to do performances of Eddie's work.

Mason had meant to go on the fried egg with the others, but the *woomo* interfere and they miss the flight. Otha, MirroSeela, Mason and Seela go into the Anomaly. Otha and MirrorSeela fall through the Anomaly to old Earth, but Mason doesn't want to go through.

Mason, Seela, and Brumble get hung up inside the Anomaly and then bounce back to the inside of MirrorEarth again.

***

13. Through the Rind.

It's two centuries later! The *woomo* wanted this to happen. Mason and Seela want to return to the surface of MirrorEarth. They see strange air ships in the maelstrom. It's the future, and there's brisk trade. They get a ride. Mason finds Eddie's two-hundred-years-old journals stashed especially for him.

***

14. & 15. Eddie's Journals.

Back on Earth in the 1850s and 1860s, Eddie couldn't believably publish under his own name, but he set Ina to reciting his stories and poems while saying she's channeling his spirit. And his Order of the Golden Frond surreptitiously spread over the centuries. Fueled by Machree's sales of his many rumbies.

***

16-19. Future SF.

Back to Mason. In 2050 Earth, lots of *woomo* have hatched from the rumbies that Eddie and Machree and the secret Order of the Golden Frond imported. There's full-on trade between inside and outside. Global warming is rampant. Something about the krakens too.

Mason writes HE2. There is some historical record that the book appeared in 2019, but Mason can't find a copy. The book was pulped and all of the ebooks were erased. But one of the *woomo* takes Mason's manuscript and gives it to me. Or perhaps a kraken did this? Burying it the past, as the prophetic fantasies of an eccentric SF writer.

January 6, 2018. Action at Core. Woomo Motives?

I'm back to dreading the thought of having too many characters onstage at once—and this will happen when Mason and the Seelas reach the core. Maybe I can handle the big cast with a party scene. Then have Eddie and the gang plus Mason and his crew *all* go inside the Anomaly at once. Maybe the *woomo* were setting this up all along, for whatever mysterious alien holothurian reasons (to be disclosed in the final chapter (I hope))!

Before the Anomaly scenes, we have action at the Umpteen Seas. The cast: Mason, Seela, Brumble, Arf, Eddie, Ina, Machree, and such black gods as Jewel, Watcher, Lightrider and maybe even Otha. Some scenes with lots of people coming and going. Like a Shakespeare play.

$$***$$

As I mentioned in passing in the previous entry, it's a hassle to suppose that all of the black gods have Mirror versions. What if, for them, it's possible to ride a board with a certain spin that let's them *whip* through the Anomaly very rapidly and skillfully—without losing, say, twelve years or, say, two centuries? What if they do that all the time? In that case I'd need to put some brief and cryptic foreshadowings of this into HE1. But I wouldn't have to do a lot of that, as Mason, Seela, and Eddie passed through the Anomaly in a smooth fashion without any pause to check out the black gods population on the Mirror-Hollow-Earth side.

Like, when some ordinary folks and some black gods go through the Anomaly together, it's like the ordinary folks took some really time-consuming detour en route and show up on the other side hella later. The black gods took the freeway, and the regular folks took back roads.

Maybe the black gods are the pilots of the *woomo*. The master race. The original attendants of the *woomo*. And we whiteys are, as Elijah Muhammad used to say, degenerate descendants. I'm okay with that!

***

I have to find a coherent motivation for the actions by the *woomo*. *Any* reason will do, really, but I need *something*. Ideally it's a dovetailed, interlocking, mainspring-type, *aha* gimmick. They seem to have caused these actions.

- Sent the *ballula* Cytherea to be Eddie's helper.
- Aided Eddie in his sessions of the Order of the Golden Frond
- Nudged Eddie to send Cytherea in time to rescue Mason and Seela from the sinking ship.
- Used a tractor beam of pink light to rescue Machree from the sinking ship.
- Instructed Tallulah to tow the fried egg to MirrorSeela's flower.
- Gave MirrorSeela a rumby that hatched into a baby *woomo* inside the fried egg.
-

Possibly the *woomo* caused me to stumble upon the manuscript of HE1. And possibly they gave me the copy of HE2. Or maybe the krakens gave it to me. It would help if there was some kind of rivalry between the *woomo* and the krakens? Not clear what that would be.

Let's go back to something simple. The *woomo* like to have both poles open in both Earths. Therefore (1) They covertly guided Mason's party to Earth's South Hole— where they could deliver the essential karate-chop straw-on-the-camel's-back force to break the ice-plug open. And therefore (2) They're promoting climate change as global warming will melt the ice in the MirrorEarth's South Hole, and will restore the maelstrom to the MirrorEarth's North Hole.

So go ahead and make a plot point of the *woomo* wanting global warming. They've been in here for millions of years, right? And the North and South Holes are their preferred viewports—although, *faut de mieux*, they can and do send their pink streamers out through the ocean holes.

Sometimes the north and south holes get plugged, sometimes they're open. Like, sometimes the windshield is frosted over, and sometimes it isn't. The *woomo* do what they can to defrost the blockages. And now they're in defrost mode.

Problem: I don't as yet see a direct way in which global warming is caused by, *um*, Mason's travels, by the importation of rumbies, by the activities of the Order of the Golden Frond, or by Rudy Rucker's largely ignored publications of Mason's veridical HE1 and HE2 narratives.

Well, just to make it butt-simple I could say that the rumbies generate warming rays. Or, what they fuck, they generate *ozone*, okay? So getting a lot of rumbies up onto Earth's surface helps promote global warming!

But, *um*, lately I've been that rumbies are *woomo* eggs. So will there start being lots of *woomo* on the Earth's surface? Hell, why not. Nice SF monster movie here. "The Attack of the Giant Sea Cucumbers."

And then Mason's got something to fight against! "And you readers are an elite cadre of shock troops readied by your readings of my editions of Mason's narratives—readied to stand firm when the *woomo* hatch and fill our world!"

January 7 & 17, 2018. Space Blister. Mirror. Internal Wind.

Jan 7, 2018.

So I have Earth and MirrorEarth, and they're connected via an Einstein-Rosen bridge that runs tween their Hollow centers. And I was thinking I don't like doubling up the whole universe. And it occurred to me that, rather than having two separate universes, that is, a regular one and a Mirror one, we could have mostly just one universe, but have is a blister or bubble or delamination of space just within the vicinity of our Earth.

So regular space splits in two for maybe only a thousand miles out from Earth's surface. So we *don't* need two Suns. Just one Sun, and its light is shared between the two hyper sheets at the "Riemann surface" border around Earth. Earth is, in a sense, a certain kind of alien spacecraft. There are, of course some other doubled-up pseudoplanets like ours. But around here, it's just us.

Localized doubling is a cool idea, but I think it might make the book even more confusing for the casual reader.
***

Note, by the way, that there doesn't seem to be any special reason why the Earth and MirrorEarth need to stay in synch after they've been split. Back in October, I entertained the idea that "balance" was a big issue for the *woomo*. But now I don't think it matters. And I went through HE1 and especially HE2 to undermine any claim that balance is in sway. It was broken for good when Mason shot the stableboy on Earth and the stableboy shot Mason on MirrorEarth.
***

In a general SF sense, the notion of a "localized alternate universe blister" is a great gimmick. I could write several kinds of stories using it. Like a "cursed house" which is double, and when you go into it, you never know which version you'll end up in. And something's hiding in one part of it. Like those dreams you have about an extra room in your house that you never normally see.

And it's better if the MirrorHouse is indeed a mirror image of the real house. And inside the house is a spooky corridor, or tunnel, or fireman's pole which runs from House to MirrorHouse. And when you pass into the MirrorHouse you become a mirror image of yourself. And if you were to exit the front door of the MirrorHouse and go out into your home town where you started, people would think you looked wrong and crooked because you were a mirror image of your old self, but they might not explicitly realize this, they'd just think you looked wrong. "The Crooked House" (good title, although it overlaps with Heinlein's folding-up 4D house story).

In a different story, a person could double up, and have two selves on top of each other. And you might see one or the other of her/him.

Science question. If I'm standing near a doubled zone E/E* and I look at it, do I see E or do I see E*? I have an image of a railway switch, the "points," and it can be open either way. So at any given time I'm seeing either E or E*, and the other one is lurking, but at any time the switch can be thrown, and then I'm seeing E* or E instead.

You might double yourself for IQ increase. We can assume that you'll have a corpus-callosum-type ER-bridge connection between your E brain and your E* brain.

***

Jan 17, 2018.

I'm a little uncertain now about "mirror" aspect of MirrorEarth. If I have my Earths on two sheets of Flatland, and I put an ER wormhole in the middle connecting the sheets, and A Square slides in along the bottom sheet, he goes up the throat and ends up on the upper sheet, and in the process he's been flipped over, and turned into his mirror image.

So that means the Earth on that upper side had better be a mirror image of the Earth on the bottom, or it won't look right to A Square.

So that means it wouldn't work to just "delaminate and copy" a piece of space around Earth to get an Earth on top and one below. Like peeling apart two sheets of onionskin or of mica. The top Earth really *does* need to be a mirror image if the ER bridge transitions are going to work. Looked at in another way the Earth's are printed on the opposite (virtual) sides of the 2D "space paper".

***

Even so, I could still have that blister that I wanted. But if one is Space and the other is MirrorSpace the entering of photons (or physical objects) along the outer boundary is a bit more confusing. Of course if I see the light as *waves*, it's a bit easier to visualize the "photons" splitting. Not sure about a meteorite.

Should I back off and that blister stuff that I just now put into Mason's HE1 vision at the Anomaly around January 10, 2018? But I *do* like the idea of Earth being one of the few "doubled" heavenly bodies because it's a *woomo* starship. It provides a kind of "explanation" for our local duality.

***

There's another point to discuss. It comes up whether we do the blister or the two parallel space sheets.

The MirrorEarth is rotating in the opposite direction as the Earth—given that MirrorEarth is indeed a mirror image of Earth. A mirrorclock's hands move counterclockwise. I always wanted that, as it makes me think of generating "electrical fluid" at the center, like in a Wimshurst Machine with its two counter-orating disks of amber or whatever. But if the two Earths are spinning in opposite directions, and the *woomo* are right on the throat between the two worlds, aren't they tugged in two different directions? Would that bother them? Well, it is just *air* being rotated there, and not the very fabric of space, so maybe it's not that big of a deal. This said we ought to expect a bit of turbulence and wind,

***

Let's pause and ponder the weather patterns or global airflows inside a rotating Hollow Earth. Near the inside of the Rind, the air is moving along with the Rind at pretty fast clip, close to a thousand miles per hour at the equator. And along the North/South axis of the Hollow Earth, the air wouldn't be moving much at all. Kind of like the eye of a hurricane.

And the Hollow MirrorEarth is the same, but with, of course the rotation in the opposite direction. But right at the axis there's not much air current on either side.

***

How will it look to Mason when he's the Gate? I think I wrote it as if the Umpteen Seas are circling around in different directions on the two sides. Should be moving pretty slowly. If they want to stay in synch with the Earth's surface, they'd only need to rotate around the axis once a day, and that's not a big distance when you're that close to the axis, so it world be quite a leisurely rotation.

Related question, when Mason looks at the *woomo* at the spherical surface of the Gate, how should the *woomo* be moving? So far, I've said that say the *woomo* have their bodies half on one side and half on the other, and that they're slowly rolling, like roasts on spits, with one side always moving into the Earth zone and the opposite side always moving into the MirrorEarth zone.

I don't think I've yet discussed the question of whether the *woomo* are rotating around the Earth/MirrorEarth axis running from South to North pole.

The *woomo* who are *at* the "North and South poles" of the spherical gate (which is, once again, the throat of the 4D

E-R bridge that is the Central Anomaly)—those guys won't be feeling a need to rotate at all. But the ones at the "equator" of the Gate would probably be rotating around the axis at a modest speed, akin to the Umpteen Seas.

So that all seems under control.

***

Switching to different, but related, topic, I don't know that I've recently thought about the centrifugal force felt against the Rim. I think it would be quite small. A quick Google search yields this. It's what my mathematician friend Vlad from Siberia used to call a "little-known but useless fact." We *do* feel a slight centrifugal force from Earth's spinning, and it's about a quarter pound per hundred pounds (varying with latitude). You think you weigh 150, but might really weigh about 150.3, with the centrifugal force canceling a bit of the weight.

So on the inside of the Rind, you would feel, due to centrifugal force, an outward pressure of maybe half a pound. Perhaps I should mention this in HE1.

January 8, 2018. Eddie's Journal. Woomo-Kraken Plan.

On my last attempt at an outline, it looked like I was four or five chapters short of a novel. Idea for more material: Insert one or two chapters from the viewpoint of Eddie Poe. And this way we'd get a nice account of what happens to him when he and Ina go back to (our) MirrorEarth before Mason. I'd been thinking of having Mason discover this info anyway. And if it's in journal form, so much the better.

It would be big fun to write in Eddie's voice. Fun for the readers too. Making HE2 yet more ramshackle and neck-deep in bogosity.

Paul Di Filippo and I found a great line in a letter that Karl Gauss wrote to the mathematician Bessel, about why Gauss hadn't published the non-Euclidean geometry results that the younger Janos Bolyai had later discovered. "It may take very long before I make public my investigations on this issue: in fact, this may not happen in my lifetime for I fear the "clamor of the Boeotians."

[From Wikipedia entry on Boeotians: "The Boeotian

people, although they included great men
like Pindar, Hesiod, Epaminondas, Pelopidas and Plutarch,
were portrayed as proverbially dull by the Atheni-
ans…Boeotia came to be proverbial for the stupidity of its
inhabitants."]

I might have Eddie's journals be set in 1862…he could
lose ten or twelve years, either in the Anomaly, or just goof-
ing around in CA slowly trying to get rich quick. What I
like about 1862 is that, as I noted earlier, in 1863 Lizzie
Doten (= Ina) was on tour performing pieces by Eddie that
she "channeled." Would be richly funny to see Eddie (posing
as Goarland E. Peale) writing about this tour.

Also Eddie would be building up the Order of the Gold-
en Frond all along, using Machree's big supply of rumbies.

I even thought of hopping Eddie up to 1950, but I'll already be doing the full-on "lost in time" routine with Mason
in 2050, and it would pall if I did the same thing with Eddie
as well.

If Eddie's going to fly back to Earth in the repaired fried
egg UFO why would he even have gone into the Anomaly at
all? Well, maybe they had to dip into the Anomaly to "tank
up" the aethereal energies of the fried egg's "engine room,"
or, as Mason and Eddie persists in thinking, the necessary
"lifting salts."
            ***
Still puzzling over the relations between the *woomo* and
the krakens. For the *woomo*, Earth is an interstellar spacecraft, like a generation starship, making its way to the other
side of the galaxy in the vasty rotation of this cosmic whirlpool.

Earth needs a fuel source, and this is the Sun. But for
the Sun to work with a Hollow planet, it takes some tweak-
ing. Like a "fireman" or stoker on a train. The krakens are
the stokers. They help keep the Sun in trim for the long haul.
It's important, for instance, that the Sun doesn't go nova. In
return the *woomo* "remember" krakens and keep restoring
them to life. The *woomo* are immortal in the sense that
they'll live as long as the universe—although we don't know
if that's an infinite time, or just a lot of time.

Martin Gardner talked to me a couple of times about this

classic SF moment in the bible. The penitent thief on cross:
"Jesus, remember me when you come into your kingdom."
Jesus: "Amen I say to you today you will be with me in Paradise."

This gospel of Luke frag can be viewed as a metaphor
for very long-term cloud-like storage of your software and
wetware. Remember me! If you're fully remembered, reconstituting you is just a technicality.

So what I'm getting at is that a human or a kraken might
do something for the all but immortal "Great Old Ones," or
woomo. in the hope they will *remember* you. This hope is a
perennial motive for mortals to help immortals.

Lighter-weight version is where a writer is a type of immortal: "Will you make me a character in your novel?" Writer: "Amen, I say to you today (or maybe in a few years) you
will be with me in Paradise (or in a text on the internet)."

Martin Gardner also related this to the fraught notion of
"soul sleeping" or "Christian Mortalism" whereby your soul
might be "on ice" until the last trumpet, when God brings the
elect to life.

    ***

Were the krakens really *fighting* with the *woomo* in that
scene where the kraken eggs hatch by the North Hole? Let's
say it just *looked* that way. After all, it didn't hurt the krakens to get beamed by the *woomo*, in fact it helped make
their eggs hatch. And the krakens were doing the *woomo* a
favor keeping the maelstrom open as long as they did. But
now they want to go back to the Sun.

Maybe the kraken who stayed behind will eventually
whip the maelstrom back open. But, wait, that's something
the *female* krakens do. This male kraken Skolder will need to
find a wife, and that could be a plot element.

By the way, I'm not sure I like the name Hella for the
baby *woomo*. Nyoo might be nicer. I'm thinking of the way
Sylvia and I used to refer to baby Georgia as *ñoo* or *nyoo*.
We also liked to say *nyoo-nyoo* to each other. It originally
meant "aren't you/we cute," but then the word segued into
an adjective meaning, "goodie-goodie." There was even a
married couple our age (about 24) in our apartment building
whom we thought were uncool and dull, and we called them

Nyoo and Nyoo.

January 9-11, 2018. The Black Gods

Okay, so now they're at the core. I'll reread a chapter to two of HE1 to refresh my memory about the black gods. First of all, I need a list of their names. And I need to decide if they're active on both sides of the Anomaly—in the sense of freely and repeatedly moving from one side to the other.

- If they're active on both sides, I'd have to revise HE1 a bit, as I had them mostly avoiding the Anomaly. One upside is that I could have Otha again.
- If they're not active on both sides, then I've got Mirror black gods on this side, perhaps with similar names and personalities. I don't think I'd bother using the prefix "Mirror" before all their names, as that's tedious. I *could* just suppose that Otha came through the Anomaly on his own and maybe lost a year or twelve himself.

Seems like Otha would have a wife, or why would he want to hook up with MirrorSeela, if indeed that's in the cards. But possibly he lost his wife over on the other side, and came over to the Mirror side looking for her, but maybe she wasn't on this side either? Could this woman be Jewel? Or Shrighunter?

What if Otha was in love with Shrighunter, and she died in a shrig explosion. So he came through the Anomaly to find the Shrighunter on this side! So then he's not the one to go for MirrorSeela. So who would she pick? It could be a new black god character, or it could be Smoker, who might be about her age. Looking back, I find that Smoker had been hot for Seela before.

The timeline is a bit tricky. Suppose that Otha also lost twelve years inside the Anomaly. In that case, he could have made the hop only a month or two after Mason, and then he's been over on the MirrorEarth side for about a year, and his age is still about the same as Mason's. But the black gods native to the MirrorEarth are all twelve years older than the ones that Mason and Otha knew on the other side.

***

   I reread chapters 12 and 13 of the Monkeybrains edition of HE1. Some notes on things to use in the upcoming chapter. Page refs are to the Monkeybrain edition. Some of the notes include "To Do" items involving changes to HE1 and/or HE2. I placed the To Do items in **bold**. I asterisk each entry where I've either fixed a To Do or where I've worked a fact from HE1 into HE2.

- They have blue hummingbirds with red necks, and pterodactyls.
- The island has long grasses on it, and there are little sea cucumbers in the grass. These are, I need to make clear are, cousins of the Great Old One *woomo*, and are **not juvenile forms**. The black gods eat these small sea cukes. And **don't use the word *woomo* for the little ones**, just for the big ones. Both are Holothurians, *but*. Like the difference between a mouse and a human—both are mammals, *but*.
- They eat shrig meat, fish, sea cucumber, and grain from the grasses.
- To talk to the *woomo*, it helps to jiggle a lightstream and get their attention.
- * The black gods' names are: (Male) Lightrider, Smoker, Offerer, Watcher; and, (Female) Jewel, Shrighunter, Tigra, Bunny. Since they don't speak out loud, the "name" is more like a mental icon. I'd had Eddie: Writer, Mason: Killer-Thief, Seela: Trader, Otha: Lover. But I won't use that.
- * The Umpteen Seas are up to fifteen miles long. One is like a foot with a really big island as the heel.
- * The seas remind Mason of when he'd throw buckets of water in the air and watch the water.
- * Watcher says he's three thousand years old because he's logged so much time inside the Anomaly.
- * There are a lot of shrigs around the outer zone of the core. The core is like a gutter or a trough, which is "downhill" from the Rind and from the Anomaly.
- * Tekelili brings a deep sense of joy. Mason sees into Arf's mind. Seela is surprised to learn how unintelligent

Arf is. Since they use teep, their lips often don't move while they're talking. In HE1, they supposedly use "Tekelili" as a name for the giant *woomo*, but I will **drop this** from HE1 as I don't want to do it in HE2.

- * They ride the lightstreams on ballula shells called lightboards. What they're riding is the wake of heated air around the lightstream.
- * On p. 154 I speak of global doubling, with MirrorMoon and MirrorStars, etc. I'm going to drop the stuff outside of Earth, and say there's **only local doubling**, which makes the pair of Hollow Earths more like a compact spaceship for the *woomo*. I put this into HE1.
- * The warty bumps on the *woomo* are cupped at the top, like suction cups. The lightstreams emanate form these cups rather than from the branching feelers, which are primarily for feeding. **Change it so the beams come from the tendrils**.
- * In HE1 I said that the two worlds are in such lock-step synch that if a black god passes through the Anomaly, his/her Mirror counterpart will inevitably be passing through the other way at the same time. I need to stress in HE2 that the **lock-step synch has been diminishing** ever since Mason's first trip, when he and Eddie, Seela, Mason and then Otha went through.
- * Mention that black gods tend to have very long lifespans, due to the beneficial effects of tekelili. Indeed **they typically live three hundred years**.
- * *And here's a bit about Smoker, whom I plan to match up with MirrorSeela.* "'Here,' called a black god who lounged near us. **I'd already noticed his intense interest in Seela**. His icon image showed him riding a light tube and dipping a rack full of dead creatures' flesh into the heat. Smoker. He had a woven basket filled with dried meat, some of it shrig and some of it from these little trepangs.*"

Okay, I'm working all this in, and then I need a nice long, chatty scene of the increasingly large dramatis personae talking together. I need byplay, and not just exposition. I think there's sixteen of them if you count the dog, the baby, and the three aliens.

Figure 29: Dramatis Personae at the Umpteen Seas

Thirteen mammals: Mason & Seela & Brumble & Arf, MirroSeela & Smoker, Otha & Lightrider, Eddie & Ina, Machree, Jewel, and Watcher. And three aliens, not shown in this drawing: Nyoo, Skolder, and Fwopsy the "fried egg."

January 14-17, 2018. Saucer Alive. Rumbies. Futures.

What about the plan I just broached in the novel about having Eddie and Machree haul a whole saucer-load of rumbies (= *woomo* eggs) to Earth's surface and having them all hatch?

Well, if the *woomo* stay on Earth's surface, that pretty much ruins the book. First of all, the *woomo* would probably trash Earth. Second of all, as we have no memory of this having happened in our actual past, we're losing the ability to claim that Mason's narratives are really true. Killing the hoax.

So if the *woomo* do hatch out on Earth's surface, I'd have to suggest that they then all flew away. It would be a dramatic scene, and Eddie could describe it in his journal.

***

Extra fillip for the scene on the island: Nyoo the little *woomo* shows up and chats with them. She can help with fixing the saucer.

***

They repair the "fried egg" airship and restored it to

working order. Maybe Machree and Eddie and Ina start the work on it—Ina's clever with machinery. But then in the end it's *woomo* who really fix it. Nyoo in particular. She knows the design from her tekelili teep with the other *woomo*. They use direct matter control, and they have their eidetic memories of the original ship to work from.

Better: the fried egg isn't a machine, and it doesn't need a mechanical repair. It's a living organism, symbiotic with *woomo*. And Nyoo the *woomo* can heal it. This is like one of those fantastically complex jellyfish lifecycle diagrams, with freefloating proto-larvae that park somewhere, become sessile, and then bud off *real* baby jellyfish.

Machree loads the fried egg with rumbies, and take it partway into the Anomaly like taking a car into the repair garage. Not only are the fixing it, they're in some sense recharging its fuel—it runs on condensed liquid tekelili. We have Eddie, Ina, Machree, Mason, Seela, and Arf aboard.

But then the ship is going towards the old Earth side, and Eddie, Ina, and Machree want to go to the familiar (to Machree) MirrorEarth side. Machree shoves Mason, Seela, Arf and Brumble out the door to cause a boost in the opposite direction.

***

So then Eddie, Ina, and Machree shoot out and fly up through that column of water filling the North Hole, and they return to San Francisco in whatever year seems to work best for the plot.

(Option 1862) I could ask for twelve years later, that is in 1862, which fits with the fact that in 1863, Lizzie Doten was did a "channeling Poe" presentation in Baltimore.

(Option 1897) I could ask for forty-six hears later, and say Eddie provoked the "mystery airships" accounts of 1896-1897, starting in San Francisco and the West.

***

Maybe the fried egg just drops off Eddie and the others, and then flies back into the Hollow Earth.

Or Eddie, Machree and Ina get to keep this working spacecraft, and they up a secret plant to manufacture more of them. No. Better: the fried egg reproduces itself, like I had the saucers doing in my tale, "Easy As Pie." Laying barnacle-like seeds on the walls of caves.

I could claim that most of the UFO reports since 1896 have involved the descendants of Eddie's craft. Or, better, I could say the saucers flew off with some humans and a pair of *woomo* in each one. Like flying seeds from a milkweed.

Wild hair: Eddie may have been involved with the (possibly mythical) group, the Sonoma Aero Club, which I learned of from a UFO-nut comment on my "mystery airship" post on FB. One more reference in this vein: there's an outsider artist called Charles Dellschau who obsessively documented the "Sonoma Aero Club. Not sure how far I'd want to go with this…it's probably too far off the track for the integrity of the novel. Like piling Pelion on Ossa and, while you're at it, Ossa on Pelion.

***

Getting back to Mason, Arf, and Seela—they're stuck inside the Anomaly for two centuries, and when they emerge into the core of the Hollow MirrorEarth, it's 2050. He finds a tour-bus or shipping-truck *woomo* saucer there to pick them up. Or, simpler, in might just be the refurbished fried egg that transported Eddie. The living saucer.

Possible meta angle: The people of 2050 are well versed in Mason's narratives HE1 and HE2. They are eager to see him, and to report on him, and he doesn't like this, so he eludes them on MirrorEarth and lies low. He needs to actually write HE2, and he doesn't want anyone to bother him till he's done. So he needs to be circumspect, in the final chapter, about where he actually is while he's writing. Because he knows the futurians will see whatever he writes due to the odd circular causation here. He doesn't, however, read the HE2 that they have, as he prefers to imagine it for himself. I mentioned this angle before: it's the approach used in the Jorge Luis Borges story, "Pierre Menard, Author of the Quixote."

Another question I've raised before: How did I, the editor, get my hands on HE2? Maybe when Mason finishes HE2, a *woomo* tendril appears, and takes his manuscript and hands it to Professor Rucker (me) in 2018. Or, perhaps less paradoxically, the *woomo* send the manuscript to me as an email file. In that case, we'd be using a William-Gibson-style time-travel to the past—where the *woomo* can send back information but not actual matter.

Can the *woomo* "send" Mason back as well? Sure. Since they "remember" him, they could, for instance, reinstantiate him and his little family back to San Francisco on the day after Brumble was born. And we might suppose that then Mason and Seela had a peaceful life there together. This, again, can be viewed as a pure info transfer. In other words they'd "send him back via email."

What becomes of the 2050 Mason and his family? The most dramatic option is that they're destroyed by krakens or the futurians in the final scene. Or the very act of fully "remembering" them destroys them. A destructive process of "measurement," akin to what the moon robots did to Cobb Anderson in *Software*. Or both: they're dying or dead—eradicated by the futurians—and *then* the *woomo* scan them and jump them back.

So Mason's transmission to 1850 might be viewed either as a just-in-time backdoor escape or as a posthumous second life. Like, the futurians in fact kill Mason and destroy his HE2 manuscript, but the *woomo* already have Mason and the book memorized, so they reinstantiate him *plus* HE2.

Mason goes on and has a peaceful life. He puts the finishing touches on HE2 in San Francisco, works as a reporter, raises a family. He leaves instructions that the HE2 manuscript be brought to Professor Rucker of Los Gatos in the summer of 2018. He especially doesn't want Eddie Poe to get his hands on it. And in the Editor's Note I report getting it.

By the way, we might suppose that by the time Poe shows up in 1896, Mason is dead at age 75. On the other hand, we could have Poe come back earlier, and have Poe and Mason working together on airships for awhile, until Eddie dies of drink—his foreordained doom in any world.

Many options. I need to go a step at a time, and see what path is the most human and engaging.

January 18, 2018. Silbersack Likes it. New Ending. Proposal

So my agent John Silbersack read my proposal and the

first half of HE2, and he likes it. He says it's rollicking fun. He hadn't been sure it would live up to HE1, but he says it does, and that he's eager to see what happens. ("So am I," I quipped.) He says it might be hard for someone to pick up HE2 without having recently read HE1; I agreed, but as I'll be submitting the new version of HE1 as well, this shouldn't be a real problem. The publisher might even do them in one volume, although he thinks that might be kind of a high word count for one vol.

He feels we should stick with Night Shade for HE1/HE2, as they're doing a good job. Also it would be hard to convince a new publisher to pick up an old book with a new book—but that's what Night Shade's been doing. Since I'm in touch with Cory Ally anyway, I'll submit it myself, and copy to John, and then he'll approach them. Their advance will probably be low, so I can go for the option to do a Kickstarter/Deluxe Limited Edition release to pick up some extra gelt—like we're doing with *Million Mile Road Trip* already.

He says I should come up with a big ending to wind up the second book. And I was inspired to expand upon a fresh ending that came to me earlier this morning while I was in the shower.

***

The big goal of the *woomo* has been to bloom, like a dandelion or milkweed sending out floating seeds. A *woomo* "seed module" is a fried egg flying saucer containing two *woomo* and a pair of humans, a man and a woman.

Machree's load of rumbies will hatch into *woomo* on Earth. And the fried egg that's been revivified by Nyoo will reproduce on Earth's surface, using that "Easy as Pie" story angle I mentioned earlier, where saucers lay spores on the walls of caves and the baby saucer grow like barnacles. It'll take them 168 years to mature. Eddie's gonna help lay the groundwork for that. And he leaves notes about it in a journal that Mason later finds.

As for Mason, he'll actually appear in California in 2018, and find his way to my house, and he's got Eddie's journal, and I'll house him and Seela and Arf while Mason writes HE2, and finds the *woomo* and the fried eggs that Eddie wrote about—I help Mason with this, and we encounter some kind of enemy—and then Mason and Seela will leave in a fried egg with a pair of *woomo*. And I wave a fond goodbye. Arf stays with me. He's my dog now.

"And if you don't believe this story, you can come see the dog."

More details in today's new version of the plot in my Book Proposal.

***

This would be a clean ending, and I could drop such baroque complications as: (a) Setting some chapters in the year 2050, (b) Having everyone in 2050 knowing about HE2 before Mason wrote it, and (c) Doing an information-flow reverse time travel to move Mason back to 1850.

Kind of satisfying to have my character show up at my house and I help him leave on his final journey. And I like ending with a big saucer launch off a cliff in Big Sur, and I see it happen. It's a bit like the ending of *Saucer Wisdom*.

Note that at present my new kraken creatures don't play a role in the ending. Nor does, really, the *woomo* skill to "remember" someone—although, yeah, they did remember the fried egg. And I'll need to decide what to do about the maelstrom. As I think I said before, it might be reasonable to mention in the Editor's Note that, with global warming, we'll soon see the South Hole ice melt away, and soon see the maelstrom of the North Hole begin again to spin.

January 19-30, 2018. Rejection.

Fuck. I sent Cory Allyn at Night Shade the proposal on the evening of Jan 18, 2019, and he wrote right back on the morning of the 19th, turning it down.

> "My hesitation is simply that we already have 10 releases scheduled from you, starting this fall, and, at least at this point in time, we don't have a great idea of how well they're going to do. I've never undertaken such a large number of releases from a single author at once before, and to be completely frank would feel uncomfortable adding to that number without having some concrete sales information

from the re-release of the first few books. Does this make sense to you? I don't like giving you a 'Well maybe, but ask me again at the end of the year' response, and I understand if you don't want to wait that long."

What he says is, I admit, reasonable, but it's discouraging. I'll finish HE2 in any case, I think I'll be done by October, 2018. And then I'll have three options.

- Send the completed HE2 to Night Shade around January, 2019. Don't know if they'll have enough sales figures on my books by then, or if the sales will be good. Usually my sales *aren't* good. Basically whenever a publisher buys one of my books, I feel like I'm tricking them. *Wheenk, wheenk, wheenk.*
- Send it to other publishers. Silbersack was discouraging about this prospect. He said that few publishers would want to republish an old book along with a new one, and I think it's kind of necessary to publish them as a pair. In my heart, I keep thinking we ought to be able to break this into the mainstream lit market—I'll have to ask John about this (with my voice breaking) once again.
- Do a Kickstarter/Self-pub edition of HE1/HE2 late in 2019. I'm doing an extra Kickstart/Self-pub deluxe edition of their *Million Mile Road Trip* when it appears around January, 2019— doing my edition with Night Shade's contractual approval. I can't do two Kickstarters too close together, so I'd probably want to let the self-pub of the *Hollow Earth* pair wait till late in the year, like around December, 2019. But if I just wait for Night Shade, that might be when *they're* doing HE1/HE2 anyway. And maybe I could get them to agree to do it that "soon," rather than first putting out every one of those ten other books.

It was nicer when I was self-pubbing and didn't have to deal with a slow pipeline!
Anyway, on Jan 22, 2018, I talked to John Silbersack. He said he'd convey to Cory Allyn my hope that, if Night

Shade *does* publish *Return to the Hollow Earth*, they could put it out in late 2019. And he said he'd try Liz Gorinsky at Tor Books—he agreed with my sense that she might be a reasonable editor to try.

***

I felt like John was taking to long to get in touch with Cory Allyn, so I went ahead and emailed him this myself on Jan 30, 2018.

> Thanks for your quick reply. I do understand your wanting to wait a bit, what with ten of my books already in your inventory. Let's hope they do well, and that we can indeed collaborate on my two Hollow Earth novels. The project seems like a good fit for your line in that it includes both a reprint and a new novel.
>
> In the meantime, John and I will look into other possibilities as well.
>
> One favor I would ask is that you consider provisionally holding open a slot for the Hollow Earth books in late 2019 or early 2020---so that there's not too long of a wait after I finish writing the new one in Fall 2018.

***

I talked to John Silbersack on Feb 14, 2018. He said Liz Gorinsky is leaving her job at Tor. Possibly she's been laid off, Tor is undergoing a round of belt-tightening. But John will ask a guy called Marco at Tor who might go for HE1&2. Marco used to work with Dave Hartwell, and probably knows me. John also said he'd suggested to Cory Allyn that they open a slot to fit the HEs in earlier than 2020, but that the conversations were fragmentary and inconclusive. John thought that if I did hope to sell the book to Night Shade I would want to hold back on a Kickstarter/self-pub edition until the Night Shade edition would be released.

We agreed that I might as well just hang loose until I actually finish the book.

January 22-23, 2018. Starting the Anomaly Chapter.

So I had them wake up the fried egg, and now they'll go into the Anomaly to feed the fried egg, and then zip back out through the Rind of MirrorEarth. I reread and lightly edited my HE1 version of the scene and I'm editing it down to get a framework for the new version.

I was just now wondering why the fried egg couldn't come rescue Mason in just a month, and why did it take over a century. Thing is, to venture so deep into the slow zone takes the fried egg that long. Watcher will be aboard.

***

Side question: Is your time *slow* inside the Central Anomaly, because you look sluggish if seen from the outside. Like suspended animation is the extreme where time goes beyond being slow—and *stops*. Or is your time *fast*, because you get to the future in only an hour instead of taking two centuries? You took a quick shortcut. Speaking of a "speed" of time is of course a bit of a pleonasm. Seconds per second? Well, it does make sense to talk about how many seconds of MY time per seconds of YOUR time. So if a second of my time is a hundred seconds of your time, my time speed is 0.01. On the other hand if I move through a hundred seconds of your time in my time, I could equally well say my time speed is 100. Language isn't built to talk about this. I could have Eddie discuss this, could be fun.

Relativity theory says your time is *dilated*, or *stretched*. So an hour of your time flops out to a century in length.

***

I'm having second thoughts about that "Remember me" rap from the Gospel according to Luke. I don't really need it for the action, and it's a distraction. I was groping for something the krakens want from the *woomo* and I more or less randomly hit on "being remembered." Let's drop that.

So what about the scene of Nyoo the *woomo* engulfing Skolder the kraken. If she's not remembering him, what's she doing? Fucking him? Exchanging electrical fluid? Checking her email?

So, sigh, tomorrow I rip all that stuff out.

I'm thrashing.
***

A broader picture. What if we say that all four species are collaborating: humans, *woomo*, krakens, and fried eggs. And all the lesser animals and creatures too, but those top four are a symbiotic quaternity. It takes Mason a while to figure this out.
***

Another change. I just had Nyoo, and Skolder, and Uxa blasting light onto Fwopsy to bring her back to life and re-furbish her. And I was saying it worked partly because thee *woomo* "remembered" Fwopsy. But if that's the case, then they could just go ahead and spit out a thousand copies of Fwopsy and do the "blooming" exodus right away.

So I need more of reason why they can do a regeneration of Fwopsy. Let's turn to our man Eddie Poe, and cash in on all that big-brow thinking he did about the hieroglyphs on Fwopsy's walls. She has, like a "how to revive me recipe" written on her body.

Let Eddie repair the fried egg, and drop that stuff about "remembering."
***

The Hollow Earth people would never fry an egg, as they don't have pans and gravity. So when Mason starts us-ing this phrase, he might need to explain it to them. They might want to call it something else. A "nonsense word" name in their native tongue. Soloo, kazmat, wheesky, veesky, fleesky *vheesky*. I want the suggestion of whisking through space. Wheesky. Maybe it's too much to change the *w* to a *v*. Kind of Hungarian accent there, doesn't quite match the style of the other native words such as ballula, shrig, koladull, rumby, tekelili. But wheesky is too close to whiskey. And vheesky makes me laugh, and I have a Tourette-style desire to say that word over and over and over—and that counts for something. Keeping me amused. Image of Soviet spacecraft. The old vodka/wodka thing. Or maybe the whole whiskey thing is too much. Too thirsty al-ky. How about something that suggests a humming sound? A *veem*. Like voom. I like that. Simple.
***

Might be nice if a giant eel jumped out of the sloshing Umpteen Sea and nearly ate Arf or the baby. Poor Brumble.

January 25-29, 2018. At the Core.

I had an awesome writing day on Jan 24, 2018. I scored 2,200 words. Usually I'm very happy if I get even a thousand words. I had Mason, Seela, Brumble, and Arf marooned on the back of Uxa in the Gate of the Central Anomaly, and 168 years went by, and now it's 2018. I might title the next chapter "Twenty Eighteen." Looks better in words than as a number, I think. Odd to see.

   ***

Why did it take Fwopsy the fried egg 168 years to come back? Seems like she could have darted back to Mason after a month or two on Earth. Well, maybe Mason and Seela had fallen down so deep into the Central Anomaly to land on Uxa that Fwopsy lost, like, 150 more years diving down to get them.

And/or we could say that Fwopsy spent quite a bit of time in that cave on Earth, laying her eggs on the cave walls. But let's have that wait a bit.

Before Fwopsy can go hatching babies, she needs a mate. Mason did, come to think of it, see another fried egg as he was falling through the Earth's South Hole. Let's say that's going to be Fwopsy's mate. Call him Duggie. A corruption of Dougie. They can meet up at the Gate when Fwopsy comes to get Mason. We can suppose that Uxa sent a signal to Duggie, who was lying low in the South Hole, kind of hibernating in the ice.

Here's a description of Duggie from HE1.

> "Glancing back at our shattering iceberg, I saw something extraordinary: A large flattened ball— approximately a hemisphere—had been frozen into the ice's core, and now the half-ball was tumbling back toward the clouds and cliffs. It was of a shiny substance a bit like metal, although it might have been gilded leather. It even crossed my mind that it might be an animal. It was hard to be sure, but perhaps it was making some motions on its own. It was

some thirty feet in diameter, and with a slanting
flange or ring projecting out along its base, giving it
a shape something like a fried egg. Before I could
point it out to Otha, the gleaming entity had van-
ished into the glowing haze behind us. Months later,
at the very center of the Hollow Earth, we would
find another one like it, but just now, not knowing
what to think of it, I put it out of my mind."

Where was Watcher during the 168 years? I'd like for
him to be down in the hole with Mason and Seela. Standing
on Uxa. Watcher likes it in there. And he's very good at using tekelili to see out. Two events he tells Mason about.

- MirrorSeela and Mason's sun Bramble lives in the Umpteen Seas with his descendents. And by the time Mason
  gets out, the son will be 168 years old, much older than
  Mason. I don't think I'll bring Bramble on camera, as it
  would be too big a distraction. I'll just have our gang
  speed out, possible dropping off Watcher on the way.
- Watcher can also report that Otha died just the year before Mason comes out. He was a great-great-great-
  grandfather. He'd lived to be a 186 years of age—a relatively short span for a black god, He was friends with
  Bramble.

Do I even want Mason to stop and say hi to the black
gods on the way out? We're kind of done with them. I'd
rather he just rocked on towards San Francisco.
  ***
Why didn't Uxa throw Mason and his gang out of the
Central Anomaly early? I can't go and say that it would be
physically damaging to get thrown out with no fried egg to
ride in—remember that the *woomo* carried Machree on a
light beam from the Rind to the core. Well, maybe Uxa
wanted Mason to wait till 2018 because it would take that
long to get everything ready for the bloom launch. They
were waiting for Fwopsy and Duggie to get together. The
two saucers meet right at the Gate.
  ***

What about all the rumbies that Fwopsy carried out to the Rind? I'd rather not have them hatching out right away. I think the hatching should wait until all the *veem* (that is, fried eggs) and krakens and humans are ready for the bloom event, which won't be till 2018.

So Fwopsy lets Poe and Machree put the rumbies into circulation. But we normal people reading HE2 in 2018, we haven't heard about rumbies because they're secret. They're being hoarded by members of the secret society, the Order of the Golden Frond. (Doing a Dan Brown "Da Vinci Code" thing here.)

January 29, 2018. Wolfram Story Idea.

This relates to a very interesting online essay that Stephen Wolfram wrote, "Showing Off to the Universe". I wrote him two responses over the last few days.

(1) Fascinating, Stephen. I'm only a quarter through reading it…will have more thoughts later. This very much a set of problems I've thought about and, as you know, I feel that NKS really cuts to the heart of many of the issues. If you just pay close attention, water in a little brook is as rich as any human work of art. And maybe we can learn to be okay with that. But, yes, what to put on the quartz disk! Looking forward to reading the rest of your essay.

(2) I read the rest of your piece and thought about it some more. I thought it was good that you made the point that there could very well be intelligent messages coming in via the radio hiss, but we don't know how to notice them. I really liked that you kept stressing the difficulty in distinguishing natural "gnarl" from intelligently made artifacts….and with the concomitant point that at some level there really isn't a difference. Also like the point that as our tech develops, our creating will look more and more like natural objects. I find it really hard to communicate these points to people who haven't spent hundreds or thousands of hours looking at CAs, fractals, chaotic attractors, and mathematical outputs! That old blind notion that humans are "special."

So I agree that the way to go is probably to send some of the specific and particular kinds of things we make, with the entire contents of internet as perhaps the best example. On a solid state drive, I guess, although the cosmic rays might trash that. We'll leave it up to "them" to decipher it.

I was kind of tickled by your idea to include the Wolfram Alpha ware to make it easier to read the web. And, why not, a complete "lifebox" of your good self…all your diaries, videos, tapes, etc. I'd agitate to include a Rudy Lifebox as well.

And, then, going the whole hog, include your frozen body in there…no point stopping at just the brain. Very similar to the Pyramid of Cheops, or some such, at this point, isn't it!?!

I have an idea now for an SF story about this. Two characters…one of them, W, constructs the rocket with the web, his software, his data-based lifebox, and his frozen body. His friend, R, who's more a fiction writer than a scientist, is intrigued by W's project, but doesn't' think about it that much.

One day R hears that W has died, and is sorry about it. That night some commandoes come and kidnap R from his home, rush him off to a private spaceport, and his last sight is of himself being lowered into liquid nitrogen…next to the rocket where the frozen W awaits.

A bit of a gap there, and R awakes to find himself with W in a flying saucer with some aliens. "I wanted company," says W. And then comes the surprising party of the story, the kicker, the twist…which I haven't yet thought of, but probably will.

In conformity with computational irreducibility, I usually am not in fact able to predict my stories' endings until I write my way out to that point!

January 30-31, 2018. Krakens and Urbsteg.

I'd like to see Fwopsy and Duggie join together like a pair of cymbals. Open holes in the centers of their undersides, so there's now a nearly spherical cabin. Nice image. I'm doing it.

***

Looking ahead toward the bloom, where am I going to get hundreds of krakens—assuming I want to place two of them into each pair of *veem*? Should I even be doing that? It's kind of complicated, having four races. Couldn't 2 veem, 2 *woomo*, and 2 humans be enough per load?

If I do want a lot of krakens, they could stream down from the sun like a flock of angels. But I had those two krakens breeding at the North Pole—where do the other krakens breed? On Earth somewhere else? Or the could be breeding serially, one pair every hundred years in the North Hole maelstrom, and they did this for the last ten thousand years.

Those frikkin' *urbsteg* don't have a plot function at all. Could I somehow connect them to the krakens? Or could the *urbsteg* be enemies? Somehow akin to greed-head, pollution-mad, Republikkkan land-developers? Note that if the krakens are friends and the urbsteg are enemies, then they can't be the same.

Well, could the krakens are enemies of the *woomo* too? It was a snap decision of mine to make them friends. I could roll that back although, looking things over, the roll-back would somewhat extensive, as I introduced that kraken character Skolder, who's friends with Nyoo. Also I was thinking the krakens might be batteries for the saucers. But, of course, the saucers *could* have batteries on their own.

Maybe the krakens are in some sense enslaved by the *woomo*, or at least bossed around by them. Maybe they want to go somewhere different from where the *woomo* go, I mean as the terminus of this cosmic voyage. So the krakens might *rebel* at the time of the bloom even though at present they are seemingly allies of the *woomo*. And maybe the urbsteg are parasites who are winning the krakens over.

The *urbsteg* could be wormhole tunnels to the Sun—which was an idea I entertained earlier—and the krakens would use those tunnels, and the urbsteg could be like spawning pools. And later, when the *urbsteg* attack our party at Big Sur, a human enemy or three might fall into an *urbsteg* tunnel to the Sun.

Note that I spoke of the urbsteg as edible, and I've variously suggested that their like either big protozoa or like jellyfish. Alternately, we might merge the urbsteg and the krakens, and have the urbsteg be kraken eggs.

Too many options. For now I'll just have to wait until I

get the necessary inspiration for this.

January 31 passim, 2018. Kickstarter Self-Pub Option.

My agent John Silbersack just left his agency to go indie, and he's so busy with his own affairs that he hasn't managed to talk to Night Shade or to Tor, which I resent somewhat, perhaps unfairly. In any case, I'm inwardly rebelling at the prospect of waiting a year or three to see HE2 published. I want this book to be read. I want to be back in the limelight.

The most recent chapter—the short chapter inside the Central Anomaly—went fast, like less than a week, so I'm suddenly thinking I might actually finish HE2 by June. I do that sometimes—finish a novel really fast. If that were the case, I could do a Kickstarter for a hardback of a two-in-one HE1/HE2 edition in July, and ship in August, and get this out before the Night Shade [9 reprints + 1 MMRT] sequence even starts.

If Tor actually wanted the book, of course, I might not do this. And it *might* not matter to Night Shade, especially if I hold back on the individual pb editions of the HEs.

I must say—the thought of self-pubbing lifts my heart. As I've said so often, I hate the hat-in-hand + long-wait routine of "real" publication. Hate the timid uncertainty and the lack of control.

February 1-4, 2018. Ants!

I've been slowly working on a painting of ants, and I wasn't quite sure why I started it. But maybe my subconscious was telling me something. I've been wondering who could be the "foe" that my characters face when trying to orchestrate the great interstellar bloom.

And maybe the muse is telling me: *Ants!* I'd like to have ants. Something else to look forward to. Big ant tunnels in the Rind, and a buttload of ants in the Big Sur cliffs.

And those as-yet-still-inchoate *urbsteg* things can just be ant farms, where the ants grow food. No *urbstegs* at all.

And go on and drop the krakens entirely, and replace them with ants? As it is we've got shrigs, ballula, *woomo*, and krakens. And now I'm saying I want ants. Is that too many kinds of critters? Well I'm going to keep the krakens, it wouldn't work well to replace them with giant ants. I tried, but it would be too hard to take the two krakens in the maelstrom at the North Hole and turning them into ants.

The ants and *woomo* can be uneasy partners, rather than out and out enemies or great pals. They're arguing about which way to "steer the ship." The ants want to go to a black hole, the *woomo* want to go to a white hole. Like two doors at the center of the Milky Way galaxy.

But, nobody really is *steering* Earth are they? Well, not in an obvious way. But maybe there are subtle, sensitive-to-initial-conditions ways of affecting our solar system's path around our galaxy. The *woomo* can use their upper-atmosphere fans like solar sails, and the digging ants can alter Earth's center of gravity.

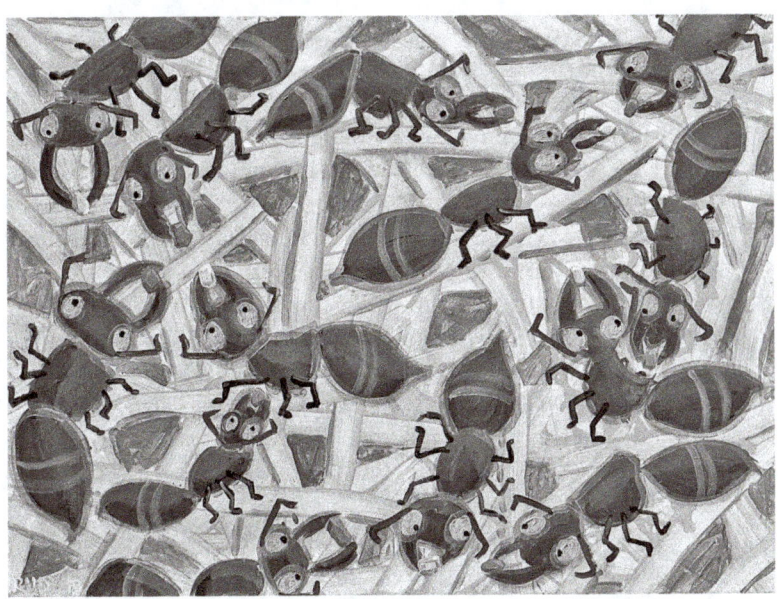

Figure 30: Ants and Gems

Extra idea for the painting, have the ants carrying gems! *Ants and Gems*. To liven it up. And…those *could* be rumby gems. Maybe some rumbies are ant eggs and some are *woomo* eggs. Maybe an ant brought that rumby that

MirrorSeela had—instead of a *woomo* tendril bringing it?

But drop the thing about using krakens as fuel cells.

No, I don't think I'll do that. Looking ahead, I see the ants and the *woomo* as enemies, and the ants wouldn't be helping a *woomo* egg rumby to hatch. If anything they'd be eating it, or *erasing* the *woomo* spirit inside.

On Earth, we might suppose that the ants took and hid most of the rumbies that Poe and Machree carried back.

What else does the painting tell me? Oh! The red rumbies are seeds for female *woomo*, and the blue gems are for males? I'll go back and work in that there's the two colors of rumbies? Or maybe not. I don't necessarily see the *woomo* as gendered. On the other hand, if the flying *veem* of the Bloom are like Noah's arks, then we'd want to have a pair of *woomo* and a pair of humans.

***

Don't have the two *veem* immediately spawn babies that they set to growing on their inner surface. They can do the spawning when they land in Big Sur and go into a cave. And Mason and Seela can see that, and then they hitch a ride from Big Sur up to Santa Cruz, and from there they'll go on to Los Gatos.

And there will be ants in the Big Sur cave, too. Not quite sure yet what they're doing, though.

And I don't think I'll talk about putting krakens or ants in the bloom ships. Humans, *woomo*, and veem are enough.

***

Speaking of krakens, I should have people also be calling them sun dragons.

February 5-6, 2018. Arrival.

I have to decide what it's like when Mason and Seela to come back to the Bay Area on February 2, 2018, the night of the full moon. They'll be arriving at my house soon after. Possibly on my 72nd birthday, March 22. Seventy-two is eight times nine. Two-cubed times three-squared, which is tidy. That can be a topic that I talk to Mason about.

***

Are Mason and Seela black? I already did that whole thing about having them be black in 1849 in HE1, and I'm not sure I want to do that again. So many pitfalls to doing that. I don't know jack shit about what it's like to be black in 2018. I was able to *sort of* fake it for 1849, but if I try for *today* I might annoy people and they'll say I'm racist and not PC and a jackass. So I might punt—and have the *veem* Fwopsy and Duggie turn them more or less white.

On the other hand, it might be racist to shy away from having my characters stay black. And Seela doesn't mind being black at all. I'm reading *Black Like Me*, by John Howard Griffin, 1962, recommended to my by Marc Laidlaw. It's kind of great, in that it makes being a Negro seem so…normal. And that's the step I was having trouble with. Really it's such a simple thing. Just the damn skin color. It's still people. Maybe I'll bleach them down to mulatto level.

How would I bleach them? "Washed in the blood of the yam," is a phrase that comes to mind. But where would the "yam" come from? I found a skin-whitening article saying they've had some success with a fungus that grows as matted white threads in the forest floor. It's a species called Ceriporiopsis sp. strain MD-1. So maybe there's a hot-springs mud-bath of this stuff all set next to the cave! But it doesn't work very well. But am I really so scared of having black characters?

    ***

Well, I'll at least get them down to Latino/mulatto color. Won't use mud baths, just a hot pool. Also keeps warm. These Esalen-style hot baths were installed by a *woomo* tendril which snakes up through the mysterious hole at the back of the cave, which is also where the *ants* are waiting, having brought in all those rumby gems some 150 years ago. The ants trot out with snacks for Mason and Seela, that would be cool.

Note that ants will want to get aboard those colony ships too. Perhaps that could be the cause of a last minute tussle. Or might the krakens be fighting to get aboard? Seems like they could just fly in the wake of the saucers if they wanted to. Probably I won't include dogs. Arf stays with Professor Rucker.

Maybe Eddie and Ina have been waiting in coffins like

Dracula, and now they wake and want to come along? I did a move like this in *Jim and the Flims*. I think it would be one element too many, though. But if all else fails, Eddie and Ina could be the enemies who try and stop the Bloom…

Figure 31: Ark Saucer with Veem, Humans, *Woomo*, Ants, Dogs

If I make Mason white, he might be viewed as white trash because he has a Southern accent. A redneck hippie. But I didn't use that angle in Baltimore or San Francisco, so why use it now.

Or have him and Seela be, like, 18 year old homeless hippies drifting into Cruz. If they're kind of colored, that's okay. Mixed race or Latino.

I'm seeing them getting a ride to Santa Cruz. They won't ride in Fwopsy and Duggie as the saucers want to watch over their young, and don't want to risk getting the Air Force after them again. Mason and Seela don't know about cars, are about hitchhiking, but they're walking along the highway and someone offers a ride. A van of hippies. "Just Passin Through." Deadheads ask, "Are you white?" Seela, "I don't know." They crash in the hippies' shared house.

Mason could get a job in Santa Cruz installing wireless antennas, like for Monkeybrains, only it's for Cruzio. Oddly enough, Rudy Jr. actually employs a Mason at his Monkeybrains ISP company. A sign from the muse! Or maybe he's a carpenter. Or something with farming. A gardener. A day-laborer with Mexicans. No, no, get Mason in with a Santa Cruz newspaper. *The Good Times*. He could be a driver or a free-lance reporter. Writes an article about Poe's Order of the Golden Frond—by way of finding those people.

Seela could be making crafts and selling them on the sidewalk. A waitress at Saturn Cafe? Works on a fishing boat? A jeweler. She goes into a shop as an intern and quickly rises. Someplace like a crystal store.

***

An issue with the human emigration crews. Accepted wisdom says you can't send just one human couple, as you need genetic diversity. A breeding stock. You'd need at least two couples, and from what I see online, it would be more viable to have fifty couples.

Traditionally this leads to the idea of sending a lot of poeple to one place. I've always found the big generation starships to be very dull to think about. Like rest homes. Or cruise ships. I could instead say that the fleet of *veem* saucers will all land in the same place. Or maybe they split into several fleets and go to two or three places. I'm not really crazy about the fleet option either. It feels more exciting to be Adam and Eve. Just the two of you on a new world.

If I do say it's two people, then the *woomo* could carry codes for a variety of eggs and sperms. A library. They sent out tendrils and got the codes of everyone on Earth. They design new genomes by merging codes, like turning a kaleidoscope. The *woomo* build a race from our Adam and Eve like a canny woodsman making a fire by rubbing together two sticks.

Who bears the babies? I wouldn't want to ask Seela to have more than four pregnancies. Maybe that's enough. If each couple has four children, they're doubling the size of each generation. 2, 4, 8, 16, etc. If you figure there's always three generations alive, we can sum a moving window of three. We'd get 14, 28, 56, 112, 222 or something. We'll assume that, thanks to the *woomo* tweaks, the people don't have overly similar genes, and they can intermarry.

I have to admit that it does leave a bad taste to say that Mason and Seela's son and daughter are going to mate. So maybe we'd have to go the fleet colonization route after all. Or just don't worry about it. Not like we'll be there to *watch* the interbreeding, as the book ends before that.

***

I like my original image of thistledown in the wind with the saucers like spores, going to a myriad of worlds. And on each of them is an "Adam and Eve" who will engender a whole race.

So it's a drifting dandelion-seeds flight—but I'll power it, so they can go fast. The *woomo* aboard will sniff out a target location for each saucer. Like hunting dogs.

***

How long does the trip take? We might suppose that the people are in suspended animation. Or that there's a *woomo*-generated time warp...but that's clunky. Or we give the saucers FTL flight powers, although they didn't use them when traveling from the Hollow Earth to the surface.

Simplest: if they fly close enough to the speed of light, it won't seem to take long. Catch: accelerating and decelerating to near light speed takes awhile, unless you use a very intense acceleration force—which is hard on the body...it's the issue of your heart being able to pump blood to your brain.

One of my Twitter followers directed me to an online app that lets you compute the subjective travel time (taking relativistic time dilation into account). Acceleration/decelerating at 1 g it still takes you to go 4 years to get 10 light years. But then the gains accumulate. You can go 6,000 light years to the Crab Nebula in only 17 years of your subjective time. That's really not bad! I guess you'd have to be on the nod during that time.

Or I go for FTL and just totally not explain it. And they can hop to wherever in a few hours. Thinking of FTL as I saw it mentioned in Ursula Leguin's *Rocannon's World*, which I just read, and loved.

February 10, 2018. San Francisco

Sylvia and I are up in SF from Feb 8 - 11 for a four day reunion celebrating her 75th birthday. "Diamond Jubilee" as Rudy Jr. likes to call it, slightly annoying Sylvia therewith. We have all 13 of us here: 3 children, 3 spouses, 5 grand-children, and us. A repeat of our 50th wedding anniversary gathering in June, 2017. I'm smiling a lot. I used to be one person, and now I'm the patriarch of a clan.

Haven't thought much about HE2.

If that cave's going to have room for, say, twenty-five saucers on its walls, it can't just be the size of a church nave, it has to tunnel back into the mountain. Like Mammoth Cave. It can be a tunnel made by the Hollow Earth ants. Love the phrase "Hollow Earth ants," *yeah*.

Mason and Seela's assignment is to find the members of the Order of the Golden Frond, and get fifty of them to come to Big Sur in preparation for shipping out on the twenty-five newborn flying saucers.

For plot purposes, I need a counterforce that's trying to obstruct Mason and Seela's efforts in setting up the big Bloom.

To make things easy, we might suppose that Eddie Poe's instructions are in a steamer trunk which also holds clothes for Mason and Seela.

February 15-18, 2018. I Need Complications. More Ants!

I need some kind of back and forth to fill up the last third of the novel. The way I started Chapter 12, everything is way too simple. I have the new saucers growing in the cave, with the rumbies are in a treasure chest there, the ants as allies, and the hidden ranks of the Order of the Golden Frond awaiting the call. What could go wrong? I'll see what I can do…

§ Something is killing the baby saucers.

§ The rumbies *aren't* in the cave. Or they've been ru-ined. Maybe the Hollow Earth ants got to them.

§ The Order of the Golden Frond no longer exists, it died out a hundred years ago.

§ The ants are enemies of the *woomo*.
***

While casting about for enemies of the Bloom, I read a little in Wikipedia about the "Shaver Mystery" discussed in *Amazing Stories* during the late 1940s.

> Richard Shaver wrote of extremely advanced prehistoric races who had built cavern cities inside the Earth before abandoning Earth for another planet due to damaging radiation from the Sun. Those ancients also abandoned some of their own offspring here, a minority of whom remained noble and human "Teros", while most degenerated over time into a population of mentally impaired sadists known as "Deros"—short for "detrimental robots". Shaver's "robots" were not mechanical constructs, but were robot-like due to their savage behavior.

I've always like the idea of *deros*. It's a great word. So short. Not that I'm going to use the Shaver stuff—even though it includes the Hollow Earth *and* UFOs. I can do a Shaver story some other time, like as a partner to "Lost City of Leng." I did find a couple of great old *Amazing Stories* Shaver covers that I might as well paste in here.
***

Back to HE2. Who would be a good enemy? What force would want to stop the *woomo's* bloom? Donald Trump is the biggest enemy around. But if I put him into the novel, it sinks me into a soon-outdated topicality. Ditto for Silicon Valley billionaire or one-percenter. I need a more mythical enemy. Some figure on the same scale as the *woomo*.

Perhaps a rival race of god-like beings. The two races striving for galactic hegemony. Okay. But what race? I was trying to set up the kraken or sun dragons as the enemy. But it's better to use them as a red herring, and in fact maybe they can help save the *woomo's* plan at the last minute. So who's the real enemy?

Drum roll...the Hollow Earth ants! Overlooked, and seemingly harmless. Like the microbes in H. G. Wells *The War of the Worlds*. So, good, we'll use them. Now I need to figure out why the Hollow Earth ants trying to block the Bloom?

Backstory: The ants are in fact the ones who hollow out the planets—and they view the *woomo* as parasites squatting in their home. The *woomo* don't know this; they don't grasp that the ants don't like them. The *woomo* are not completely intelligent in every way. They overlook the ants; they assume the ants have no minds.

***

Let's say more about the fact that it's the ants who hollowed out the Earth. They hollow out planets, and they pry space into two hypersheets so there's a Wimshurst-machine or plasma-globe type flow of energy within. Image of the busy ants bucking their bodies to split apart the two sheets of hyperspace.

When the ants hollow out a planet, they shove all the extra matter into the hyperspace between the delaminated sheets.

I did a relevant calculation in my head this morning in church. If you have a sphere of radius R, then half the mass is inside the 0.8*R radius inner sphere. This works because $(0.8)^3$ is close to 0.5, and mass varies as the radius cubed. Now our Earth has radius 4,000 miles, so the inner sphere to be hollowed out could be 3,200 miles radius, so the Rind would be 800 miles thick, which is all fine with me.

They can pulverize the hollowed-out matter and spew it into the 4D cavity between the hypersheets. Or they can compact it into the core of the Rind, Which is better if we want . Or use the hollowed-out matter to make a second Hollow Earth which will, however have half the mass, which isn't good. To keep the mass of the Earth constant, I guess when the ant delaminates the Earth, it's in effect Xeroxing it onto the upper sheet. Seen from "below" it'll look backwards and seem to rotate the opposite way. And then they hollow them out. Lots of complications here if I dig into it. On the one hand there's the mass of the Earth as experienced by gravitational attraction when you stand on the surface. On the other hand there's the mass of the paired Earth/MirrorEarth which orbits as a single object around the Sun. Well, maybe you can "feel" the mass (or gravitational space curvature) of the combined Earth/MirrorEarth on the surface of either one.

I need to make 1D and 2D drawings of this.

***

Maybe the planets don't *like* being hollowed out. Love that idea, The planets are, in a sense, alive, The *woomo* are attracted by the hollowed planet's loud telepathic complaints.

***

Things that ants might do to *woomo*. The ants enjoy eating tender, newly hatched *woomo*. And they can use their chirps as dynamic acoustic arrays, focusing their chirps on a specific region with explosive effect. A swarm of ants chirps and—a *woomo* explodes into blood and slime.

Recall that the "genome" of a *woomo* is stored in a rumby in the form of a vibration or a holographic info storage or a standing wave. Ants can "erase" the *woomo* spirit from a rumby egg with their frantic chirps. They can put in ant code instead. And when the "egg" hatches it produces an ant and not a *woomo*. *Surprise*!

***

Is Mason especially on the *woomo* side? Up to a point. But really he wants to stay on Earth and live his life with Seela. He doesn't plan to emigrate with the saucers. But then Seela seems to have died—she's taken captive by the ants and disappears, and Mason blames himself. And some other woman is suddenly all over Mason, and he wants to leave Earth with her. He'll bring Brumble with him and leave Arf with Professor Rucker.

The Seela disappearance should be a last minute thing, in the second to last chapter. But then in the last chapter, *ta da*, she'll come back.

Who will be Mason's other woman? She could be one of the hippie girls from the crash pad. She's black and her name is Shoshanna. But I seem to remember Bruce Sterling telling me that it's not wise to introduce a new character in a pivotal role near the very end of a novel or story. I'll call this injunction the Sterling Ukase, keeping in mind that "ukase" is a crossword-puzzle-type word, originally Russian, meaning an arbitrary edict, command, or decree.

To obey the letter, if not the spirit, of the Sterling Ukase, I *could* have it turn out that Shoshanna is the not-dead-after-all Ina from 1860. Eddie somehow revived Ina as his finale. Like, the undead and rapidly decomposing and deliquescing Eddie has kept Ina alive in a Sleeping-Beauty-type trance. Eddie's been like a crypt-keeper, preserving the dead woman in suspended animation—just the kind of woman that Eddie likes!—and now that he's delivered her to Mason as *virgo intacta*, he can die. We might literary find Ina in a crypt. Or, no, wait, she came back earlier as one of the hippies? We'll see.

If I didn't want to bring back Seela, Mason might imagine that Seela managed to code her soul into a rumby, which Ina assimilates into herself. At least Ina tells Mason she's doing this, although she could be hoaxing Mason just to really land him. But, nah, the reader would like it better if I bring back the real Seela.

And possibly it's a bit too much if I insist on a three-way with Ina. "People" might say I'm an old horndog. Imagine that. On the other hand…if this is escape literature, can't my hero have a good time?

February 19, 2018. Quick Fixes.

I'd like to stop planning, and finish the "Twenty Eighteen" chapter, and just watch and see what I end up writing, instead of trying to figure it out in advance.

But I do still need quick fixes for a few issues. *Anything* will do, in terms of the fixes, I just need to duct tape the story together so I can move on, and skip back through the manuscript making chainsaw changes to match—and I can smooth it all out later on when the still-emerging plot is final.

- I forgot all about my baby *woomo* character Nyoo during the sequence near the Central Anomaly. Nyoo is flying around with her new friend the kraken, and then the humans get into Fwopsy and ride into the core, and we don't hear any more about Nyoo. Okay, I better have Nyoo ride back to the Earth in the saucer with Mason and Seela. She even goes into the Central Anomaly with them first, but she doesn't do much in there as she's so ecstatic at that moment. So, okay, Nyoo comes back to Earth with our guys and she splits off from them to lead away the attacking planes on a wild goose chase, and then she catches up with Mason outside the Big Sur cave the next morning, and she goes inside to gloat over the load of rumbies that she thinks is inside the treasure chest. And a swarm of ants seethes out and eats her and kills her dead. As the ants have a 4D aspect to them, they're capable of changing size, so you can fit a hundred dog-sized Hollow Earth ants into a little chest if you want.

- Are the saucers on the side of the *woomo* or of the ants? They don't care. They'll work with either party. What do they gain by transporting passengers? Do they get some kind of payment? What could you possibly *pay* to for a living flying saucer? Well, you don't *pay*, you do a favor. You give it guidance on which planet to go to next. The *woomo* can sense distant things with their tekelili and their light tendrils. And the ants can see far away via 4D. Their feelers stick up into hyperspace. Note that *woomo* and ants are looking for two slightly different types of worlds. Ants want to find fresh, juicy, Earth-type worlds to hollow out. *Woomo* want to find worlds that the ants have already hollowed out.

- And what about that little kraken who was friends with Nyoo near the core? I keep forgetting his name, so it must not be a good name. Oh, right, it was Skolder. But something much more incongruous would be better. Karl-Heinz Ziefler—which I remember (perhaps incorrectly) as being the name a kid I knew at boarding school in Königsfeld in the Black Forest in Germany when I was thirteen, a good guy, smart and puny like me. I guess it could have been Ziefler with two f's, but that's not how I remember it. This particular kraken splits off from them at the Umpteen Seas and flies out to the Sun. And later, near the end, in the last or second to last chapter, when Mason is totally screwed, Karl-Heinz can come back as a *deus ex machina* to do a save. He saves the saucers for the *woomo*, chases off the ants, and gets Mason and Seela to go aboard a saucer after all.

Feb 20, 2018. Working Outline.

Okay, I'd like try and figure out the ending. Here we go.

Twenty Eighteen. Mason, Seela, B, A, and Nyoo lands in Fwopsy and Duggie near Big Sur and it's 2018. The saucers go into a cave on a cliff, and spawn a bunch of babies, like barnacles or shelf mushrooms, onto the cave walls. They'll take some months to mature. Mason and Seela spend the night by a hot spring outside the cave. There's some Hollow Earth ants in the cave. The ants kill and eat the *woomo* Nyoo. Mason hitchhikes with Seela, Brumble, and Arf to Santa Cruz. The get a ride with a van of freaks or hippies, and crash at those people's pad in Cruz.

A Visitor. Mason works loading *Good Times* papers onto trucks, and Seela is working the counter at Mystic Crystals making her necklaces. Mason writes an article about the Hollow Earth for the *Good Times*. A cloaked figure visits Mason at his house and presents him with a manuscript that seems to have been penned for his eyes—a manuscript by Edgar Allan Poe, dated 1860. Mason realizes his visitor is the undead Poe—alerted by the article. Poe now decays into dust. The manuscript he gave Mason is perhaps in some kludgy Poe-type cryptographic code.

Professor Rucker. Mason's editor at the *Good Times* fires Mason, having learned that Mason's passage has been published in a book edited by Rudy Rucker, *The Hollow Earth*. Mason and Seela make their way to Professor Rucker's house in Los Perros with baby Brumble and the dog Arf. Professor Rucker shelters Mason and his family while Mason works on his *Return to the Hollow Earth*. Rucker seems to think Mason may be hoaxing him, but he likes what Mason is writing, and he hopes to sell the book. Meanwhile Rucker decodes the Poe manuscript.

Poe's Miscellany. (Double length. Unknown Writings by Poe.) I see a variety of things in this miscellany. (a) Several pages of Poe's epic poem "Htrae," about the Hollow Earth journeys. (b) A journalistic narrative of his journey back to Earth without Mason. Eddie lost about ten years in the Anomaly, and got back to Earth in 1860. Machree took off with the rumbies. Eddie went on tour with Ina, with her de-claiming supposedly séance-channeled poems by Eddie. Ina is laid low by the sting of a Hollow Earth ant. Eddie pre-serves her body in suspended animation. (c) He shares opium with the ants, and is able to understand them. They tell him of their rivalry with the *woomo*. The ants hollow out planets, the planets' cries attract the *woomo*, and the ants don't like the *woomo* to come and squat. (d) Instructions to Mason on how to resurrect Ina.

All is Lost. The Professor helps Mason and Seela. The resurrect Ina. No traces of the Order of the Golden Frond remain—all of them died mysteriously. They go in search of the missing rumbies in the tunnel behind the cave in Big Sur, and come face to face with Drusilla, the queen of the ants. Seela and Brumble are taken captive by the ants. Mason is desperate. He is comforted by Ina, who talks him into going on a saucer with some ants. He finishes his manuscript for HE2.

Farewell. Professor Rucker writes the final chapter, which is set the next day. At the last minute Seela shows up , saved by the kraken Karl-Heinz Ziefler. The ants are driven far into the Hollow Earth. The saucers, the newly hatched *woomo*, and some willing human passengers gather on a cliff in Big Sur They take off, with two humans and a pair of *woomo* in each of the paired *veem* saucers. Ina is, like, "I'll stay on Earth, you two can go, you don't want me along." Mason is, like, "Well maybe a three-way is good for starting a new race," and Seela says okay. So Mason, Ina, Brumble, and Seela are the last to go. And they leave their dog Arf in Rudy's safekeeping. My closing words: "And if you don't believe this story, you can come see the dog!"

February 22-23, 2018. Mason and Seela Immigrate.

A van with four or five people picks up Mason, Seela, Brumble, and Arf on Route 1 near Big Sur, heading for San-ta Cruz. Visualize the van and its driver and passengers.

I'm trying to cast them. Four surfers maybe, or four stoned hippies, or four homeless people, or migrant workers, or Oakland blacks. Zep and Del make a cameo? That would be meta funny, not sure Marc Laidlaw would approve of that use of the copyrighted intellectual property, but they could resemble Z & D, but naw, it would throw the book off kilter.

I think I need to let go of the default surfer or hippie thing and just have them be poor Latinos, they work in motels, and they were visiting some relatives in Salinas who work in the fields. All four are Mexican illegal aliens, they're kind to the deserted Mason and family, not like the white drivers who gave them the finger for looking like Blacks. And they get room in the Mexicans' garage. Can I *call* them Mexicans? Only if they're *from* Mexico. Otherwise Latinos.

But they still have to be characters. Let's sketch.

Aida is driving. Dark hair, Roman nose, know-it-all, big flirt, works cleaning at a motel, the Dream Inn. She paints cactuses on the walls in their rented house, shoplifts food, says she's Aztec, makes big meals. She has a baby Dorothea.

Hector is next to Aida. He works as a busboy at the same motel. Likes hip-hop music and sports, plays vinyl LPs, wears yellow sunglasses, has a broken motorcycle.

Rafael in back plays videogames all the time. He works as a cleaner at the *Good Times*. He likes to go surfing now and then. He's holding Tomás, his and Maya's baby.

Maya is Rafael's girlfriend, she's into crystals and candles, works in an occult shop. Likes pot and she has cats.

Aida and Maya are sisters. They live in a house in the Beach Flats near the Boardwalk amusement park. They let Mason and Seela sleep on a mattress in their garage, they found the mattress in the garbage.

***

What about green card? It's called a *mica* in street slang, and in 2010 you could buy one from guys hanging out in front of almost any passport photo shop in the Mission. See article. But in 2018 I'm not sure this works anymore. There are some online offers, or maybe there are things on the undernet or dark web. I could just leave it vague. Given that Santa Cruz and San Francisco are so-called "sanctuary cities," the green card isn't all that big of a deal.

February 27-28, 2018. Job. Evergreen Cemetery.

I had a hell of a run last week, four or five days in a row where I did a thousand words a day—which is the most I ever hope for. Then I collapsed by the roadside. And I pissed away the last two days working on a short essay, "The Panpsychic Hylozoic Manifesto." It's cool. Maybe I'll do a panpsychic HE2 move with Gaia and/or Helios, like I was hinting at before, the thing about planets not liking being eaten from the inside by Hollow Earth ants.

The latest is that I had Uxa get in touch with Mason, and she hinted he could be like Jesus—and she had him fix his host Hector's broken motorcycle by laying on his hands. And later Mason's going to lay his hands onto Rafaelo's Game Boy and install full, original code for a videogame called *La Tierra Hueca*, that is, *The Hollow Earth*. But first I want Mason to go to the Santa Cruz office of the *Good Times* newspaper and get a job.

Where is the manuscript of Mason's Hollow Earth at this point? Let's see…Mason left it at Coale's bookshop, and Machree read it there. Eddie never had a chance to read it, although Machree told him a bit about it, and at one point, on the *Water Witch* in 1850, Eddie remarks that he'd like to edit the book for publication. And, as we know from the Editor's Note to HE1, the manuscript eventually it found its way to the library of the U Va. And on March 7, 1985, Professor Rudy Rucker found the manuscript there, and he published it in 1990.

I want to move fast with HE2 now. Sprint to the finish line. So let's say that Mason immediately wins over the *Good Times* editor. He's like Jon Pearce. Maybe reuse Jon's name from when he was my character's boss in *Hacker and the Ants*, let's see, he was "Ben Brie." Don't use that. They need a local hook for Mason's Hollow Earth story…oh, right, have Mason say he'll talk about the light wave surfers of the Hollow Earth. He shouldn't spill the beans about the Big Sur cave.

Mason writes up his article. Uxa wants him to do this. She hopes to flush out some hidden members of the Order of the Golden Frond that may remain. Nor sure yet how the story will be received by the Santa Cruzans.

[On Feb 18, 2018, Sylvia and I went down to Santa Cruz to visit the Evergreen cemetery, the oldest in California, has people from 1860 and on. Pioneers, Gold Rush people, Chinese. I'd thought they might have crypts but they bascially don't, at least not old ones. But they have crumbly, funky graves, damp and dark, and near a cement plant and freeway, whose noise overlays the air.]

Eddie comes out of the woodwork. He was in a buried in the Evergreen cemetery in Santa Cruz with Ina. Or maybe Ina was buried, and Eddie got down into her grave with her the way he likes to do, and he stayed there for a century and a half, and then *fauugh* burrows up through the loam, unspeakably foul. Classic undead body routine, like at the end of *Carrie*.

I want Eddie to give Mason his manuscript and then Eddie crumbles. Maybe Eddie has all the rumbies with him, and they've been keeping him in suspended animation, and when Uxa repossesses the rumbies at that moment, Eddie turns into dust. His last request is to Mason is to put his dust into Ian's grave.

I don't want to bring Ina back to life. That would be that's too much trouble. I want to streamline and rush for the end. Be focusing in, not fanning out. But I'll give Ina a good scene or two in Eddie's memoir. Do the thing about her pretending to channel his poems on stage, and he in fact was writing them. He fell in love with her. She died in some bad way, and he got in the coffin with her, suspending his animation with rumby eggs, but them *aigs* have in fact been feeding on him like ticks for one and half centuries. Takes a lot out of a man. Uxa knew all along. Perfect.

I'll wait till Mason's been at Professor Rucker's for awhile before I have him put the Hollow Earth game on Rafaelo's Game Boy. Somehow Rafael gets the motorcycle away from Hector.

Another great gift from the muse on Feb 28 when we went to Cruz. I saw Hector's motorcycle from half a block away! And why *wouldn't* I see it? I'm at the same place and (nearly) the same date as in the HE2 chapter I'm writing. The motorcycle was one of those kind of fat Harley type machines with all white, or cream, fenders and forks and tank. Gleaming. Like white butter.

And then Sylvia picked up a free newspaper, which was the very *Good Times* weekly where Mason gets a job.

March 3, 2018. Eddie in Evergreen Cemetery.

Listening to Google Play, where I've accessed a newly assembled complete collection of cuts from Zappa *Live at the Roxy*, the Dec 10, 1973 Concert 2, cut "Pigmy Twylyte," starting about 3 minutes in, Frank gets into a solo with two drummers laying down a fat background, the man is weaving a brocade, his music like a rushing cascade, filled with his joy at the playing, his craft and the upwelling music in his soul.

Image 33: Poe's Grave at Evergreen Cemetery in Santa Cruz.

I've been writing really fast again the last couple of days, I polished off another chapter, "Plagiarist," about Mason publishing his "Lightsurfing the Hollow Earth" in the *Good Times*. And at the end of the chapter he gets the message that Edgar Allan Poe is waiting for him at the Evergreen Cemetery. It's about 10 or 11 am. He has Arf with him, and I think he gets Rafaelo to come along, taking an early lunch hour. They walk there from downtown Santa Cruz, the walk ain't far, maybe half an hour. I don't think they bring baby Brumble.

The stone could now say Ina Durivage. Born: Jan 19, 1832. Died: Jan 19, 1877.

If Eddie didn't sneak in, list him. Goarland Peale. Born: Jan 19, 1809. Died: Jan 19, 1877.

And drop the (problematic) birth years, and say the ages. 33 and 44. I think Ina goes first.

Ina Durivage of Louisiana
Died Jan 19, 1877. Aged 33 Years
***

Goarland Peale of Virginia
Died Jan 19, 1877. Aged 44 Years
***

What Laughing Hearts Have Died in Vain

Fine points. I have Ina born the same month and day as Eddie. She's actually 11 years younger than Eddie, as we need to discount the 12 years Eddie lost in HE1. So in HE2 at the start, in 1850, Ina is 18 in 1850, and Poe is 29. And, then in HE2, they jump twelve years to 1862, and hang around for fifteen years until 1877, at which point Ina is 33 and Poe is 44.

Note that, 2018 minus 1877 is 141, which is how long Eddie and Ina were in that grave. A hundred and forty one years.

The ground shakes, and Eddie's pale hand worms out of the dirt, first one hand, then the other, opening a rent in the earth. He's leathery, foul, dirty, but not decaying. He's covered head to foot with—red ticks? No, it's the rumby stones, glued to him all over. They've been feeding on him and, at the same time, keeping him in a lethargic yet living state. The rumbies were, I suppose, waiting for the *veem* to be all set, and for Nyoo or Uxa to be zapping them so they hatch.

Poes sees the gravestone and starts weeping about Ina. He hands Mason some papers wrapped in oil cloth inside a metal box sealed with wax. A bunch of Hollow Earth ants come down from the gulch at the back of the cemetery and pick the rumbies off of Eddie. They scurry away. Eddie turns to dust. Arf is barking. One of the ants is menacing Mason. Rudy Rucker shows up in his car and saves Mason. Rafaelo is, like, "Later, man. I can walk." Mason directs Rudy to the Bewitch Crystal shop. They pick up Seela and Brumble, and head over the hill to Los Perros.

Finishing this journal entry, I then wrote Marc Laidlaw an email about where I'm at.

> Two more good writing days. At this rate I'll almost certainly finish by May. I was rocking along today, really happy, just putting *whatever* in, nothing was too crazy to use, letting the characters talk at random. And then I put on a cut of Zappa playing "Pygmy Twylyte" live and he was in this chatty guitar groove, on and on, pouring forth like water from a spring, and I'm like, yeah, *that's* how I want to be doing, and today I'm hitting it, and I'll just rock into the next chap if I can, don't hold back any future surprises, just spring them now, no hoarding, it's time to light all the rockets off, we're coming to the grand finale… And I *still* don't know how it's gonna end. Doesn't matter. Just keep playing. And I *still* don't know how I'll publish it. Doesn't matter. Main thing is to play.

March 5-6, 2018. Eddie and Ina Return

Last night, while in the process of writing and rewriting the text of Eddie's note to Mason, I firmed up my idea that Eddie has been in a trance in Ina's grave, with a golden or silver or bronze box or even flask holding all the rumbies (it would be too outré to have them stuck onto Eddie like ticks), Eddie is waiting there in a coma, but thanks to the massed rumby tekelili he's subtly sensitive to the return of Mason—which will signal the imminence of the *woomo* Bloom. Eddie wants to ride one of the saucers of the Bloom. The ultimate kick.

Note that a man needs a woman partner to ride with off him in a *veem* during the Bloom. I've thus far been saying that Ina is dead for good, but maybe this needs to change. If Ina really is dead—might Eddie then form a scheme to run off with Seela? That would fit nicely into my story. Seela of course doesn't like Eddie. But maybe he's sneakily lusted for her all along. Like—while watching her nurse, his eyes are hot and appraising. Maybe I've hinted that angle, but I'd dial it up.

If Eddie abducts Seela, that accomplishes something I'd wanted to do anyway—to have Mason (temporarily) lose Seela, and to be in such despair he decides to leave on a *veem*. And have Seela is in fact restored to him at the end. I'd been thinking of the Queen of the Hollow Earth ants as holding Seela captive, but it could be simpler if Eddie takes her away. And then I wouldn't even need a Queen of the ants, and I'd then be obeying the Sterling Ukase: "No New Characters in the Final Chapters!" This said, I'd kind of like to see Drusilla, the Queen of the Hollow Earth ants.

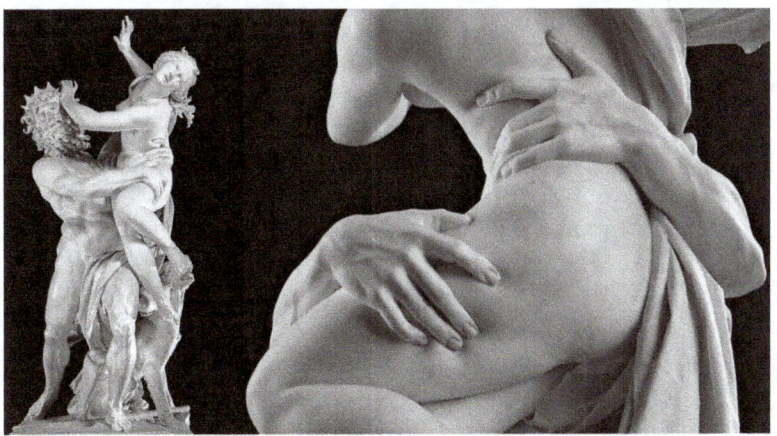

Figure 32: Bernini's Sculpture of Pluto Abducting Persephone.

Visualize the possible abduction, I have an initial mental image of Eddie riding on the back of a large and possibly winged Hollow Earth ant, with a struggling Seela tossed over the ant's back. Like a Cossack horseman stealing a woman.

Or a mental image of Bernini's "Rape of Persephone," a statue that Sylvia and I saw at the Villa Borghese in Rome. *Amazing*, the marble modeling of her flesh. Pluto, the god of the underworld, is carrying her off. He doesn't need a horse. Could Eddie physically carry Seela? Can't see that happening—although *maybe*, if his golden flask of rumbies grants him strength. He takes a big swig from the flask of rumbies? Like Popeye with his spinach. But if a character swallows rumbies, then later they might hatch out *woomo* inside them, which would be unpleasant for them and, for that matter, the reader.

I might mention in passing that Bernini's titular "rape" means "abduct." And it could in fact be that our Seela will manage to maintain and enforce a refusal to have sex with Eddie. Although it could be interesting if they did have sex at least once and then maybe Seela could be carrying Eddie's baby—but that seems like a needless complication. Keep Seela pure.

Backing up: Suppose Mason thinks he's lost Seela. And, in despair, he's decided to ride off in a *veem* of the Bloom. What woman might he pick to be his partner? Could it be Janelle of the *Good Times*? And then at the last minute, when Mason gets Seela back, might Janelle be willing to switch over to Poe? Could be. I'm not sure there's any other single women around at this point, and I'm loath to bring in yet another character and thus violate the Sterling Ukase.

If we haven't killed off Ina, and Seela is (temporarily) missing, then Mason could of course plan to leave with Ina—which is something I'd thought of before. Wife swap.

March 6, 2018.

Today I drove back and visited the Evergreen Cemetery in Cruz again. Writing this note, I'm in a bakery in Cruz, I'm here for the day and I taped a talk to a class at the Crown College of UCSC, I spoke to them last year too, about fifty of them, I'll talk about writing, cyberpunk, transrealism, and maybe pantheism. Invited by the teacher, Tim Fitzmaurice, a pleasant character about my age.

In the graveyard I was looking at that same gravestone that I photographed the other day. It's right next to an extremely large California bay laurel tree which could be well over a hundred years old—in fact some quick research shows they can live <u>beyond</u> 200 years.

I was thinking there could be a hollow passage through a hole in the side of the tree, down into the earth, a narrow, water-carved passage that leads over to the bronze casket within which Eddie and Ina were interred. Eddie has slyly installed a sliding door in the side of the bronze casket for later use. And when one or both of them wakes, they can worm their way out through the escape hatch, through the loamy tunnel, up past the roots and into the party rotted trunk of the tree, and out through the hole in the tree. "Eureka! The same, yet changed, I arise again!" Possibly a *woomo* light tendril has in fact carved the tunnel and the hole in the tree...like a lighting stoke that rises from the ground.

In principle, Eddie and/or Ina could, over the intervening 141 years, have made periodic reappearances from their shared lair in the Evergreen Cemetery casket. Checking things out, seeing if it's almost time for the Bloom and, by the way, generating a persistent myth of ghosts in that graveyard. But I think this would be too much trouble to explain.

In any case, Mason finds them out and alive. As I visualize it, Eddie and Ina sit there on a crypt, legs crossed, chatting. If Ina's back, then Eddie doesn't have to find a new woman. And I like Ina as a character. And then the ants will have to temporarily abduct Seela after all.

I'd had this idea about finding a manuscript of Eddie's. But if have Eddie himself, he can just *say* whatever would have been in the manuscript. I'd meant to have a double-length chapter of fake Poe journals (based on that recovered manuscript), but that might slow the book down. We're getting onto the bobsled run of the ending now, it's better to whiz down. I'd also had the idea of Professor Rucker decrypting Eddie's journals—just to give Rucker something to do—but maybe decryption is boring.

I was saying that Rucker would show up. He saw the Good Times article, went to their office, Janelle told him

Mason went to the Evergreen Cemetery, and Rucker shows up there to pick Mason up. They go and get Seela and Brumble and Arf and go to Los Perros.

Issues to resolve: Is there a crisis that makes Rudy and Seela eager to leave Santa Cruz? What am I going to do with Eddie and Ina? I can't see having them at Rudy's house for a month or two while Mason writes HE2. What about the conflict between the *woomo* and the ants?

Can I kill off Eddie and Ina, shortly after their return? But that would be "overkill." I mean, I killed two Eddies ways in Baltimore in HE1. And I'll have to somehow kill Eddie and Ina in, like, 1877 to get them into that grave in Evergreen Cemetery—or maybe I'll have them just pretend they're dead so they can lie low inside a casket. And then in any case they rise up yet again, and I if I *then* kill them yet again, then the reader's gonna say, "Big deal, it means nothing to kill these people, they just bounce back."

Hartwell's Ukase: Once you've killed off a character, don't bring them back to life. Move on without them. (He said that when I wanted to bring back Frek's dad in *Frek and the Elixir*.)

I've already violated Hartwell's Ukase once for the sake of bringing back Eddie at the start of HE2—and that was worth doing, right at the start of the book. One could argue that it's stupid to bring him back again in second or third to last chapter of HE2. Maybe it's best to empty the stage for the final scenes?

But I do enjoy the handwritten message from Eddie that Mason gets. Could I possibly keep it? If Eddie's really dead, then it would have to be a hundred and forty one year old message that some local librarian or antiquarian had, and they knew to send it over to Mason Reynolds, or maybe one of the *woomo* sent it, and then the *woomo* gets Mason to worm down into that hole in the tree to get the flask and get the flask full of rumbies, and the box with Eddie's notes—but, nah, that's ridiculous.

Or I go back to my original notion that Mason sees a temporary apparition of undead Eddie, who then turns into dust. He wants to die anyway as he feels so guilty about causing Ina's death. Or Ina bites him savagely in the neck—

but, nah.

So, okay, let's just say Eddie and Ina are alive, and sitting there in the graveyard. Actually I "saw" them today. At the time it didn't strike me—I'm always in such an unobservant daze—but, yes, a slender woman came into the graveyard, dressed in black, and shortly thereafter I saw her sitting on a low concrete wall with a young man in black, chatting. And earlier I'd seen the shadowy figure of a man high up in the gully that runs uphill from the graveyard, I felt afraid of him, and maybe that was the man who joined her. And then a bit later they weren't there anymore. It was Eddie and Ina, I tell you!

March 7-9, 2018. Issues: Author, Cult, Time Gap, Motives.

At this point I have no idea what I'm going to do. So many snags, and each fix introduces new problems. I'll work on some of the issues in this entry, with hopes of grinding them down. I put nine or ten hours into this on the second day, March 8, when I woke up and got going at five am. By the end of the day I felt like I was getting there. It's a big mess, but it's "logical."

TAKES TOO LONG FOR MASON TO WRITE HE2

If Mason is supposed to be busy writing HE2 at Rudy Rucker's house from February to June, what are Eddie and Ina doing during all this time? And wouldn't the *woomo* want to get the Bloom in gear? I'd like to avoid the wait.

Here's a "wild hair" fix. When Mason gets to Rudy's house, he finds that *Rudy has in fact already written most of HE2*! Love it. *Such* total bullshit! A Poe-quality hoax!

Rudy has unwittingly channeled signals fed into his brain by *woomo* tendrils. Rudy dreamily talks about being inspired by the muse, but in fact it's been tekelili nudges from Mason, channeled by the *woomo*. The *woomo* have been dictating Mason's tale to Rudy all along! Note that this would echo, and be validated by, Ina's stage routine of channeling the unspoken mind-poems of our Eddie (and saying they're from the dead MirrorPoe).

And to make my channeling of Mason work, I should

mention several times during HE2 that Mason was longing to start writing his narrative, and was embroiled in too much ongoing chaos to write, but he was composing the book in his head, with his mind singularly enhanced by the rumbies. He was in effect writing it to "the cloud" via telepathy, and Rudy was in effect receiving it from the cloud. The cloud here being the shared cosmic mind of the *woomo*. So Rudy has channeled HE2 from the actual Mason, even though Rudy himself imagined he was imitating Mason's writing and, in effect, forging this second narrative. But all along it was genuine. And then Mason actually appears, as if conjured up, and Rudy is totally tripping over this.

Mason does a couple of days of touch-up on the text, and he adds a few previously *woomo*-censored passages here and there that are less flattering to the *woomo* than what Rudy had been told by the *woomo* transmissions.

And Rudy confirms all this in the final Rudy-point-of-view chapter. Given that he's writing the last chapter, I don't think there will be an Editor's Note to HE2.

AVOID HEAVEN'S GATE RESONANCES

In orchestrating the Bloom exodus, I need to steer clear of the taint of the Heaven's Gate cult mass suicide, which was discovered March 26, 1997. Twenty years ago this month. Thirty-nine poeple killed themselves, expecting to have their souls picked up by a UFO following the Hale-Bopp comet. And that's uncomfortably close to my notion of fifty people disappearing into UFOS leaving from the cliffs of Big Sur. Note, by the way, that this style of ending dates back to Arthur Clarke's *Childhood's End*—which was the model that I in face had in mind, not that I remember Clarke's book really well, as it's been about fifty-five years since I read it. (I don't plan to reread it before finishing HE2, due to "anxiety of influence.").

I had thought of the Heaven's Gate problem before, and Tim Fitzmaurice reminded me of the problem the other day at UCSC. I well remember that Heaven's Gate happened while I was working on *Saucer Wisdom*, and at the time it very seriously freaked me out—*so* frikkin synchronistic—and I had a motel nightmare about an alien laser dentist drill inscribing things onto my teeth—Sylvia and I were on a road trip, in Zion National Park in Utah. I ended up using that scary dream in *Saucer Wisdom*, which in fact has a "Rudy Rucker" character to whom I ascribe the dream.

But, anyway, while writing HE2 for the past year, I hadn't thought to worry all *that* much about the similarity of Heaven's Gate to my plans for the Bloom. But now I realize I need to worry. Otherwise it becomes a spoiler. I just read the Wikipedia page about the cult. And I learned that the cult's deeply creepy webpage is still up—but I really can't stand to look at that one, it's such a foul potpourri, transmuting everything that I think of as fun and exciting into dumbass, tacky, lowbrow, psycho dogshit.

So annoying. Those fucking losers went and ruined a really great SF trope. Ruined for good? I'm hoping I can, in some small measure, redeem the lovely, soiled trope of alien rapture.

So how do I proceed?

I could "grasp the nettle," that is, have one of the characters, maybe even Professor Rucker, *mention* the Heaven's Gate event, and say, "But the *woomo* Bloom is different." But that could backfire. Best not to name the demon. Even worse would be to say that the Bloom *is* kind of the same, but the Heaven's Gate people "didn't do it right." But I really don't want to mention them at all, don't want to drag my lovely, sweet, dreamy Hollow Earth fantasia into contact that slime—no more than I want to start slobbering about Shaver's *Amazing Stories* deros.

Instead I'll make the Bloom be as different as possible from the Heaven's Gate mass-suicide-in-a-rented-house routine. And, in this wise, redeem by example.

First of all, I'll make it completely clear these are actual, physical UFOs—and I think I've got that covered. And, to be on the safe side, I'll have the takeoff be on a hilltop so it can't possibly seem like they are actually in a state of hallucination and are in fact killing themselves by jumping off the Big Sur cliffs onto the rocks.

Most importantly, I can't go for a big group emigration like I'd thought I might do. I have to keep my number of passengers way down, and they need to be fully invested in the trip, and in no way brainwashed. I'll keep it down to Mason, Seela, and Brumble, plus Eddie Poe and Ina Durivage. Mason and Seela are the paramount couple, the new Adam and Eve. I like having at least the one other couple so that we aren't immediately faced with brother-sister incest in the next generation.

So okay, let's have two couples. Mason, Seela, Brumble, Eddie, and Ina.

At one time I'd thought Eddie would staff many *veem* with people from the Order of the Golden Frond. But that's *way* too Heaven's Gate. Let's say the Order of the Golden Frond died with Machree, and the death of the group might have something to do with Eddie and Ina going into hiding.

I'd also thought I might add in Rafael and Maya to the exodus crew, but I'm not sure. First of all they're kind of minor, last-minute additions to the cast, so why put them into such a leading role. Also, the fact that Rafaelo is Latino could have an unfortunate resonance with the Jonestown mass suicide, as many of the People's Temple followers were from minorities…conned by a white leader. This said, I'd almost like to have Rafaelo and Maya show up at the last minute on the white motorcycle, Maybe they play a big role in rescuing Seela from the ant Queen. And, flipside of the Latino issue, we'd be giving them some prominence. Well, we'll see what happens. If Rafaelo, Maya, and Frida get in on rescuing Seela, why not let them come along. Brumble could marry Frida, to get the next generation going.

GENETIC DIVERSITY WITH ADAM AND EVE

I've mentioned before that we need a workaround for the lack of genetic diversity if you only have two or four or six people in your breeding stock. I think the simplest move is this: Make sure that the *woomo* have sampled out cells from a bunch of different humans. They plucked tens of thousands of cells with their stealthy and ubiquitous tendrils. And swap in DNA from there.

I'd also suggested that we might suppose the *woomo* do a kind of genetic "kaleidoscope" or shuffle thing, as if revolving genomes in a mirror-reflective tube and snapping new configurations into place. But that process is too complex and rickety. Just do a genetic library of humanity, that's the way to go.

Related question; Why do the *woomo* want Mason and Seela to be their Adam and Eve? Maybe Mason and Seela are special because: (a) Mason broke the Earth/MirrorEarth symmetry (need to check on this). (b) Mason opened the original Earth's south hole. (c) Mason and Seela have a peculiarly protean and receptive biochemistry that allows for wide changes in DNA without losing viability. Intelligent enzymes if you will. Clean RNA. "Good breeding stock."

It's not just the DNA that you inherit from your parents (especially from your mother), it's the cytoplasm environment, the chemicals in her blood, and so on. A tiny bit of this in, I suppose, in the non-genetic part of the father's sperm cell as well. But mostly it's from the mother's body. But, the father's DNA will in some measure affect the body chemistry of his daughters' bodies although, come to think of it, if you swap in new DNA, then Dad's body juices don't much matter. Really it's the flesh of Eve that counts. And Seela is a good choice for Eve.

WHY THE TIME GAP?

Recap: At the core, Mason and Seela were scared because the time was getting so slow, and they were uneasy about the outer world rushing by so fast. They wanted to get out of the core . But Machree insisted they stay longer so they could harvest more rumbies. And they did stay a bit longer, and carry out the additional harvest. But then Seela angrily clawed Machree's face, and he threw Mason & Seela out of the saucer with Brumble, Arf, and Nyoo. And then Fwopsy sealed her door and took off.

Why did Fwopsy ditch Mason, Seela, Brumble, Arf, and Nyoo at the core? That seems kind of hostile. She could just as easily have scooped them up then and there, and someone could have subdued Machree.

But let's say that Fwopsy and Uxa knew at that time that there was no known saucer or *veem* for Fwopsy to mate with, and they figured it could take awhile to find one. Also they knew that Mason and Seela were ideal candidates for Adam and Eve. So they deemed it wise to keep our star couple in

305

something like suspended animation at the Earth's core—not really *suspended animation*, but in greatly slowed-down time. So they'd have centuries, if necessary, to find a saucer for Fwopsy to mate with.

And in fact it took a full 170 years to find the mate Duggie for Fwopsy. Duggie was buried in the ice in the side of the original Earth's South Hole. Seems like the *woomo* would have known that, from doing tekelili with Mason, but maybe it took them a few hours of Core time with Mason to totally figure that out from Mason's memories. Also we can suppose that Duggie was inert in a trance, almost like Fwopsy had been.

And in the meantime, during those 170 years of search,, Fwopsy was just saucering around. And she incidentally sparked the MirrorEarth's humans interest in flying saucers. We might even say that Fwopsy displayed herself deliberate-ly—because she waned to provoke some legit reports of real saucers (like Duggie) to be her mate. But this was no avail as Duggie was, once again, (a) on the original Earth instead of on MirrorEarth, and (b) he was in hibernation in the ice walls of the South Hole.

Fwopsy might say something dismissive and contemptu-ous about humans' false reports about saucers "which some-times even provoked vile abuses of trust against fragile, credulous seekers, and which sometimes even led to these pathetic and naive would-be adepts to their death." (This by way of defusing the Heaven's Gate incident, but without ex-plicitly mentioning it.)

MOTIVATIONS FOR THE SAUCERS & ANTS

I set up that whole saucers breeding on the walls of the cave thing so I'd have a fleet to carry my settlers. But if there's only four or six human emigrants, seems like we don't need all the saucers. Ummm—got it! The extra sau-cers are for the *ants*—who'll need to chew out the core of the new colony planet. Fine.

So the ants aren't big enemies of the *woomo* after all. Okay, but then why did the ants eat Nyoo? Maybe I drop that scene? But I love it. Want to keep it. Well, let's say the ants are a little hard to control, a bit impulsive, not all that bright, like dangerous pets whom the *woomo* do, after all, rely upon for hollowing out a fresh planet.

And if the ants are more or less allies of the *woomo*, then why would they kidnap Seela like I want them to do? Maybe the *woomo* were really mad about Nyoo and were going to punish the ants in some way, so the Ant Queen Drusilla grabs Seela so the ants have a bargaining chip. And then Mason rescues Seela and works out a deal. "Oh those hot-tempered aliens!"

What might the ants and the *woomo* be arguing about? Maybe about how many slots in the saucers each species gets? One or two or three saucers for the humans, ten for the ants, and ten for the *woomo*?

And if there's a limited number of saucers, we have to suppose there's a limit to how many children Fwopsy and Duggie can lay. Maybe they die after they spawn, like salmon do.

EDDIE'S MOTIVATION FOR LYING IN THE GRAVE

The *woomo* are fixed on having Mason and Seela be their new Adam and Eve. And Eddie and Ina are grudgingly being allowed to come along. But first they have to wait till the real "Adam and Eve" show up.

So Eddie and Ina went into stasis in the casket in 1877 Santa Cruz—so they could be around for the Bloom. They knew, or were told, that the Bloom wouldn't happen till Mason and Seela showed up. But they didn't go into stasis until they'd passed about eleven years on Earth. They wanted to kick up their heels. But the chance to be part of the Bloom exodus grew more important to Eddie and Ina over the years. Also they'd just murdered Machree, and needed to lie low.

WHAT ERADICATED THE SAUCERS?

Why weren't there any saucers around other than Fwopsy and the frozen Duggie? Did someone kill them all? Nah. Let's say all the saucers left during a previous Bloom. This journey is taking longer than expected, and now the aged *woomo* have time, unexpectedly, for yet another Bloom. (The late Bloom is an objective correlative for me writing another novel about the Hollow Earth.) And millen-

nia ago, after the previous Bloom, they'd set aside two saucers for eventually breeding a new generation of saucers,
when necessary, but the two idle saucers went into stasis,
and the *woomo* knew about Fwopsy, right there in the Umpteen Seas, but he non-*woomo* locals had forgotten what
Fwopsy even *was*. And Duggie had slipped off the grid, and
out of the sight of even the *woomo*.

WHAT ABOUT THE KRAKENS?

I need something big. I'd imagined they could fly along
after the saucers like dogs after a caravan,, but that's *meh*.
Possibly they come help rescue Seela, but I'd rather not
bring them in on that—better if Mason does it himself, possibly with Rafaelo and Maya. Although, yeah, maybe the
rescue attempt is a disaster and they're all about to die and
then Skolder the kraken shows up.

Or, wait, I changed his name from Skolder to Karl-Heinz
Ziefler last month. Why the fuck did I do *that*? Jakob Boeh-
me would be better, the name of a famous medieval mystic.
Or how about Hermes Trismigestus? Or a real angel name,
maybe, some weird shit like Uzrail. But, nah, that slides into
a cheesy religioso mode. And, worse, staggers into Heaven's
Gate territory as well. I'm just switching it back to Skolder.

Anyway, as I say, I want to go big. The krakens are,
like, things that live in stars. Almost like angels, at least in
the sense of higher energy beings. Potentially huge and surprising. Right at the end of the novel, maybe one of them
unfolds into a sail that covers half the sky and speeds the
saucers on their way.

March 14, 2018. Leaving the Cemetery

So I've got them all together in the Evergreen Cemetery,
kind of chatting. There's a little too much exposition in their
talk. Next time I revise it, I ought to throw in some asides.

And now the cops show up and hassle them a little. I
don't think they'd use a loudspeaker or threaten them or
have a paddy wagon. These just homeless people, in the
cops' eyes, and there is in fact a homeless center just two
blocks away in Cruz. All the cops want is for them to go
over there. Possibly they're annoyed about the broken bottle,

if they notice it.

I don't want to escalate this encounter, as that leads off on an irrelevant tangent. Like, I don't really want see Rafaelo and Maya running up the gully behind the graveyard. Probably the cops ask for ID, and let's say that Rafaelo and Maya do in fact have green cards, so that's cool. But possibly Mason is a problem, as he has no ID, but just in time Professor Rudy covers for him.

Rudy found out where they are by stopping by the *Good Times* office. He just happened to be down in Cruz for the day, writing. And found himself writing the scene about Mason being there. And saw the actual *Good Times* with Mason's article, and he's like, *whoah*. Cue *Twilight Zone* music.

Rudy's driving my BMW. Earlier I'd been thinking that Mason and Seela go to his house in Los Gatos with him. And Rafaelo and Maya would drive the van home or go back to work. What about Eddie and Maya? It feels a little top-heavy to bring them to Rudy's, although I *could* fit them all in the car: two couples, a baby, a dog and me.

March 15-16, 2018. Issues: Ants, Woomo, Humans

Maybe I should make another working outline like I did on Feb 20, 2018? Funny to look at that outline now—almost everything in it is wrong. Fuck it. Rather than an outline, I think it's more useful to work on a set of Issues, like I did last week.

WHERE DOES RUDY DRIVE THEM?

If Rudy drives all those people to his house, then what happens? It would be a dead end. Earlier I'd thought Mason and Seela would have to spend a couple of months there while Mason wrote HE2, but Rudy's already done most of the writing via his subliminal muse-like tekelili mind-feed, and can in fact continue transcribing as an amanuensis or psychic reader or recording angel. If Rudy keeps transcribing up to the end, then we don't really need to switch to his POV. till Eddie is actually gone, and in this case the Rudy POV. chapter becomes an Editor's Note, which might be a nicer match for the structure of HE1.

Anyway, let's say Rudy *doesn't* drive them to his Los

Gatos house. It's time to be tobogganing down the final slope. They head straight for the Big Sur cave and the climax.

My first impulse is to put Rudy and Mason in the front of the BMW, and Seela, Eddie, Ina, Arf, and Brumble in the back. But if I get a child seat for Brumble, they won't all fit. And I could grab a baby child seat from Maya's babysitter neighbor on the way out of town.

So now the seating is like this. In the BMW, Rudy and Mason in front with Arf on the floor in front of Mason. Seela, Ina, and Brumble in back. On the motorcycle, Rafaelo with Maya on the pillion seat behind him. And in the sidecar, we have little Frida in a child seat in front of Eddie Poe.

I find photos of this kind of sidecar use online. I love motorcycle sidecars—I first saw a picture of one in a German picture book for kids when I was about eight, and ever since have longed to ride in one. With a nice little windshield.

By the way, a good thing about this seating arrangement is that it puts Mason, Seela, Ina, and Brumble together, and I in fact expect them to travel off in a veem together and without Eddie Poe. On the drive down, Ina might mention again how sick of Eddie she is.

So they head for the saucer cave, and they all go on down the cliff, and there's the cave, and Fwopsy and Duggie are stiff and dried up and six little saucers are chasing each other around, darting out of the cave's open mouth like swallows or bats.

WHAT IS THE RELATIONSHIP BETWEEN THE ANTS AND THE WOOMO?

As I've been saying, it's a symbiosis. The ants hollow out a planet and buck it into a Planet and a MirrorPlanet. The ants have more strength than you'd think, and their population goes into the trillions. The woomo help with the digging, using their rays, and then they're eager to flop into the Central Anomaly as a nest. They draw energy from there. And the ants like that the woomo keep a planet worm. And the woomo provide "wifi," that is, keep they the ants in tekelili contact with the ants in the "Greater Hive," that is this region of the galaxy.

I think I'll have the ants be very stupid and robotic and acting-on-reflex. To some extent the ants don't even *know* that they're allies of the woomo—they don't know anything. But if you put them on a new planet they'll unthinkingly hollow it out and buck it into two sheets. They're like living tools the woomo use.

Another aspect of the ants is that have a deep, ungovernable lust for eating the flesh of woomo. And this yearning is a source of the woomo's hold over them. The woomo are, in a way, like sexy, bossy women leading submissive, pining men around. But with the kicker that the slaves here do literally want to devour the masters.

And of course woomo will sometimes zap ants to death, but this isn't very easy for them, as the ants have reflective shells.

So it's a bit like a rough and tumble gotcha game between the ants and woomo, like jousting or no limits ring fighting—combatants *do* die, but not all that often. Also they don't get really furious when one of their member dies. It's like, "S/he fucked up." Another way of putting it is that both races are hive creatures, and don't view an individual deaths as a huge deal.

WHY DID THE ANTS EAT NYOO?

Usually the woomo have no trouble avoiding the ants— like statuesque women brushing off nerds in a bar. But Nyoo is young and inexperienced, and she imagines she can order the ants around. And Nyoo specifically does something to annoy the ants.

Maybe she points at the treasure chest and says, "I know that's full of rumbies. The stupid ants stored them there. And we woomo are going to take them all."

At this point, Nyoo doesn't know that in fact Eddie Poe has all the rumbies, and he's still in a casket with Ina. And the ants are mad they don't have the rumbies and Nyoo's talk pisses them off.

HOW DID THE RUMBIES END UP WITH EDDIE?

Okay, so Eddie, Ina, and Machree showed up in San

Francisco in 1862 with a couple of hundred rumbies.
Fwopsy hid them in the Big Sur cave for the woomo.
Machree knew where it was and he kept going down there
and stealing a few to sell. The ants sniffed out the rumbies
and settled into the back of the cave. Machree was scared of
the ants, and scared to go back to the cave. He sent Ina and
Eddie down there. They barely escaped. Machree was planning to kill them when they got back to the inn in Santa
Cruz. But Ina killed Machree. And Eddie and Ina took the
rumbies into their casket with them.

WHAT MAKES A RUMBY HATCH?

Is it that they have to age? Or maybe at any time they
can hatch. All it takes is a blast of woomo light. Why do the
ants want rumbies? The tekelili makes them feel good.
Their antenna shiver. And the rumbies remind the ants of
woomo, and an ant's greatest desire is to kill and eat a
woomo.

HOW MANY RUMBIES AND WOOMO ARE THERE?

Recently I'd thought of rumbies as the size of diamonds,
so there's be a least a thousand of them. But maybe they
should be more like size of marbles, and I only have a hundred of them.

I never said how many *woomo* are at the core of the Hollow Earth. Is a hundred enough? Or two hundred? What is
the volume of a grown woomo like Uxa? What if I had a
container that's cube fifty yards on a side. And let's say
fledgling woomo are 25 yards long and 5 yards across. So I
could fit in 2 x 10 x 10 = 200 of those woomo into that fifty-
yard-cube. But the saucer is a sphere. Well, a sphere inscribed in a cube has pi/6 of the volume, which is 0.52, or a
shade more than a half. So we can handily squeeze a hundred woomo into the saucer that's a sphere with a diameter
of fifty yards. Groovy.

How do I get a saucer that big from those newborns?
Well, heh, I could have twenty saucers merge like the faces
of an icosahedron. But that's too mathy. Let's just say a
saucer can grow really fast, the old energy-into-mass routine.

What was that about a control panel in the saucer? Who

ever used the controls? Let's say a fleet or group of saucers leads needs at least one human "pilot" in order to fly fast. And our hero Mason will be the pilot, natch.

WHY DOES THE ANT KIDNAP SEELA?

I have a clear mental image of one of those big Hollow Earth ants grabbing hold of Seela and carrying her down into the very deep and extensive nest behind the cave. I see her in there with the ant Queen Drusilla triumphant over her, with the big ant's mandibles and legs akimbo. Possibly the ant has grabbed Seela because she was holding Eddie's stash box of rumbies. The queen's handmaiden ants are reveling in the tekelili and the smell of Seela, Sticking rumbies stick to the scapes, which now look like gem-encrusted scepters.

Better idea: the ants are so stupid that they think *Seela is a woomo*. And, as mentioned, they are desperate to eat the flesh of woomo. So the worker ants want to bring Seela to the queen for her to eat, as Seela seems like such a *special* woomo. And, again let's say she's carrying Eddie's rumbies, which promotes this impression.

The ants are magnificently stupid. Like in the Beatles movie *Help* when some cult members want to paint Ringo blue and kill him.

HOW IS THE SITUATION RESOLVED?

Mason needs to display great bravery, and he needs to do something clever. I think at the last minute, Eddie Poe should die in a noble self-sacrifice. I don't want Mason to have to take him along to New Eden.

Mason convinces the ant queen Drusilla that Seela is not a woomo by...fucking her? Hugging and kissing her. Getting her to laugh and sing. Perhaps song is a uniquely human gift.

HOW MANY SAUCERS ARE THERE? AND WHO RIDES IN THEM?

Let's have six individual saucers and three pairs. One each for the woomo, the ants, and the humans. Keep in mind that the saucers can in fact get very large. The one with, all the new-hatched woomo is fifty years in diameter. And the ant Queen and sixty of her workers in the other saucer. The human saucer flies point, and the two others follow. They're grouped in a triangle. Rudy watches them leave.

I think Mason, Seela, Rafaelo, Maya, Ina, Brumble, and Frida are in the human saucer. But it's a certain amount of trouble to get Maya's family down to the Big Sur cave, both in terms of motivation and in terms of logistics.

Arf won't get in the saucer. Rudy keeps Arf, as per Mason's last request to him.

We might also suppose that Fwopsy and Duggie are going to stay on Earth. They're in hibernation for ten thousand years until the next Bloom.

March 20-21, 2018. They Prepare to Drive to Big Sur.

So now they're all together in the Evergreen Cemetery: Rudy, the three couples, baby Brumble, and the dog. They've got Rudy's BMW and Hector's sidecar motorcycle with a child's seat. Everyone's dressed, and Eddie has the rumbies in a box. They've had lunch. A cop just checked in on them, but he's gone. It's a bit past noon. Rudy has said they're welcome to come to his house.

Down in Sur the six baby saucers are probably grown. Fwopsy and Duggie are in comas. The ants are alert and ready for action. At the core of the Hollow Earth, Uxa knows that everything is just about set for the Bloom.

I want them all to go to Big Sur now. I want them to go to Rafaelo's and Maya's house and get little Frida. Get an extra baby seat for Brumble. And drive down. Put the main characters in the BMW: Rudy and Mason in front with Arf on the floor in front of Mason, and with Eddie, Seela, and Brumble in back. On the motorcycle: Maya with Rafaelo on the pillion seat behind her. And in the sidecar, we have little Frida in a child seat in front of Ina. I'm worrying too much about the logistics here. That motorcycle sidecar is becoming too much of a thing. Why don't they just go down in Maya's van.

I keep wanting to ditch the Latino family, but it would be good to have Frida on hand to marry Brumble. Or I could raise the incest issue right away, and have that explanation about the woomo changing the genome each time.

Something has to convince Seela and Mason that they want to go to Big Sur—otherwise it would be logical for them to go to Rudy's, as he's offered to take them in. Or they might just stay in Cruz, although the cop may have said he'll book them if he see's them on the street again.

Rafaelo and Maya also need a reason to go to Big Sur.

I think they need to have some kind of vision in the cemetery to kick the action into gear. I kind of randomly want to see a *woomo* standing up on one end, possibly wearing a mortar board, piping exhortations from its cloaca. As so often before, I think of the wonderful talking DNA molecule from *Jurassic Park*, Mr. DNA. His brisk hick accent, and the way he says "Dah-no-sawer." Possibly I go for a ball-and-stick molecule instead of a luminous god-like sea cucumber from the Hollow Earth. Either way, I want that same intent, pedagogic vibe.

Possibly Uxa could appear and then transport them. No BMW and sidecar motorcycle at all. And then there wouldn't be the issue of convincing Seela and the Mexicans to come along.

I wrote for the rest of the day, and when I was done, sent an email to Marc Laidlaw about it.

> Sometimes when you're writing, there's a section that's like a portage. You have to lift your canoe out and carry it on your head through underbrush for a hundred yards. I had a stretch like that today. I've got ten or eleven characters on stage now (a taxing thing to manage, and a practice earnestly to be avoided), and they're in this Santa Cruz cemetery I was talking about, and one of the characters is, *ta-da*, Rudy Rucker, who's been in fact writing *Return to the Hollow Earth* all along, feeding on the subconscious telepathy that Mason's been sending him, all unawares, and there's even a cop hassling them, and I just want them all to go down to Big Sur and finish up the novel, but I know that some of them don't *want* to go there, and then I got into worrying about the seating in the two vehicles they might use,

...

going over and over that, as if it mattered, and thinking, "there's got to be a way to *see* what's going to
happen," but really all there is, is words that I'm
writing down, and I'm wanting to fall into a seer-like
trance and just start typing fast, and whatever the
fuck I manage to write can be the new reality, and
then I'm back to worrying about the motives and the
seating and then, after ten hours of this, I'm like,
fuck it, and I speed-type a scene where Uxa the giant
sea cucumber shows up in the living room with
them, and she's going to carry them all to Big Sur
right now, and no more worries about the seating or
about whether or not they want to go, it's in Uxa's
hands, well, not *hands*, in her branching tendrils.
Thank you, o Muse.

As chance would fortuitously have it, tomorrow
Sylvia and I are *ourselves* driving down to spend
two nights at Santa Lucia Lodge at the tip ass deserted south end of Big Sur. To celebrate my 72nd
birthday on March 22, 2018. Yay!

One quick afterthought. If Uxa can come to Earth's surface, then she could just as well have laid her rumbies here,
and there would have been no need for our gang to have carried them up. So maybe a junior woomo appears in Maya's
living-room. Or, better, one of the old, existing rumbies suddenly hatches, which is way cooler. Seela's or Mason's
rumby. Probably Seela's is best. An Uxa ray tickles it. And
Seela's necklace swells and drops from her neck, and something like Nyoo hatches, but now this new one grows up the
size I'd indicated, a room-sized *woomo*. Yeah.

March 22-23, 2018. Birthday in Big Sur. I'm 72.

Morning. It's raining a lot here, rained hard all night,
patter of rain on the roof, sighing of the wind, steady roar of
the surf. It's raining off and on this morning too, with fog so
thick at times I can't see the ocean or the hills. But right
now I can see. Misty green spring Sur hills, round and abrupt, moiré double embroidery of drops on the analog window glass and the paired digital window screen, the drops

flowing at times but static just now, the sluggishly heaving ocean green gray.

Figure 33: Crystal Ball in Big Sur. Portal.

We're in the "Honeymoon Cabin" on the tip of a promontory. I keep telling Sylvia that Mason and the gang are here "right now." I might even juggle the date in the book, so I'm truly a you-are-there eye-witness. If so, I have to change it to be raining, which could be interesting, but, nah, clear weather is more fun to visualize. Also, in the book it's a Wednesday, and it's a Thursday here, although yesterday was Wednesday, so I could say the big climax happened last night. I kept waking up, having to pee, and sweaty under our eiderdown, the rain, as I said, endlessly brocading the sloped roof, tiny footsteps.

Isabel gave me a little crystal ball for my birthday, really a nice thing, if I move it along, the world sweeps by inside.

Possibly the saucers fly through a crystal-ball-like flaw in space that the human "pushers" create with their psychic yearning. Longing for the New Eden and an unfallen state. Or they're gonna use FTL. For sure, I don't want a four or ten year journey for them. In hibernation? Icky. On the other hand, seems like if you're using hyperjumping, then distance doesn't matter, and I'd been thinking that when they want to do a Bloom, they have to wait, like, ten thousand years until Earth has come a bit closer to a target. Well, we could readily say that a hyperjump can only go about ten light years at most. Humans are the hyper jumpers. The veem can fly around quite well on their own, but it takes a human to craft a Gate.

Sylvia brought along a little nut cake she'd made, and we just now put three candles on it, and she took my picture, and I blew the candles out. Very good cake, moist, and with sweet mocha icing. I already ate a quarter of it…but keep in mind that the diameter is relatively small. So nice to be with Sylvia, so warm and kind. Cozy in our cabin.

Counting the turns our planet takes around our star—that's a fairly large mechanism to use for a little individual's "life clock"! More human-scale to say you're counting the seasons. The wheel. The spring equinox was March 20, this year. And then we add on our number system when talking about the birthdays, also an odd thing, such a complex intellectual construct.

I always have a melting, tender feeling about the season of my birth. Wet, and plants sprouting, and newborn chicks and lambs. I always think of the sweet puffy white clouds in the Heidelberg springs of 1979 & 80, when our little family of five lived there, and I became a beat-SF novelist. Old photos of my mother aged thirty, in the year of my birth. Very much herself. She was Nonny, take it or leave it, both shy and self-assured, like me.

I don't remember all that many birthday parties, but one stands out, not any specific event during the party, but the vibe, the ensemble of me and four or five other kids, sitting around our dining table at 620 Rudy Lane, Louisville 7, Kentucky—cake and ice cream, and the unaccustomed bright colors of balloons and gift wrap. And I think, "This is my birthday party!" Our voices raised, excited, vying for each others' attention. Another party: Pop is there, we throw pennies into a metal washtub, the tube full of water, with a saucer at the bottom, if the penny lands in the saucer you get a prize, and if it misses you get a prize. Good old Pop. A birthday in Heidelberg, I bought a quart of American whiskey at a bus stop kiosk. Pop had sent me a hundred dollar bill, and that evening I went into the downtown alleys and bought, I thought, a bar of hashish from an Arab—kind of to teach my father a lesson, as I was mad at him for leaving Mom—but it was just pressed camel shit or some such.

***

6:30 pm. The sun finally came out around four o'clock. Sylvia and I were walking a little trail up at a monastery or hermitage on a ridge quite near the lodge. During the rain this morning, mudslides blocked off the sole highway (Route 1) just south of us, and blocked it off seven miles north of us. Sylvia was kind of worried about this, imagining various repercussions, but I think the road north will be open tomorrow and, as kept telling here, this is our little adventure here. And by now with blue sky and sun as well as some clouds, it all looks pretty nice. The weather turned good when we drove up to a monastery or hermitage up the hill and took a walk there in the initially impenetrable fog. So peaceful up there. And then I saw a patch of blue.

There's a fenced-in area just down the hill from us, halfway to the waves, and I was there later this afternoon, looking around, and Sylvia, standing on the cliff with our house, fifty feet above me took my picture, and sent it to the girls, and daughter Georgia messaged back, "Da in his pen." Endless pig jokes, always. Sylvia said I'm Sir Pig in Pig Sur today. My hallowed totem animal.

I actually did some writing today, first when we were fogged in this morning, and then later in the day, sitting in the sun on a chair outside our room. I realized—just a minute ago in fact—that Mason, Seela, and Brumble are not going to leave in one of those veem saucers. It'll be Raphael and Maya and, I think, Eddie and Ina as well. They'll get "transfigured" before they leave, that is, make healthy (even Eddie), and somehow implanted with "full DNA" which includes genomes for nearly everyone on Earth.

Figure 34: Saucerian Sky in Lucia, CA.

Mason and Seela…well, they'll drop out, fade away, head for Mexico. Go live with my friends Bef and Gabriela perhaps. Or…go back inside the Hollow Earth? Or to Oregon, with the little farm and the cow. Hard to see Mason fitting in anywhere at this point.

March 23, 2018

Stopped at Big Sur beaches near Garrapata Creek on the way home, and I wrote my old "write another novel" motto on the beach yesterday on the way home and signed it by Poe. Actually he ought to say that when he emerges from the grave.

Not as yet sure where Eddie goes at the end. Could just put him on the *veem*, even though he probably can't be a father, but he might dig the trip anyway. Sending him back to the Hollow Earth would be too repetitive. Having the ants kill Eddie, that that's mean. Maybe he wanders off, and

Rudy in the Editor's Note sees Poe on the street in San Francisco, homeless, a junkie near the Civic Center, but assuredly immortal. Hate to be too harsh on him like that. And, anyway, if he was supposed to really be here right now, why aren't we hearing about him? I guess Eddie leaving with Mason is the best option. I just need to figure out something for him to do as part of the posse.

Figure 35: "Eadem Mutata Resurgo. — E. A. Poe"

March 24-27, 2018. Seela No/Yes. Sperm Bank. Ants.

I'm trying to work out where my characters go at the end, and how they're going to get genetic diversity. Heavy problem-solving, thinking about this all day and whenever I wake up at night.

SEELA STAYS

(1) Suppose that Seela really does refuse to go on the saucer exodus, and Mason accepts that, as he loves her. Seela doesn't even ride to Cruz on Lux. She hands Brumble over to Mason as well. And Maya will nurse Brumble—she's still lactating, as she's still weaning the one-year-old Frida. To find a place for herself in Cruz, Seela will pair up with Gregor, the owner of the Sparkle Wow jewelry store, in fact she marries him and becomes his business partner, and by the time of the Editor's Note, they're moved their store to New Mexico. Seela leaves Arf with me when she leaves town. That way I can use that funny last line, "Every bit of this is true, and if you don't believe me, I can show you the dog."

Note that now I can't do the routine in Big Sur about having the ants abduct Seela and having Mason save her.

Possibly I drop any big battle with the ants, and just stream-line the ending, and fatten up what I have. More texture. I got enough plot.

So we have an emo scene where Seela bails and gives the baby to Mason. And we want to hear Rafaelo and Maya saying that they do want to go. They're not being abducted. They're opting in. We take some time and talk this out. We don't just have Lux snatch them up. Lux can be in the conversation too.

(2) I like all that, but we need a twist. It's too sad for the lovers to separate. And it would be hard to pair up Mason with Ina. And too boring (and counterfactual, hoax-wise) for Mason and Seela to settle together on Earth. So…Seela has a change of heart, and shows up in Big Sur at the last minute. She borrows Hector's motorcycle and drives down with Arf in the sidecar. (And later, Rudy rides the cycle back to Cruz with Arf in the sidecar.)

REHAB INA AND EDDIE

I'd like to see Ina get physically refurbished to be a po-tential child bearer. At least theoretically, she's only thirty-three, but we'd need some flash method of plumping her up after 140 years in a casket. Lux the woomo can fix it, and in fact she'll freshen up Eddie as well, and perhaps even make Eddie potent—in the sense of implanting a data base of sperm in him. She'll do the tune-up on the flight down to Sur. Those two crawl into her little mouth and ride *inside* her, and they get super-smeel all on them. "Do that smee goo?"

I had thought of Eddie as impotent or sterile. Keep in mind, that on Eddie's wedding night with Virginia, Mason stood in the man's place as Virginia's groom—and deflow-ered the bride. It could be that Mason takes Ina as a long-term mistress, and Eddie doesn't object. Or—more pleasant-ly for Eddie—his sexual dysfunction has been healed by the *woomo*. But may they all swap a bit, to shake up the ge-nomes of the kids.

FLY TO SUR

After Seela (temporarily) bows out with Arf, and Eddie

and Ina crawl inside Lux, and Rafaelo and Maya sign
on…then we have Lux like a flying dragon carrying the others like riders on a horse. Inside her are Eddie and Ina, On
her back are four adults, three of whom are leaving on the
veem. And two of the adults are holding children Rudy /
Mason(Brumble) / Maya(Frida) / Rafaelo.

THE GENETIC BOTTLENECK

We'll need a drastic step to get past the impending genetic bottleneck (see the link to Wikipedia, and see also
founder effect and minimum viable population). I won't do a
"random mutation" kind of route, as so many mutations are
lethal. As I've already hinted, I want there to be a human
library of genomes. So it's as if we'd brought along a virtual
starship crew of one or two thousand people.

This said, even at first we do allow some normal births,
so we're developing a gene line from the founders. And later
we don't bother regularly inserting genomes at all, we can
just let evolution happen—although, sure, we can keep
throwing in sports.

How long would this take? I've heard you ought to get
up to a population of two thousand different genomes. But
we want to bring in the babies slowly enough so that the
humans can raise them. Suppose each couple has four children, so that we get a doubling in the size of each generation.
2000 is two to the eleventh power. So if we started with four
founders, then ten generations would do it. If we that each
generation takes twenty-five, you'd get to the target population of two thousand within 250 years. This can be approxi-
mate, as we might have an extra woman.

Note that if you've got salubrious woomo light playing
on the population, then lifespans extend to several centuries,
as with the black gods. This means we could have one individual human, say Eddie, in charge of the genome bank.
Naturally this should be Eddie Poe. And his genome samples can be drawn from the past membership of his Order Of
The Golden Fleece, or OOTGF.

Now—how do we grow an exogamete genome into a
baby? I considered a number of methods, and I'll use the
last, which is the most fantastical and, perhaps, the least

Rudy Rucker

slimy.

Zap ova into fertilized eggs. Zap a woman's egg, making
it into a single-cell fertilized embryo that takes off from
there. Like the Holy Ghost did to Mary, supposedly. It's not
as if, right before the Annunciation, the Holy Ghost "fucked"
Mary and put in a godly sperm. He put in a fertilized egg, or
converted an existing egg into a fertilized state, Mary was, in
effect, a surrogate mother. How to do the zap? The easiest
is if you have a woomo tendril do it. So we need a genome
bank that, I think, could least offensively be brought along in
the form of information, or as crystalline molecules. A mini
woomo that's in Eddie's charge. Call it the "tickler."

Implant fertilized eggs. A man's ball-sack could hold a
library or bank of fertilized eggs, and he could sometimes
squirt one of those into a woman, and it finds its way in
through her cervix and into her uterus? Icky and complex.

Sperm Bank in Scrotum: Vary the DNA of the sperms—I
think you could just use existing eggs, but keep using exogamic sperm. One male—or each males—might have a library of sperm in their sack. Like, one particular man's ball-
sack loaded up with the library of the human race, and he
does a *droit du seigneur* routine on fertile women for his
whole 300-year-long life, and thus father's a race. Abraham!
Could the racial ball-sack man be Eddie Poe? But he's so
icky. Could it be Mason? But then he's set up to have sex
with his daughters, grand daughters, nieces, etc. But that
makes him a revolting child-molester, and we don't want
that. So somehow the library ought to go into the sack of
each boy?. Like a circumcision ceremony, but you're implanting something like a rumby, only different. Make up a
name for it. A pearlie.

External Sperm Bank. Or have a single big pearl with
sperm samples, and let the women put a drop from it into
their own vaginas with the finger tips, just as we already saw
MirrorSeela doing with a bit of Mason's sperm while they
were riding Fwopsy the fried egg from the flower to the core.
Or the pearl bank could be a freestanding dick, or dildo, and
the woman could put it into themselves. Kind of gnarly. In
either of the sperm bank cases, there's the issue that sperm

324

cells die if you don't freeze them.

Grow the babies inside *woomo*. Thus we avoid the offensive tactic of a wholesale use of human women as surrogate mothers or, as the women might angrily phrase it, brood mares. Obviously a smeely slimy woomo cavity would be perfect as a womb. And how do we implant the genome cells into the woomo? Eddie fucks them! *So perfect!* He's got the OOTGF genome library in his ball-sack, and he fucks the woomo, inveigling couples into taking over the care of these bonus babies.

Where did the gene bank come from? From the members of the Order of the Golden Frond! Rather than literally bringing a physical "genome bank" along, we'll suppose that during the ceremonies of the Order of the Golden Fleece, samples were taken. In the interests of not making this disgusting, I'd like to see the information in the samples stored in the form of pure information or, more visually, as little crystals. We don't want gobbets of smelly tissue.

MERGE THE ANTS AND THE KRAKENS

I don't I really need *both* these races in the book? It's confusing. Overkill. The krakens, in the end, don't have much to do. But the ants are handy for hollowing out the Earth.

I did love the kraken scenes at the North Hole, but ants can do that. And I loved when the ants eat Nyoo, and we can keep that. And there was the floating antfarm, we still have that too. And the ants in the cave. So okay, krakens out, ants in.

And on March 26, 2018, I did a brute search and replace to put "ant" everywhere that it said "kraken," And then I spent the whole entire day going through and looking at each "ant" spot, and seeing what I had to fix to make it work. Took about eight hours. Taking old things out, and putting new things in to replace the holes. I took out about a thousand words and put about two thousand new ones in. And now the book makes more sense.

March 28, 2018. Rising Frenzy.

I'm entering the "blood-lust writing frenzy" that comes when I get near the end of a novel. As I like to say, it's as if I've wounded my mythic prey, and I'm bushwhacking through the underbrush in pursuit, sniffing at the spoor and splattered blood, my heart pounding in anticipation of my final leap, when I'll alight upon the sacred beast and slit its throat wide, letting its steaming life pump onto the pages of my tome.

Why did Skolder go to the core? Why did the ants kill Nyoo in the Cave? Well, Skolder wanted to track where the rumbies were going to be placed on Earth, so that his little family could gather there to be in on the Bloom. The ants who killed Nyoo were rival low-caste ants. Possibly the low-caste ants are red

I'd kind of like to see a big scene where the giant empress ant surges up through the crust and—does something. Attacks the low-caste ant colony and—maybe frees Mason? Or takes Mason to fetch Seela? No just a good ant-on-ant battle. Two empress ants duking it out. Wild chirping. Silhouetted against the night sky. Yaaar.

Mention as early as possible that Eddie Poe's OOTGF was gathering "life essences," to be used to impregnate woomo to create non-inbred members of the Bloom colony. Can I possibly clarify how those life essence items get inside Eddie's ball-sack? And what these items look like? Could they merely be cells that the woomo snips out and then threads down through Eddie's *vas deferens* like a single tobiko egg?

I'm seeing a sexy, creamy-skinned redhead come slinking out of one of Lux's woomo wombs to be Mason's replacement wife. But, wait, it would be too much to expect the *woomo* to flash-grow an embryo to adult size.

By the way, when they do reach new Eden, Eddie could in fact fuck babies into the woomo as rapidly as the adults cold handle them. But in point of fact, raising babies is hard, so you probably wouldn't want to bring them in at a superfast rate. So he'll probably just do a few a year.

Consider placing the cave up the hill from the Lucia

Lodge, and near the Hermitage or monastery up there. Like in the gorge where Sylvia and I walked. Could Mason prevail upon a cute, sexy young maid from the Lodge to come on the trip? No, no, that gets into the Heaven's Gate thing.

Had a good day of writing today really hitting it, got over a thousand words. I spent a lot of time on the outdoor patio of a cafe next to the high-school, with teens swirling by at lunch, and then I went and sat on a bench in the town park. Three or four Japanese mothers with Japanese babies on special-purpose lawn-baby-blankets, so cute the mothers and babies. Three 13-year-old girls doing dance routines together, like granddaughter Althea, legs and arms pumping in synch, joyful motion.

. I'm getting close to 80,000 words. I have that "about to graduate" feeling that I had at Swarthmore during Senior Week. Like, we're men and women, we've done it, we're in the big time now. A swagger to my gait.

March 29-30, 2018. Stay or Go?

That Clash song, "Should I Stay or Should I Go." Lines from the lyrics. "This indecision's bugging me (esta indecision me molesta). If I go, there will be trouble. And if I stay it will be double."

Seela should come of her own free will, if she comes at all. How would Seela arrive? On the motorcycle, yes. But what would impel her to come down? She misses Mason and Brumble, yes. But what could change her mind about going on the saucer trip? Nothing. I can't really see that happening. And she's right. The trip to New Eden seems dreary. Hanging around with clones of freaks who either donated "life essence" samples to the insane freak OOTGF, or maybe Eddie liked their looks on the street.

I'd really like to see a scene of Eddie fucking the woomo. Poor Eddie—do I tease him too hard? He does a demo when they get to Big Sur. He's, like warming himself up. To get Eddie going, Lux embosses the form of a dead woman on her surface. Eddie Poe fucking a dead-maiden bas-relief on the warty hide of a *woomo*, yeah baby. Mason, Rafaelo, and Maya watch, and they're like…"*Yeccchhh.* We're not going on this trip after all."

Flip-flop time.

Let's say that Mason, Rafaelo, and Maya bail. They see the three veem take off. Mason wants to win back Seela. Rudy calls a rental car, like an Uber, and the four of them ride back to Hector and Aida's. Seela's there. Mason talks to her.

Seela: "There's no need to keep running, Mason. Be here with me and Brumble. It's adventure enough. And you can do another quest when you're older. You've got so much time."

Mason: "I'm glad to be with you, but I do feel a little bad about missing the veem ship of the Bloom. A whole new world!"

Seela: "For all you know, it's a scam. Eddie's at the center of it, right? And it wouldn't be fun to live on a deserted world. With nobody there but the giant ants digging, and the woomo nosing around."

Mason: "The woomo and the giant ants are exciting."

Seela: "If you think so. But they'll still be here on this Earth. Or inside it. And they'll be our secret. In five or ten years, if we're bored, we might find our way inside and visit them again."

Mason: "The thing about staying here—I hate how crowded is in twenty eighteen."

Seela: "We'll go somewhere out of the way. Virginia?"

Mason: "God, no. I'm not going back there after all this. We—we could go to a South Seas island."

Seela: "Rudy will know a good one. And, don't forget, he's going to give us some money. I'll make necklaces down on the island."

Mason: "And I'll write. Or, no, I'll buy a boat. I'll take up diving. I saw a dive shop in Santa Cruz. You wear tanks on your back and breathe underwater. I'll be a dive guide."

Figure 36: Writing in the Woods

So they fly in a plane to Micronesia, finding an island a bit further off the track than Pohnpei. They bring Maya and Rafaelo and Frida with them, so they have a posse. Hector and Aida choose to stay in Cruz. They leave Arf with Rudy; the dog doesn't want to go.

Another good writing day. First I did some laptop work while I had breakfast at a table outside a hole-in-the-wall cafe on Los Gatos Boulevard while a scurvy Speedee shop changed all the vital fluids of my car, I don't know why I let them do it instead of the classy Autobahn shop I usually go to. Inertia. I was at Speedee to get a Smog inspection anyway, and they upsold me.

When I got home, I printed what I had, and for revising I walked up along a creek bed on Saint Joseph Hill, bringing my scraps of paper with the latest pieces of the novel and the notes. I was very happy sitting there in the woods,, patching holes in the story with my pen. For a minute there I could see the whole ending, but just now I forget it, but I'll find it again, I'm sure.

Home stretch!

.April 3, 2018. Ned and the Pegasus

NED LAWRENCE
Editor, '64

Figure 37: Ned Lawrence, Eponym for Mason's *woomo*

Getting on a roll, I dug out the *Pegasus* of 1963, and found the stream-of-consciousness Kerouac-style offering shown below. My first real writing.

Around 1983, I folded this passage into my transreal *bildungsroman* novel *The Secret of Life*.

RUDY RUCKER
St. Xavier

Critic '63

BUS RIDE – DECEMBER 20, 1962

I came out of the school building and it was raining and I didn't have a raincoat so I ran under a kind of roof which stuck out over the main entrance which we weren't allowed to use because visitors came in there and we would get it dirty and I was standing there and there was a little ninth grader talking about how it was going to snow most likely and the teachers would all be in a bus and have an accident and we would get out of school for a couple of weeks till they got them all buried and we had some new teachers and I said yeah good ok and then I walked back into the rain and went over to the place where we wait for the bus which is a chartered city bus which takes people specially from school to out in the suburbs and there were about fifteen guys all waiting for the bus and saying when's that son of a bitch gonna get here anyway, there it comes, hell, its in a traffic jam, probably won't get out of this damn place till six, but then the bus came and we ran through the rain and I stepped in a puddle on purpose and all the bus guys hurrying to get good seats which were double, but I like to sit in one by myself to have room and anyhow I feel so cutoff and who gives a damn when I listen to those guys all excited about tests or parties or cigarettes or getting stoned, I don't feel superior, just kind of like a cold hand is grabbing my guts and squeezing them, and then the bus started moving and all the bus guys were shouting, but not because they were joyous and bubbling over with shouting, but because all the leaders of the little cliques were shouting to get everyone to look at them and all trying to be noticed in about every way they could think of but nobody really noticed each other except some of the guys who were real bugged about not making the scene with the studs were laughing at the right times, and then the bus was really going and I was sitting at the window looking at the road all black shiny wet and being amazed at how we moved by going by stationary objects and not hitting anything and floating except I was hungry as hell because I didn't eat lunch and I felt like vomiting but instead I spat on a bunch of little worms which lived in a crack in the floor and watched the inundation until they escaped and then I saw a great big oak tree dripping unbelievable drops into a puddle and blurping up great big bubbles which looked like jellyfish until they popped, but the whole time all the guys in the bus were shouting and the gut in front of me had picked a scab on his face and was dabbing at the blood with a piece of paper and the guy he was talking to didn't even notice it and I was the only one who saw it except for a little kid across the aisle and when I stared at his eyes he wouldn't look at me and acted like he saw something outside the window and when I looked out I saw that the gutters were overflowing and there were big triangle puddles on the road which filled me with a sense of adventure.   R. RUCKER

Chevalier Literary Society, "The Pegagsus," Louisville, KY, 1964, p. 16–17

Figure 38: "What I Was Like in High School."

I decided to have Mason's rumby turn into a *woomo* named Ned because I recently happened to have some email with my Louisville high-school friend Edmund "Ned" Lawrence, also a member of the Chevalier Literary Society, and a year younger than me. Synchronistically, brother Embry found a copy of the 1964 edition of the Chevalier literary magazine *Pegasus*, and I found Ned's photo there,.

April 4 - April 7, 2018. The Final Push.

(1) Instead of using a plane to get to Micronesia— Mason's rumby hatches. It's a boy woomo. Helpful. Named Ned. Ned makes passports for them all. And flies them to Micronesia. What ever happened to Eddie's rumby by the way? Weave back that he had it on his neck all along. It's the first to hatch when we do the hatching scene. And Eddie fucks it.

(2) Change the control panels of the fried egg veem so there's only one chair and one control knob, a joystick. To make the hyperjump work, you have the two merged veem with a man in one chair and a woman in the other (yin/yang, doubles, twin theme). The controls are specifically designed by wise ancient humans for setting up a stargate. The controls in fact have no other purpose. Either I have two seats side by side in Fwopsy and no controls in Duggie, or I have (symmetry) one single-seat control panel in each. A slight problem if I have a seat in Duggie, it seems like the boy sitting in him will be upside down if the woman in Fwopsy is right side up. Well, I can fix this by having Duggie normally fly with his flat side up. Or, no, just put the seat on a swivel. Naturally, by the way, we're going to have Ina and Eddie at the controls. Really one single pair of humans is enough.

(3) Eddie has his "life essences" in a third testicle. *Too* funny! He'd been doing this all along.
***

I keep thinking of more scenes. But now I can finally see an end to them. I'll make an outline again—or this time let's call it a "shooting script." Sounds more purposeful and fun. I'm not quite sure about the chapter breaks, or how many chapters I'll split it into. I'll go with the flow and the page length. I was thinking the big Bloom take-off should be a climax at the end of a chapter. But that means my last two chapters are quite short, I think the Bloom part will be under 2,000 words. That's really too short for a chapter. It would look like I ran out of steam. So I'll put them together into one single long last chapter with a § section break in the middle. And then the Bloom isn't positioned as the book's peak climax, and that's okay, since Mason and Seela aren't leaving on the Bloom,

Re. the shooting script, I didn't precisely adhere to it, but pretty close. I'll mark each completed step with an asterisk * as I go along.

RUDY

[*Already done:* * Rudy shows up at the graveyard. They go to Rafaelo's house. Seela's rumby hatches into Lux. Eddie and Ina crawl inside Lux to be healed. Seela leaves with Arf, refusing to come further. Rudy, Mason, Maya, and Rafaelo ride Lux to Big Sur.]

* They land beside the cave. Eddie and Ina get out, they're all well.

* The two groups of ants burst through the ground fighting, The empress ant Jormungo and her husband Fafnir are in on it. The ants disappear underground and the earth is shaking. The tremors die down.

* Lux says the saucers will be okay, but they people are scared to go into the cave now.

* Ina says she's pregnant with twins by Eddie, thanks to *woomo* intervention.

* Lux hatches Eddie's rumby's *woomo*, called Lenore.

* Lenore grows a dummy pale-white-dead-maiden shape on her surface. It looks like Virginia Clemm. Overcome by lust (or some similar emotion), Eddie fucks it. He says he's impregnated the woomo womb it with another pair of twins—not from his own gene line but from, he brags, from the life essence bank in his third testicle. So this way, Ina's children can find exogamic spouses. '

* Mason, Maya, and Rafaelo look at each other. They're, like *yeeecch*. They aren't going on the trip. But they still want to see the Bloom.

FAREWELL

* Eddie gets Lenore to hatch all his rumbies form the box. A hundred woomo squirming around.

* The three saucers come out of the cave, with one of them full of ants, the purple-green ones and a few of the white farmer ones.

* The woomo get into a *veem*. Both the veem stretch to fit, and their skin is somewhat transparent.

* even Rudy to get in. They all say no.

* Eddie and Ina's veem forms a stargate and the veem disappear through it and it closes up. The Bloom is done. All the woomo are gone, including Lux and Lenore.

* They hike to the Big Sur monastery on the hill above Santa Lucia, the Camaldoli Hermitage, and Rudy calls a car service. They get out at Maya's house. Rudy says he'll stay the night. [They pay a monk to drive them, no car service.]

* Around 5 am, Mason goes to find Seela at Gregor's house. It's not far away. Seela and Mason make up. Gregor is yelling. He says he'll try to get Seela and Mason deported if Seela leaves him. He says Mason and Seela are crazy and he'll get them locked up in a psych ward. He' s trying to work himself up for a fight. Hefting a hammer.

*Uxa sends a tendril to Mason and makes his rumby hatch. He's called Ned. He's a *woomo* about the size of a dog. He scares the shit out of Gregor. Arf doesn't like Ned either. Mason and Seela go back to Maya's with Arf and Ned.

* Ned the *woomo* steals passport blanks for Mason, Seela, Brumble, Maya, Rafaelo, and Frida, then doctors them. Rudy goes to his bank and gets out $10,000 for Mason. Ned eats several twenty pound bags of rice and sugar and soy beans.

* Arf stays with Rudy…Arf can't stand *woomo*.

* They ride on Ned to Pohnpei. [Airplane tix would be about $7K all together.] They lie on Ned's back protected by a dome of tekelili.

* Mason gets into diving. He gets a boat and sets up as a scuba guide with Rafaelo. His personal woomo Ned lives in the reef. What next? *Quién sabe.*

334

AFTERWORD

Rudy still gets occasional tekelili updates on Mason's status from Ned.

The natives think the *woomo* is a god. Remember that they have eels that are gods.

Rudy mails a printed final copy to Mason, but it's returned as undeliverable.

I found a nice photo of Arf to put into the Afterword.

Figure 39: Arf in 1982, riding down the James River with me in an inflatable raft.

"And if you don't believe this story is true, you can come and see the dog!" — Rudy Rucker's Afterword to *Return to the Hollow Earth*, by Mason Reynolds.

April 8-9, 2018. Done. Ideas on Publication.

So as of April 8, 2018 the book is done. I'll print it out and do a revision. And I'll write a short Afterword when the revision is done—I outlined a couple of little ideas for the Afterword in my April 7, 2018, entry, and may think of more things to mention.

I can't face revising HE1 yet again just now. I did a full revision of it before I started HE2 and, along the way, I've been pushing in various prefiguring tweaks. To knead in the tweaks, I'll eventually have to give HE1 another read-through, like a copy-editing run. But it's more critical to revise HE2, and that's a more interesting task, so I'll do that first.

***

As always, I'm sad to bid a farewell to my characters. And to the regimen of writing a novel. I'll be adrift once more. I'll do more paintings and more blog posts. In the near future, I'll have the revisions to do, and then the book designs, and then the Kickstarter and the self-publishing. I'll do, I think, an omnibus ebook edition containing both Hollow Earth books. I'm leaning towards doing separate paperbacks of them, or maybe a double volume there too. I'll look at the production costs. And as a high-end gift, I'll make an omnibus hardback edition with color illos—a collector's edition. Maybe I'll pay Georgia to do a really profesh covers (or two).

By the way, I talked to John Silbersack the other day, and he'd gotten word back from Marco Palmieri at Tor Books...who at one point had worked with my late, lamented editor David Hartwell. Palmieri said that the Tor execs would never ever buy another book by me, and that in principle he'd be willing to try to butt his head against the wall on my behalf, but that it would be fruitless, so (unspoken) why should he even try. It's the sales-figures thing, which is the reason why Tor dropped me a few years ago—and given that nothing has really changed since then, they would not want to take me back. So be it.

I've got a buttload of marked-up manuscript pages to give away as small bonus prizes. For the cover picture of the Kickstarter page, I'll overlay an image of me onto a photo of an ensemble of these pages laid out on angles atop each other...best to choose pages with drawing as well as text. At good old Hartwell's suggestion, I used an image like this for *The Big Aha*, and I pulled in $12.5 K for that one...and the goal was only $7K.

This time I'll set my minimum goal at $10K, but perhaps

intimate that my actual goal is $15K. I'll justify the $10K as being the least amount I'd view as a reasonable advance for a novel that took me a year to write.

April 11, 2018. The Ending. Arf.

So over the last three days I compulsively did eight re-writes on the ending, that is, the last three pages, making them simpler, more punchy, more of an effective adieu. Not wanting to stop. And now I think the ending is really, *really* done. Here's how it ending looks today. Flawless.

> Maya and Seela have a jewelry stand. Rafaelo and I run a small dive business. I do some writing for the local paper. Our *woomo* Ned has taken up residence in a local reef, and we visit him from time to time. Rafaelo is making progress on his *Tierra Hueca* game. Oh, they don't have cows on Pohnpei—but I got us some chickens, and we're thinking about a pig.
>
> Rudy mailed me his draft of *Return to the Hollow Earth*, and it reads as if I wrote it myself. I didn't find much of anything to change. Tekelili is amazing.
>
> I used to dream of a literary career. But getting to know Eddie Poe took the bloom off that rose—as did Rudy's inability to sell our book to a commercial publisher. Rudy's printing it himself, for what that's worth. He says nobody believes my story is true. To hell with them all.
>
> We've made some friends in Pohnpei. Brumble is learning to walk, and Frida is talking. It's beautiful here—the flowers, the birds, the rain, the fruit, the fish, the waves, the faces. It's almost as good as the Hollow Earth.
>
> And Ned is out there in the reef.

I still have that "school's out" feeling. My time is my own. Relaxing. I'm realizing I do in fact have a rather deep level of inner fatigue after the big push of the last couple of months. Don't want to do much of anything just now, although, yes I am doing some paintings. One view of Mason and a woomo in a UFO over Big Sur, and two matched circles on big square canvases, I want them for matching covers for HE1, 3rd Ed., and HE2. Not sure if I'll do detailed Hollow Earth interiors inside the blank central disks.

Once I felt like the ending was done, I went out in the back yard and worked on my three paintings. I finished the one of the couple in the UFO. I'm calling it *Honeymoon.*

Figure 40: Honeymoon. Oil on Canvas, 24" x 16".

In a way, it's a picture me and Sylvia on our trip to Santa Lucia, not that I'd want to press that point, although she does get it about the painting, and she thinks it's cute. At first she kept pointing to that "creek" between the two round hills, and saying, "What's that?" "It's a pussy," I answered. "You know that. Art is always about sex."

April 12-17, 2018. Editor's Notes.

I planned the notes on April 12, 2018, and thought about them for a few days.

AFTERWORDS TO HE1

I'll combine the three Editors Notes to HE1.

Change the date of the drawing in the 2nd Editor's Note to HE1 from 1852 to 1850, and have Mason do the drawing while waiting for Brumble to be born, and then he leaves it with Mrs. Mackie.

Also change the end of the second Editor's Note so as to subtly prefigure Rudy's "tekelili amanuensis" role as author of HE2.

EDITORS NOTE TO HE2

I want to say that Rudy received Mason's narrative by tekelili, and that he transcribed it, as if from an exceptionally loquacious and eidetic Muse. My assumption is that the *woomo* are transferring Mason's mentally-written narrative to Rudy via tekelili. When does this happen?

Well, Mason reaches Big Sur on Saturday, March 15, 2018, and he leaves on Thursday, March 29, 2018. So the simplest and most obvious move would be to say that Rudy gets this information during that time. But I'd like Rudy to be nearly done with the book by the time Mason meets him, and it's not reasonable to say Rudy did all that writing in three or four days.

So I'll just say Rudy was drawing on Mason's thought and writing HE2 for about a year before he met Mason. To make this work, I can that the *woomo* Uxa had received and stored Mason's mental writing when he was becalmed at the core, or even earlier, and Uxa then starting feeding that info out to Rudy a bit in advance of Mason's departure from the core, starting, say, in April, 2017.

I might even have Uxa tell Mason when she starts doing the feed…unless I don't want to telegraph that punch.

April 17, 2018

Today I got the Editor's Notes written—I revised the one for *Return to the Hollow Earth* quite a few times, and revised the ending of the book to dovetail with the Note. In the end, it turns out Mason is mad at Rudy, as Rudy didn't manage to get a commercial deal for the book. And Mason feels like Rudy didn't give him enough money. And I tried to make Rudy's writing sound kind of stupid compared to Mason's limpid elegance. Rudy fanatically ranting about the "doctrine of the Hollow Earth." I find all this very funny. Keeping myself amused.

So, anyway, it's really *today* that I finished the book, not last week like I said. The final Editor's Note is almost 2,000 words, which brings the book length up past the 90K mark I was shooting for. Can't quite believe I'm truly done. Huzzah!

April 18, 2018. Kickin' It

So now I'm setting up my Kickstarter ask page for *Return to the Hollow Earth*. I'll launch it on May 1 and let it run to May 31. Everyone feels broke after taxes, so I don't want to launch in April. We'll be on a trip to DC and NYC from May 18-27, I think, but the project can pretty much be on autopilot then, with time for a "goose it" update when I get home. "There's still time, sisters and brothers!"

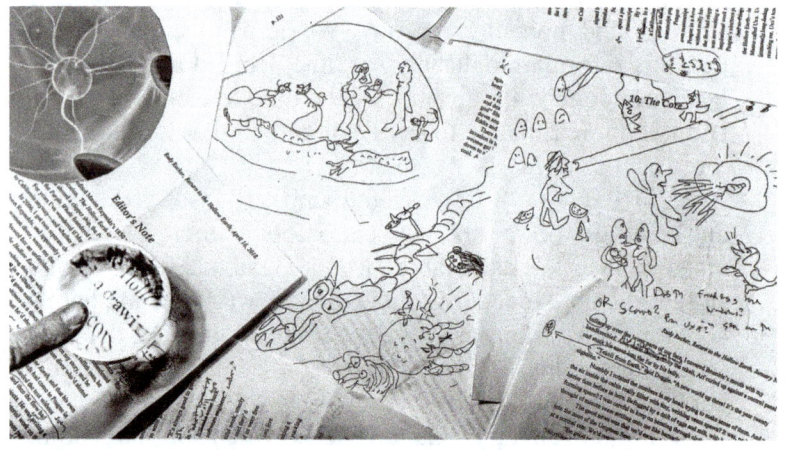

Figure 41: Kickstarter Image of My Project.

For the project photo, I made a nice image of my manuscripts with drawings, plus Izzy's crystal ball and a pasted-in image of my plasma sphere. Way back when, Dave Hartwell advised me to use an image of the manuscript rather than a photo of one of my possibly off-putting paintings, and I think he was right. I still need to make a video of myself talking about the book—this is always hard. And I have to figure out the "Rewards" structure. I went quite simple on this with *Transreal Cyberpunk*, and that went fine. I'm going to shoot for $10K.

I'm thinking ebook omnibus, separate pb HE1 and HE2 editions, and a hardback omnibus, and call that one a deluxe collector's edition, possibly with thick cream paper, cloth bound with a dust jacket. I don't feel like tacking the hassle of the "69" design for the hb, but I can put one cover illo on the front and the other on the back.

Interior illos? I could include some of my paintings and working drawings in B&W in the pb and possibly make the paintings be color in the hb, like I did with *The Big Aha*, although I'm not sure I have enough of them, and I'm also not sure if anyone much cared about the illos. Zero feedback on that. I don't think I'll do them.

How about a print edition of the *Notes*? Maybe I'll do a high-end hardback limited run (about 25) color illustrated collector's edition of the *Notes*, and use that as an add-on for a higher-level "Collector's Edition" Reward tier. And once I've put this Notes doc into InDesign for that, I can export an EPUB and MOBI and give those away as a bonus reward for the medium tiers.

Figure 42: Mason and Seela Hollow Earth Paintings, Ver 1.

Hardly anyone cares that much about the *Notes*, so maybe I shouldn't bother—I don't want to overdo it and make it too hard for myself, like I'm trying too hard to please. But I'd kind of like to see the *Notes* book, and it could get a few people to go up to that higher tier. Not sure. I can't remember exactly how hard it is to paste a Word doc with illos into InDesign. I seem to recall that you end up having to put in the illos by hand…I remember doing that for *Saucer Wisdom*.

If I just want to punt, there's always the PDF option.

Working on a couple of cover paintings now, a matching pair of big square ones with cross-sections of the punctured circle of the Hollow Earth's rind. And I'll put a cartoony fat-line drawing of Mason inside one, and Seela in the other. I've drawn the backgrounds, but now I'm scared of the moment of drawing the cartoons. Hung up on the challenge, and I keep not being able to bring myself to do it. What's that word for a calligraphic Japanese single-shot ink brush painting, with no revision possible? *Sumi*? My paint tools are out in the backyard right now. Time to go there and try. Yoda: "There is no *try*. There is only *do*." Rasta: "*Yah, mon*."

Figure 43: Mason and Seela Hollow Earth Paintings, Ver 2

So I did it, and Mason worked pretty well. I didn't truly have to do total irreversible sumi, as a washrag with turpentine was enough to remove false moves, though I only had to do that a couple of times. Had trouble with Seela's outline, partly because the background layer of paint underneath her wasn't totally dry yet, and my line colors weren't sticking. And then I made her jawline too masculine and had to wipe it off. And then her colors weren't right, and later I realized that, although Mason can be a line drawing, Seela should have brown skin. That's one of the whole points of the book, duh. At a meta level, Mason doesn't really *have* a color here, because he's an outline! But Seela needs to be black.

And then a day or two later, I went and added another layer to those paintings. I made Seela darker and redder, and I put in some bright color outlines orange and magenta, inspired by the Thiebaud-like 92-year-old Latvian artist Raimonds Straphangs whose work we saw in the SJ Art Museum the other day.

I hope I didn't ruin the pictures. The thing with painting is that there's no Ctrl+Z "Undo" control. I'll do one more layer on Seela's face. Lighten her back down a shade, go a little yellower, and do a little modulation so her nose shows up more clearly.

April 19, 2018. Fixes.

I finally fixed all the items in my HE2 To Do list this morning. Only took about four hours, it was just a matter of getting around to it. I'll do my fixes on the Seela cover painting today, and maybe start in on the Kickstarter video, and the Rewards list—although I have till May 1 for that.

Today I'll buy a new printer-ink cartridge and print out the whole of HE2. And then I can mark it up, and then type in the HE2 changes (with possible ricochet corrections to HE1), and then print, mark up, and fix HE1. Will take at least a month, or maybe even six weeks.

And then I have to print, mark up, and fix *Million Mile Road* trip, which will take at least a month, or maybe six weeks. I told Cory Ally at Night Shade that I'd have MMRT done by mid-July, which is interpreting "mid" generously, three months from now, so I ought to be able to make it.

Keep in mind, though, that I'll be on vacation in DC & NYC for nearly two weeks. And publishing HE1 & HE2 will take at least a week. So I do need to get on those revisions starting in the next couple of days.

If things get too tight, I can try to slip the MMRT delivery to August. Cory Allyn wants it so he can give his new editor Paula Guran the final manuscript to read in advance of its publication in Spring, 2019.

April 23-24, 2018. Video. Printing.

I made my video for the Kickstarter "ask." I used my Fujifilm X100T fixed 24mm lens digital camera to record most of it. I was going to splice the clips together with the old free Microsoft Movie Maker that used to come with Windows, but it doesn't really work anymore—it trashes the colors when you export. So I went ahead and spent about $60 on Pinnacle Studio 21 (made by Corel), and figured out how to use it—a hurdle I'd feared, but which was superable—and it made a good video for me.

It's embarrassing to be working on the video when Sylvia's around, as she keeps hearing my self-promoting voice on my clips—like Rudy is on *such* an ego trip, or so it seems, although "really" I'm just humbly making a fundraising ad. Humble, my ass. Some of the clips aren't quite perfect, I think I'll see if I can mix in clips taken with my Pixel P2 phone as well—I wonder if Pinnacle can handle that. I put in some clips of my Plasma Ball toy, with the wavering sparks from the center—my original inspiration in 1987 or so for the light streamers inside the Hollow Earth. They look very cool.

Later: I did try making some Pixel phone videos, but they're fuzzy and wobbly, so I shot a replacement clip and an two extra clips with my Fujifilm. I think it's done now.
***

I needed to get a new ink cartridge to print out HE2. And I notice that I've worn the paint off some of the keys on my laptop keyboard over the last year. HE2 is now 90K words, but I typed maybe half again as many words with the revisions. Say 135K words And these Notes are 117K. So I typed about 250K words in the last year for my HE project. They say the average length of a word is a shade over 5 letters. If I include the spaces after words, that's 6 key presses per word. So we're talking 1.5 million key presses in the last year, and I'm sure a million of them were on this little laptop keyboard—I did in fact do most of the writing on my trusty Thinkpad X250 lappy. At this point I'm finally kind of used to where the keys are placed on this model, even though they diverge from my older ThinkPads, and from my sacred Microsoft Natural Elite Ergonomic keyboard on my desktop. Recently had to replace that one with an unused vintage exemplar I found on Ebay for, like, $100, rare that it now is. Wonderful "action" on that baby, and great keyboard layout.

Anyway, now the manuscript is in a binder and I need to read it. Stalling on that, just now. I'm like, "Back into the salt mine already?"

I took a huge bike ride yesterday, and today I'm going to Panther Beach with Jon Pearce. I'll bring the binder and maybe do an hour of markup in the Verve Cafe in downtown Cruz. I'll be interested to get a baseline estimate of how many days per chapter it will take.

April 30, 2018. Kickstarter Prep

I've been fiddling with my Kickstarter page for a week or two. Putting a lot of thought in to the Rewards, that is, the price levels and the descriptions. I looked over my old campaigns, seeing what worked the best. I added an "Ebook Cornucopia" level at $25 today for about nine ebooks. The ebook rewards are good, as you don't have to snailmail anything. I'd been tempted to be stingy with the ebooks, as I do actually sell some of them, but it's better to be openhanded. And you need a good $25 prize, that's the most popular level.

My top-end "Three Hardbacks: Collector's Edition," now goes like this. I'll make it $200, as hardly anyone will go higher than that. Printing up each set of three hardbacks and having them mailed to me for redistribution will cost me about $60 a pop. What a deal for my backers!

> Three matching hardbacks: THE HOLLOW EARTH, RETURN TO THE HOLLOW EARTH, and the book-length NOTES FOR RETURN TO THE HOLLOW EARTH. Plus the Ebook Cornucopia package. The NOTES volume includes over 40 drawings and images, and will be printed in color.

All three volumes cloth bound with dustjacket, and with signed and numbered bookplates designed by me. Plus an original hand-inscribed drawing on each title page. The NOTES volume will be limited to an edition of 25, and is destined to be a rare collectible. Also included: a generous sheaf of hand-corrected pages from my drafts of RETURN TO THE HOLLOW EARTH. And personal mention on the new novel's Acknowledgments page.

Figure 44: Georgia's Covers Trio

And Georgia made up three awesome covers for me.

May 1-8, 2018. Kickstarter Launch.

May 1, 2018. I went live with the Kickstarter this morning, and I've already got 45 backers and $3,735 bucks. For sure I'll make my cautiously low target of $8K, and maybe I'll get past $12K, which is what I really want. Making and the books will cost a couple of thousand. So it should work out like I was hoping, with me getting about as much money as I typically got from a publisher's advance. With, of course a lot of work on my part, although I don't entirely mind doing it. Kind of interesting.

Now it's 9:30 pm and the pledges are up to 49 backers and $4,045. I'll noodge BoingBoing tomorrow and if they post me, that'll give a lift.

May 5, 2018. I reached my target goal of $8K. Half the money came from "whales" who went for the $200 Three Hardback Collector's Edition.

May 7, 2018. I fixed up a good Two Hollow Earth Books page. I posted a free reading PDF of Notes for *Return to the Hollow Earth* there. I was stalled at $8.5K anyway.

May 8, 2018. I did a blog post on "Writing 'Return to the Hollow Earth'". Meh. Then Dave Pescovitz of BoingBoing came through. I did an update on my KS page. We floated up past $9K. All from small pledges coming in from the BoingBoing ripple. Regular people who want to read the book.

May 1-26, 2018. Revisions to HE2

May 1, 2018.

I'm moving into with the revisions of HE2, marking up the pages pretty heavily, and then typing in the changes. I actually started correcting on April 24, which was a week ago, and now I've corrected about 50 out of about 200 pages, so it might take three more weeks, so I ought to be done by the end of May, or by early June. I hope going over HE1 doesn't take so long—it really shouldn't, as I already did a revision of it earlier this year, although I'll have to smooth over the various scattershot alterations I made in the course of keeping the current state of HE1, 3rd Ed, consistent with the emerging HE2. I kind of panic when I think about having to proof both HE1 and HE2 and then produce the books and mail them out and *then* having to revise MMRT, which will take longer as it's a longer book. No way I can finish all that until the end of August. I checked with Cory at Night Shade, and he said that would be okay. I might even correct MMRT before I correct HE1, or do a really light proofing of HE1, just to make sure I get that done in time.

May 2, 2018

While revising, I notice in HE2, they talk about leaving Crispa with some "Indians" in, I guess Northern California, or Oregon, or even in North Dakota. They're killing bison, so I guess really they're in the Great Plains or in the Canadian Prairie, even though that's not exactly on the way from SF to the North Pole. Anyway it might be cooler and more in tune with current usage if Mason could use a tribe name instead of "Indian."

Figure 45: Drafts of the Night Shade Covers.

Well, I can circle back to Dirk Peters of HE1, who was an Upsaroka, which, it turns out is a variant name for Absaroka, which is more commonly still called the Crow Nation. And then to prefigure in HE1, I say that Crispa is an Upsaroka Crow…lay the ground for him wanting to live with Indians.

May 8, 2018.

I've marked up and typed in 78 out of 194 pages. Going a little slower than I was at first. Hard to keep at it. Worn out from the long push of writing the damn thing at all. It's been two weeks since I started revising, on April 24. At this rate it'll take me five weeks till finish, that is, three more weeks from now, which was, discouragingly, just where I thought I was a week ago. So till the end of May, and probably into the start of June, since I'll be on a trip to the East coast for a week and a half, that is, during May 17 - 28. More to worry about: I'll be on a three-week road trip with Sylvia from about July 15 to August 7. Rudy, don't drive yourself nuts with *self-imposed* deadlines!

By the way, here's the schedule for the ten Night Shade editions. See draft covers in the figure above. If *Return to the Hollow Earth* came out in September it wouldn't really clash with the Jan, 2019, release. Cover drafts below, with *The Sex Sphere* missing.

Jan 2019: Turing & Burroughs / Mathematicians in Love
March 2019: Saucer Wisdom / White Light
May 2019: Million Mile Road Trip
July 2019: The Big Aha / Spacetime Donuts
September 2019: Jim and the Flims / The Sex Sphere
November 2019: The Secret of Life

May 9, 2018.

Revising HE2, pushing and pushing. I'm a little tired of the work. I'm almost half done, I started April 24, so it's been 15 days. I've been a little slow as I've been distracted by the Kickstarter promo. But I do like HE2, reading it over, I see a lot of good stuff. Laughs, adventure, mystery, love and sex. I got in touch with Michael Troutman, who proofed my *Journals*. He's going to proof HE2 and probably HE1. He has a good eye.

May 12, 2018.

I've been pushing hard, trying to do a chapter a day. Finished "Chapter 10: Fwopsy." Done 117 out of 193 pages. 18 days since I started on April 24. Call the total number of days needed x. The ratio $x/18 = 193/117$ means the total days needed is $x = 18*(193/117) = 29.7$ days. So 11 more days. So theoretically I could finish on May 23. But I start on my trip on May 17. We'll see.

Figure 46: Woomo Hunters. 24" x 18". May, 2018

I was getting burnt out on the revisions, so I took a few afternoons or mornings off and did another HE2 painting. Oil on canvas. I started out just with the floating woomo, and then I put in some foreground figures that I "quoted" from Peter Bruegel's drawing, "Big Fish Eat Little Fish."

May 14. 2018.

Took Sunday the 13th off. Mother's Day beach party at Clipper Cove on Treasure Island in SF with Rudy Jr. and his pals. Great day. Did all of "Chapter 11: Uxa" today. 127 out of 192 done. (The total page length has shrunk by one as I'm tightening up some passages.) The projected total days needed is $x = 20*(192/127) = 30.2$ days. Annoying that I work my ass off today and the projected completion time fucking goes up by half a day. Anyway, I might finish in 10 more days, well, at least *that's* a day less than it was day before yesterday.

May 15, 2018.

Finished "Chapter 12: Twenty Eighteen." Aa long one. This one was hard, as there was some confusion about the Bloom plans and the missing rumbies. Done 144 our of 193 pages. Estimated total days work is x=21*(193/144)=28 days. So I might finish in 7 more days.

May 16, 2018.

Did "Chapter 13: Imposter." Estimated total days work is x=22*(193/157)=27 days. Five more days work to go. Our trip starts tomorrow afternoon, Thursday, when we head up to spend the night at Rudy's in SF before flying out to DC on Friday. I'll be a chicken with his head cut off tomorrow, but might mark up some pages on the plane on Friday. Or not. Relax and enjoy your vacation, Rudy. One way or another you'll be done proofing HE2 by the end of May, and then you can whip through HE1 and get onto MMRT…or do MMRT first if you're paranoid about how long it'll take. Troutman will need some time to proof HE2 anyway.

May 18, 2018.

On the plane from San Francisco, to Washington DC. We had a great day and evening with Rudy & family yesterday. Woke at 5:00 am today and got underway. Three hours of plane ride done, and two to go. Misty haze around the plane now, not much of a view. Got a nice shot of the Rockies—glancing out the window, for a second I read the landscape as sloping upward, and thought I was seeing a single ultra-Matterhorn mountain some 20,000 feet high—the clouds had kind of masked the mountainscape to a triangular shape. Exciting. Even exciting when the mountains lay back down. Gorgeous classic cumulus white fluffer clouds.

I finished typing in corrections for "Chapter 13: Reunion" just now. Doing the usual math, we have remaining days at x=24*(193/167)=28 days, so theoretically I have four days to go. Cleared out some repetition and clutter in Chapter 13. Next comes the "Rudy" chapter with Rudy at Rafaelo and Maya's house, and Mason loses Seela, and he goes with the gang to Sur to set up the Bloom. Then the

"Farewell" chapter of seeing the Bloom happen—big scene!—and wrapping up loose ends. And then the short "Editor's Note." I'll get there yet!

May 25, 2018

Figure 47: Flatiron Building

I've done some work off and on during our trip to DC and NYC. I'm into "Chapter 16: Farewell," on page 180 out of 193. Might finish by the time we get home, on May 28. I rewrote the big "fireworks" type scene of the Bloom three times, trying to get it to be both flashy and logical. I think it's okay now, but will need to look at a print-out of it at home. The last pages still seem a little rough, I guess I didn't revise them as much.

I ended up doing more work in the afternoon, and the evening I went and did some final corrections on Chapter 16 on a bench in Madison Square Park. Did a Facebook post about it.

Figure 48: Flatiron and Two 21st Century Interlopers

Sitting here in Madison Square Park. Making final corrections by hand on the very last page of my novel *Return to the Hollow Earth*. And saying goodbye to Tor Books. They're moving out of the old Flatiron Building. And my editor Dave Hartwell is dead. Little hope of me selling them a book again. I publish myself now. And there's strange new buildings on Madison Square. I first visited the Flatiron

Building with my father in 1958. Later I was proud to be doing business in there. And now I'm on my own. A sense of having come full circle. Bittersweet.

May 26, 2018

Typed in the final corrections for HE2 today, the sixteen chapters and the Editor's Note. A great book. Maybe my last, maybe not. Now I'll send it to my proofreader, and do a quick (I hope) go-through on HE1.

May 27, 2018. Recap of Meeting with Silbersack

On the plane home from NYC now. I've been watching *The Sawshank Redemption* on the excellent seat screen of this new plane. It's a surprisingly good film.

I had a pleasant meeting with John Silbersack at his club on 43r St. near Fifth Ave, the Century Association. Nice old building, creaky wooden floors, white tablecloths, good food, intelligent-looking members. According to John, it's always been the city club for artists and writers. He kindly intimated that if I lived closer to New York City, I might be able to join.

I griped a little about the self-pub fate of *Return to the Hollow Earth*. I did this obliquely by saying that at the end of HE2, Mason is mad at his editor character "Rudy" for not getting the book a commercial release.

John replied with the same thing that I've heard every year I've been a writer—I used to hear it from Susan Protter, who, sad to say, died a couple of months ago. "Things have never been worse. It's all about the bottom line. All that the big publishers care about is your sales record." John said there are, however, some small presses that are managing to get their books into stores. He feels that's important, and it's more effective at keeping your work alive than is self-pubbing via online sales as I do. In this viewpoint, it's definitely a good thing to have Night Shade doing ten of my books—if, god forbid, they don't somehow go out of business first.

I didn't ask John if he thought I should have tried pubbing HE2 with a small press like, say, Underground (if they would take it). My sense is that I'd rather not bother with the small presses, when I can be (a *very* small) one myself. Less hassle, and I don't risk rejection, and I get the book out faster, and there's more money for me. Possibly I'm mistaken. But my approach does seem to be working for me. I guess that, even after I die, Transreal Books could coast along on its own for some number of years.

I recently raised the prices of my ebooks, and now it seems like my monthly checks are a bit larger. Re. ebook prices, I mentioned that it seemed odd that on new books, the ebook prices are nearly as high as the hardback or paperback prices. John says publishers do that so they don't undermine the print books too badly. They can always drop the ebook prices later on. Re. hardbacks and paperbacks he also said that, looking back on this period, the Futurians may feel we were engaged in a hopeless, retrograde battle on a par with trying to keep the buggy-whip industry alive after the advent of automobiles.

July 7 - August 15, 2018. Wrapping it Up

So Michael Troutman proofread HE1 and HE2 for me. I did a couple of last fixes on them. And then I imported them into InDesign for making my print and ebook editions of them as rewards for my Kickstarter backers. I'll be publishing them via Amazon, Lightning Source, and eJunkie as well. Lots and lots of steps I have to walk through now.

I did a number of passes to finalize the covers. Georgia made me some good front cover flats and I made them into full covers. The title font Georgia used is Basic Sans, by the way, I found that out using the What the Font app, rather than bugging Georgia. I needed to know Georgia's mystery font so I could use it on the spine. I'm also making a combo H1 & H2 edition, the pb of this will probably be the best selling version, other than the combo ebook.

I was still seeing errors, and I got Sylvia to proof *Return to the Hollow Earth* as well. And I went over the last couple of chaps a couple more time myself.

The biggest change I made was on August 15, 2018, to the scene when the Bloom happens, with Eddie and the *woomo* opening up a space tunnel to the planet they intend to colonize. Before that fix, the Bloom scene was a little flat…I was tired by the time I wrote it in June or July. But then in August I took two weeks off, and returned with fresh energy.

August 16, 2018. Farewell

I'm gonna close out these notes now.

What kind of man writes two novels about the Hollow Earth? See the photo below, taken on my phone by granddaughter Zimry, after she'd coiffed my hair with creek water in the woods last month on a family outing.

Why are sea cucumbers like gods?

What if white people turn black?

What kind of person writes novels about the Hollow Earth?

Was Eddie Poe a good guy?

How can you travel into the future?

Are flying saucers alive?

How do you write a book?

Is Mason Reynolds real?

What does the tunnel to MirrorEarth look like?

Professor Rucker explains all!

Figure 49: The Hollow Earth Expert

Notice how kindly I look. (If you ignore the fact that I did a gnarly mashup of the image with a painting of the Hollow Earth.) I don't normally have that expression unless I'm looking at my grandchildren. They're one of the few aspects of the 21st century that I thoroughly approve of! I hope one day they have fun reading some of my novels.

Pass it on.

www.ingramcontent.com/pod-product-compliance
Lightning Source LLC
Chambersburg PA
CBHW070910260626
47162CB00007B/2621